Copyright © 2020 by Jeffrey Marcus Oshins

Deep Six Publishers

Johnson & Associates

PO Box 4072

Santa Barbara, CA 93140

805-683-1200

Lake Barcroft is a work of fiction. Names, characters, businesses, places, events and incidents are either the product of the author's imagination or used in a fictitious manner. Any resemblance to actual persons, living or dead, or actual events is purely coincidental.

Printed in the United States of America.

Library of Congress Control Number: 2020913526

Publisher's Cataloguing-in-Publication Data

Oshins, Jeffrey Marcus, 1950-

Lake Barcroft/ Jeffrey Marcus Oshins - Santa Barbara, Calif.: Deep Six Publishers c. 2020

p. ; cm.

ISBN: 978-0-9831981-9-2 (ppb) ; 978-1-7350612-1-4 (e-book)

Summary: In the 1960's the counterculture emerges among the children of the elite in Washington, DC. who struggle to avoid scandal and political ruin while dealing with their rebelling children.

1. Jeffrey Marcus Oshins (author)–Fiction. 2. Politics – Fiction. 3. Washington, D.C. –Fiction. 4. Rock and Roll– Fiction. 5. Virginia suburbs of Washington, D.C.–Fiction. 6. Abortion – Fiction. 7. Washington D.C. scandal– Fiction. 8. Adoption– Fiction. 8. California political campaign – Fiction. 9. U.S. Senate – Fiction. 10.. Santa Barbara, California– Fiction 11. Catholic adoption –Fiction.

Cover art: JM Oshins, drawing of house Lily Spandorf

INTRODUCTION

L ake Barcroft is real. Built around the old reservoir for the city of Alexandria, Virginia, a post-World War II ideal of peace and prosperity. The fortunate first generation of Lake Barcroft children were plentiful. We played on traffic-free streets, in open yards, boats, beaches, and lived in new custom built homes. Fathers were politicians, government officials, high ranking military, businessmen, and diplomats. All were middle class and white except for the maids who helped raise us when parents pursued careers and pleasures.

Janey's dialect is racist because this was a racist time. Segregation was the law and practice in Virginia. I describe the love between Beck and Janey, the Black community on other side of Columbia Pike from Lake Barcroft with its own schools, churches, and stores. Ebonics is how I remember the voices.

The drawing on the cover is by the Austrian-American artist Lily Spandorf. This is the house I grew up in and the model for Beck's home.

Only one child in the Lake Barcroft community drowned as I recall. We organized our own pickup games–baseball, football, basketball–free to swim, skate, and sail with minimal parental supervision.

As long as you stayed in the neighborhood, parents and maids didn't ask where you were going, whom you were playing with or what you were doing. Return for dinner, ask permission for a sleepover and you could govern your own life with the confidence of parental love and protection.

The assumption that we were good kids was for the most part true. We kept our secrets, shared pleasures, pain, and dreams, went to friend's schools, churches and synagogues to worship, celebrate passages, and dance.

We committed unpunished acts of juvenile delinquency, snuck out at night to roam quiet streets, hang out at the community beach, explore sex, form bands to play songs heard on the radio and self-taught.

The challenge to write from the female point of view arises from a conceit of fascination with women—what they think and feel—and heartfelt literary portraits by male authors and artists.

This novel is a mixture of children I knew from the neighborhood, the bands, and later the adults. I knew of no teen-pregnancy.

We did go to the White House to eat in the mess and explore the Oval Office, had prime seats at presidential inaugurations, and suffered with our parents at the assassinations of their friends—the Kennedy brothers.

One exception is the character of Randall—modeled closely after my best friend—Roger Stanley. His mother did teach piano and his father was a colonel who worked at the Pentagon.

Rog was an early and popular member of the original 60's garage bands. He enticed me into music with the girls who loved him and covers he sang. I don't know if leaving Lake Barcroft at the height of his high school fame contributed to his death in Florida, but I like to think that he would have gone on to write his own music and sing his own words as I have been inspired by him to attempt.

Jeffrey Marcus Oshins

Santa Barbara, California, 2020

Dedication

To Roger Alfred Stanley.

And the children of...

ONE
SONIA-BARTON–1964

B eck's new stepsister cooed at Beckette. "Come here, baby."
Clipped hair and cut nails as if prepared for this moment, the poodle
wagged up from the aggregate stone of the recreation room porch, to
be lifted, held atop the redwood picnic bench.

A tickling warning raised hair on the back of Beck's neck.

That's my dog!

Nostrils flared, fists clenched to trap the burning in her crazy place. Eyes
closed, she trembled, and the madness passed.

Beck would have to share Beckette, her father, friends, the house,
everything with Sonia-Barton.

Weakness and remorse pulled shoulders to hips, surrender and
submission. Who was she to demand anything? She was fourteen, Sonia-Barton
fifteen—a canyon Beck could barely see across. Even Sonia-Barton's hyphenated
name declared *I'm older*. Rebecca Penelope Lyons didn't have the same ring, a
mouthful—just Beck.

A diamond glinted in Sonia-Barton's pierced ear as she scratched the pink
skin beneath Beckette's curly white coat.

Sonia-Barton kind of looked like a gypsy, Beck thought. Her straight black hair was cut like an awning over a pale forehead and arching, wide eyebrows.

Beck's ears weren't pierced because Panda said she wasn't a gypsy. Beck flipped her strawberry blonde shoulder-length hair still layered cut for the wedding the day before when her father had married Sonia-Barton's mother.

Mrs. Elloitt had said she'd be pleased if Beck called her Mama. "You're my daughter now *jist* like Sonia-Barton."

Mama was what Beck called her mother when she spoke to her in prayers and dreams. But Beck had lowered her eyes and said, "Yes, ma'am…Mama Elliott."

Mrs. Elloitt's trill had made Beck think Mama Elliott thought her funny not willful.

"Jist Mama, now darlin'. You *jist* call me Mama."

Sonia-Barton caught her stare, studying Sonia-Barton's blasé attitude, tilt head, eyes asking *is this all?*

Beck's eyes fell to her tank top—a nursery wall pattern of butterflies and strawberries. Her eyelashes fluttered as if surprised to find herself in a dream where you don't know how you got there or what to do.

The night felt real. Muggy air raised a faint sheen of perspiration on her forehead. Katydids chattered and crickets sawed—mad flamenco dancers snapping heels on the hard surface of a Virginia night.

"Want one?" Sonia-Barton held out a pack of cigarettes as if that was why Beck had been looking at her.

Beck raised her eyes with an upturn of lips, relieved Sonia-Barton had misinterpreted her attention, an escape.

"Go on take one," Sonia-Barton held out the red and white pack as if it was nothing to leave childhood behind.

"Thanks."

With a casual reach that belied she didn't smoke, Beck plucked the filtered tip from the tight order, a soft tube between her fingers. The match flame wavered beneath her focus. Sweet cherrywood first-lit tobacco mixed with tolerable heat trapped in puffed cheeks, held on her tongue, too hot and acidic to take into her lungs.

Sonia-Barton contracted glossy lips to send smoke rings spinning up into the heavy air, Bette Davis attitude, forefinger positioned against the thumb, cigarette pointed to the feathery ferns of a drooping mimosa tree.

Beck exhaled a ringless miasmatic cloud.

"Know any boys with cars?" Sonia-Barton drawled–different than Virginia– New Orleans with long sensuous expansion.

"I know a lifeguard at Virginia Beach." Her voice sounded singsong to her– too high a register, too cute, too eager to please.

"What about around here?"

"Can't think of anyone right now," Beck said with a throat rebelling half-cough.

Sonia-Barton wanted boys with muscles, barely imagined sexual prowess. She'd just moved in and was already bored with being a little girl at Lake Barcroft.

"I'll meet some guys. Then we can go places."

"That'd be nice."

The promise of boys to like them, grownup days coming, caused Beck to smile modestly like she was sharing a joke with herself.

She took a tentative inhale just as a large figure in a gray maid's uniform filled the screen door from the rec room.

Smoke grabbed her lungs. Burning fingers reached beneath ribs. "Put it out," she coughed, and threw the cigarette toward the cover of twisting English ivy.

Sonia-Barton whipped the evidence behind her back, and said dismissively, "What's she going to do?"

Janey moved as if to stomp out a flame. "What ya girls doing?"

Sonia-Barton considered her, sizing up an adversary. "Nothin', just a couple of gals talkin'."

"Sonia-Barton, yo mama a told me not to let ya smoke."

Sonabaaten–Janey's vowels were Tidewater, colonial southeast Virginia, a dropping and slurring.

"I wasn't," Sonia-Barton said as if the smoke and smell were the fault of unseen, departed guests.

Janey had come with Mama from a community of maids and workmen who'd served the first families of the Tidewater since the colonies.

After the drowning, Janey's soft body had been a refuge when Beck's skin turned cold with fear. Her strong, meaty hand led Beck, lost between awaking and dreaming. When a neighbor returning from late duty at the Pentagon had found seven-year-old Beck alone in her pajamas, walking in the middle of Lakeview Drive, Janey had moved into her room and slept by the door to intercept Beck's nocturnal walks.

As far as Beck knew, she'd not sleepwalked since her body went through the change and the rages started. Maybe she could only have one condition at a time.

When she was eleven, she'd awoken with blood in her bed. *I'm dying,"* she'd shaken and sobbed on the phone to Panda.

Her grandmother had laughed and told her what was happening was probably perfectly normal. She'd picked Beck up and had taken her to Dr. DeVoe near Fairfax Circle.

DeVoe, with a long face and forced smile, had explained menstruation and told Beck she could now get pregnant. The shocking but grand news had been that Beck was a woman.

"And Becka, don't ya start with that stuff. It'a get in yo hair an a smell up yo clothes."

"I won't." The sweet, obedient child was back.

Janey locked a *you or me* stare on unflinching Sonia-Barton.

"Honey, ya gonna be a living here, ya got to have to understand something. I'm like Santa Claus. I know when ya been bad, so be good for goodness sake, cause if ya don't I'm a gonna a wail on yo butt. Now give me them damn cigarettes for I call yo mama!"

Sonia-Barton lifted her pointed chin with a haughty dismissal, her drawl a cavalcade of privilege. "Who the hell you think you talking to girl?" Sonia-Barton challenged the law in the house.

Beck leaned back. Beckette's nails clattered on the wood as she skedaddled off the picnic table.

"About done talking." Janey said and pulled the cigarette from Sonia-Barton's hand and the box from beneath her skinny thigh.

Beck's throat tightened. She knew what was coming next if Sonia-Barton dared more sass. Janey had a wooden spoon she called Suzie. Memory of Beck's brother Colin's cries of protest, hips pushed forward to lessen the blow on his bottom had been enough for her to respect even the threat of Suzie.

Sonia-Barton pulled back at the audacity and power of Janey. "Wait until my daddy hears about *this*," she muttered.

"Smoking's bad for ya." Janey dropped the cigarette on the aggregate stone and disintegrated it with a twist of a black and white oxford saddle shoe.

"Humph," Sonia-Barton pouted.

Janey silenced her with a sharp look, then her shoulders slumped, and a pleading tone entered her voice. "Please girl, don't cause me a no trouble. I know what it like to be young and wile. My job to see ya don't git hurt. Ya can have all the fun ya want, jist don't git pregnant, beat up, nor sent to naw hospital. That's all I ax, and don't smoke no mo."

Beck pursed her lips, amazed as if Janey had been stripped naked. Sonia-Barton worried her in a way that went beyond spankings for sass.

Janey should act like a servant in Sonia-Barton's eyes.

Janey picked up the destroyed cigarette and walked the tobacco into the house with an imposing sway of her wide hips. "Yeah, OK, young and wile and me a having to track ya like a damn houn' dog. Dear Jesus, don't the troubles ear neva en?"

TWO
CRAZY

—————————————————

The sleepwalking returned the night Sonia-Barton came to live at Lake Barcroft. A dream walk down the stairs to the beach, to find her mother.

"I'm wet." Beck awoke Janey.

The strong, warm hand, the body wafted in sleep scent walked Beck back to her bed, careful not to awake her because that would make Beck angry. Her bedroom door was locked from the outside because of Beck's dreams.

* * *

The black and white wake of the cruise ship sailed on at the end of The Gail Storm Show.

Beck looked at Sonia-Barton to see if she'd been inspired by Gail's perky, can-do problem solving.

Sonia-Barton frowned and looked out the wall of window with a wistful tilt of her head as if missing someone.

They could go out on the Arkansas Traveler rowboat (only the lifeguards were allowed an outboard engine on the back of their boats). She had some Nancy Drew books she could let Sonia-Barton read.

Sonia-Barton turned to her with a glint of an idea.

"Come on, I'll show you how to make yourself up, bring out your lips and eyes. You got a decent bod and good features. You might be able to get yourself a boy with a car if we fix you up."

Heat spread across Beck's scalp. Her father had told her she was beautiful, but to hear even vague praise from Sonia-Barton held greater promise. "At Lake Barcroft?"

"Neva' can tell. Got to be prepared. Let's go out and see what we can stir up in this sleepy town," she said as if she was in a movie and Lake Barcroft was hiding some exciting secrets.

* * *

To show Beck how, Sonia-Barton dressed in a Mary Quant mini-skirt, white go-go boots, scented herself with Chanel N⁰ 5 perfume.

"Let's see what you got to wear."

Beck shrugged. "I don't have anything like you." She'd hoped Sonia-Barton would share some of her clothes, even if Beck was taller than Sonia-Barton, just not as filled out.

Across the hall in her bedroom, Beck opened the sliding door to reveal a Janey-arranged procession of hanging blouses, pants, and coats. With desperate hope, Beck pulled out the sleeve of the bridesmaid dress she'd worn to the wedding two days ago.

"Don't you have something sexy?"

Beck breathed in, askance at a word she'd rarely heard, much less used. The idea of looking sexy was to attract a man who would fall in love with her the way Ashley loved Scarlett or maybe a scoundrel like Rhett Butler in her mother's copy of *Gone With the Wind*. She had trouble imagining her father feeling that way about Sonia-Barton's mother.

Beck turned back to the closet as if a sheer cocktail dress might magically appear. "No, I'm afraid I don't." The confession trailed, ending in embarrassment.

"Let me see what you got." Sonia-Barton pushed childhood and school clothes aside like annoying hindrances.

The blame or thanks for her clothes belonged to her grandmother.

Panda–a pet name given when Beck's brother Colin had mispronounced her name, Penelope–was the sergeant of a squad who took care of Beck because she didn't have a mother to shop, drive her to the dentist, doctor, birthday parties or school.

Beck had shopped with Panda when they were at the Homestead in January for the annual Battle family reunion or in New York for a cousin's wedding last year. Mostly Norris, her grandmother's driver, would deliver square, thin boxes, tied with string and imprinted with a picture of Woodward & Lothrop Department Store. Beck would wear whatever sized clothes her grandmother guessed her to be–often wrong since she'd grown from the juniors to the women's.

"What's this?" Sonia-Barton pulled out a hand embroidered white fleur-de-lis kaftan her father had brought her from Paris last year.

There was a rumble of distant thunder. "Think it's going to rain," Beck looked outside at the graying sky, hoping Sonia-Barton wouldn't want her to go into the neighborhood dressed like the sultan's daughter in *One Thousand And One Nights*.

Sonia-Barton held the exotic loose tunic and inspected it. "Might be a little long on you. What else you got?"

Beck again looked into the hanging proof of her immaturity. "Nothing, I guess."

"That will have to do until Mama gets back and we can do some shopping for you."

"That'd be nice."

Sonia-Barton spoke as if she'd found Beck living in deprivation and squalor. Maybe she was. If she had clothes like Sonia-Barton, boys would want to be her boyfriend. Except she already had a boyfriend, a real boy, and he'd be angry if she went with another boy. Or maybe he wouldn't. "I have a boyfriend," Beck made a weak plea.

Sonia-Barton raised her eyebrow. "You mean Randall?" She sneered. She'd met Randall at Beck's birthday party in June because he was the only boy Beck knew to invite.

Beck looked down and meekly argued, "He gets angry if he thinks I like another boy."

That might be the *dream* Randall who did things she liked more than the *boy* Randall who'd she see when she went over to his mother's for piano lessons and wouldn't ask her to play with him and his neighborhood friends.

Sonia-Barton shook her head. "Too short. He looks younger than *you* do."

That was true and he was two-years older. Randall had been Colin's best friend. After the drowning, when Beck had come back from her grandmother's, Janey had smiled shyly and said, "Randall's been coming round axing for ya."

She'd become *his* best friend, like filling in for her brother. Except she loved him more than her other friends and when she was eight she'd let him see her naked.

They'd played getting married in the rec room, him pounding the Wedding March on the upright piano and then over to where she stood with a lace tablecloth draped over her head, to hold her hand and promise to love, obey, and cherish.

"Now you have to take your clothes off for our honeymoon," he'd said with a shy smile.

Her confidence had then seemed irrepressible. "You have to kiss the bride first."

His lips, tender and soft against her closed mouth, had been her first kiss.

In the furnace room by the light of a workbench, she hesitated at the final act of exposing the main difference in their bodies. Naked, his thing sticking out like a thumb on a balled up fist, he'd eagerly stared at her finger frozen in the elastic waistband of her panties.

The thud of Janey coming down the stairs over their heads had set off a rapid redressing and quiet giggling as Janey had searched for them.

The older he got, the less Randall wanted to play with her. Last year, he'd started high school and she'd stopped her piano lessons at his house. She didn't see boy-Randall much, but dream-Randall held her hand and said, "Then we'll get married," like he had before.

Dream-Randall would surely be hurt if she found a taller boyfriend with a car.

No greater evidence of change in the house than her father's bedroom—new bed, wallpaper, pictures, and Mama Elliot's makeup table. Gone were the pictures of Beck's real mama in a ballgown talking to Mamie Eisenhower, contented with Colin on her lap on a fallen tree in the wild forest of the house before landscaping. Arrayed on the blonde wood bottles of perfume, jewelry boxes, and an earring tree stood like a conquering army. Lifting the tabletop revealed a cabinet with a mirror, eyeliners, tweezers, clips, creams, and foundations.

"Sit on that stool there," Sonia-Barton instructed.

Beck looked at herself in the light-framed mirror and saw the same tanned and freckled girl whose arms and legs extended like wild growing branches. Small breasts, mostly nipples, pillowed her chest. Her nose was too pointy. Her chin out too far like her father's, a neck better suited for looking over a hedge than holding a big head.

"Can't do much about your hair." Sonia-Barton dismissively flipped up Beck's stringy strawberry shoulder-length cut. "When Mama comes back we'll go to Stephen. He'll get you cut right."

Beck smiled at her reflection. "That'd be nice."

Sonia-Barton showed her the painful but necessary process of plucking stray eyebrow hairs, the brushing out of eyelashes, drawing with mascara, the touch of rouge on cheeks, and the selection of the right shade of lipstick. The oily taste was unpleasant as Sonia-Barton showed her how to smooth and glisten by smacking and running her tongue over her lips.

Beck's reluctance to leave the house was overcome by a tingling in her legs and quicker breaths. Dressed like girls on the television show Sunset Strip, they walked up the flagstone entrance, her not-ready-for-viewing concentration camp-thin legs hidden by the trailing Arabic robe. Down the middle of Lakeview Drive, through the neighborhood she'd charted on her bike, her friends, houses, yards, the lake and community beach where they played. She knew who had children, pets, where the father's worked, who had the best candy on Halloween.

Sonia-Barton swung her hips and lifted her pug nose as if everyone would be coming to their windows or out the doors to see them. Beck kept her eyes lowered as if they were.

Bad luck–they'd barely reached Beach One, the beach for people in Lake Barcroft who, like Randall, didn't have lakefront houses, when Wayne Conrad rode his bike down Tollgate Terrace. He had muscled up young–a leader of the boys–always scoring in the pickup football at the beach or baseball in the circle in front of Beck's house. The boys never let the girls play with them, not that they wanted to.

"Hi Beck, didn't know that was you." He straddled his red Schwinn beside them, staring at Sonia-Barton.

Beck's blood boiled. She closed her eyes. Heat spread down her scalp across her face. They were at the worst possible spot in plain view from the floor-to-ceiling living room windows of Randall's house.

She looked up with a grimace and lowered her gaze. "Hi." She squeezed the exhalation from her constricted throat.

Sonia-Barton ignored him as if he wasn't worth her time.

"Hello," he said with the trepidation of confronting a dangerous dog.

Sonia-Barton glanced at him. "Have any cigarettes?" Her French Quarter accent descending into a sigh.

Wayne compressed his eyes and mouth from amazement to shame. "No."

"Don't suppose you have a car?" Sonia-Barton disparaged.

Beck thought Wayne would laugh at Sonia-Barton's maneater behavior.

"I'm getting my ll...learner's in a couple of months."

Her cruelty was proven by his stricken humiliation as Sonia-Barton sashayed away. She was teaching Beck how to make a boy suffer, how to assert your womanhood. "See ya, Wayne." Beck looked over shoulder and tried to put some warmth and sympathy into her voice.

"Bye Beck, nice meeting you," he said to Sonia-Barton's back.

She pshawed a derisive laugh sending Wayne peddling away in a humiliated scald.

Dark clouds piled above them. A flash followed by sharper boom shook the air. Wind blew in their faces and heavy drops plopped, leavening a summer smell of cut grass and street tar. Beck had to hold the tunic up to run. Sonia-Barton was in the house before she reached the top of the driveway.

Beck stood beside her, wet in the living room looking down on the lake.

"My gawd, what a storm."

Something about Lake Barcroft had finally impressed Sonia-Barton as sheets of rain and wind drove whitecaps cross the darkened water.

"We can go out after it stops," Beck said and wiped the sting of running mascara from her eye.

"Naw, there's nothin to do here. This place is dull, dull, dull."

LAKE

BARCROFT

Jeffrey Marcus Oshins

Deep Six Publishers

Beck looked around the barren fireplace, Scan Design couch and matching chairs, a bar, and sound system. "I know," she frowned.

* * *

Lake Barcroft might be boring to a fifteen-year-old girl from New Orleans, but on a summer Sunday afternoon drunken conversations and excited cries of playing children carried across the water as families partied on beaches, drank gin or vodka tonics on battery-powered party barges, and entertained city friends out for the suburban life eleven miles from the U.S. Capitol. A flotilla of flat-bottom sailboats with single rainbow striped-sails raced around a triangular three-buoy course.

Beck sat beside where Sonia-Barton lay face down on a terry cloth towel on the hot off-white sand of Beach One. They could have gone to their own beach, but Sonia-Barton was unlikely to meet a boy with a car there.

From the corner of her eyes, she watched Wayne stride down the grass hillside that lead to the sand, weave through the bodies and random groups on the sand toward them. His biggest-in-the-neighborhood muscles were out.

"Hi." His voice was several decibels lower than she'd heard before.

Sonia-Barton looked at him as if trying to decide if he was worth sitting up.

"Got some cigarettes, thought you might want one." He held out a red and white pack of Winston.

Beck was impressed with his bravery. He was closer to being a man than Randall she decided.

Sonia-Barton arched her back off the towel and with magenta-colored nails pulled a cigarette from the box, propped on her elbows waiting for a light.

Wayne stared at Sonia-Barton's Annette Funicello spotted bikini top. His hand trembled as he held the match.

"Don't you got a Zippo?" Sonia-Barton sat up and turned her back to him and smoked.

Beck hugged her knees and looked at the sand to hide from the adults who might report their misbehavior.

"Want one, Beck?" Wayne asked holding the open package out to her.

She shook her head. "No thank you, Wayne. How generous of you to ask." She tried to sound as nice as Sonia-Barton was mean.

The next time they saw Wayne, he was with two neighborhood boys in the asphalt parking area of Beach One, practicing popping open the silver lid of a Zippo with a castanet-like snap.

* * *

The atmosphere in the house thickened when her father and Mama Elliott returned from their honeymoon. At first it was fun, the feeling of growing up, shopping in the women's section at Garfinkle's for clothes and cosmetics, a trip to a Georgetown hairdresser as if Gail was Sonia-Barton's partner in reshaping Beck. Life became more complicated. Gail asserted herself as the lady of the house, telling Janey how to dress with a white apron, ringing a small cast brass bell to call her from the kitchen to serve them at the dining room table.

Her stepmother, blonde hair perfectly sculpted and frozen in place, dressed for company even when there was none, did not know you could stop acting perfect all the time as if you were being watched and judged. You'd go crazy if you had to be that way *all* the time.

Sonia-Barton was a lot like her mother. She never wanted to go out in cutoffs and T-shirts. They had to dress like they were going to meet some boys even if Beck knew they'd see the same neighborhood kids.

Maybe Gail would go crazy. Sonia-Barton would leave to live with her father in New Orleans. Beck wouldn't be able to see her until she *was* grown up. Maybe not so bad if the house returned to the familiar rhythms before the marriage.

* * *

Excitement and challenge put a briskness in Beck's step as she and Sonia-Barton walked to Beach One. Warm air blew softly around her bare legs. Beckette trotted beside them. Fireflies blinked in the elms like Christmas lights, easy to catch and put in a jar to smell like cucumber, too childish a game for Sonia-Barton. Tomorrow would be their first day at Miss Madeira. Beck would know a few of her new classmates from Burgundy Farm Country Day School, a family friend or two. Change was fine. This summer was about change. She'd have Sonia-Barton with her to insure social survival.

"I wish we could go to public school," she said because Sonia-Barton wanted to.

Sonia-Barton exhaled a languid cloud of cigarette smoke. "When I turn 16 my daddy is going to buy me a red Mustang convertible. He promised. Then I can drive us to school. We won't have to board."

"That'd be nice." Beck hesitated and said with a sideways glance, "Then you won't need to meet a boy with a car," she tried to joke.

"Yeah. I'll be gone, gone, gone." Sonia-Barton was serious.

Her daddy never came to visit and didn't call. Sonia-Barton had to telephone him and lots of times he wasn't available. She'd told Beck he had a girlfriend only ten years older than she was.

Beck watched her stepsister cross her legs, look out at the lake then at her. They sat on the grass hill that sloped down to the crescent of sand disappearing into the nightscape of lights reflecting on the placid surface of the lake. Points of grass tickled the back of her legs and she pulled up her knees to her chest.

"What's with the Leader teasing me?" Sonia-Barton asked.

Gail called him Leader because he was the U.S. Senate Majority Leader and that's what people around the Capitol called him. Maybe Sonia-Barton was more comfortable calling him Leader than Daddy. Beck had started referring to him as Leader too because it was more grownup than Daddy. She called Gail, Mama, because that's what Gail had asked.

"It's like he's always joking, you know like sometimes I think he just likes making fun of me all the time."

Beck sat more erect, ready to defend her father. Sonia-Barton was complaining because the Leader didn't think Sonia-Barton was as great as she thought she was. "Well, I don't know if that's it exactly, Sonia-Barton." How could she attack her father? He was admired around the world. "He's kinda of joking sometimes."

"I don't think he likes me."

"He *does*."

"Why is he always making fun of my clothes and make-up? Does he want me to dress like you?" she asked as if the idea was too preposterous to consider.

Beck's back stiffened. She wasn't the country cousin. Dressed in a denim pinafore and Indian thong sandals from Jelleff's, she had Sonia-Barton's style if not glamour and sophistication.

"What do you mean like me?" Anger crept into her voice.

"I mean like you *used* to, you know white socks and Mary Janes, like we're little girls. And how come he never takes us out with him to any parties where we can have some fun, meet some boys?"

Beck's hands balled. Anger lowered her voice. "What do you want him to do?"

Sonia-Barton smirked. "Take us to some real parties. When you come down to New Orleans with me and stay with *my* daddy, *then* you'll see what a good time is. Why we can drink and smoke and the boys there are so good lookin' and sexy."

Beck looked out at the dark lake and imagined Sonia-Barton drunk and going with men. "That'd be nice," she said but sheshe wasn't sure she could be that way anywhere–even in New Orleans. People would judge them because they were the daughters of a famous politician. Acting up might cause her father to have to answer for their behavior.

"We have to be careful because he's the Leader," she tried to teach Sonia-Barton.

"Pshaw. What are they going to do to me? Send me to my daddy's? I hope they do."

When Sonia-Barton talked about her daddy, she'd become cross, bullying, showing she didn't like living at Lake Barcroft.

"You miss your mama much?" Sonia-Barton asked.

Beck's chest clenched like it did when people talked about the drownings. "Sure."

"What was she doing out on the ice anyway?"

Beck leaned forward. Her voice pressed. "Getting my brother."

Sonia-Barton pulled back her head and glanced at her. "I was just asking."

Beck's voice was of the other girl, disembodied, dangerous. "I just don't like talking about it, OK?"

"Don't go crazy on me now."

Beck looked at the lake. Her hands tingled.

"You were five?"

The prickling burst in a blinding corona of fury. "Shut up!"

Sonia-Barton laughed. "You act like it was your fault."

"Arrrh," Beck threw herself at Sonia-Barton.

The surprise attack gave her a momentary advantage, but Sonia-Barton was a field hockey player and punched up with a blow that shocked Beck into awareness. She relaxed enough for Sonia-Barton to roll her over, sitting astride her chest.

"Let me up." Beck tried to roll free.

Sonia-Barton pinned her arms to the ground with surprising strength. "You are crazy as you can be."

Beck sobbed. "I'm sorry."

"You're a wild animal. That why they lock you in your room at night."

Beck convulsed with tears beneath the weight of Sonia-Barton. "I said I was sorry."

Sonia-Barton warily released her and stood ready for another atta[...] climbed to her feet.

"I don't know what happened to me," Beck lied and brushed cut grass fro[...] the back of her neck.

Sonia-Barton quickly laughed. "You lost your mind is what happened. Mama warned me you had a condition."

The revelation of her illness caused Beck to sob deeper, lowering her head between her shoulders, weak, exposed. "I just don't like talking about it, OK?"

"Sorry, I brought it up. That was very thoughtless of me." Sonia-Barton was the gracious victor.

Beck wiped her cheeks with the back of her hand. "I get confused sometimes."

Sonia-Barton pulled her into a hug. "Stop crying. I won't bring it up again."

Her pity raised more sobs.

Sonia-Barton released her and stepped back to study her as if she might completely break down.

"I can't help it," Beck gasped.

Sonia-Barton didn't know what it was like to be her and she couldn't explain the explosions in her mind that came on suddenly and were quickly over, leaving her ashamed and weakened. Janey would vacillate between threatening a beating to holding her until the shaking and sobbing stopped. Once her father had spanked her at the Homestead. She'd screamed so loud he'd hissed, "Be quiet. The police will come and take you away."

"It's all right. Come on, pull yourself together. We got to get on home, get ready for school." Sonia-Barton turned up the grass embankment.

hting to trap the crying in her raw throat.

told Beck was crazy. What had Gail told her?

revelation squeezed Beck's eyes and lowered her

ames, she'd lived with the uncertainty of memories

…colors and smells, acting normal. The violent rages started when she was twelve—two different realities—two different girls.

After attacking the bully Megan Clematine at Country Day, she'd been sent to a psychiatrist. Her father didn't her what she had. Panda said she couldn't go back to the psychiatrist because of people would talk. Panda said she should stop making excuses and use strength of character to control herself.

Beck learned the names of what she had in a letter on her father's desk in the corner of the rec room. Maybe he'd left it there for her to read because it had been right on top so she couldn't help but see it. Maybe that was his way of telling her.

Beneath the heavy scroll font of the doctor's name and titles was an underlined word in the body of the letter—diagnosis.

DRC–Dream-Reality Confusion and Intermittent Explosive Disorder brought on by the trauma of witnessing the drowning …

Beck reread the letter but found no mention of cure, only assurance of confidentiality.

Beck positioned the letter where she'd found it so her father wouldn't know she'd been snooping.

"Don't tell anyone," Beck pleaded.

Sonia-Barton glanced over at here as they walked down the empty dark street. "About what?"

"I mean that I'm crazy."

"Oh, for god sake, you should hear me when I throw a fit."

The idea that others, even Sonia-Barton, might suffer from the same ailment gave Beck comfort. Maybe she wasn't the only one. But in the deepest place of her awareness, she knew no one who'd watched their mother and brother drown.

* * *

Some truths are so big, so obvious you can't put them into words. Some feelings are like clouds that can't be held and shaped, but blot what is bright and hopeful in you. She couldn't stop reliving those minutes as if this time she'd find a way to change what had happened. Beck could tell herself Sonia-Barton was right. The drowning wasn't her fault. But her mother and brother would be alive if she'd not been so helpless. She could have gone for help. She could have rescued them.

Colin went on the ice by himself. She'd been six, he eight. She'd followed where he led her, on adventure, to the beach behind their house, ducks swimming in a keep clear space of ice.

"Look it's OK." He stepped off the frozen sand of their beach.

"Colin, no! Come back," Beck begged.

The more fearful, the more he teased, how brave he was. He's slid his shoes pretending he was ice skating.

"Colin! Come back," Beck had pleaded, crying now. "Mama is coming! Get back."

"Colin!" Mama shouted from the top of the stairs an eternity up the steep slope. "Get off that ice. It's not safe."

"It is," he'd shouted, twenty yards from the beach.

A pinging like something trying to escape from below and his arms threw up in the air like someone was there to hold him when the ice broke beneath him.

"Colin!" Mama screamed, run down the stairs, stepped onto the ice beside Beck.

Thin surface broke into planes pointing to grey sky. Hands windmilled, head above the surface to swim to Colin. For a moment, Mama held him up.

"Get help, Beck," Mama pleaded but Beck was frozen.

"I'm cold, Mama," her brother said his last words.

"Beck, help," Beck heard in the middle of her screams for help.

A hand pulled them below the caramel surface. Mother and child held each other and were gone.

Ambulances had driven the bagged bodies, past press and neighbors in the circle before the house, comforting each other if not the bereaved, awed by the cruelty that took so quickly from those who had so much.

* * *

Beck had lived at her grandparents through the winter and summer until school had started. She'd been happy to come back to live with her father at the lake, grown accustomed to the empty house, missing her mother and brother as if the roof was gone.

A half-step ahead, Sonia-Barton looked at her over her shoulder. "How could your father stay here after that?"

Beck wasn't going to get angry and say *I thought you weren't going to talk about it.* She wasn't going to stop Sonia-Barton from poking at the always tender wound. She wiped her forehead with the back of her hand over her hair and down past her ear, thrust her chin like her grandmother and said what Panda would say. "We stayed to face our fears."

"What?"

Beck's jaw relaxed into an expression of confusion. She didn't know why they'd stayed. Probably because Panda had said they should. Would it have been easier to forget if they'd moved? Were you braver if you always kept your fears in front of you with constant reminders? Would she feel less guilty, less accused if she didn't watch ice form and melt on the lake, shiver in a winter freeze when the ping of bubbles sound like the cries of her brother? She was the one who spent the most time here. But the choice had not been hers. Nobody asked would it be better for her if they moved. Maybe she wouldn't be so crazy if they'd moved.

"I think we stayed to be near where they died," her voice trailed to a whisper.

Maybe they'd stayed to punish her, to remind her she shouldn't have let Colin go out on the ice. She could tell herself that was unfair. Her father wasn't cruel. He loved her. But regret would seep through into thoughts and envelop her with the question–why she was alive and her mother and brother dead.

THREE

RANDALL

D ressed in a plastic-coated mini-skirt and white go-go boots, her hair straight along her face and curled at the shoulders, Beck watched Sonia-Barton perform final touches to her eyelashes, black needles pulled into air. The two girls in the mirror over Gail's makeup table looked to be teenagers ready to go on a date, except it was Columbus Day vacation and the quiet streets of Lake Barcroft was their destination.

Beck went into the hall to escape the sharp lavender smell of hair spray mixed with the complex scent of Gail's French Guerlain.

"Don't leave that room no mess," Janey said.

Beck watched her place folded towels in a linen closet between the bathrooms.

"Where ya two fancy ladies a going today?" Janey straightened, a smile pushing her checks like she was ready to laugh.

Beck put her hands on her hip and bent to the side. "We're going to Paris, and then Rome, and to a yacht in the Caribbean."

Janey snorted, "Might as well a go to them places if ya can. Me, I think I go to California."

"Why?"

"Cause they treat colored better out there. Ya can buy a house and live where ya want."

Beck thought Janey was happy here. Her father was working on laws to make things better for the colored. Maybe Janey would leave and have a house and family in California.

"Come on, Beck. Bye," Sonia-Barton said.

Janey laughed. "Ya gonna get cold out there in them little dresses."

Beck closed the front door behind them and stepped into the sunken entrance way that climbed in two steps to a path up the sloped gravel driveway.

"Even the maid laughs at us," Sonia-Barton complained.

"Janey's just trying to take care of us."

"The help don't act like that back home."

Where *was* Sonia-Barton's home? Beck had to hurry to keep up with her busy footsteps like Sonia-Barton was going somewhere, escaping being fifteen at Lake Barcroft.

Janey was right. The wind blew cold around Beck's legs–the first change of season, a great day for football at the beach. Beck bet there would be a game. Maybe that's where they'd end up letting the boys show off for them as they pretended to ignore them.

Low bass notes and faint reverberations of cymbals and other instruments signaled something different in the neighborhood. They stopped in the street to listen more closely. Sonia-Barton's dark eyes narrowed with interest. "Sounds like a band."

"It's Randall. We can go in if we want," Beck turned to her stepsister looking for approval.

Sonia-Barton scrunched up her pert nose in a dubious expression. "Randall's in a band? What kind of band?"

Beck sometimes wondered if Sonia-Barton didn't think much of Randall because Beck had said that he was her boyfriend. When she thought of Randall as Sonia-Barton did, she could see he was a bit awkward. His father made him wear tied shoes not loafers, and he always had his hair cut in a military buzz.

"You know, rock and roll. They're high school kids. He said we could come to their practice."

"Let's go see." Sonia-Barton swung her arms forward to stride up the driveway, turned across the Zoysia lawn, thick grass beginning to brown for the winter, beneath large angled-windows that looked out on the street and the lake. She bent over a window well trying to see the source of the music. Beck hoped nobody was watching. They could go to the door. Mrs. Malloy would be happy to see her.

Sonia-Barton crouched lower looking through cobwebs that waffled against the brick. The idea of trying to spy on Randall seemed so odd Beck started to giggle.

"They sound good. And look even better." The brazen girl led Beck to the front door as if she was the one Randall had invited.

"I got dibs on whoever's car this is." Sonia-Barton nodded at a burgundy GTO convertible parked on the steep asphalt.

The other car was an old tan Rambler. Beck wondered if she would get the boy who drove that car.

Mrs. Malloy answered their knock. "Oh Beck, come to hear the band? And Sonia-Barton, I've heard so much about you."

"Hello, ma'am." Sonia-Barton knew how to act like a good girl.

Beck wondered how Randall had described her to his mother.

Like most of the neighborhood women, Mrs. Malloy stayed home to take care of the children and the house. Beck thought of her as beautiful, poetic, happy even if you saw a distant, troubled expression in her eyes like she was missing something or somebody. Once she'd picked Beck up from Burgundy Farm when a girl in the third grade had turned suddenly and jabbed Beck in the back with a pencil. Mrs. Malloy had taken her to her bedroom plush with satin pillows, sweeping thick curtains, and strange pungent scents of creams and oils. She'd lain on the bed while Mrs. Malloy took out the lead point of the pencil with ruby-colored and shaped fingernails.

Years of Tuesday afternoons in her basement learning to play scales and simple music made the house familiar. Mrs. Malloy had cut Beck's fingernails with big black paper scissors—a means that Beck had used until Sonia-Barton had showed her how to shape and paint her nails.

"They're in the rec room," Mrs. Malloy said as if proud of Randall. The fried flour scent of chicken wafted from the kitchen as Mrs. Malloy opened the door for them to the basement.

Randall's father, Colonel Malloy, had finished the basement with wood paneling and a bar. Down there was the upright where Mrs. Malloy taught Beck and other children piano. A beautiful, big black grand was in the living room reserved for Mrs. Malloy and adults.

The music came up so loud the wooden stairs shook. A set of circus drums—pearl inlaid cases and multi-sized brass cymbals. Black curled cords attached to guitars with sunburst paint jobs—their long blonde necks held by unfamiliar boys–old enough to be juniors or seniors in high school. Randall played an instrument encased in red plastic with a row of switches running across a bank above a keyboard set atop a black metal two-legged stand.

The sound was WEAM-AM but more immediate. Amazing boys from Virginia playing rock in Randall's basement.

Silver buttons up her crack.

What did that mean? Had she heard right?

Don't know how to do it, show you how to walk the dog.

A riveting, beautiful boy with long eyelashes and thin, wide shoulders beneath a striped Gant shirt grasped a bass guitar and whistled calling a dog, lips a passionate contortion of meaning. He smiled at them and shook his Elvis hips.

"Whew," Sonia-Barton shouted. "Bourbon Street." She started to dance a go-go, pulling an imaginary robe up between her legs.

Beck looked upstairs. Mrs. Malloy had closed the door as if she didn't belong in this teen world.

Beck's eyes glistened with a rush of independence and teenage freedom. With her head down like somebody might notice and tell her she didn't belong here, she crossed to a couch along a far wall. The basement smelled of cigarettes and Old Spice. She could look at the boys–their faces, hair, lips–because they were performing. The drummer, bangs to his eyebrows, hit white skins with sticks and pumped his feet. A tall guitar player moved long fingers with calm assurance in coordinated patterns on metal strings. Black amplifiers filled the basement with music.

When the song was done, she clapped along with Sonia-Barton who'd stayed in front of the band so they all would notice her. Randall's big almond-shaped eyes blinked and he pressed his lips together as if trying not to smile.

"Aren't you going to introduce us, Butch?" the bass player's movie voice boomed around the room.

Randall spoke into a microphone, his voice large with reverb. "That's Beck and Sonia-Barton. They live near here."

"Way to go, Butch," the drummer said and flipped the plastic-tipped drumsticks in a quick roll on his snare drum.

Beck's fists clenched.

Randall had a silly gasp of a laugh like he was trying to hold something back. They were teasing him for his short hair by calling him Butch. She thought his military cut made him stand out, look older, highlighting his long jaw line and bringing out his blue eyes. Sitting behind the keyboard, you couldn't tell how short he was.

"Yeah, beautiful women. Way to go," the bass player said. "I'm Robbie Puckett." the bass player said into the microphone.

"Robbie Fuck-it, you mean," the drummer said, and the guitar player laughed. Randall kept his casual grin as if these boys could do or say anything and he'd do nothing to stop them.

"Fuck you, asshole." A further obscenity echoed from the amplifier.

"My name is Richie Johnson," the drummer rose from his round cushioned stool and bowed over the big round drum between cymbals.

"Otherwise known as Dumbfuck."

Beck's eyes widened. She shouldn't be part of this disgraceful association. A good girl shouldn't socialize with these kinds of boys if she wanted to stay a good girl for long.

Sonia-Barton lit a cigarette.

Beck leaned deeper into the couch at the outright rebellion erupting around her.

Robbie, the singer, took out a cigarette.

"Where's an ashtray, Butch?" Sonia-Barton asked, completely ignoring propriety and joining the disreputable behavior.

"Over there by Beck."

Randall was now Butch.

"What's the name of your band?" Sonia-Barton asked as she moved to Beck's side.

"Needle-Dick and the Bug-Fuckers," Richie the drummer said.

"It's his family name," Robbie the bass player cracked.

Sonia-Barton's delighted laughter rang with a twangy note. "Are you serious?"

"We're the Pirate Heroes," Randall said with a gleam of pride in his eyes.

Robbie grinned, followed Randall's gaze at Beck and winked. "Let's play *I Want You* in G, Butch."

* * *

A peppery scent of first bloom crocus blew by Beck in the back of Richie's GTO. The spring air was still too cold to have the top down, but they did because they could.

Through the opening of the bucket seat, she saw Richie slide his hand far up Sonia-Barton's exposed thigh below her dress.

Beck was going to be fifteen that summer–then maybe someone would take her out, touch her like that.

Since meeting the band, fall and winter had passed quickly and slowly at the same time waiting for weekends when they could escape their private girl's school world into the swirl of public school and modern styles of dress and hair. If it wasn't for the band, they'd be stuck with school dances, debutante parties, hoping for dates with brothers or friends of the girls at Madeira.

Congressional on the way to Annandale was the private school Beck had gone for Cotillion when she was thirteen. Once a week during the winter, Mrs. Malloy had driven her and Randall to the formal dances arranged for the boys and girls who would be coming out or presented at debutante balls. Beck had dressed in a gown purchased by her grandmother at Lord and Taylor. She'd curtsied to a fat woman and a bored-looking man in a tuxedo and had passed from partner to partner in a line. When she'd danced with Randall, she'd been taller than he even though he was two-years older. It was only this year that he's started to become a man.

Pirate Heroes set up their equipment on a stage in the cafeteria, then went to the bathroom to change into their Pirate uniforms–striped gondolier T-shirts and pants torn down by the middle of their calves. The Pirate was a bar and restaurant on the waterfront in Georgetown owned by Richie's father. He'd given the band shirts with Pirate Heroes printed on the front.

The tables had been cleared and the open area filled with high school kids from all over Fairfax and Arlington. Everyone except the janitor who turned down the lights was white. Robbie sang, *"Got rocking pneumonia and the boogie woogie blues."* Richie slammed his stick down on his drums. Jack played exciting high Chuck Berry notes on his guitar. Randall smiled happily and swayed, singing into a microphone during the chorus, *"So roll over Beethoven and tell Tchaikovsky the news."*

A boy came up to Beck. He was olive-skinned, maybe Cuban from one of the families who'd fled Castro. He'd stammered when he asked her to dance. After the song he spoke quickly, "I go to Jeb Stuart. I'm in the tenth grade."

She only smiled, not wanting to tell him she was only fourteen.

The band played *My Girl* and she stepped close to him, laid the side of her face against his shoulder, and moved her feet side-to-side, a remnant of the Cotillion dances. He was wearing a pleasant lemony scent she liked. The feel of him between the fabric of their clothes caused a warmth to expand down her thighs. When the song ended she relaxed her stiffened posture to do the stepping back and forward moves to the fast number the band was playing.

"We'll be back in snap," Robbie said into the microphone, leaving Beck to see if the Cuban boy would stay with her.

"Thanks for the dance," he said.

"You're welcome." Maybe she should have spoken to him, acted more interested. She moved alone off the dance floor looking for Sonia-Barton.

Robbie walked by and casually took Beck's hand. "Hey, girl," he said sexily.

She blushed as the warmth spread back through her.

"Let's go outside." He took Beck's had.

Did that mean go kiss?

"OK." She fluttered her eyelashes the way Sonia-Barton did when she flirted with Richie.

Weakness of being led mixed with anticipation and a rush of sexual arousal as he led her out a side entrance to where a lawn sloped down to the road.

There was a commotion off to the side in the dark. "Fight," someone shouted.

Two boys wrestled each other. Wayne from the neighborhood was fighting a greaser who played in another band. Friends of each pulled them apart and glared at each other like there might be a West Side Story rumble.

Robbie pulled her farther into the darkness. The warmth shot into her breasts and held so tightly she could barely breathe. His tongue probed inside her mouth. The shame of not knowing how to respond like two snakes darting and twisting against each other made her wilt against him.

"What are you doing?" Randall, shoulders hunched, eyes narrowed, menacing, ready to fight, pulled Robbie from her.

Robbie stepped back and raised his hands in submission. "Sorry cat. Sorry I kissed your girl."

She looked from one to the other, exhilaration causing her to clutch her hands before her like praying. Randall *was* her boyfriend.

"Plenty of fish in the sea," Robbie turned, black pants cut tight around his narrow hips and ankles sashayed back to the dance.

Beck glanced to see kids watching them and followed Randall when he stepped deeper into the shadows of a boxwood hedge. He looked down at her and hesitated as if unsure how to explain what he'd done. "I just don't think that you should be associating with people like Robbie."

She looked about again to confirm nobody could hear their whispered conversation. "Why? I like him."

Randall fell urgently into his argument, raising his hand for emphasis. "He's got a reputation, you know. He wants more than a kiss."

"Don't lecture me. You're not my big brother."

Even the hint of a reference to his dead best friend seemed wrong.

His jaw locked. "Maybe I don't want you kissing anyone...until you're older." He hastened to add the qualifier.

She tilted her head to study him, savoring the idea that he was jealous. Her expression softened and she sighed in relief to be safe with Randall again. "You're taller than me now."

He grinned. She knew how to please him, how bothered he'd been by not maturing as fast as his friends. "It's about time," he said.

Richie came up. "There you are. Show time, Butch."

Her eyes flitted to Richie and back to Randall who shrugged. "Some things you just know," he said mysteriously to her.

She walked with Randall and Richie to the fringe of the crowd gathered along the walls of the school cafeteria. The Cuban looked at her and turned away, not interested. She felt more confident. Two boys had fought over her. She was desirable. Her eyes closed for a moment, marveling at how exciting her life had become so much promise for the future.

She watched Randall climb on the stage where the band were picking up their instruments. What did he know about being sixteen that she didn't? That she shouldn't ever be with anyone but him? The idea seemed prosaic, from another age or country—a fourteen-year-old girl only knows one man and is betrothed to him in childhood. Her family would never go along with that idea. If Beck was destined for anything her marriage was to be magnificent to a well-chosen mate.

She looked at three girls standing along the wall, waiting for a boy to ask them to dance while Randall sang, "Come on up and have a good time."

This wasn't a dream. This was growing up—fights, kisses—like a blinding light she was rushing into—good or bad. She didn't want him kissing another girl either. But if he did and fell in love with someone else so would she. They could always come back to each other.

FOUR

FIFTEEN

S aturday morning, Beck sat in a wooden schoolhouse chair in Panda's office, a small room near the kitchen filled with recipes, account ledgers, the Green Book, invitations, stationery, letters to be answered, bills to be paid.

Panda had white hair, worn in whatever style was fashionable, now short and swept back behind her ears. Beck wished she had her deep blue almost purple shade of eyes instead of her greenish ones.

Dressed in a silk kimono robe, perched on the edge of an old parlor chair, Panda spoke in a Petersburg's accent–a British-inflected drawl old movie actors had imitated to sound sophisticated. Petersburg was in the Tidewater part of Virginia, Panda had lectured, because the first colonists–their people–had settled there while the later arriving Catholics had to live in the mountains.

"When preparing your guest list think like a cook. There are your basic ingredients–the right mixture of types. The greater skill is in knowing personalities. Season your party with the right mixture of the spicy, lively personality to offset the common tart serious souls."

"Well, we have Sonia-Barton for that," Beck smiled.

"Yes, we certainly do." Panda rewarded her with a slight chuckle and wrote down Sonia-Barton's name with a fountain pen on lavender, embossed paper. With reading glasses half-way down her narrow nose, Panda looked at Beck like a bird ready to catch a worm. "Is she behaving herself at school?"

"She wants to go to public school. She likes the kids better there."

"What about you?"

"Oh, it's fine."

"It's a very good school," Panda said. "I attended Madeira."

"I know."

"I hope you can exert a good influence over Sonia-Barton. Does she go with boys?"

"Panda!" Beck blushed and looked down.

Her grandmother smiled. "I suppose you have a special someone you want to invite?"

Beck's reddening deepened and she fidgeted her hands. Was she *supposed* to have someone? Was this a trap to get her to reveal improprieties? As if she had any chance to meet boys going to Madeira. Panda knew the regulars at the Homestead. "I don't know many boys."

"What about Randall?" Panda asked.

Beck had invited him to her birthdays and Panda had let her bring him to her box at D.C. Stadium to watch the Senators. Did Panda know about the boys in the band? Had Janey told her? No, Janey was loyal. Maybe Gail who was always bending over backwards to please her mother-in-law had said something. Panda had powers. Beck should never assume she could *ever* hide anything from her grandmother.

"I guess."

"Shall I put anyone down?"

"Randall plays in a band, you know. If I invite him, I probably should invite the rest of his band. They're musicians. I'm kinda of friends with them."

"You know I don't like *you know* and *kinda* is not a word, dear. Shall we hire them to perform?"

Beck quickly shook her head. "Oh no, I didn't mean that. They might think that I only invited them to play."

"Well, we'll worry about the entertainment in time. Let's finish this list."

* * *

More than anything, Beck wanted the afternoon birthday in the garden to be a success. She would have preferred to have the party at Lake Barcroft at night where the kids could sneak off to drink and make out. She prayed nobody tried that here. All the guests except the band were from families Panda knew, so there probably was not much to worry about unless Pirate Heroes started to act up. Had she made a mistake inviting them? They were her real friends.

The June weather was good—azaleas and day lilies still in bloom, the first magnolias casting their perfumed scent. Beck wore a pink party dress with a bow at the waist. Her figure had filled out but not as much as other fifteen-year-old girls who looked womanlier than her tall and skinny figure. But her makeup of lipstick, rouge, and eyeliner provided sophistication. Panda's hair stylist had fluffed her hair and parted it off center with buns on the side.

Randall was the first to arrive carrying a wrapped gift. Panda was ready. Dressed in a tight bodice and full skirt hemmed below her knees, she met him and his mother at the front door. Mrs. Malloy bowed her head and didn't come in when Panda invited her. She said she was going to see the new stores at Tyson Corners. "I'm very proud of you," Mrs. Malloy whispered loud enough to hear when she said good-bye to Randall.

Panda went to see about the food, leaving Beck to stand with Randall to greet people. Beck glanced at him and wondered if people would think he was her boyfriend. He still had a baby face. The first bristles of his blond beard were on his upper lip. He no longer wore the butch cut that had earned him his nickname but still cut above his ears.

"I got you some Ray Charles and Jimmy Smith," he said and tried to give her the records wrapped in circus theme paper.

"Thank you, Randall. Would you mind putting them on the table inside?"

When he returned to her side, she shifted her weight and looked at the driveway. That would be all right if the girls from school thought he was her boyfriend. But what if Robbie wanted to kiss her again? She contracted her eyes, guilty for betraying Randall. She definitely didn't want Panda thinking he was her boyfriend.

"There's going to be a colored band playing, a blues band. They are setting up in the back if you want to go see them."

"What are they called?"

"The Chaps."

His eyes expanded. "You have the Chaps for your birthday! How did you get them?"

"My grandmother hired them."

Randall considered Beck as if she was a painting.

"What are you looking at?"

He gave his quick swallowed laugh. "It's like you're somebody else."

An immediate, irresistible rush of fear clenched her heart. "Do I look all right?"

"You look good, like a lady, all grown-up."

She sagged with relief and smiled. "Thanks, Randall, you look very nice too."

His gaze dropped to his blue blazer. "My Mom bought me this at the Varsity Shop. She acts like this is my big chance to make it in society. She's been talking about this ever since I got the invitation. I never got a printed invitation to anything before. Why did you invite Robbie?"

"I invited all the guys in the band."

"You know what they call you?"

Beck didn't want to hear.

"Dodge."

She looked down then up. "Why?"

"They like you, really. Dodge is a cool name. It's from a song I wrote about you. I didn't want to use your real name."

He wrote songs about her. The idea was so romantic she didn't care what he called her. She looked up at him and her eyes glistened. "Of course not. I'd love to hear it."

A very elegant woman and fashionable girl stepped from a black limo. Diplomatic, Beck decided, an ambassador's wife and daughter. As if knowing when to appear, Panda rejoined Beck at the door.

Randall openly gawked.

Panda introduced them as the Viscountess the somebody and her daughter the...

Beck shook hands with a girl her age who looked at her with a kind of helpless pleading that she had an image to uphold or she would be more fun.

"This is Randall Malloy," she was forced to introduce him because he was standing by her. Panda frowned at the implication that he was a host or maybe acting too familiar.

Before Beck could say something to send him into the party, Robbie stepped from his Rambler and gave the keys to a red-coated valet. His hair parted in the middle hanging over his ears, Beck thought he looked daring the way he was dressed in stovepipe pants tailored tightly around naked ankles in pair of maroon Weejuns.

"And who are you, young man?" Panda grilled him.

"I'm Robbie." He shook her hand with a cock of his head and a gleam in his eyes as if sure Panda would immediately fall under his spell.

Panda gave him the freeze because of his hip dress and lack of formal manners. "Robbie whom?"

Robbie smiled and Beck was afraid he might outright laugh at her grandmother.

Randall interjected to save the day. "Robbie Puckett. He's a friend of mine, Mrs. Lyons. Thank you for inviting him."

"Well go on inside, and behave yourself, Mr. Puckett." She pronounced his last name as if it were a curse.

Beck lowered her eyes from Robbie's grin, embarrassed for her family's elitism. Robbie didn't seem to care if her grandmother thought him lower class. He handed Beck a small wrapped box. "Happy birthday, gorgeous."

"Why thank you, Robbie. How very thoughtful of you. There's a table inside for the gifts." She led him away from her grandmother's stern expression into the entrance hall where the round table was already piled with presents.

Robbie softly whistled. "Whew, look at this place."

An arch opened into a vestibule below a curved flight of stairs. Matching copper statues of toga-clad slaves held aloft orbs.

"Looks like a museum."

Beck wished she'd had her party some place normal. Heatherford had been in the family since before the War of Independence. To reach the manor house, you traveled up a long driveway lined with tall pointed pines and firs. There used to be more land, a plantation that had been broken up to build other estates. Her ancestors had been contemporaries of Washington, Madison. Robert E. Lee had been a neighbor. Many had been in politics. A President had lived in the house, a congressman, ambassadors. There were scandals. Panda had told Beck cleaned-up versions because scandal was the most fearful thing to a politician. The President hadn't really lived there. He'd visited a mistress who nobody acknowledged in polite society. A bad great-great uncle had come into the family because a daughter had gone riding in a carriage with him without a chaperon and hadn't come back until dark so the family had been forced to marry her to him.

Every couple of generations a relative knew how to make money as Beck's great-grandfather had, before a boom had knocked him off a ketch into the

Chesapeake Bay during a sudden squall–the *Chesapeake drowning* as her grandmother referred to that episode of the deadly curse that seemed to stalk their family.

Sometimes in the many lonely days Beck spent in the big old house after her mother and brother fell to the curse, she had fantasies about the man she'd bring into the family, maybe one of the Kennedys–Robert and his large brood of boys was a neighbor–both wealthy and a good politician.

"Man," Randall distracted Robbie. "Guess who the band is? The Chaps."

"Bitchin."

"Please don't curse," she said in an urgent low voice.

They looked at her and smiled. "We won't, promise. I'm going to go check out the band, OK?" Randall said as if she might not want him to abandon her.

"That'd be nice. I have to stay and greet my guests."

She returned to Panda's side and waited for the lecture about being careful to choose her friends. But Panda was too busy showing her how to be a hostess for a warning that would certainly come later.

After the party had filled, Panda took her in tow for more social lessons. Panda lectured as if this was a task Beck would soon have to perform, "A party should circulate. What you must do now is take guests and introduce them to other guests. Mix them in a way that creates interesting conversations."

Beck sighed, more an advanced form of cotillion than a fun party. The yard was too big, permitting the guests to distance themselves. How was Beck supposed to bring them together? The girls from school sat at round metal tables and chairs near the tennis court. They giggled and glanced shyly without much practice around boys. The sons and daughters of Panda's friends and social connections stood silently by themselves by the pool. Pirate Heroes were by a wooden dance floor laid on the grass near the rose garden. Sonia-Barton openly smoked a cigarette–something she'd just dared to do.

A colored man in a tuxedo passed with a silver tray serving hors d'oeuvres. Another waiter, the husband of the maid, was behind a bar on the patio serving soft and fruit drinks.

Under Panda's watch, Beck introduced a girl from her school to the son of a senator. They mumbled a greeting, stood awkwardly until the girl moved to a group of girls.

Panda stayed at her side, the patient teacher.

"What do you do when they don't want to talk to each other?" Beck asked.

"This is a peculiar age. Who are those boys with Sonia-Barton by the musicians? They seem a lively sort. Move them around."

Beck's head turned and her eyes widened that her grandmother had said something approving about the Heroes. But she wasn't released to join them because her grandfather replaced Panda as her escort.

Tall and thin like her father, he used to put her on his knee and sing Gilbert and Sullivan songs to her. Since she went through the change, he acted with reserve and didn't kiss or hold her like he used to. She still called him PawPaw.

"I better go check on the others," Pawpaw said.

"OK Pawpaw. I'm going to go be with my friends."

He smiled. "You go right ahead. Might as well have some fun with your friends. Believe I'll join mine too."

Only Randall looked at her when she walked up. How long could she stay before having to go back to her social duties? She looked back to see Pawpaw entering the house to go drink and socialize with the adults. Randall turned his attention back to band.

A drummer, sax, bass, guitarist and singer were dressed in matching tight suits with jackets of a material that looked embedded with metal blue flakes. After they finished a slow blues number about *dat gal of mine*, the singer smiled at her as if he knew her.

"How ya' doin' birthday girl? You got anything special you want us to play?"

"Willie Dixon," Randall said. "Play *Wang Dang Doodle*."

The band leader laughed. "How you know about that song?"

"We have a band," Randall said.

"Well, you boys study your books, don't go off and be no musicians."

"I *am* a musician," Randall said.

Beck tilted her head to look at him. His certainty amazed and impressed her. When she looked into the future, she saw only haze where Randall seemed to see a clear path. Perhaps if she could see with his clarity, she'd have more confidence instead of blindly placing one foot before the other, fearful of a fall.

The singer and other members of Chaps laughed harder, showing their bright white teeth.

"What you play, young man?" The guitarist asked as he carefully set a glass of iced tea on his amplifier.

"Keyboards. I want to get a church organ, a B-3. All I have now is a Farfisa."

The guitarist nodded, "Yeah, that's the sound, with a Leslie speaker. But that's a load. You'll need a truck to haul it."

Beck was pleased that Randall had an intense expression, excited to be taken seriously.

"I've written some songs. I'm going to take them up to New York this summer. You know anybody up there I can talk to?"

The guitar player looked at the lead singer with a knowing smile. "Man, that's hard," he said. "You got to be good and lucky."

The singer laughed. "Yeah and be willing to sell your soul to the man. Come on, boys, let's gig now," he said.

The Chaps started a version of a Rolling Stones song, or maybe the Rolling Stones had played a version of their song.

The music attracted more dancers. Sonia-Barton and Richie started to dance.

"Want to dance?" Randall asked her in an almost joking tone as if he knew that she wouldn't.

"No," she said morosely. "No fun for me. I'm the hostess."

Lucy Baines Johnson, the President's daughter arrived and apologized that nobody else from the family could attend. Beck believed her. Ladybird, the First Lady, probably would have come because she was Panda's friend.

Beck moved from group to group, cut the cake, opened her presents–Robbie's first, a bottle of Ambush. She gave him a warm thanks as he stood with Randall watching her. He winked in way that caused her to quickly turn her attention to another present. Robbie wasn't afraid of Randall or anybody.

* * *

Beck lay in her bed a cloud of jasmine from Robbie's Ambush, frowned with her hands behind her head. She was fifteen now. This was the year she'd spread her wings and have more fun. Her first choice was to be out with her friends with their cars, music, and dating.

The band was fun but the society she'd been born into was more important and was where her responsibilities lay. She sighed and turned over to her side. Life just got more complicated, harder to figure the older you got.

* * *

Panda took her to her box halfway down the third base line at the new ballpark for a day game against the Yankees. Both of them wore matching large straw Rattan beach hats with black ribbons. Some of the veteran players knew Panda and called out, "Hi, Mrs. Lyons," as they emerged from the dugout to the on-deck circle. Whenever a lefty would come to the plate against a right hand pitcher even if Panda was talking, she'd keep an eye on the plate.

"You know darling, it's very important for you to wisely choose your friends. One is known by whom they associate with."

Beck turned to stare at her grandmother to act as if she was intently listening even if her mind was wandering. Sometimes, she was interested in Panda's stories, mostly she just wanted to appear attentive.

With her eyes on the field, Panda repeated her fundamental warning that the Lyons were different. "People will just be waiting to talk about you. Boys will try to have their way with you and believe you me, they will talk, and the world will know of your fall."

Beck didn't have to feign interest now. She watched her grandmother as she would a threat.

Panda used family history as she often did to make a lecture more immediate and important. "We had a cousin, a Petersburg Battle, who let a man have his way with her. She said she was forced and maybe she was." Her grandmother intently eyed the plate.

A foul ball sliced their way. Beck flinched, a scream stuck in her throat as the white bullet rocketed toward her. A fan sitting above them reached over and caught the ball with a loud *whack*. His glove hit Beck's forehead. The near miss shook Beck. The catch was so phenomenal that many in the crowd cheered. The man modestly accepted the accolades by raising the ball in her right hand. He leaned over and handed the ball to Beck. She thanked him to be polite but decided she hated baseball.

When everyone's attention had returned to the game, Panda continued her parable as if nearly being knocked silly was part of the game. Beck stared at her. She was supernatural.

"Cousin Winifred was sent away to Europe, married well there, returned to Petersburg with a child *and* a title, but could never escape the whispers. She tried very hard for the rest of her life to regain that which had been given to her freely and in abundance before her disgrace. But once lost, to regain one's reputation is like chasing a train through a station—one rarely looks one's best."

Beck could count her kisses: Randall—she'd never played husband and wife with him again—, and a quick peck by a boy at the Homestead when she was twelve, the real kiss by Robbie. Sonia-Barton gave sex a good reference.

Beck looked at her blouse. "I don't even have a boyfriend."

Panda chuckled. "Oh, you will, darling, you will. And he will tempt you. But the foundation of good character is moral strength. You must resist temptation until the moment is right, and then," Panda smiled and batted her drawn out eyelashes. "All your waiting will be more than worth it."

Did her grandmother expect her to be a virgin when she married? Was life easier for girls who didn't have famous fathers? People treated her like she was a princess. It might be ten years before she married. Beck wasn't going to wait that long.

The Senators lost. Eddie Yost, the manager, said he'd have the team sign the ball Panda had caught for Beck.

* * *

Sex came to Beck quicker than ten years. Two weeks after her birthday, she, Sonia-Barton, and Gail were going to Europe. Her father would join them in London. She was excited about the trip but would also have happily stayed with her friends at Lake Barcroft who had taken to sneaking out at night, meeting at Beach One, and sleeping during the day.

The night before they were to fly to Paris, Robbie came over with Richie to say good-bye. Beck had not been expecting Robbie. She was dressed in shorts and a thin blouse.

"Let's go to the beach," Sonia-Barton said.

Beck only had time to quickly spray Ambush on her neck before they walked through the quiet neighborhood. Sonia-Barton and Richie held hands. Though the orchid smell of the cologne surrounded her, she wished she'd rolled some Dial beneath her arms. She was intently aware of Robbie tapping his hand on the side of his leg, wondering if he was bored. The intimacy of where he might be leading her made the sounds and lights of the neighborhood, the warm, still air, a place of promise. She wiped her forehead with the back of her hand and twisted a friendship ring with her thumb. The crickets were rubbing a constant racket. The lake had a feral scent of old cut flowers. Lights from houses and a lone cruising electric barge reflected off the serenity.

Sonia-Barton and Richie went into the darkness on the grass that sloped down to the sand. Beck could see their dark shapes as he lay atop her. She sat next to Robbie on the grass. He looked at the lake. Was he afraid of Randall? She trembled in the darkness.

"You know I don't have a boyfriend," she said in a near-whisper, nearly a sigh.

"I'll be your boyfriend," he said.

Flushed with excitement, she closed her eyes as his lips moved toward hers. In a smooth motion he pushed her back. Her open hands pressed against the hard contours of his chest before clumsily moving to the back of his head. She rolled a leg over the other to keep him from laying atop her.

A blade of grass tickled, and she turned her head. His lips moved to her ear, a new startling sensation. He moved slightly to the side which was a relief, reached under her blouse, pushed the cup of her bra up over her right breast. That too was uncomfortable. He rolled her nipple between his fingers. That was pleasant. She opened her mouth and concentrated on the play of his tongue against hers. His words that he'd be her boyfriend played over in her mind filling her with a euphoric feeling that spread through her in a warm wave.

His hand rubbed over her shorts. She would have stopped him if he tried to open her zipper, but he was too clever and experienced. Was she letting him go too far by allowing him to touch and push on the outside? The way he moved his fingers up and down made her want him to touch her more. As if knowing her desire, he unbuttoned the top of her shorts and pushed his hand down underneath her panties.

Now, she was definitely letting him go too far. Embarrassed by her wetness, she placed her hand on the back of his head, feeling the softness of his hair. She involuntarily pushed up against his hand, causing him to move inside of her—his finger up and back causing the exquisite sensation to grow.

He seemed to be willing to do that for as long as she wanted, kissing her, moving his finger. After the first awkward minutes, she relaxed and enjoyed his incredible touch and the thought he was now her boyfriend. When he rolled off of her, she was glad he'd stopped because of the uncontrollable, embarrassing sounds, she started to make.

He took out a foil-wrapped square from his wallet. Sonia-Barton had told her about rubbers at Peoples Drug Store. *They keep them behind the counter. If a boy wants one they place their fingers on the counter.* She'd made the shape of a V or spread legs with two fingers. Sonia-Barton knew a lot about sex.

Beck watched fascinated while he released his penis from inside his pants. She'd seen them on statutes and paintings in the National Gallery, and Randall's little one, but never swollen and erect in moonlight, a domed animal that rose from a dark cavern between his legs. Not until he reached for her shorts did she feel involved. Could she say no after all that she had let him do to her? She stood and buttoned her pants. He reached for her and she ducked under him and ran down to the sand, starting to laugh.

She couldn't see his face to judge his reaction. He came after her. She wondered what he had done with his penis. Was he still erect and hard in his shorts? He was quick and strong. She dodged him twice but he caught her and was on top of her reaching for her pants again.

"No," she said.

Amazingly, he obeyed her. "I thought you wanted to."

"Get off me."

He let her up. She brushed the sand from her hair.

He looked at her quizzically.

"Sonia-Barton," she called into the darkness.

There was no response.

"I'm going home," Beck said.

Robbie reached for her, but she ducked away.

"Come here," he said. "I won't do anything if you don't want me to."

She decided to trust him. He tenderly pulled her to him and kissed her in a way that started to excite her again. She stepped back from him.

"Dodge is a good name for you," he said. "You're hard to read."

What did that mean? That she was a snob? Just because she didn't want to go all the way?

Sonia-Barton emerged from the darkness. "Hey, let's go to Hot Shoppes," she said.

"I'll be right with you," Robbie said. "I have to go cut my dick off."

Beck laughed with Sonia-Barton at the word as they watched him go over to the shadows near a stack of canoes and rowboats his back to them as he pulled the thing from his pants. Maybe she'd hurt him. Sonia-Barton steered Beck by the arm. "We'll meet you at the car," she said to Richie.

Away from the boys, Sonia-Barton whispered, "How far did you go?"

"Almost all the way," Beck reported.

"Why was he chasing you?"

"You saw him?"

"I wasn't going to do anything, unless you screamed or something."

"He put a rubber on."

"You went all the way?"

Richie came within earshot.

"Remind me to tell you about it sometime," Beck said—using a phrase Panda said when she wouldn't reveal the most interesting part of a scandal.

On dark Lakeview Drive, Beck pulled free from Robbie's hand holding when they passed Randall's house.

Robbie looked up at the big windows over Randall's lawn and laughed at her. "I won't tell him."

She laughed back like she could take a joke. Randall might be watching them. Robbie was more of a catch, a real boyfriend as Sonia-Barton would say.

He reached for her hand again as if he knew she wouldn't resist.

FIVE

GIVE ME BACK THE WORLD

H er trip to Europe was filled with thoughts of Robbie and frets that he wasn't really her boyfriend. She missed him in a way that made paintings in museums, even stained-glass images of saints raise an ache and a distant daydream focus where she'd imagine being with him. At night in the dark, laying in a bedroom with Sonia-Barton in another bed beside her, she'd intimately touch herself and pretend it was him. She'd written Robbie a postcard of Michelangelo's David without writing the strong, naked power of the statue reminded her of him. She told him she missed him, not daring to write she loved him. Maybe she should have sent him a lighthearted card of fat Bacchus, the god of wine, riding a turtle, but she hadn't.

She continued her study of Sonia-Barton and wished that she had more of her daring careless attitude. Sonia-Barton had snuck off to sit in a cafe in Paris, drank wine, flirted in Italy with men who followed them, pushed up against them in crowds, and whispered passionate pleas in their ears in funny English— *happy, happy, go with me.*

On the Lido, Sonia-Barton had smiled at a remarkably beautiful man named Giovanni del Verrocchio.

Gio had followed them for two days in Venice then to Florence. They'd be shopping, sightseeing, or walking after dinner and he'd be there–his brown eyes impossibly large, full lower lip quivering–begging Sonia-Barton to come with him saying he loved her more than a sailor loves the stars. When they'd last seen him on the Spanish Steps the night before they'd flown home from Rome, he'd wept, saying he'd swim to America to be with his *bella, bella, bella.*

Beck understood Gio better than Sonia-Barton who laughed at his passion. She'd swim home to be with Robbie. Her longing was a pain that only he could heal.

* * *

They returned to Washington early in the morning. The Leader's driver picked them up at Dulles and drove Beck, Sonia-Barton, and Gail home before taking the Leader to the Capitol.

Lake Barcroft reflected a calm, safe welcome. The streets and houses appeared smaller–different–as if moved to the side, off-center. She looked out the car window as they drove past Beach One. The memory of sex excited her. Robbie would find her more sophisticated now. What did he know of Paris or Rome? She looked away from the beach and frowned that he might think her unapproachable because of who she was.

They'd been home an hour when Randall came over.

She and Sonia-Barton sat on the picnic table on the rec room porch while Randall stood before them.

"What did you like best?" he asked Beck.

"How old everything was, how different yet the same."

"I wish I could go there."

"You will someday."

"How's the band?" Sonia-Barton plucked a loose piece of tobacco from her tongue and looked down her nose at him.

Randall shifted his black Keds. "We're pretty much broken up. We only played once, at a pool party. Robbie's got a job playing at Ocean City in a beach band. He's eighteen now so he can play in the bars."

The news struck Beck hard. She trapped tears in her throat and turned toward the lake. Robbie was gone—three years older than her—playing in bars full of college girls.

"What about you? You're seventeen aren't you?" Sonia-Barton asked.

Randall smiled, the future bright. "Robbie and I are going to put a band together in the fall. I've been writing some songs."

Sonia-Barton looked at a red Italian shoe dangling from her foot then at the sky as if uttering a prayer. "God, give me back the world."

Randall considered her.

"What are you looking at?" Sonia-Barton asked.

"I'm going to use that. It's a good line. Hope you don't mind."

She twisted her lips. "Use it for what?"

"A song, something about longing."

"Oh yeah, sure great, can't wait to hear it," Sonia-Barton mocked Randall.

What difference did it make if he wrote songs? Beck thought. He was an artist, like van Gogh. Someday people would appreciate him. Beck smiled. "I'd like to hear what you've been writing."

"You will some day, when I'm ready. Soon," he said.

Though Beck thought he'd be better served by trying to get into a good college she tried to encourage him. "I think it's wonderful you have a plan. Working toward something," she said

The love in his eyes made her look down, embarrassed but happy she'd pleased him.

"Maybe you'll make some money," Sonia-Barton said.

Randall furrowed his eyebrows. "I've got an idea for the melody. I'm going to go see if I can figure it out." He hurried up the gravel path to find the notes before he forgot.

"That boy is so strange," Sonia-Barton said.

Beck stared at where he'd gone. "He's not writing music for the money."

"Yeah, right. Think he knows about Robbie almost popping your cherry?"

Sonia-Barton could be crass, like vulgarity was part of being a teenager, to say things she'd never say in front of an adult.

Beck looked to where a small flat-bottom sailboat was tacking in a breeze on the lake. "No. I hope not. Randall would be hurt."

"So? Who is it Robbie or Randall? It's like you're already married and you're not even going out with him, so weird."

Beck didn't want to face the question. She looked at her beaded sandals. "I never want to hurt him."

Sonia-Barton frowned and shook her head. "Yeah, but you love Robbie. I can tell."

Beck blinked as if startled by the truth. "I know, but oh well, who knows, he's probably forgotten me."

"That's one thing you don't have to worry about Randall."

Even though Sonia-Barton had said it like it was a curse, Beck felt tenderness relax her jaw. When she kissed Randall, she *would* be his girlfriend and could never go out with anyone else. She was too young for that, and desired Robbie in a way she'd never felt for Randall.

* * *

Sunday morning in the Ocean Front Avenue beach house in Virginia Beach, Beck was dressed in a white terry cloth jumper that reached down to mid-thigh and covered her bikini. "Going to the beach, Daddy," she said as she walked by him on the screened porch.

"My god, you're all grown up."

Sadness in his voice caused her to turn slowly, unsure of what she'd see.

He wore an old pair of slacks and a short-sleeve shirt. The Sunday New York Times and the Washington Post lay out around him. These August days were when they could be more like a normal family. He'd slow down gradually like one of the navy ships gliding past Cape Henry. Then he'd go to movies with her, play games, laugh more. She knew the process. Now, he was still the Leader—nearly spending as much time on the phone as in the office.

He smiled still with a wistful expression in his eyes. "You are very beautiful."

"Thanks."

"Come sit with me for awhile." He moved a pile of newspapers and a briefcase stuffed with memos to make room for her beside him on the cushioned couch.

She sat close to him and leaned into his side, comforted and pleased to feel the protection of his arm around her shoulder. A few years ago she'd have sat on his lap and kissed him. She raised her head and kissed his cheek.

He looked down at her. "You are beautiful, you know. Men will say things to you and tell you things so that they can have their way with you."

He was able to say things, anything and pull it off, forcefully, but politely, with a slight tone of humor.

She buried her face in his side to hide her blush. "I know about that."

He laughed his deep, rolling, gut buster. "I hope you do, because you're going to knock them dead."

Why did her family think she was a tart, liable to run off with the first man who came along? Maybe she was, seeing how she'd behaved on the beach with Robbie. She quickly looked into her father's eyes and saw the twinkle there. He was complimenting her.

"What about Randall? He still your beau?"

Did everyone in the world think she should be with only him? "We're just friends."

He laughed again. "You're right to play the field. You've got a lot of growing up to do."

She blushed and lowered her gaze in confusion. Talking to her father about dating was disconcerting. Here was an opening, an opportunity to talk like adults. Her confusion was replaced by pride that he thought her old enough to speak about such things. But she couldn't find the words, looked up and said, "I know, Daddy. And thanks for caring."

His bushy eyebrows narrowed to accent the lines on his forehead. "I'm never too busy for you, my darling. You're my number one concern."

She could see and hear nuances in his expressions and words. Like those magic eye images if you stared at them the right way you'd see a unicorn among the random colors. He was an expert at making people believe him. She could read him better than anyone else. She knew when he was uncomfortable, unsure, or untruthful. He didn't really know how to talk to her about dating. He was trying to fill in for her mother who would have known better how to better advise her on being a woman.

* * *

The third Friday in September, Randall invited her to the first performance of his and Robbie's new band Pearl the Angel. She'd not seen Robbie since the incident on the beach.

She'd surreptitiously kept track of him by asking Randall casual questions without giving him reason to know how deeply she cared. Robbie was working in his father's vacuum cleaner repair store at Culmore and going to community college at Bailey's Crossroads.

Their time on the beach had only been an opportunity for some quick sex. Maybe, as Panda feared, to brag about what he'd done to Beck Lyons. What had been magical and enrapturing for her had meant little or nothing to him. If he cared about anything, he'd be more worried about not angering Randall...*kissing his girl.*

The hard facts had little effect on her emotions. In an instant, at school or sitting on the sidelines waiting to go into a field hockey game, she'd be sucked into sorrow and longing with a thought of Robbie and how hopeless her love was for him.

She dithered for days about what to wear, finally settling on a psychedelic black and white pattern dress that barely hung below the top of her thighs, cut low across her chest with billowed cuffs over her wrists. A stringed shell pattern belt rested on her hips with white go-go boots ending mid-calf. Before leaving her bedroom, she sprayed the Ambush Robbie had given her around her neck.

Sonia-Barton whistled when she saw her. "Loaded for bear, tonight, *eh?*"

Beck frowned. "Nothing special."

"Yeah sure," Sonia-Barton smiled. "Robbie bear. Well good hunting."

A boy from Jeb Stuart High School nicknamed Pluto helped Randall load his keyboard, amplifier, microphones and box of cords into the back of an old Dodge station wagon Randall had bought with his band earnings. Pluto was small, with bad acne on his chin and checks, festering red pustules. He'd walked from the other side of Columbia Pike near where the colored people lived, through the woods to their neighborhood to help Randall.

Mrs. Malloy came to the kitchen door dressed in a thin flower print blouse and black slacks that stretched around the circle of her stomach. Colonel Malloy, thick neck and tall emerged from the brick house to watch their son leave. "You two have fun, now," he said.

"Don't they look cute together?" Mrs. Malloy asked.

"Beautiful, just beautiful," Colonel Malloy said.

Beck frowned slightly. Maybe if everyone didn't assume she and Randall were together, she might feel more like being his girlfriend. The Leader was right, she needed to go out with other boys. If not Robbie, she'd meet someone else tonight and tell him that Randall wasn't her boyfriend.

"Bye," Randall waved with a happy smile as if excited to be doing what he loved.

Pearl the Angel was opening for bands with records played on the radio, a soul singer with a hit love song and a longhair band from New York called the Express had top billing and would go on last.

The atmosphere was different at the Elks Hall on Route 50 than the school dances. A fat, middle-aged man tried to organize everything.

"You're on first, kid," he said to Randall. "You'll play a half-hour set. Put your stuff up in front of the other band's equipment. After you play, you'll have to get your gear off the stage while the other equipment is being set up. You ever done anything like this before?"

"Well, we opened for the Beatles at the Coliseum," Randall said.

The man sneered. "Wait until the other bands have their stuff on stage. Get your shit set up as fast as you can at the front of the stage. Where's the rest of your band? Your drummer has to..." The man kept talking rapidly as he surveyed the hall as if searching for something else to worry about.

Beck became aware of a man looking at her. She glanced at him out of the corner of her eye. He was sitting against a metal shipping case on wheels, smoking a cigarette, tall and dressed in black with long hair and a wan face.

"Fucking big-time," Randall exclaimed as they walked out to unload the car.

* * *

In a crowded room behind the stage, Beck stood in front of some empty equipment cases. The band members of the *Express* sat in the center of the room in the only chairs with their entourage, including women in their twenties who didn't look like they'd come from Northern Virginia. The Negroes dressed in matching blue suits and had pointy black shoes practiced harmonies, quietly singing together in a corner. *Pearl the Angel* was supposed to go in five minutes. Everyone in the band was there but Robbie.

"What are we going to do if he doesn't show up? Pete, the drummer asked. He clutched two drumsticks in his hand. Randall shrugged and leaned closer to the guitar player. They practiced singing in harmony like the Negro band.

Beck wondered whether to stay or go out and look for someone she knew. She wanted to be there when Robbie arrived, but she didn't want to look as if she was waiting for him.

The musician she'd seen when they first arrived, pale skin on a long, thin face, moved to her side. "I'm Mick Pickford from the *Express*." He introduced himself like she should be impressed.

Beck shook his hand and blushed at the way he leaned close to her. "What's your name?" he asked.

"Beck," she said because her grandmother had taught her a long time ago not to let people use her familiar name until you knew them."

"Well, Beck of Sunnybrook Farm, we're going to have a little get together in our motel after this. Why don't you come over after the show?"

As if he knew the man was flirting with her, Randall moved to her side, close enough to appear as if they were together.

Beck smiled at Mick. "I'm only a sophomore. I can't stay out too late."

Mick laughed. "You're old enough to party, aren't you?"

Just then, Robbie arrived with a pretty blonde, distracting Randall. "Come on, man, get your stuff on stage. We're about on."

Beck didn't think Robbie noticed her.

"You can stay here with me," Mick said to her.

"What do you play?" Randall thrust out his jaw and squinted at the taller man.

Mick looked down at him. "Drums."

"You do any of the song writing?"

The man shifted uncomfortably as if Randall had exposed a weakness. "I help."

"You're on, kid," the fat promoter rushed into the room.

"Come on, Beck, you can't stay back here while we play," Randall said.

"Sure she can," Mick said.

Randall's face reddened. "She's the daughter of a senator, all right?" His voice trembled.

Beck closed her eyes and clenched her fists.

"Kid, are you playing or not?" the promoter asked?

Randall looked at Beck as if it was up to her. She knew him. If she did not go, he'd stay to protect her.

"What's going on?" Robbie came back from the stage. "We're already to go, Butch. Time to boogie. Hi, Dodge."

"Come on, Beck," Randall took her by the elbow and started to guide her to the door.

"I can go by myself." She pulled away, feeling childish.

"You sure have a lot of names, Beck of Sunnybrook Farm," Mick laughed.

She smiled quickly at the man because she didn't want him to think she was a snob because her father was a senator. "Got to go," she said and followed Randall and Robbie to the side of the stage. Randall must not have much faith in her to think she'd be interested in a creep like Mick.

Robbie hung his bass around his shoulders, looked over and winked at her as if he knew she was there to watch him.

The fat promoter on the stage, stood in front of Robbie and spoke into his microphone. He sounded excited and talked about what a great show, how happy he was to be part of such a "great opportunity to hear the latest, most popular bands in the country...and here to start things off are a local favorite..."

The band started with an up-tempo song that caused stirring in the crowd and a movement toward the stage.

If Beck was going to meet another boy, it wouldn't be here in the wings of the stage. She saw Sonia-Barton talking to a tall strong man that looked older than the high school kids. The way his hair was cut, Beck guessed he was military.

She climbed down the steps at the edge of the stage and stood next to Pluto. He smiled at her, but she knew that he wouldn't ask her to dance. On stage Randall's eyes searched for her. When he found her, he smiled as he sang, "I got the real thing."

What did she expect coming with Randall? It wouldn't be right if she ended up with someone else, but she could still dance with another boy, couldn't she?

She watched Robbie and he looked very sexy the way he shook his hips and pouted his lips when he sang. She wasn't the only girl looking him. At least she'd not let him go all the way. She'd been too open, too naive that night on the beach. No, she should not expect anything more from him. They were too young to remain faithful for that amount of time—faithful to what? Nothing. She was embarrassed that she'd signed the postcards from Europe, "Love, Dodge." No, that was all right. They were just friends. Maybe there would be another time and she wouldn't expect so much afterwards.

She looked around the dancers, groups lounging by the walls, boys dressed in sports coats and ties, some with the longest hair wore jeans, girls is skirts and blouses, short dresses like hers. A couple kissed in a dark corner, their open mouths working against each other, eyes closed.

Maybe there was something about her that made boys not want to ask her out. Maybe what Randall had said—the daughter of a senator—as if she was some kind of princess or something. But Sonia-Barton was the daughter, stepdaughter, of the same senator and she could find a boy in a minute. Beck was just as pretty as Sonia-Barton. Something inside of her repelled boys. She had to find out what it was and do something to get rid of it. Maybe she needed to smile more.

A handsome boy moved toward her. She smiled at him and he stopped next to her. Beck hadn't noticed Robbie's date standing near. The boy, tall and skinny with bangs over one eye, asked Robbie's girl to dance. The blonde smiled and went on the floor with him, right in front of the stage. Robbie would be able to see her. Don't take everything so seriously, Beck told herself.

An overweight boy stammered an invitation to dance. She went with him and sympathized how hard it would be if *she* was the one who had to ask someone to dance.

The audience clapped for *Pearl the Angel* at the end of each song. Her dance partner was polite about not pressing against her during the slow songs. When the band was between songs, he joked and appeared jovial. He was very intelligent and spoke like an adult. His name was Mark Brandenburg. He said that his father was a banker. They had just returned from Hong Kong where they'd lived for the last four years. He said that they had servants in Hong Kong who had done everything for them. "It's still really very British influenced," he said. "What does your father do?"

"Oh, he works in Washington." She said softly and looked down. She didn't want to say he was a senator because she sensed that would make him even more nervous.

When the band was done, she said that she had to go backstage to meet her friends. He stared at her for a moment as if to judge her intent. "Thanks for the dance," he smiled as if to leave open the possibility of more contact.

She felt mean as she turned her back on him, but he wasn't her cup of tea as Panda would say.

The members of the band and Pluto were moving their equipment off the stage through the back room out to their cars. A crew of workers set up the stage for the Negro soul singer and his band.

Randall and Pluto loaded his equipment into his car. "Do you want to leave?" Randall asked her.

"Don't you want to hear the other bands?" she asked.

"I don't care," Randall said.

"Let's stay."

"I want to go."

Beck put her hands on her hips and cocked her head at him. "I know you want to stay. I want to stay too."

"All right, we'll stay."

Robbie came up and put his arm around Beck's shoulder, as if not caring what Randall thought. "How you been, Dodge?"

"Fine as could be? How's tricks?" She imitated Sonia-Barton.

He gave her a quick squeeze. "Good, good, good. Couldn't be better. Life is grand. Hey, man," he removed his arm from her and spoke to Randall, "there's a party at the Express' motel after the show. We're invited."

"That's cool." Randall shrugged, "But I got to get her home on time."

"Come on go," Robbie smiled, and she wilted.

"Let's go. It could be fun, interesting," she said.

Randall frowned.

She watched Randall with a gleam of anticipation, wanting him to be responsible for her misbehavior.

He shrugged. "Yeah, OK, for a little while."

Watching Sonny B. Madison perform was fun. Hair greased and teased into a shiny helmet, he held the microphone and leaned forward, eyes closed, singing passionately even if there were only white kids in the crowd. Sonia-Barton was with the soldier, a Marine, she said in a whisper. Robbie's date joined Beck and Randall. Beck danced with Randall and then Robbie. She was proud of how popular Randall was. A beautiful girl said how much she liked his music. He asked her to dance and that was the group.

Mark Brandenburg stood against the wall looking at her with a dismissive expression. With squared shoulders and free dance moves she was protected in her group.

Sonny B. Madison played his hit, a slow love song. Randall danced with his new friend. Robbie's date went to the bathroom, leaving him to dance with Beck.

There was nothing shy about Robbie. He pressed against her intimately and held her close. She lay her head against his shoulder and felt the warmth spread through her as he swayed against her.

"Your girlfriend is pretty," Beck said.

"Not as pretty as you are."

"Sure, you're just a talker."

"Not always, if a girl will let me do more."

She ignored the shocking proposition. "Where did you meet her?"

"Ocean City. She goes to the University of Maryland."

Outclassed, no doubt the coed was happy to let him do what he wanted. Why not if his touch felt as good as on the beach?

"How was Europe?" Robbie asked.

"It was OK."

"Thanks for the cards," he said,

Over his shoulder, she saw Randall dancing a polite cotillion distance from his partner. Beck's eyes met his as if to share a promise. But she looked away and allowed Robbie to hold her close.

"Been meaning to call you," Robbie said his breath hot and exciting in her ear.

"Well, why haven't you?"

"Oh, you know, Randall. He's real gone on you."

Was he saying he'd be her boyfriend if not for Randall? "I'm not *going* with him or anything, you know." Her stomach contracted at her wanton betrayal.

Robbie harrumphed. "Wouldn't bother me, if you were." His hand fell down and brushed against her bottom so that she jumped slightly as if shocked.

His playfulness disoriented her, lost in a place she didn't belong. He was in control waiting to take her when and how he wanted. Her desire a weakness, she pulled her hips back from the pressure of what she'd seen in the dark on the beach.

The Express launched into a fast song with Mick twirling a drumstick in a black-gloved hand. Robbie's date returned and he danced with her, leaving Beck without a partner, until Randall bowed and asked, "May I have this dance?"

His smile as they faced each other, moving in the uncoordinated step forward-step back dance of youth, comforted her. As long as she was with him, there would be order and she'd belong wherever he was.

SIX

LEAVING LAKE BARCROFT

W ith a tremble behind her knees and gleam in her eyes the excitement and misbehavior of going to a party so late made the old motor court seem exotic like the Rainbow Cabins where Marilyn Monroe stayed in the movie *Niagara*.

Late, late, late and getting later, Beck told herself what difference would another hour make?

The party was in the last cabin. Lights and noise caused her to hesitate and look toward Route 50. Randall would take her home immediately if she asked, but she didn't want to appear fearful.

Too many people were crammed into the smoky bedroom with two beds, a kitchenette, liquor bottles, beer, wine, pretzels and potato chips on the counter. Members of the Express and Sonny B. Madison's band smoked cigarettes and held beers and glasses of liquor. A 45 rpm record plopped down a central cylinder. A needle riding a plastic arm played Eve of Destruction.

You're old enough to kill but not for votin',
You don't believe in war, but what's that gun you're totin',

Mick grinned to see them and shouted a greeting at Randall over the party noise. "How you doing, man? Glad you could come Beck Dodge Beck. So, is your father really a senator? What's his name? I'd like to meet him."

The idea was a threat. She looked around to see if anyone was listening and almost didn't answer, but that would have come across as snooty.

"Richard Lyons," she said softly.

"The Majority Leader? You're kidding?"

She smiled slightly in the modest way she responded when people found out who her father was.

"I'd like to talk to him about Vietnam. It's wrong, you know. We shouldn't be there."

The war in 1965 was growing more unpopular, one of those topics she didn't feel qualified to discuss. The President was sending more troops. Demonstrations were breaking out on college campuses. The Leader said we had to support the troops and she supported him. Sonia-Barton in her conservative Southern way had said the protesters were traitors and should leave America if they didn't like it.

Mick spoke passionately about a friend he'd grown up with who'd come back in a bag.

"I'm sorry," Beck said, afraid he'd blame her father.

"Sorry," Randall echoed.

"It's wrong." Mick leaned over her. "The war is wrong. You need to educate yourself. Talk to your father about cutting off funding."

Whenever she was in public with her father people constantly spoke to him about what he should do. He'd listen as if paying close attention and say,

"Thanks for bringing that to my attention." Or, "Please contact my office." Beck had never spoken contrary to any of her father's views, never asked him to vote for something. She liked to get up early and sit at the dining room table as Janey served them breakfast and he read the papers. When he was done, she'd read the Washington Post, and New York Times, more interested in the social sections and comics than the news. She was informed by his comments and grousing about a column or editorial. The idea that she could influence national policy by talking to him seemed rebellious, misbehaving. Maybe when she was older and really cared about something.

The noise of the party increased. Two members of Sonny B. Madison's band and Robbie were smoking marijuana. Beck had never seen the drug. But she knew from the sweet pungent smell and the peculiar shape of the cigarette a Negro passed to Robbie they were flagrantly breaking the law.

"Better get out of here," Randall said.

Mick looked to the drug use with consternation then back at her. "I'll give you my number." He moved to a desk beneath a television mounted on a wall.

"Sorry, got to go, man," Randall said and led her to the door as if the police might arrive any minute.

"Nice meeting you," she said to Mick in with reflexive politeness.

He looked at her with curled lips as if losing a chance and gave her a quick wave.

As she and Randall hurried across the parking lot as if to escape, she lectured herself to be more careful about the company she kept. She could trust Randall to protect her but could she trust herself? She was the one who'd wanted to go to the party. Robbie had showed himself to be a drug fiend. What if the police had come? What a scandal that would have been. Panda was right. People were waiting to talk about her and use her to tear down her father.

* * *

They let Pluto off in front of his small house near Ellen Glasgow Middle School across Columbia Pike from Lake Barcroft.

Randall wasn't talking to her.

She glanced at his frown and shoulders hunched over the wheel.

"What's wrong?" she asked. "Is it something I did?"

"No, it's me. My life."

She spoke to his profile. "What's wrong with your life?"

He sighed. "If I knew that, I'd know what to do."

"Oh," she said, but couldn't figure out what he was talking about—maybe being a teenager. Her life was ordered, preordained. She'd be happy if she had a boyfriend. "Don't pull into the driveway," she instructed when they drove in the circle.

In front of her house, she stood beside the car door Randall closed, leaving them in darkness.

"I had a really good time," Beck said and patted him on the forearm, ready for him to kiss her like Robbie had.

"I'm thinking of going up to New York."

Knowing him so well and the serious tone of his voice she sensed he was not talking about a visit or holiday.

"Robbie's cousin has connections in the music business. Wants to put together a band and get signed."

She shivered in the fall air, cold in the skimpy dress she'd worn to entice Robbie, not sure what being signed meant. Her foot tapped at the thought he might be thinking of running away.

He looked down giving her the opportunity to study his face for clues.

"When?"

"Robbie's ready to leave."

"But you're still in high school."

He swept his arms around. "I don't want to live and die in Lake Barcroft."

How could he want to be her boyfriend and leave for New York and take Robbie with him? Her wish to play the field seemed like a yawning challenge of the unknown.

"We want to make it in the music business, tour like those bands we heard tonight."

So that's what had set him off. "You can someday." She spoke soothingly but thought his plan rash.

He scratched the side of his head. "Yeah, I guess."

"You need to go to college. You can study music there."

He looked at her with squinting disparagement. "That's not how it's done. None of the bands come out of college."

"But if you don't go to college, what will you know then?"

He pursed his lips in distaste for her conformity. "If I stay in this structure, I'll grow into its shape. I don't want that."

She thought of saying *what about us*–like a girl would on the soap operas she watched with Janey. Her family would never approve of her marrying a musician.

She straightened and did not keep her disapproval out of her voice. "You should do what you want."

"Yeah." He sighed. "Time to hit the road."

"I better get in there." She looked toward the house, then back at him, leaned forward and kissed him on the cheek. "I had a great time. Call me tomorrow, OK?"

He put his hand on her waist and held her for a moment. "They'll never be anyone else but you. You know that, don't you?"

She leaned closer. "I know. Good night, Randall." She gave him another quick peck on the cheek. "See you tomorrow or today." She laughed that it was already another day and walked up the sandstone path to the house.

Questions she didn't know whom to ask gripped her and dragged her to despair as the childhood dream she'd marry Randall died. Maybe he'd be famous and...no, then he'd have plenty of girls. His promise that there would never be anyone else but her would be meaningless if he left. And if he stayed, he'd be unhappy, and would she want him anymore than she did now? Could they be with others and know they could always come back to each other? They were growing up fast. There was so much she didn't understand or feel prepared to meet as an adult.

SEVEN

ABOVE REPROACH

The Mustang Sonia-Barton's father had bought her was not in the driveway. Lights came on in the hallway. Fear clutched her heart. Who or why would anyone be up? Had there been a tragedy? She abandoned her intent to go through the private entrance to her room on the lower patio and quickened her steps to the door.

Gail was sitting in the living room off the front hall.

"Is everything all right?" Beck asked.

Gail stood and came to her. They were about the same height at five feet seven. Dressed in a long light blue satin robe trimmed in lace, her usual perfect hair was fallen around her cheeks, making her appear more vulnerable to Beck.

She looked beyond Beck into the darkness outside and back at Beck. "I'm waiting up for Sonia-Barton. Do you know where she is?"

Beck expelled her breath in relief. "Oh, I sure she's fine. She met someone at the dance, a Marine."

"Where did she go?"

"Give her a few minutes. She stays up late sometimes. I'm sure she'll be home soon." Beck turned from her stepmother, hoping to end the interrogation before having to answer for her own behavior.

"And what are you doing coming in at this hour?"

Challenge in Gail's voice caused Beck to end her retreat to her room. She turned to see a struggle between anger and concern in Gail's pursed lips and narrowed eyebrows.

"I was just out with some friends."

"I can't handle this. I *must* wake your father." Gail said and turned toward the hallway leading to the bedrooms.

Beck eyes widened and she stepped forward to stop Gail. "Why?" she practically sang the plea.

Gail quickly shook her head. "Beck, I don't know what is expected of me. I *must* have some help."

Beck took hold of Gail's sleeve to physically restrain her. "It can wait until morning. Daddy's probably exhausted."

Gail pulled away and turned down the hall.

"I'm not going to come between you and him. He would want to be awakened."

"*Please.* I don't think so." Beck hurried after her stepmother. "No, *please.*"

Short of physically holding her, Gail could not be stopped. Beck followed, heart pounding to her father's bedroom. The sound of his snoring, and a smell of deep sleep reminded her of being a child and coming to his bed when she had a nightmare. This was a living nightmare. Here was the punishment she'd feared for stepping out of line. "*Please don't!*" she begged.

"Richard, wake up." Gail turned on the light.

The Leader awoke immediately.

Gail's expression was tight. "I need your help. Sonia-Barton has not come home."

The Leader looked at the clock by his bed showing 1:14, got up and put a robe over his pajamas.

Beck stepped back in the hall, and almost fled to her bedroom but stayed to defend herself.

The questioning moved to the living room. Large, angled windows reflected the light against the darkness over the backyard and lake. Beck sat by herself on a couch, her knees pressed together, her hands clenched and pushed into her lap.

Beck admired the way he comforted Gail. Someday she would have someone to be that way to her.

"I'm sure she's OK. She met a soldier. Maybe they're talking." Beck pressed a weak case to cover for Sonia-Barton.

The Leader and Gail shared a worried glance before he glowered at her, ominous in his disapproval. "Why are you dressed like that?"

"This is how kids dress now, Daddy."

"Not my daughter. You look like a strumpet."

She wasn't sure what a strumpet was, but bet it wasn't good. Her eyebrows rose in shock that he'd spoken to her that way. She wasn't his little girl anymore. She should have gone to room let Sonia-Barton handle her own trouble. "I was out with some friends."

"Randall?"

"He just drove me."

"Maybe Randall knows where she is," Gail said.

Beck squinted at the stupidity of the idea. "He doesn't know where she is. We were just at a dance together where he was playing. He had to pack his equipment and take someone home who helped him."

"You going to call him or you want me to?" the Leader asked.

She was sure her father believed her but was doing what his wife wanted.

She raised her hands. "What's the point? I'm telling you he doesn't know. She left with the soldier."

"Then I'll call him," he said and strode to phone.

Beck rose quickly to follow him. "Daddy, no. He doesn't know. Why don't you believe me?" Pain in her voice moved to a sob as she half-reached to stop him.

"Randall's father is a colonel, isn't he?"

The Leader opened the cabinet beside the stairs leading to the recreation room and found a Lake Barcroft community directory.

"You can't call him now." Beck opened her hands palms up. "It's too late. He'll get very mad."

"He'll stand at attention with his finger in his ear if I tell him to," the Leader muttered.

"Please, Daddy," Beck gasped and pulled on his arm.

"Behave yourself," he ordered.

She stepped back, eyes lowered and swayed as he dialed the number.

"Colonel Malloy, Senator Lyons, here."

"Yes, sir." Beck heard the colonel's faint reply.

Humiliation and shame flushed through her. With a wail, she fled down the stairs to her bedroom. Her father was ruining her life. Randall was going to get killed. His father was a stern, ponderous man. He'd been shot down over Germany in the war and had a bad back. He'd never tell Randall what had happened, only it was tough.

The heavy thud of the Leader's steps preceded his angry demand. "Open this damn door, immediately, Beck."

"No." She drew out the vowel.

The Leader rattled the round handle. "Let me in!" His voice was crisp, demanding.

"I don't know where Sonia-Barton is. She's not my responsibility."

"I want to talk about *you!*"

The Leader furiously shook the door. "Things are going to change around here. You are grounded for a month. Any future dates are to be cleared with me or Gail. We were obviously wrong to trust you."

She lay facedown on her bed in the meager shelter of her room and pressed her face into arms. Her sadness drained all hope. Her life was falling apart like a shell breaking, leaving her exposed and vulnerable. She didn't deserve this. She wasn't bad. Who would speak for her? Who knew her for who she was? She barely knew herself in this woman's body subject to lust.

Randall might think he could leave Lake Barcroft, but she had a higher calling and standard to live up to—well-groomed, polite, associate with the right people. She'd been where people were smoking marijuana with colored musicians far from the way her family thought of her, the way she was supposed to be. Her bad judgement for following Robbie, for allowing him to fondle her, had come home to roost. No secrets would not be revealed–no sins would go unpunished.

She didn't want to disgrace her father, be written about in newspapers and gossiped about by constituents and strangers. She was public. She must resist or at least be more careful. After she was in college, away from home, with a separate identity she would be released–be responsible for herself, not the reputation of her family.

* * *

Sonia-Barton's screams and threats awoke Beck after she'd barely fallen asleep. "I'm leaving. I'm going to live with my daddy."

The Leaders calm rumble indicated he was being nicer to Sonia-Barton than he'd been to her.

In the morning, Beck stayed in her room until nearly eleven. The house was quiet.

Beck read a note by the phone at the top of the stairs written in Gail's practiced elegant cursive on lavender think paper embossed with her name, indicating she was asserting herself as a disciplinarian. *Your father and I have gone to a reception. Janey will be watching you. You are not to go anywhere.*

Beck went into the kitchen and made toast spread with peanut butter.

Janey came in carrying a load of sheets.

Beck greeted her with a lowered head and a quick "Hi."

Janey set the load down in the laundry pass the breakfast nook. The maid's hair had started to gray. Fat hung on her elbows and she looked tired as she came back into the kitchen. "Ya know ain't no trick to get in a trouble. What make a life hard is staying out a trouble."

Beck drank orange juice and kept her head down, not responding.

"That girl downstairs, the one a going to get ya in trouble. What they a talking about that boy, Randall? He not the one a gonna to get ya in trouble."

"I have homework to do." Beck headed out of the kitchen carrying her sandwich on a plate.

"Ya know ya not a suppose to carry no food round the house," Janey said with more sympathy than reproach.

Beck sighed, came back and sat at the table. The house felt confining. She was being imprisoned for a false crime. She wasn't like Sonia-Barton. All she wanted was a boyfriend, to be a normal girl. She wasn't bad. Neither was Randall. Now, even he couldn't be her boyfriend. Maybe he didn't even want to be her boyfriend. Maybe that party scene with Negroes and marijuana was what he wanted, to be like Mick, so proud of having a record played on the radio.

She quietly went into Sonia-Barton's room where her stepsister lay beneath her blankets curled into a tight fetal position. Beside a desk cluttered with beauty products was a shelf of records. Another pile of albums, some out of their jackets lay scattered on the floor by her stereo.

Atop a jumble of dirty clothes were panties and the turned-out skirt Sonia-Barton had been wearing last night. The bridge of Beck's nose furrowed at the sight of a pasting of red blood and something yellow.

She quickly found the album by the Express and left the room.

In the living room, sunlight reflected off the lake. This was going to one of the last hot days of the year. A couple of boats were already out on lake. Beck put the record on the stereo and sat in her father's reading chair to listen.

Such a lonely girl,

Didn't know what she wants

Until love came along

Love came along like a light

Love came tonight

She'd heard the song before, pretty, but hadn't paid much attention to the words. Music could take her to a dream where the musicians were telling how *her* love would come, without knowing what she wanted, like a light.

 Maybe Randall wanted to speak to other girls that way, take them into a dream where he was singing beautiful, emotional messages.

She looked at the cover—a color picture of the band lounging around a train station. In the background Mick, the drummer, stood next to an old gray metal luggage scale, dressed in a satin shirt with frills on the cuff open across his hairy chest. He had a bored distant expression. She'd met famous people all her life, but these musicians were different as if they didn't care what old people thought of them, living on their own terms in ways her family couldn't understand, barely perceive.

Randall wanted to be part of a rebellion. They would grow apart because she wouldn't follow him. She was satisfied and comfortable in the traditions of her family, the class consciousness of her school, in the life she'd been placed at birth. She'd be waiting to bring him back, make him respectable again. Maybe she'd talk to him. He'd understand. He was still young. There was time for him to go to college, get a job, marry, have a family.

When she was a little girl, after the drowning, she'd kept a kitten she'd found in the woods in her room for a week, sneaking food, hiding from Janey.

Beck hadn't been allowed to keep the pet who had gone to live with Randall. Her family would never let her keep anyone as exotic as Randall wanted to be.

She didn't have the guile or cunning to hide him. She'd made bad choices. She didn't want to lose the security of the Beck who was good and admired by adults. She mustn't do things and be things that would expose her to disgrace.

She looked out at the lake and silently asked her mother what she should do. She prayed for her guidance to a place of quiet and order, where she'd be known for her virtue and good deeds. Her life that had seemed to be opening up before her with the promise of excitement and the thrill of discovery now seemed scary and ominous. "Who'll guide me, Mama? Who can I trust?"

* * *

Randall didn't call or come. She fretted he was mad at her. Why should he not be? He'd probably been grounded too. Maybe he'd already run away with Robbie to New York.

She resisted the urge to call him or walk by his house and waited for Sonia-Barton to wake.

* * *

Hot enough to be in their bikinis on their beach, Beck sat in a folding chair beside Sonia-Baron who sat on a beach towel on the sand, smoking silently, her arms wrapped around her knees. Beck wanted to know what she suspected from the evidence she'd seen in Sonia-Barton's room. She shielded her eyes to look at her stepsister illuminated in the sunlight. "Did you get in much trouble?"

"They say I am."

"Me too."

"Called my daddy."

Beck studied her. Was Sonia-Barton going to leave her too? "What did he say?"

Sonia-Barton frowned. "He's got someone staying with him, a new whore I guess, says now's not the time. Said I could board if I want." Sorrow and disgust mixed in her words.

"A strumpet," Beck used the word she'd learned from her father.

"A what?"

"You know a whore." She'd looked it up.

Some junior high boys were paddling slowly by in a canoe, looking surreptitiously at them. Sonia-Barton did a pantomime for them as she stood, straightened out her towel, her bikini stretched tight across her ass. The boys stopped even the pretense of paddling and stared at her.

"That's Byron Walters' little brother."

"Who?"

"The one in the boat."

Sonia-Barton looked at them and shrugged. "I sure as hell am not staying around here for a month, they can forget that noise."

"Where were you last night, anyway?" Beck asked.

"The Marine, Marty, wouldn't let me go."

"You like him?"

"He's all right."

Something confessional in Sonia-Barton's voice prompted Beck to study her. "What do you mean he wouldn't let you go?"

Whatever she'd thought she'd seen or heard disappeared as Sonia-Barton countered with a thin grin. "What about you? I hear Miss Goody-Wonderful came dragging in pretty late herself."

"And caught all hell because Miss Trouble's Mom was waiting up for her."

Their chuckles were a mix of admiration of their wit and acceptance of their situation.

"I went to a band party after the show," Beck said.

"How was it?"

Beck shook her head. "Good thing you didn't go. We had to leave cause of the drugs."

"What?"

Beck was satisfied by Sonia-Barton's wide-eye shock.

"Some colored guys from Sonny B. Madison." She protected Robbie.

"God, Beck! You were at a party where some colored guys were using drugs?" Sonia-Barton whooped.

"Shhh!" Beck held her finger in front of mouth. "Sounds travel on the lake."

Sonia-Barton leaned closer, their heads together.

"What about you, what did you do?"

"Got my cherry popped, that's all."

Evidence confirmed, this was big news. Her revelation paled in comparison. Beck pushed her head closer to her stepsister.

"My period wasn't over. It didn't stop him. Took me in the back seat of his car, pulled out the Tampax and went to work."

"Oh God, Sonia-Barton." Beck covered her mouth. "Did you want him to?"

Sonia-Barton stared at her a moment. Her lips pursed. "Girls got to get it out of the way sometime. At least I won't get pregnant."

This was wrong. Sex was supposed to be the culmination of love.

"It was real quick. I never had time to say a word. He's so big and strong. The next thing I knew...whoops, no more virgin."

Sonia-Barton looked away from Beck's horrified expression as clearly something sordid had happened to her. Her mother had been right to be worried about her.

"Sonia-Barton, you were raped."

"No, I mean, it..."

"Yes, you were. You were raped."

"Maybe I shouldn't have told you." Her lower lip pouted and she reached for another cigarette. "Maybe I'll see him again. And this time it's gonna be 'cause I want him to."

Beck exhaled loudly and stared into the distance feeling somehow complicit as if she was to blame for Randall playing at a dance where Sonia-Barton met a rapist. "I went into your room to get a record this morning. I saw your clothes. You'd better wash them out before Janey sees them."

Sonia-Barton took a drag off her Virginia Slim. "Guess you're right there. Don't want everybody in the world to know."

The scandal, the talking to the police, so many people knowing, what would she do if she was raped? When her time came would it be her choice or like on the beach when Robbie touched her in a way that made her lose control? Life only seemed to be getting more complicated.

* * *

Sunday morning, they went to Christ Church in Alexandria as a family. Sonia-Barton wore a maroon A Line dress with perpendicular buttons lining her waist. Beck dressed in a more traditional yellow skirtwaist dress. The church was over 200 years old. George Washington had attended the high Episcopalian service there.

She was old enough to sit with her family in their pew but went to Sunday School because she was training for the youth ministry.

Father Dorfman said to the rapt attention of the 6th-8th graders, while looking directly at her. "The fruit of real love can never be picked from the illicit tree of lust. There will be many temptations. But always remember, no matter what happens, never lose your faith."

Beck forced herself to keep her eyes on the priest's compassionate expression as if he knew how strong her urges were and wanted to tell her if she succumbed she must remember the teachings of the Church and not fall into greater sin.

After the service, the family went to lunch at the Evans Farm Inn—a special place normally reserved for birthdays and holidays—as if the family were trying to demonstrate what they'd be missing if the girls strayed too far.

The usual stares of recognition were directed to the Leader—strangers who whispered to their children, wives, and dates, nodded or pointed. They could be constituents, government officials, diplomats or lobbyists, a blur of roles. A White House official stopped at the table to talk to the Leader.

Beck had a way of listening when people spoke to her father with her eyes averted so as not to show she was listening. The Leader never asked her what she thought. Eavesdropping was more for her education when he or Panda would discuss events with her. The man from the White House was only being friendly and didn't talk business. He said he hoped he hadn't disturbed their meal. Beck smiled with practiced modesty, easy to feel special. The hard part was to act normal.

When they'd placed their orders and a waitress in colonial dresses served hot popovers from a cloth-covered basket, they were just the family. Dickie Lyons was the son, the pride and joy of Panda and Pawpaw who sat at the round table with them.

Panda looked across the glasses and cutlery at Sonia-Barton with a twist of her lips and stern expression Beck knew meant trouble.

"Sonia-Barton," Panda said with her Petersburg drawl of drawing out the "a" into an "ah"

"Yes, ma'am." Sonia-Barton's respectful response did not match the proud, defiant tilt of her head.

"You are fortunate to be known as a member of this family."

"Yes ma'am?" Sonia-Barton indicated she didn't know where this was going but was ready to meet the challenge.

Beck looked down, fingers of embarrassment reaching around her eyes.

The Leader cleared his throat in a nervous manner as if he too dreaded what was coming from the defender of family dignity.

"To be a member of a respected family comes with great benefits, but..."

Oh god, here it comes, Beck thought. Had the Leader or Gail revealed what had happened Friday or was this Panda's supernatural powers to see through any subterfuge or sniff out misbehavior?

"...also, great responsibilities and duty to conduct oneself in a manner above reproach."

Beck looked up quickly. Her grandmother's purple eyes shifted momentarily to her, confirming the lecture was for her too, before returning to bore into Sonia-Barton who did not flinch in meeting her gaze.

"On account of your unfortunate lineage you face a greater challenge."

Beck's breathe froze. She couldn't avert her eyes from the attack.

Sonia-Barton glanced at her mother as if to ask are you going to stand-up for us or do I have to? But Gail only had a glazed expression of submission. "What are you referring to, Mrs. Lyons?" A catch of anger lay within the question. Sonia-Barton kept her eyes locked on Panda's, but she wasn't going to win. Panda was ruthless.

Pawpaw George and the Leader stiffened with anticipation of the coming cut, but Beck knew they'd not intervene.

With a quick movement in her chair as if to better position herself to deliver a blow, Panda said, "Your father is a well-known scoundrel. I fear you are in dire risk of following in his footsteps."

Don't go after her father. Show mercy, please, Beck prayed and twisted her hands in her lap.

Sonia-Barton trembled. Beck couldn't tell if she was going to cry or shout. Sonia-Barton's eyes swept from her mother to the Leader, saw no help, placed her napkin on the table. "I'll believe, I shall wait outside," she said with exaggerated dignity and started to rise. Beck thought this was how someone with good breeding should respond to a personal attack.

"Sit down, Sonia-Barton," Gail said with steel in her voice that surprised Beck. "Listen to Grandmama Lyons. She is absolutely correct."

Sonia-Barton glanced at Beck as if she was her last hope. But Beck looked down, frozen by embarrassment.

Sonia-Barton submitted with a fury in her clenched jaw and a distant focus as she put her napkin back in her lap.

Panda was not done. "You are fortunate to have Beck as an example of good breeding and a proper upbringing. Follow her example and you'll do fine," she said as if the answer to Sonia-Barton's challenge was to accept Beck' superiority.

A quick smile and a near laugh nearly escaped Sonia-Barton. Beck was certain Sonia-Barton's reaction would tip her grandmother to Beck's lack of virtue.

Her fear was confirmed as they left a meal where Beck and Sonia-Barton had been seen but not heard.

"Stay here, Beck," Panda said.

As the rest of the party moved back to their cars, Beck stood with her grandmother at the edge of a lawn bordered by a split log fence surrounding a pond and white gazebo.

"I want you to listen to me, and hear me very clearly," Panda said with the urgency of desperate message.

"Yes, ma'am." Beck was taller than her grandmother but felt as if she was shrinking before her intense scrutiny.

"You must come to me immediately if anything untoward happens. Do not speak to anyone else, confide in no one but me. Scandals will happen. There are ways to deal with them if they can be contained early enough. Do you understand?" she sternly asked.

Beck almost asked what scandal but sensed her grandmother was not referring to anything in the past but warning of grave coming danger.

"Yes ma'am."

"And do try to keep an eye and caution against that slattern Sonia-Barton."

Beck had another bad word to look up.

As she walked back to the Leader's blue Lincoln marked with the Virginia license plate US Senate *1, she inwardly cringed at the prospect of dealing with Sonia-Barton's fury. Her stepsister would want to prove herself, challenge and not accept submission.

The Leader drove, his eyes visible in the rearview mirror as he looked back at them seated in the leather padded seats separated by a cushioned armrest.

"Sonia-Barton I want to compliment you on how you handled yourself in there," he said.

Beck perceived the tone and aim of the politician to mollify someone whose support he needed.

Sonia-Barton was susceptible to the flattery and the tension in her expression lessened.

The Leader's eyes returned to Leesburg Pike.

Gail joined the peacemaking. "I was proud of you Sonia-Barton. I'm always proud of you," she hastened to add.

Sonia-Barton misinterpreted their diplomacy as alliance. "Who does she think she is? The Poydras are one of the great families of Louisiana."

"I know, dear." The Leader said. "A great family, proud family who have made great contributions to the nation."

He was going into speech mode, Beck thought.

"I know what it is like to be unfairly attacked, have my name slandered, believe me. I'm afraid I went into the wrong profession for my mother. She feels she must defend me and the dignity of our family against all who attack us."

From her perspective, Beck could see him smile slightly in the way he did when he was trying to win someone over.

"She's like a tormented dog sometimes," he said.

"A bitch is more like it," Sonia-Barton said.

"Sonia-Barton!" Gail exclaimed, the pride gone.

But the Leader reflexive laugh was more genuine than anything he'd said in the car. Beck frowned at the thought her father respected Sonia-Barton's spunk more than his meek daughter's obedience.

* * *

In bed that night, moonlight shined faintly around the edges of the closed blinds on the door that led outside. When the Leader married Gail, Beck and Sonia-Barton had been given their own downstairs bedrooms. Beck had been both excited and terrified about having a private entrance that someone would come in and take her.

The sound of the Tonight Show came from the recreation room where Sonia-Barton was watching television. Beck wasn't sure Sonia-Barton still trusted her and believed she suspected Beck had said something to cause Panda's lecture.

Panda had seemed to warn the coming teen years would bring unimaginable dangers to body and soul. Beck wished for a place she could be protected, virtuous and unassailed. She wanted to be happy. Since the drowning, darkness always seemed to wait for her. Only in dreams did she feel strong and happy. She said a prayer to God and then her mother, the angel watching over her. "Mama, show me how to live in peace."

Randall was all she had. She could tell him anything. If he left, she'd have nobody. She should kiss him, do whatever it took to keep him with her. Her thoughts of blessing fell to sin as she ran her hands down her chest and imagined Randall's touch, his body against hers.

Drifting closer to sleep, she was drawn quickly to consciousness by a tapping on the window. The old fear that someone would come through that door made her cower beneath the sheets.

"Beck, its Randall."

She had an irrational thought that he'd been drawn by her thoughts of sex with him. Had he or other boys been watching her? Had she been careless about leaving the curtains open.

"I have to talk to you," he said.

She moved quickly across the dark room and without opening the two locks, whispered, "What do you want?"

"To say good-bye."

She fumbled in the dark for her robe to cover her nightgown and opened the door a crack.

"Come out with me," he implored.

"No, I'm already in enough trouble. Go away."

"I am. I'm hitting the road. We're leaving tonight."

"Tonight?" This might be her last chance to talk some sense into him. She opened the door, showing only her head.

"I didn't want to leave without talking to you, make sure you're going to be all right while I'm gone."

"Randall," she sighed. "Wait a minute I'll get dressed."

She came back out dressed in a gray dreamer T-shirt and jeans. "We can't stay here, we'll get caught."

"Let's go to Beach One."

Walking down the deserted road, Beck imagined all the ways her disobedience would be discovered. Maybe she'd be sent to board. Maybe being in the dorms at Miss Madeira would be better than being alone at Lake Barcroft.

Randall seemed lost in his own thoughts as if he'd forgotten what he wanted to say to her. Where the road dropped from his driveway to the community beach, he said. "I'm picking up Robbie at the Hot Shoppes."

Did Randall want her to be part of his plan, an accomplice? Was he leaving because the Leader had called his father? "What did you want to tell me?" The question sounded cold, hiding what she wanted to tell him.

He looked at her and back to his walking. "Not to give up on me. I don't want you going off with someone else just because I'm not here."

"You're leaving me alone. I don't know anyone else," she said pathetically, closer to the truth.

He stopped in the street, turned to face her and took her hands. "Remember, I said there's some things you just know?"

"Yes." Emotion rose at his touch as they leaned closer to each other.

"I've just always known about us. I don't know how or why, it's just always been there."

His arms around her waist were a gentle touch, his lips soft against hers. She closed her eyes and put her hands on his shoulders. The contours of his muscles were different than the Randall in her mind, the kid. Their bodies fit together nicely. She felt him bigger, stronger than she'd imagined. Warmth spread through her, and she trembled as happiness overflowed a barrier.

"I'll always be there for you," he whispered in her ear and released her.

How was leaving being there for her? What had he hoped to accomplish by coming to her window like a thief? He was still leaving, and she didn't know the words to stop him.

Before he turned and walked out the circle in front of her house, he kissed her once more, hugged her and said, "We're going to be all right."

The confidence she'd prayed for was his not hers. Back safely in her bed, sadness washed over her like a dark wave. A single tear rolled down her cheek. Randall was her lifeline to happiness and now he was gone.

EIGHT

ALL THE GIRLS IN NEW YORK CITY

J aney said, "Randall's mama a wants ya t'caw her."

Mrs. Malloy had called her before about piano lessons. But his was different.

She knew Mrs. Malloy wanted to talk about Randall—unnerving, an adult challenge. To ignore the request would be too rude. And Beck was curious.

"Oh Beck, thank you for calling me back."

"*Er*, welcome," Beck paddled in the conversation waiting for Mrs. Malloy to tell her what she'd already dreaded.

Beck leaned forward clutching the telephone cord at the table closet on which the hall phone rested.

"Randall wasn't home this morning. I'm so worried, I can't see straight."

Beck inhaled too loudly. He'd done it, jumped over the side of the ship that was to carry them to lives like their parents, with jobs, homes, and children of their own. Her chin lifted in admiration for his bravery. "I'm sure he's OK." The meager reassurance was enough to reveal she knew where he'd gone.

"Has he gone to New York with Robbie?"

Beck hesitated. "I don't know."

The lie came so easily and sounded so sincere she'd surprised herself with a talent she didn't know she had. She'd seen her father flatter to avoid the truth, her grandmother's defense of the family name in all manner of behavior, but the lie rolled off her tongue like she could never be caught, never held accountable for her an easily exposed falsity. All Randall had to do was tell his mother that he'd told her where he was going, and Mrs. Malloy would never believe her again. Beck would be typed as a liar.

Maybe because she'd lied herself or Mrs. Malloy knew Beck better than she thought, Mrs. Malloy knew she was lying.

Randall mother's voice relaxed to acceptance as if she too would protect her son as long as he was safe. "I guess he's run off to be a musician. He took his band equipment with him."

Beck joined Mrs. Malloy's fatalism. "That's what he wants."

"But you know he's all right?"

"I hope so."

"If you hear from him, please tell him that he can call me. I'll understand."

Beck blew a stream from her pursed lips. This was so grownup, forming alliances with adults to manipulate someone you loved.

But what about the colonel? Were they supposed to conspire against Randall's father?

* * *

Randall telephoned that night on her private line. She leaned off the edge of her bed and held the pink phone as if the curled handset cord was a lifeline to him.

"Just want to let you know I'm OK. Can't talk for long, I'm on a pay phone."

Beck kept up her end of the bargain she'd implied with Mrs. Malloy. "You should call your mother. She's very worried."

"Tell her I'm OK. Just not where I am. My father will call the cops."

"I told her I didn't know where you were."

"You did?"

Tension rose in her throat—anger that he was surprised she'd lied for him. "Don't make the messenger to your parents."

"Did you tell them where I was?" Alarm and suspicion in his voice showed his doubt that she'd be on his side.

"I lied for you. But she knows where you've gone with Robbie."

"She does?"

"I don't want to talk about it anymore. Do what you have to do. It's not my business."

"OK, sorry. I get it. Sorry I put you in that position. Maybe I'm living out my mother's dream. Did you know she was a singer in a band down in Florida when she met my dad, had me?"

Beck stared without focusing on her desk imagining what Randall meant. Mrs. Malloy had been young like her once not knowing what she would be, then she had Randall. Was she married when she got pregnant with Randall or was he the reason she married the colonel and stopped singing in a band?

Beck didn't ask questions that Randall might never have been told the answers because they were to be hidden.

* * *

He was right to worry about his father. A week after he ran away, the colonel telephoned on the house line. The novelty of talking to a parent had worn off enough for her to sound confident in her greeting.

As if he'd just sobered up enough to realize he was talking to a 15-year-old girl he'd known since she was a child, he coughed and said, "Just want to make sure you know that we're..." he paused, as if fighting to get it out, "very...ah...worried about Randall. Perhaps I should call your father about this."

Her head rocked. "No, I'm sure Randall's all right and my father would be...he's busy...and."

"Yes, I see....ah...thank you. Sorry to bother you."

Unnerving to realize how weak the adults were, how little they knew about their children.

What if Mr. Malloy did call her father? Was she supposed to lie to him too for Randall?

* * *

Her father said he wanted to speak to her about *something very serious.*

She sat on the caramel-colored Scan sofa in the living room while he stood before her like a lawyer asking for her testimony. "His father has asked me to help locate him."

The Leader had told her once *if someone lies to me, I never believe them again.* His warning resonated in her answer. "I'd rather not say." She'd leaned forward, obvious in her discomfort.

Her father looked at her with sympathy. "You know Randall is very special to me. I'd want to help if he's in trouble."

As was her skill, she detected the truth beneath his practiced demeanor built to inspire trust. Randall was a piece of what was left of Colin, in his way a stand-in for his son who would be the same age growing up at Lake Barcroft had he not died. What would he think if Colin had run off to play music? Admire his spunk like he seemed to do with Sonia-Barton while she was only good Beck?

Her first loyalty was to her father. She took a deeper breath. "He's gone with a boy in his band to New York. He wants to be a professional musician. His father ordered him to quit his band."

The Leader nodded and frowned. "Because I called his father about him?"

Beck shrugged. The call might be the immediate cause but not wholly. "He wants him to concentrate on his studies, go to college."

"His father asked me to nominate him for West Point."

Randall, a soldier—the idea seemed silly enough that she tilted her head and looked at him as if he had told a joke. "Did you?"

"I would be happy to if that's what he wants." Her father smiled slightly as if he too knew that Randall was too soft to make a good solider. The lines around his blue eyes deepened. "How do you feel about what he's doing?"

The question beyond whether she approved caused Beck's skin to flush. He was asking if she was in love Randall. "I miss him." She looked up from hands clenched in her lap to see his reaction.

He blinked and smiled slightly. He could see beneath her words too. "He's been a good friend to you. But perhaps it's time for you to go your separate ways. Let him follow his dream."

Was he saying that she could make Randall do what his father wanted?

"Are you going to tell his father where he is?"

"Not if you ask me not to."

The politician was back. What was the deal—that she not be Randall's girlfriend?

"I don't think we should get involved. He's doing what he wants. His mother knows he's OK," Beck said with conviction.

Her father said his decisive manner. "I'll speak to the colonel. Tell him we believe Randall is safe and with friends."

She admired him for his concern for something as minor as Randall with so many important demands on his time. They were on the same team. She stood up. "Thanks, Daddy. Well, I have homework to do."

He opened his arms and she snuggled against his left shoulder.

"I'm very proud of how well you're doing in school, but I hope you find some time for some fun."

In other words, find some new friends.

She went down to her books and wondered where exactly she was supposed to find friends, not like Randall—out in the world unlike anyone their age she knew—on his own, removed from family, doing what he wanted, facing danger from not only the unknown but his family. Pain throbbed at the thought of Randall with girls, prettier, older, sexier than her. He would have no trouble making new friends while she sheltered in her fifteen-year-old life.

* * *

Ten days after he ran away, she came home from school.

"Ya got a letter," Janey said.

In her room, she threw her book bag on the bed and tore open the white envelope. The letter was mostly about the band.

I got an ID says I'm eighteen so we can play in the bars. Joe, Robbie's cousin is writing the songs. He's pretty clear about it being his band. Just wants me to play what he wrote. That's OK, as long as I'm learning the business but between you and me I think his songs sound like everybody else but at least they're not covers.

Sorry my dad called you HOW EMBARRASSING. He's the kind who would come and drag me back home or turn me in for being a truant. He'd like it if I got drafted.

I have to be careful getting in touch with them. I'm old enough to be out on my own. I think it's because I don't want them holding me back or trying to turn me into someone they want me to be. I guess I'm just being selfish and trying to find what it is that I do want to be.

Talk about being selfish! How are you? I hope I'm not putting you in a tough spot having to cover for me. I want to be honest–always honest with you, never lie, but sometimes you just have to cover your tracks.

I hope you're not missing me too much (ha, ha) or think I'm not sincere about loving you. I need to grow up, get some experience–here I go talking about myself again–can't help it I guess. What was I going to write songs about? Living on the lake, playing other peoples songs? Even if the lyrics are stupid they belong to them, not me. The only thing that came out sounding half-way intelligent was when I wrote about how I feel about you. I guess everyone, everywhere knows about that kind of love.

I'm going to be a real musician, able to survive anywhere. Then I'll come back to you and you'll see...

She reread the part about love. What kind of love was that? Strong enough to withstand the girls he'd meet playing in the bars? And what if in the end he was going to be a soldier anyway? The war in Vietnam, the dread of a young man killed in his youth, came home to her.

She pulled her shoulders back. Randall loved her more than all the girls in New York City. It was OK if she didn't meet anyone new. She had something precious in his love that could withstand temptation, be true and loyal through all.

* * *

He gave her a PO box address and she'd written him back immediately. *I don't know what you're looking for, but you know they say at the end of all our journeys we'll arrive home and know it for the first time.*

That had drawn this response from him.

I love you because you are so smart. You understand what I am doing. Your quote was right on. When I come home it will be so that I will be able to understand and write songs about what I cannot now see.

* * *

Two months after he'd run away, Saturday morning, the air cold and bright, the leaves of late November scarce—red and yellow fluttering on dark skeletal branches. Beck wore new fall clothes—a red plaid wool Pendleton shirt, black slacks, and brown leather boots.

She hesitated outside of Randall's house, but she'd accepted Mrs. Malloy's invitation to visit and hear about what Randall had written to her. What was she afraid of? That afternoon, she was going to the White House with Panda for a visit with Ladybird Johnson. If she could handle that she certainly should not be afraid of Colonel Malloy. Maybe, she thought, he might be her father-in-law someday, a more complex relationship than being a neighbor.

She walked up the slope of their driveway and knocked on the door beside the carport.

Mrs. Malloy must have been watching from the large trapezoidal windows that overlooked their front yard and street and opened the door as soon as Beck knocked.

She held both of Beck's hands as she leaned back and looked at her. "Oh darling, you look so beautiful."

Beck blushed at the praise. Mrs. Malloy could tell her things about boys and dating if Beck knew how to ask. Could you only have one boyfriend, a boy you'd been in love with since you were a child? Not that Beck was much older than a child now.

She'd started to believe that she was good looking enough, saw the way boys checked her out when she walked past, but no boyfriend, unless you counted Randall and what kind of boyfriend was he? She'd at least like to have the opportunity to make a choice in being faithful to him.

Since Randall had run away, she'd had one date, a double with Sonia-Barton, who seemed to be trying to prove that she could have sex when she wanted—an attitude popular with boys she found attractive. The date had not gone well. The boy was in college. He talked about the relationship between love and desire, and how Beck was going to *grow-up to be the kind of girl that he could respect*. Afterwards Beck had felt as if he had not liked her because she was not smart enough.

Maybe next year when she was sixteen and could drive, she'd have another boyfriend or at least some dates.

"Colonel Malloy is at the hardware store, so we can have a little visit by ourselves."

"That's nice."

"May I get you anything? How about some grape juice and cookies?"

Beck hadn't thought she was hungry but the gooey comfort smell and sight of a plate of fresh-baked chocolate chip cookies was too enticing.

"Let's take them into the living room." Mrs. Malloy led her past *her* piano— a large black Steinway, where she'd play with bewildering skill and force that made Beck wonder why she wasn't famous, her face on sheet music with Nelson Eddy and Jeanette MacDonald, Patti Page, and Ozzie Nelson—posing handsome and serene in black and white photos.

Beck sat on one of the clear vinyl-covered sofas on which they'd not been allowed when they were children, juice and cookies resting on an end table.

Mrs. Malloy sat in a stuffed chair facing her, studying Beck as if to judge her manners. While Beck ate, Mrs. Malloy smoked, clouds from her Kool wafting around her face. She'd grown stout and developed a worried look centered in her deep, dark eyes. Thick black hair had streaks of gray she didn't bother to color.

"You were always a pretty child, but now you are just gorgeous. Randall has always been crazy about you. Ever since he was a little boy he's been saying that he's going to marry you."

Beck held the glass of grape juice and looked at the straw pile carpet. This was too embarrassing.

"Oh, I shouldn't say things like that. He'll get mad at me." She relayed information Beck already knew about Randall in a rapid manner as if Beck would be bored if she didn't. "He promised he'd be home for Christmas."

That was news. He'd made peace with his father.

"I guess my boy just left home a little earlier than most," Mrs. Malloy said with a sigh.

Through the windows, Beck saw the colonel's car turn into the driveway.

"I guess I could have just told you all this on the phone, but it seemed a good excuse to see you."

"Good to see you too," Beck said too stiffly.

"You know Randall would never do anything to get you in trouble. He had no idea where Sonia-Barton was. I hope the senator knows that."

Beck pushed back her hair. "I'm sure he knows. He likes Randall. He was worried about him too."

"Oh, I know. I know." Mrs. Malloy's waved her hand with the cigarette if chasing away a bad thought.

Beck glanced nervously at the sound of the front door opening.

"Well, look who is here." Colonel Malloy's skin reddened.

Beck resisted the urge to stand, remained seated her legs together, knees pointed at a 10 degree angle.

His nervous laugh was similar to Randall's–*haw, haw, haaaaw.*

"Isn't she gorgeous?' Mrs. Malloy asked.

"Pretty as a picture."

"I was just telling her Randall's latest news."

The colonel scowled. "I hope you can help us talk some sense into him."

Mrs. Malloy frowned. "Now you promised not to say anything."

Lines around the colonel's mouth deepened.

"You are the one who has put this foolish music business in his head."

Were they going to fight in front of her? She wanted to leave.

"He is very talented." Mrs. Malloy turned to Beck as if she was the judge. "I think he think he's going to be very famous, make us very proud, prouder than we already are."

Beck had a sudden empathy for them, growing old, missing their only child, robbed of their last year with him. Randall should be here with them, maintaining a balance in the house.

Beck put the half-drunk glass of juice on the end table beside the plate of cookies. "I'm sorry. I have to go. I'm going to the White House with my grandmother," she said so they'd think nothing less could shorten her visit.

The colonel straightened almost to attention.

"Will the President be there?" Mrs. Malloy asked.

"Maybe. It's a family thing." She hated the idea they'd think she was trying to impress them. "Ladybird is a friend of my grandmother."

Both walked Beck to the door.

"Thank you so much for the cookies."

"Stay here, Mae," the colonel ordered and walked Beck to the top of the driveway.

"I know Randall doesn't have a chance with you."

Beck looked down at her feet, her shoulders tightened, leaning back as if in repulsion.

"You and your family stand for everything that is great about this country, the way they serve the people."

She forced herself look into the crazed intensity in his face.

"Here's a chance for you to help someone just like your father does every day. Randall really cares about you. If you could use your influence to try and make him see that this music business is just a hobby. He's going to get drafted. That'll straighten him out."

Beck nodded. "Yes, sir. Good-bye." She quickened her steps home, not daring to look back but with a strong sense he was watching her.

She didn't want to be the colonel's ally in controlling Randall even if she agreed with him and thought she might have told the colonel she didn't have any control over Randall but that would have been a lie.

* * *

Gail let her off in the driveway of her grandparent's house, performing the duties of a driver, not invited or expected to come inside. Beck had spent too much time dressing before settling on a tried and true plaid princess panel with gusseted sleeves that she wore to official functions with her father.

Tardiness was not tolerated by her grandmother. *What if the right foot decided it would rather lay back a little or the left hand thought it might be nice to sleep in that morning*–was one of Panda's favorite aphorisms.

If she was late Beck could blame Gail.

She entered through the kitchen. The maid, Geneva, was sitting at a wooden table shelling peas from the garden. Her husband Norris was reading the Evening Star at her side. They were light skinned and lived behind the mansion in an apartment above the garage beside the tennis court.

"Miss Beck." Norris stood, beaming a wonderful smile.

"Don't she look lovely?" Geneva exclaimed.

Beck paused long enough to be polite but was anxious to let her grandmother know she'd arrived.

Norris, dressed in a dark suit, reassured Beck. "Your Panda be right down."

"Norris you go get that car and be waiting outside like you supposed to be," Geneva lectured.

"I'll wait for her in the parlor," Beck said. She passed through a formal dining room into the hallway that split the library and parlor, what would now be called a living room. A piano and portraits of Beck's ancestor's, a tall grandfather clock whose face was turning from being a sun to the moon, a quarter of two. She was right on time.

Panda dressed in a dark dress with a hat, carried a mink stole and leather gloves down the grand marble stairway with its two bronze statues holding globes of light.

"There you are, darling. I'm glad that you are on time. That is one of your best qualities, one of many but one most rare, you are punctual."

Beck kissed her grandmother's cheek and smelled the complex scents of her expensive makeup and perfume.

They walked around back where Norris was waiting beside the black Lincoln.

"Where's Pawpaw?"

"Where else? Chevy Chase playing golf." Panda was younger than her husband, who'd started a law firm in Washington. He would not miss his weekly game of golf for anything short of *hell or high water*. Beck had gone with him once when she was eight. They were having a good time until he cursed at missing a shot. He apologized for his language, had told her never to talk that way, and had never asked her to come golfing with him again.

Beck sat beside her grandmother in the back seat as they were chauffeured past the bronze winged horses on the Memorial Bridge.

"Ladybird asked me to bring you. I think she misses having the girls around. When was the last time you were at the White House?" Panda asked.

"I went with Daddy, last summer for a party."

Panda turned and looked at her. The late afternoon sunlight illuminated the side of her powdered face, her startling purple eyes accented with flesh-color makeup at the inner corners.

"You should spend more time in Washington. You are part of both worlds remember, Virginia and the Capitol. How is your social life, any beaus?"

Beck smiled at the quick non sequitur sneak attack. Was she supposed to find beaus in Washington? "So many that I have to take my phone off the hook to study."

Panda arched a precisely drawn eyebrow. "I should think so, though I don't know how you find proper dates these days. Do you see any of the young men that came when you were presented?"

The all white National Debutante Cotillion and Thanksgiving Ball had been held in the Mayflower Ballroom with old world pomp and tradition. Randall had not been invited. Beck, dressed in a white formal gown with a billowing bell-shaped skirt from her narrow waist, shoulders bare, silk elbow length gloves had been paired with a boy from St. Albans school who said he'd be going to Princeton next year if not Harvard. They'd entered and swirled around to Tchaikovsky's Serenade–stiff and unnatural after the freedom of the dances where Randall played.

"No, I'm too busy studying."

"That sounds very dreary, but tell me, darling, has anyone talked to you about how to behave around a man?"

Beck flinched. Here it comes, she thought.

Her grandmother leaned closer and lowered her voice as she did when speaking of a scandal. "We had a cousin from the Richmond Wards. Her mother passed on quite young as your darling mother did and left this poor girl in the care of her father. One day she turns up with child. Nobody had an idea how it happened. It turned out that not a soul had thought to tell this sweet pretty young lady that one had to be careful of such things."

When was this–a hundred years ago? "Oh, I know about that," Beck said with too much confidence.

Panda looked down her narrow nose at Beck with a suspicious expression.

"I mean," Beck said, "Gail talked to me about it." An uncomfortable, blushing conversation when her stepmother had first tried to define her role as her mother. Gail had asked a similar question and then said, "I want you to know you can always come to me with any questions or problems. Anything you tell me will never be repeated."

Beck bet Gail's daughter had never shared any of her sexual adventures with her. Beck had learned a lot from Sonia-Barton. Last month, Sonia-Barton had met a boy from Episcopal at a Miss Madeira school dance and after making love to him, had turned him into a crying, pleading wreak with her indifference.

Beck looked out the window and did her best acting job to appear too embarrassed to speak. She was visible to Panda, who could read her thoughts.

Panda forced her to look back and appear attentive with another lesson about advantages and disadvantages. At least the embarrassing assault was not in front of the family like Sonia-Barton's had been–only Norris as if he wasn't sitting inches in front of them and could hear every word.

"The fact of the matter is people are waiting to use you to tear your father down. You would be the prime actor in a scandal. People are much more interested when one like yourself is indelicate, because we have something that most of them never have, a family name which signifies. You have advantages, and disadvantages too. The disadvantage is that there are far more ears waiting to hear the first whisper of a scandal involving Beck Butler Lyons."

They were turning past the Willard Hotel, a block from the White House. Panda spoke more quickly, urgently "I want to tell you, my darling, you must trust nobody with an indiscretion. Men, all men are beasts. They will lie, cheat, use brute force to have their way with you. I am not so old-fashioned that I do not know a girl in this day and age cannot be expected to have the same morals as when I was your age. It is not the act, it is the trusting. A boy whom you let have his way with you will most certainly spread the word about you. You cannot win."

Beck smiled inwardly at her grandmother's euphemism–part of her old world gentility–opposed to Sonia-Barton, the girls and boys her age who spoke graphically and crudely about sex.

Panda continued more rapidly and urgently as they neared the White House, "If you ever find yourself in a situation where your reputation will suffer, come to me, trust no one else. We will take care of it in our own way. Confide in no one for that is how every rumor starts with a confidence. And be very careful of Sonia-Barton."

"I shall Panda, promise."

Had her grandmother forgotten she'd given practically the same lecture word-for-word only weeks before? Was it so important that the admonition be repeated? Beck felt the dread of her grandmother's premonition. Why did her grandmother worry so much about her? She was the top of her class. No boys were interested in *having their way with her.* If anything, they were intimidated by who her father was and treated her like she was elevated, untouchable. Randall had given her one kiss and run away. Some beast he was.

Panda took out a white invitation engraved in gold and passed it through the window at the Northeast gate. The uniformed Secret Service agent looked at them and smiled, "Welcome to the White House, Mrs. Lyons. Drive straight out after you let them off, and wait in the Executive Office Building parking lot," he instructed Norris.

"Yes, sir, I certainly will, sir," the driver said.

"You should have told him that your father was a butler here, Norris," Panda said.

Norris laughed delightedly. "Yes, ma'am. I have been here a few times before, I certainly have."

A Marine opened the door in the north portico for them.

Maybe, Beck thought, she'd live here some day and then her grandmother would be confident of her morality.

In the family room, Ladybird was sitting alone watching television. Last year, Beck while reading at the dining room table, had overheard a conversation between Gail and another senator's wife sitting in the living room. They'd talked about a female reporter who'd slept with both President Johnson and President Kennedy. The two older ladies had tsk-tsked about the way men thought they could get away with that and condemn a woman for the same behavior. Panda was right, all men were beasts. But what about her son? Was the Leader a beast?

Ladybird made a fuss over Beck. She and Panda were friends from the days when Lyndon had been the Majority Leader.

They had tea in the private sitting room. Fresh baked, delicious iced pastries and small sandwiches on white bread with the crust cut off were served on an elaborate silver service by a waiter. Beck only ate one of each. She could get fat on all the goodies people were feeding her today.

Besides being in the White House the affair was like others to which her grandmother had taken her. Beck barely spoke unless to respond to a direct question. Timid by nature, she admired forceful women like Panda and Ladybird. The meek may inherit the earth but probably because they were told to.

The door opened and the tall figure of the President entered dressed in a casual lime-colored shirt that clung to a roll of fat around his waist. Beck started to rise but remained seated because Panda and Ladybird did.

"Hello, dear," he said when he shook Beck's hand, holding it longer than he had Panda's.

Beck was shocked he wanted to speak to her. She intently followed his words as if she might be tested on what he'd said.

"I want you to tell your friends that I grieve over having to send so many of them to war."

His broad shoulders shrugged around his unusually big droopy-eared head. Deep set eyes and lined face showed signs of little sleep.

Panda and Ladybird looked at Beck as if she might say something intelligent.

"Yes, sir," Beck said.

"I want this war to be over with as quickly as we can. Tell them I hear them out in the streets and on the campuses with their cries of protest. I hear them," he said with a profound sigh of fatigue, patted her once on the shoulder, and strode out the door to the West Wing.

"This Vietnam situation is just tearing him apart," Ladybird said to Beck when her husband was gone and turned her attention back to Panda and discussions about maneuvers in the Senate with the expertise of two professional gamblers handicapping a pennant race.

To whom could she give the President's message? Randall if he got drafted? Mick Pickford? Even if she could get in touch with Mick, she couldn't imagine telling him the President felt bad about his friend getting killed. Mick wouldn't believe her. And if Randall were to be killed in Vietnam, she wouldn't believe him either.

NINE

CHASING JOY

S onia-Barton set her up with Al, the best friend of a boy she liked. They went to his house in Hollin Hills because his parents were gone. Here was the beast Panda had warned her about. Al was a football player, stocky and strong. The boys and Sonia-Barton drank Pabst Blue Ribbon beer in a living room laid out in an expansive manner with windows looking out on a stand of mulberry trees. Beck held the open can of beer Al gave her and tried to drink some but didn't like the bitter taste. Sonia-Barton and Gary went upstairs to a bedroom leaving Beck alone with Al.

He was handsome enough and maybe if he'd been gentler, she'd been responsive. She fought him off by pushing him away and saying she had a boyfriend. He wasn't a rapist and when rebuffed seemed nice enough and told funny stories that made her laugh. She enjoyed his company and would have gone out with him again if he'd called, but he didn't.

* * *

When Randall returned for Christmas, Beck thought he'd changed. Aside from his long hair, a clear rebuke of his father, he seemed to be able to know things she could barely imagine. The two-year difference between them had not seemed so great since was she six and he was eight after the drowning when he'd been her idol.

At night, they walked to the beach. The nighttime air was near freezing, pavement wet from afternoon rain, houses and trees outlined by Christmas lights.

He reached for her hand. His touch released a confusion of emotions. She wanted to be hugged—to flee. She pulled her hand from his.

"What's the matter?" he asked.

"I just want to be friends."

"Friends hold hands."

She pouted—sensing how mismatched they were now—her sorrow as ill-defined as the dark gaggle of Canada geese floating atop the water.

They walked beside the edge of the lake, sand and mud hard with frost beneath her boots.

She didn't want him to see her like this.

"Are you all right?" he asked.

"Are you just going to leave again?"

The reason for her anger suddenly clear to both of them, his eyes narrowed with a sympathetic smile. "Yeah, I am."

As morose as she was, he was excited. His voice and expanded chest carried pride and confidence. "I got asked to play in a San Francisco band. Think I'm going to give it a try. Lot happening out there."

She twisted her lips. Did he expect her to wait while he went here and there playing music?

"What about school?"

He shrugged and nearly laughed. "Guess I'm a high school dropout."

"What about Robbie?"

He smiled at her arguments against doing what he wanted.

"He's sticking with his cousin, playing the bars. Don't worry about him. He's having a ball."

I bet he is, Beck thought. "You're going to get drafted," she repeated his father's threat.

"Yeah, when I'm eighteen. I am worried about that."

"If you went to college you could avoid it."

He scowled at her blatant parroting of his father. "Sure and be like everyone else. Just send the poor kids to war."

"They draft college kids too."

"So why bother to go if I'm going to get drafted anyway? Not really though. Most are poor or joined because they need the money."

"The President told me he hears the protest. He wants to end the war."

Randall squinted, tilted his head and looked at her like she was a princess in a tower trying to understand how the common folk live.

If he loved her, he loved a memory. They were hopelessly mismatched now.

"I'm cold," she said. "I need to go home."

"Come with me. Just for awhile. I've written some songs. I want to play for you."

"Oh, Randall. It's not going to work this way between us." She heard herself sounding like a soap opera.

He wore his emotions on his face. Her rejection registered in a downward glance and frown. But he again showed new maturity by smiling and shrugging his shoulders. "Maybe it's just puppy love by me, but I don't think so."

Even that indirect expression of love melted her resistance.

He held her hand as they walked up the road and didn't speak. A calm pleasure being near him. She wanted him to love her, welcomed his desire, but was confused about how she should respond, afraid of being ruled by her emotions.

"Want me to walk you home?" he asked at the foot of his driveway.

"It's a dangerous neighborhood."

He laughed at her stupid joke. "Yeah."

"Thought you were going to play me your new songs."

"Love to." His step quickened as he led her up his driveway as if afraid she might change her mind.

She was happy to please him. Maybe love was giving pleasure with simple acts.

At the basement piano, he hesitated as if trying to remember something, took a deep breath, and hit the keys with a series of chords that hung in the air while his left hand started a rhythmic, rock bass pattern.

The lyrics sounded too wordy to her—not like the songs on the radio—not about *baby this*, and *love that*. He was singing about Lake Barcroft, about her, about them.

When you're born,
When you're young,
Find yourself
Not on the map.

Where we're from.

Not me,

Not her,

Don't live in the city,

Don't live in the town.

Where we're from.

Times that last and last,

Always, always,

Virginia.

He played for an hour, a strong performance. Some songs were beautiful, capturing feelings. Others were angry, passionate about love and peace. She thought the shouted verses and loud chords would bother his parents, but they didn't come downstairs. Perhaps the Malloys were sitting in their living room as awed as she was.

He sang about her.

Dodge's there when I need her.

Nobody can touch her,

Cause she's my friend.

What comes after that

doesn't matter much in the end.

What came after that did not matter much in the end. Randall left her in the last days of her childhood to be precocious beyond his seventeen years.

She was angry and missed him.

* * *

The Miss Madeira Junior-Senior prom was held at the Army-Navy Country Club in May. Beck was invited because she was the president of her sophomore class and needed to learn how to put on the prom for the seniors next year.

The all-purpose room decorated with bunting, balloons, and tables set with floral centerpieces featuring tulips was already filled with her schoolmates dressed in brocade tulle formal gowns and young men in tuxedos. A band played on the stage. Sonia-Barton and her clique of girls danced together with the most handsome boys.

Beck waited for Randall near the door. She'd not seen him since Christmas. He'd written embarrassing letters and telephoned her private line at odd times of day and night to tell her what he was doing, but she suspected he was not telling her everything. Hippies had become famous. Magazines delivered to the house—*Time, Newsweek, Life* carried stories of free love, marijuana and LSD—a drug that made you see things. Pictures showed young people with long hair and funny old clothes, girls with no bras—far beyond anything she could imagine wearing. Had he gone too far into that world for her to understand him?

Beck didn't know anyone else she felt comfortable asking and had already turned down two arranged dates with friends of Sonia-Barton. Randall would be flying in from San Francisco to be her date. That was impressive—if he ever showed.

When she'd asked him, Randall had giggled in his stupid-kid way, sounding as eager as life away from Lake Barcroft hadn't changed him much. He promised he'd come right from the airport, and she'd agreed to meet him at the dance.

Why had she ever come without him? She stood inside near the front door, thinking about leaving, caught between the paper streamers over the dance floor and the tables where couples sat.

Sonia-Barton sent her date to ask Beck to dance.

Beck looked quickly past him to the door and accepted to be polite. When she was an old lady somebody would remember the prom night when she was stood up by damn Randall Malloy.

After dancing, she went to the pay phone inside the portico to call Gail to come take her home. A stir of conversation and a girl's laughter came from the portico. Randall stepped from a black limousine looking like a rock star, with hair longer than any boy at the dance, silly in an emerald frock coat and yellow frilled shirt like something from Edwardian England.

She was sorry if he'd spent his money to come to her prom and rent a limousine, posing as a rock star, inappropriate, clownish.

Beck hung up too happy to pretend she hadn't been waiting for him.

He carried an orchid in a small covered box.

"Sorry, I'm late," he said. "Here."

She took the box.

"Want to ride in the limo?" he asked.

Tempting to leave, not be embarrassed by his bizarre dress. But she was stuck. At least she'd not been stood up. "No, we should go back in there for a while, I guess." She pinned the corsage to the décolletage of her dress while he watched.

"You look so beautiful. I haven't met anyone in the world who looks as pretty as you."

"Sure. You're such a talker." She hooked his arm and led him in the door.

Nothing for it now, but to go through the motions, ride out the mistake she'd made.

"Ms. Goodridge, may I introduce you to Randall Malloy."

The headmistress remained seated. "You have been expected, young man."

With an embarrassed grin, he bowed slightly like they did back at cotillion and shook her hand. "Sorry, I'm late."

Beck *showed him the room* as Panda would say. He was handsome in a rock and roll way, arms clasped behind his body, relaxed with social ease, confident in who he was, used to being admired. They danced and she lay her head on his shoulder.

He pulled her closer and whispered. "Let's go, I don't want to get in trouble for getting you home late."

She smirked. "We're older now."

"I want to ride around in the limo."

"No, you can do that when you're a star. Behave now."

After a late dinner at the Dumbarton Oaks mansion of a girl in the senior class, nearly one in the morning, the limo let them off in front of her house.

Randall gave the driver a tip and he drove away.

"Let's go to the beach," he said.

She glanced down at Gail's full-length Oscar De La Renta (*It will never fit me again*), she had altered. "In my prom dress?"

"Go inside and change. I'll wait."

She examined him and felt challenged by his lack of boundaries. "No, I don't want to get in trouble again."

"Yeah, that was fucked up."

His coarse language was further proof how he'd changed. She frowned in disapproval, intimidated by him. "You should go home. Have you seen your parents yet?"

"They're asleep."

"I bet they're waiting up for you. Your Mom is so excited. The colonel is too. I saw him walking Barney the other day and he said, 'The boy is coming home," Beck imitated his serious and slightly hurt voice.

"You're home for me, now."

Something tightened in Beck.

"Don't I even get a kiss?" he asked.

"Thanks for coming." She kissed him on the cheek.

"Jeez, I fly three thousand miles and that's all I get?"

"Sounds like a lyric to a song."

"Maybe a country song."

"Good night, Randall. Thanks for being my date."

She turned and started to walk to the door.

"Why did you invite me?"

She looked back over her shoulder and smiled at him. "Because you're the next teen idol."

"Come on. Go to the beach."

She stopped three steps from him and turned back.

"It's not that late, people are supposed to do things on their prom night."

"That was not my prom."

"Well, your practice prom night or whatever it was." He moved to her and placed his hand on her shoulder.

She quickly brushed it away. "It's not like that."

He giggled, "Yeah, I forgot."

"Good night, Randall."

He may want to flaunt convention, but she was comforted and supported by the structures of her life, wanted to be a good girl. If conservative meant obeying and pleasing her family then she was conservative. If he really loved her, he would not be so rebellious, so different.

* * *

She liked to think that he returned home, straightened up because of her, flattered herself that she was a good influence on him. More likely it was to avoid the draft. He'd passed a high school equivalency exam and was registered at the local community college. She grew used to him kissing her, and then slowly more until he regularly touched her in ways that were intimate and intensely pleasing.

Late October, a fall chill in the air, nobody was home at her house. Janey had the night off. Her father's election was in two weeks. He and Gail were campaigning. Beck could stay up as late as she wanted.

They stood on the beach behind her house. The scent of decay in the air and lake life had given up its summer aspect of boats and parties. The tempo of insect chirps and strokes had slowed with the falling temperatures. Small wind-waves lapped against the retaining wall. He held her hand. She wanted him to kiss her. He talked to her in a soft voice as if telling a bedtime story. "Do you ever feel like stepping out of yourself?"

"I had a dream last night that we swam naked in the lake at night," she said. "Let's do it."

"No, thank you."

Suddenly, he pulled her.

She shrieked and fell over with him into the four feet of water. He was laughing like a maniac.

The water was cold, her soaked sneakers weights. The blind heat came over her and she rocketed out of the water hands extended for his neck, screaming.

He reeled back and was underwater, her hands holding him down when the awareness returned. He came up, blinking, sputtering. "You're strong when you're mad."

"Randall, you are insane. The biggest jerk. I can't believe that I ever went out with you."

"Oh God," he wailed, clutched his head, fell back into the water.

Maybe she'd ruptured an artery in his brain. She flashed to the memory of the drowning. Was it going to happen again? She reached down in the darkness searching for him with her extended arm.

Randall emerged as if coming up through a pane of dark glass. "Boo."

She pushed through the water, her clothes heavy, and climbed up the railroad tie steps to the beach.

Randall followed her and reached for her as she opened the patio door to her bedroom.

Uncontrollable fury rose as she pulled away. "Don't touch me," she warned and closed the door in his face.

Her lips turned down, her eyes closed to press back tears, anger swallowed by sorrow. How could she live without him? Sobbing, she dropped her wet and sandy clothes onto the floor beside a shaggy bathmat and stepped into the shower.

The cleansing water calmed her. She'd forgive him. Only one love, what Randall said he knew. He was growing into a man leading her. Her lower lip drooped. She missed him, wished he was there with her.

She stepped out of the shower, wrapped a towel around her head, and put on a blue terry cloth bathrobe, opened the door to her bedroom and stifled a scream.

Randall had taken off his shirt and stood like a swamp creature in a B-movie in her bedroom.

"What do you think you're doing here?" she demanded.

"I came to apologize. I really feel like a jerk."

When he was this bold, he wanted change, was going to break a barrier.

"You shouldn't be here." She clutched the robe over chest.

"Take the towel off your head." He spoke confident she'd do what he said. The beast Panda had warned her about came to her. She shouldn't stand there, fight, order him to leave immediately.

He removed the towel and smoothed the hair gently around the side of her head.

"When I look in your eyes, I see someone totally different."

"Whatever are you talking about?" Her breath trembled.

He confidently held her waist and kissed her softly on the lips. She had revealed too much of her desire to him.

She put her arms around his neck and kissed him as if they were standing in the shadows.

He parted the robe and touched her bare skin.

"No." She pushed away.

"I love you." He moved to her as if in slow motion.

Her nerves fired in response to his hand running up her back. "Don't."

"I love you so much. We don't have to do anything."

He backed her toward the bed, slow dancing, kissed and caressed, suckled her breast, warm and compelling. He moved on top of her, his weight a pressure to release a flood of pleasure.

The thought of being pregnant made her push against his chest with her hands. She groaned, and he pushed down harder on her.

Her hymen tore with a burning pain and his penis moved far into her. She cried out. He pushed inside of her and she moaned. "Please no." She pressed her hands up against his shoulders. He moved in a way that caused her to position herself to meet him yet not accept him. For the first time, she heard the sound, the song of her sexuality, a humming rhythm, which built to crying moans. She tried to silence herself, to stop him.

He shuddered and warm moisture spread down her leg.

"What if I get pregnant?" Her voice trembled.

"You won't. I didn't come inside of you. It's difficult the first time. It'll be better, you'll see."

How did he know so much about women and sex?

He took her into the shower, the hot water flowed a cleansing stream between their bodies, down his chest and across her belly. Her desire for him made her pull him closer and kiss him without care.

He took her back to her bed, to her wet bedspread, and pushed her legs apart.

"No." She twisted and turned over on her stomach.

He tried to come at her from that position, hurting her in a different way.

"I'll get pregnant," she said.

He rubbed her back. "You won't."

He kissed the back of her neck and she turned over. He pushed her legs farther apart and kissed her in a way she could never have imagined, shocking, filthy but oh so pleasurable–things he'd learned in San Francisco being a hippie. She cried out and then her song began again. The pleasure was for him–for love.

They joined into a single presence, sparkling happy heart. Ecstasy grew into an euphoria she'd never experienced, shivered, hugged him tighter. His touch was immediate. Happy to be where she belonged. This–everything–freedom–freedom of the wires that spiral around until you can't breathe. She could breathe, run, laugh, make love–be herself.

Randall was rising and falling on her more rapidly, their skin making a slapping sound. He was groaning an urgent love song, a kind of rasp, that sounded here, now–everything was now.

Beck moved wildly beneath him in a primitive frenzy. She was too young to be in prison. Here with all this love, all this love, was where she belonged.

"Wait, softer, more slowly." She reached down and held him, swollen and pulsing. She guided and moved him to increase her pleasure. He shuddered, then lay as if stunned atop her. Another moment of pleasure as he slipped out of her.

He lay quietly by her side caressing and kissing her until he was ready to start again. The next time, he moved atop her for nearly an hour. No longer was he Randall, but a force, a passage to pleasure that made her lose touch with herself, that changed her bed and her room to a cloud on which she floated through the night. She fell asleep in his arms with a primordial feeling of security and awoke in the deepest part of the night to the hot sensations of him making love to her again.

Afterwards, she forced herself to stay awake. Five-fifteen—she had to have him out of the house. She listened to the regular breathing of his sleep, and lay in the crook of his arm, surprising to know her deep love for Randall had never really passed. She ran her hand down his body. He awoke and was ready to start again.

"You have to leave," she said.

"Please," he begged and kissed her. He rose atop of her and began again. Instantly, they were in the other world, moving with each other, merging and parting, merging and parting in an eternal dance. She cried out when she came, her body shuddering through her first complete orgasm, followed immediately by another and then a third. She frantically pulled on his shoulders and rubbed her breasts across his chest.

They lay against each other until Beck saw the clock. The thought her father might come home from a campaign swing at any time, his schedule hard to predict made her panic to have Randall out of the house.

Randall cooperated and quickly dressed. "I love the smell of you on me. I'm not going to take a shower this morning so I can smell you all day."

The quirky comment made her realize that after all Randall was in her room.

"I can't wait until tonight." he said.

"We have to be careful."

"I don't want to leave you now." He held her again.

"You have to." She pushed him toward the door.

"I'm going to stay here. I don't ever want to be away from you."

"What are you talking about? I know you're going to leave when you want. I won't stop you."

He considered her, then reached for her and gently kissed her. "I know what I have to do. Thank you for tonight. It was the best night of my life." He turned and ran up the path to the road.

He'd known that she wanted him to lead her where he'd already been, to touching and love magnified by commitment–from mixing to melding into a single emotional being. A blessing that they'd found each other so young, more time to grow together. They were an old-fashioned couple, mated for life like Canada geese. If one were to die, the other would live a life of solitary sorrow.

Randall was not the husband her family had planned for her. Someday, she hoped they would understand there could be no other man for her. Feelings swirled–high to low, certainty to doubt, smiles followed by sighs.

TEN

TRUTH

B efore her gynecologist, Dr. DeVoe, would start Beck on the birth control, she had to pee in a cup–to run some tests.

She sat in his office ready to be instructed on the use of birth control.

The doctor opened her file, read quickly, looked up and said. "I can't give you contraceptives while you're pregnant."

Beck leaned forward then collapsed into her chair as if the air had been squeezed from her lungs. She closely examined the doctor, looking for something in the droll delivery that indicated a joke or the possibility of mistake. Her mind raced looking for an escape. "Are you sure?" she managed to say.

"Yes, very recently pregnant I would say." He had a faint smile that indicated he'd seen this situation before.

She nearly panted trying to free her breathing. "Is there a possibility that it will go away?"

He shrugged and looked at her down the tip of his long nose. "Do you mean miscarriage? Yes, that happens. But you're young, healthy. It's not a high probability. Is there someone you can discuss the alternatives with–perhaps your grandmother?"

"Don't tell her," Beck panted in a rush.

"I don't intend to. I was only suggesting that perhaps you would like to."

The news hit like a cosmic laugh of scorn as God said *I told you so*. Who would rescue her?

Panda had known. Repeated the admonition that she should come to her. What would she do? Send her to Europe like in the old days?

What about sex was so unforgiving for her? Sonia-Barton could carry on as if nothing could touch her and Beck had *this* happen. Sonia-Barton had said there were places a girl could go to have an abortion, no questions asked, you received safe treatment. She hadn't said where–maybe New Orleans. Beck had also heard about coat hangers and knitting needles–girls bleeding to death.

She could do nothing–wait and see if she had a miscarriage. How long would it be until she showed?

She'd started her junior year, less than two weeks to her father's election. She'd be expected to appear with him when he won. She'd be a joke.

She mustn't harm his reelection. A lot could be made of a pregnant sixteen-year-old daughter. People would laugh behind his back. He could lose because of her.

With eyes barely seeing the road, Beck turned onto Old Dominion Drive that would take her to Heatherford. She'd see if her grandmother was home.

From the front of the four-car garage she saw Panda in her vegetable garden dressed in old dirty clothes, a straw hat and thick white gardening gloves, bent over pulling out dying or dead tomato plants. Maybe if she'd been out, Beck would have turned around. She parked the new green Dodge Charger, the one she'd made love to Randall in the back seat, two days ago. She'd said they should wait until she got birth control. He'd used a rubber. It must have been the first night. When was that? She did the calculation. Her baby would be born...no she couldn't have a baby. Panda would take care of this. She'd be furious but she'd do something. Beck walked into the garden, not smiling her head hung in guilt.

"Darling, what a wonderful surprise. I was just thinking about you," Panda greeted her as she walked up the walk.

After Beck hugged her, Panda held her at arms' length, leaned back to study her. "What's the matter?"

Beck sighed. "Do you remember the cousin you told me about who had to go to Europe?"

Her grandmother closed her eyes for a long moment so that Beck thought she might have not understood what she was saying. Without speaking, Panda hooked Beck's arm and led her on the brick path beside the walled planting areas to the lower level of the estate. They sat on a marble bench set beside a pond framed by bare branches of weeping willows.

"I used to sit here when I was pregnant with your father," Panda said wistfully as if remembering a youthful happier time.

Beck studied her grandmother's face with complete attention. Was she going to forgive her? Understand? Be happy for her? Save her?

"Do you mean to tell me that you are pregnant?"

"Dr. DeVoe told me. I just came from his office."

"Whom have you told?"

"Nobody. I can't believe it." She gave her grandmother a fearful look and turned away. She'd known this could happen, been warned, felt stupid for wandering into this disaster. Randall had said he was being careful. He was to blame. He'd come to her bedroom, forced her when she'd said no.

"Were you raped? Did he force himself on you against your will?"

Her eyelashes fluttered and she saw the way out of the blame. She could truthfully say yes, the way Randall had seduced her when she'd said no. He would be arrested, jailed. But that would have been too great a lie. She'd tried to stop him but not the times afterwards. She'd wanted him. "No, we were just careless."

"And whom is it?"

To say his name would forever condemn him in her family's eyes. "Randall," she whispered.

Beck had seen that expression when Panda described political opponents of her son—a compression of lips and squinting of eyes reserved for the most hated and reviled of real and perceived enemies.

"Was he the only one? Were there others?"

Beck squinted back tears and shook her head. "No." A sob drew out the denial.

Her grandmother's expression reddened to fury. "You did this on purpose."

Her tears freely unleashed, Beck wailed. "I didn't mean to. He said he was being careful."

Her grandmother's lips twisted into a tight scowl of disgust. "You, foolish, foolish harridan. After all I've done to properly raise you, you do this to your father."

Beck clutched her hands before her white school blouse. Was her sin so unforgiveable that her grandmother would turn her away? "I need your help," Beck sobbed. "You told me to come to you."

"You've told no one?" Panda peered at her as if searching for a lie.

"No, I told you. I just found out a half-hour ago."

Her grandmother pursed her lips and sighed deeply. Color drained from her face. "At least you came to me first. We can be thankful for that. We're going to have to take care of this. You'll stay with me—not leave my sight until we do."

Beck leaned back. Her grandmother was strong, would know what to do. All Beck must do is submit and obey as she'd always done, and she'd be saved.

* * *

Only Janey was home. Beck went to the storage closet built beneath the stairs. She moved ice skates her grandmother had given her for her fourteenth birthday that she'd never taken out of the box and carried a travel bag to her room.

Her grandmother followed, close enough to stop her if she tried to run.

In the midst of her shock, Beck saw the scene of the crime as Panda might. How could she have fallen here in her father's house?

Beck packed as if going on a weekend campaign trip for her father and carried the bag up to her grandmother's car.

Did her grandmother mean to arrange an abortion? Panda now appeared unfamiliar, unpredictable, desperate and capable of anything. Was Beck going to die? She wondered if she should have turned to Sonia-Barton. No, she had to protect her father. Panda was more reliable.

"I forgot something," she said to her grandmother at the car.

"Don't you try to call anyone. If you tell that boy, I won't have a thing to do with you. Your father will have to come and take care of you."

Beck entered through the private entrance to her room not wanting Janey to see her, quickly packed a red TWA bag with her Bible, a picture of her mother and brother taken the Christmas before they drowned, and a novel she was reading about a French heroine. Beck listened in case her grandmother was coming and glanced to confirm Panda was not coming through the patio door to her room.

Beck picked up the telephone to call Randall, frowned and hung up.

The telephone rang as immediate as if she'd placed a call.

She stared at the pink phone. Panda could be coming to check on her. Beck lifted the receiver.

Randall, as if there in spirit, cheerful, loving, inappropriate for her circumstance.

"I can't talk now. My grandmother's waiting."

"In your bedroom?" he asked mirth in his voice.

"Randall." The tremor in her voice was a broken shudder.

"What's the matter?"

"I'm...my grandmother doesn't want me to talk to you. I shouldn't be talking to you."

"What's wrong?"

Dangerous for him to think anything was wrong.

"Beck, tell me, trust me."

"I have to go campaign."

"Beck."

"Goodbye." She hung up before he heard her sob, and climbed the inside stairs chased by the faint ring of her phone.

Janey watched her leave with a sorrowful expression, not saying goodbye. Certainly Panda hadn't spoken to her, but Janey would know, just like Randall—some people knew her too well.

Panda drove her out of Lake Barcroft.

Beck's hands trembled over her womb where a baby was growing. Thoughts of bulging figures, birth, pain—the sudden end of childhood.

"Will you tell Daddy?"

Panda's lips twisted as she spat out condemnation. "I don't know how to tell him what you've done to him. What were you thinking? I spoke to you about this very problem. Were you just trying to vex me?"

The ego, the lack of concern for her lashed Beck. Gone was loving good will, replaced by scorn. She was merely an appendage to her father, a bad pet, in her grandmother's eyes.

"I'm sorry." Her apology as light as the breath that carried the words, incapable of gaining sympathy.

"Your father has worked too hard to let some gutter snipe ruin everything. You did this on purpose to ruin him, didn't you?"

Beck covered her face with her hands and sobbed. "Why are you talking to me like this?"

"Do you think the world is going to be as kind to you? When a girl loses her reputation, she loses everything."

"It's my reputation, not yours, not Daddy's," Beck wailed.

Red ran up her grandmother's neck into her cheeks. "You know nothing. You are an appendage of something bigger–better than you'll ever be. You know nothing of how hard it is to earn respect, how easy it is to lose a good reputation. What will people say about a family with a child like you?"

Beck's shoulders heaved. *People* were more important than her. To what depths had she fallen? Stripped of love and support why had she turned to her family. Randall loved her, wanted what was best for her. She'd tell him. His parents would take her in, understand.

Panda was hunched over the wheel as if aiming to run someone over. "You think you are so grown up, well you are going to learn about being grown up. You've had it too easy. You'll find out about pain and sacrifice now."

The ominous doom in her voice caused Beck to turn and stare at her grandmother's florid profile, lips pulled back in a near snarl.

"I'll go to him. He'll marry me."

Panda slammed on the brakes, nearly causing an accident, and pulled over on Leesburg Pike. "Get out. Leave. I wash my hands of you."

Beck stepped from the car. Whimpering, she leaned in the still open door. "Just tell me what you expect me to do."

Rarely had she seen Panda cry, not since her brother had drowned. With eyeliner-darkened tears, she shook her head. "You've ruined your life. Hasn't your father had enough tragedy? How could you do this to him?"

Beck stepped fearfully back into the car, leaving the door open, unsure Panda would allow her to return. "I'll have an abortion. Nobody will know."

Panda's tears evaporated as her head spun to Beck with a mocking bark of a laugh. "Do you know how many women I know of who have had *secret* abortions? It's laughable. Get in or get out. I haven't all day."

Beck closed the door, choosing rescue over abandonment.

Panda drove into the traffic past Falls Church.

"Do you know where I can get an abortion?" Beck asked.

"How in heaven's name would you expect me to know that?" Panda asked in a tired defeated voice.

"If I have the abortion quickly, nobody will ever find out. I'll be careful. I'll never let it happen again."

"Oh, be quiet and let me think."

* * *

Five days of quarantine at Heatherford, paralysis, thoughts shifting by the moment–from clear resolution to obey her grandmother to a dream of Randall taking her hand with his certainty –*I'll make it OK*–to abortion. She could do nothing until she spoke to her father. Did he know? All was for the Leader. She mustn't do anything to distract him in the last days of his election campaign. She was his protected and treasured child. He would know what to do after the election.

Caught between fantasy and mystery, Beck wandered in the past, revisiting parts of the mansion she'd explored as a child, through cobwebs to a subterranean kitchen where slaves had prepared meals for their masters in an open hearth, massive hand hewn beams of virgin wood, old forged extensions to move heavy cast iron pots, the remnants of shacks where they'd lived by their own small gardens.

Upstairs adjoining her bedroom–called the nurse's room from when her grandfather's younger brother and sister had died of whooping cough–she reread Rapunzel–waited for Randall to rescue her.

* * *

With a paper due at school on Hemmingway, Beck sat in a high back judge's chair at her grandfather's desk–a carved wooden behemoth like so much in the house with ancestral provenance.

She was reading the Atlantic about the author in Cuba, turned the page and saw the start of another article entitled–*One Women's Abortion*.

She devoured the information–in a *major American city*, last year. The woman's decision had not been done in secret but after a discussion with her husband–a careful calculation of what would be better for them. The couple could not afford or properly raise a fourth child just as she was in no position to have a child. With quick footsteps, Beck carried the magazine to Panda's study. Her time of indecision over–she'd have an abortion.

"I thought you were doing your schoolwork." Panda held a fountain pen above the letter she was writing.

"Look what I found." She offered the article like a valuable gift and laid it atop of Panda's lavender stationary.

Panda's eyes fell on the magazine and rose to confront Beck.

"Do you propose now to be a criminal? Aren't you causing enough trouble?"

Beck shrunk from the contracted lips, narrowed-eyed condemnation. "But...we can talk about it, can't we?"

Breathing heavily through her nose, Panda leaned forward. "How would your father explain this to the Catholics? Have you no sense? How could you be so ignorant?" She dropped the magazine into a wire trash can beside her desk as if contaminated.

Defiance, a burst of courage straightening Beck's back. Her voice rose in volume and pitch. "Nobody need know. It's my life. My body. Nobody will know."

Her grandmother leaned forward, her face red, speaking in a low guttural fury so not to be overheard by the help. "You, you...are nothing. You are incapable of making a proper choice. Now either get out or go back to your homework and stop trying my patience."

"But what are you going to do? Where am I going?"

Panda sat back into her seat. "When I know I'll let you know. Now leave me be."

"Aren't you even going to consider what I want to do?"

Panda closed her eyes and appeared to be composing herself. Her voice moderated. "I hope you're learning the lessons of scorn. This is what happens when you fall. I have no trust in what you might want to or reason to consider what you want to do."

"Are you just going to keep me locked up here?"

"If the accommodations aren't to your standards, please do leave."

Tears swelled in her Beck's eyes at the futility of arguing with her grandmother. Hands clasped before her, Beck cried. "Why are you being so mean to me?"

Calmly, Panda spoke as if explaining an obvious truth, "I am going to send you away. I'm making the arrangements now."

"When?"

"After the election."

"Maybe my father won't want me to go."

"If you want to remain in the gutter, cost your father his seat, leave, walk down the street asking for an abortionist."

"I very well may!" Beck cried in exasperation and spun away from the mocking dare to prove her independence. She'd get her purse, walk to nearest pay phone and call Randall. The article had said an abortion cost $500. He had money now. He'd understand, protect her, come to her in a minute.

Or she could call her father. She was more important to him than Panda. He'd find a doctor. The woman in the article asked five friends and each knew a doctor who would do it. It's almost legal. There was some pain but the operation done in 45 minutes. She'd be back in school and none the wiser.

What if he didn't know? Panda hadn't told him, didn't what him hurt with the truth of his despoiled daughter.

* * *

Election night, Norris drove the hundred miles south to Richmond.

Beck sat between her grandparents in the backseat of the Town Car. Her grandfather's courtly manner—a mixture of manners, humor, and love—provided no evidence that he knew. Panda behaved as if there were no issues between her and Beck, offering observations about politics and the way different populations of Virginia voted. Beck asked no questions and made no effort to demonstrate interest.

The closer they came to Richmond, the stronger her conviction she'd find a way to speak to her father. Sometimes, before he'd remarried, on Janey's night off, they'd go out to dinner at the S&W cafeteria. If nobody recognized him or at least did not come up to talk to him, they'd be quiet with each other, speaking almost in whispers. Sometimes they'd laugh at the funny way someone had done something–as the time when she was ten and a fat lady had dropped a bag in the upper corridor of Seven Corners shopping center. The lady had said to the smaller man with her, "I believe that I am in need of assistance."

Then, Beck and her father would say to make each other laugh–*I believe I am in need of assistance.*

Beck walked between her grandparents into the Jefferson Hotel–the embodiment of Virginia grand hotel decor with its Carrara marble Thomas Jefferson statue–into the euphoria of election night. Who knew? What was she supposed to say about where she'd been–what she was going to do?

As they stepped off the elevator on the seventh floor, Panda reached for her hand and held tightly as if she might run.

Beck's hair had been styled into a beehive, teased and back combed into a large dome, centered with a red barrette. A full-length red silk dress and for the first time in her life a girdle Panda had purchased for her–cinching her shame. A chiffon scarf attached to one shoulder, wrapped around the neck and draped down her back. Her makeup was a modest gloss on her lips and a touch of rouge on her cheeks.

A young man with a crewcut admitted them to the private victory party with a leer that made her feel better about how she looked. Family, friends, senior campaign and senate office staff gathered in the hotel suite. Beck's great-uncle, Judge Harry Battle, a thin male version of Panda, kissed Beck on the cheek, held her at arm's length, and drawled, "You look like the pride of the South, darlin."

She saw her father seated by a telephone surrounded by campaign staff.

"Got to go say hi to Daddy," she said to her uncle.

Panda followed like a censor.

He looked up at them, smiled, and went back to a conversation about a race in Alabama, too far into his political side for her to get a read on his reaction at seeing her. She wouldn't discover if he knew here and this was not the time or place to tell him.

Gail beamed with happiness, thrilled to be married to a great man. "I hope you're feeling better," she said to Beck.

What had Panda said was wrong with her?

Gail drawled, "You've never looked lovelier. Is that a new dress? It makes you look so mature, so grown-up."

Sonia-Barton, up from New Orleans for the election, dressed in a mini-skirt, a black wool horseback riding jacket and leather pumps–stylish as Beck would have liked to have been–was grinning, happy, effusive with her greeting, "Hey Beck, how ya been?"

"Fine as could be," Beck forced life and happiness into her voice.

"Mama says you have a nervous condition. What's that?" Sonia-Barton was teasing as if everyone knew what was wrong.

Beck led Sonia-Barton away from where anyone might overhear them and obeyed Panda's order not to give Sonia-Barton a clue.

"I don't know what she means. She's the one who has the condition."

Sonia-Barton nodded–suspicion replaced by a more obvious truth. "Why don't you come back to the lake with me?"

"Naw, I'd better stay with her for a few more days. She's really been crazy lately."

"She seems the same old madame to me," Sonia-Barton said. "At least let's get away from this scene. There's some cute guys here. That one definitely has you in his sights.

Beck glanced to see the young man from the door who was staring at them.

A cheer went up as the news came over the television that Richard Lyons had been reelected. The party formed to go downstairs for the victory speech.

"Randall coming tonight?" Sonia-Barton asked.

Panda moved toward them.

"Not that I know of." What if he did? She could tell him, run away with him.

They took elevators to the mezzanine and descended stairs duplicated for the mansion in *Gone With The Wind*.

The Leader flush with victory waved to supporters standing in the alcoves among the faux-marble columns. Sonia-Barton waved to someone.

A band played, *Carry Me Back to Old Virginny*. Clapping grew when the Leader stepped to the microphone on a stage hung with American flag bunting and the Virginia flag. Beck kept her eyes locked proudly on him feeling like an actress—she wouldn't give a clue.

"My good and loyal friends. How can I ever thank you enough?" His voice amplified by a small public address system silenced the well-wishers. Beck heard the projected voice as an echo. The crowd responded with more cheers. Bathed in bright stage lights, she stood behind her grandmother as a shield, and glanced at the audience. Her eyes passed and then flitted back to Randall in front of staggered bodies and bobbing rows of smiling faces, and away as if she shouldn't look at him, then back incapable of not meeting his smile.

Dressed in a pressed blue shirt, a narrow tie, he waved at her, at Panda. Hair combed back, mature and handsome, blue eyes shining like a sunny day. He grinned like an idiot, trying to make her laugh.

He would know, did know something was wrong.

She quickly shook her head at him. *I can't, Randall, not until I talk to my father.*

The speech stirred the crowd to more cheers, prolonging the torture of standing before Randall, the click of cameras. After a moment of confusion when the family stepped off stage, supporters surrounded the Leader, friends from Petersburg greeted Panda. Beck stood alone.

Randall appeared beside her and led her behind the stage. She didn't resist, allowed him to take her hand. Her legs wobbled and he held her up. Hidden by a curtain, he kissed her quickly on the lips. "Hi."

"I can't," she gasped.

"Beck." Panda's harsh whisper caused Beck to flinch as if she'd screamed in her ear.

Face mottled, Panda's voice trembled as she seized Beck by the wrist. "Coward," she hissed at Randall. "White trash."

A red wave of embarrassment clouded Beck's sight. Her grandmother was insane with false pride. Beck turned to see Randall pale, jaw agape. "I'm sorry," she mouthed as her grandmother led her in a near drag past the family.

Sorry I didn't take your hand and run.

BOOK TWO

ELEVEN

THE BETTER LIE

H er father was in the Virgin Islands on a post-election vacation. He'd return to Virginia tomorrow, and surely would come for her. Saturday afternoon after the election, Beck was in her room sitting by the window reading *Angélique in Revolt*. A passage about the French heroine's love for her dead husband executed by the king on false charges sent Beck into a daydream. Her breathing slowed and she was Randall responding to the glisten in her eyes, reach of her hand. *"We'll be together always."* She pressed the book to her chest. Randall was her true love separated by a wrong. *I'll find my way back to you.*

The door opened. Norris carried a large suitcase into the room, followed by Panda. "Put the boxes on bed bench," Panda instructed.

Beck stood and watched Norris carry in eight boxes of various sizes from Woodies. After the servant left, Beck asked, "Where are we going?"

"To the theater. You'll find a new gown, coat and shoes," Panda said.

"Thank you, Panda. In Washington?"

"New York. I must go make arrangements. Dress in the evening gown and shoes. Pack the rest and your belongings. Be ready to leave by 4:30."

She was to be sent away before speaking to her father. Janey would know how to reach him. Beck could sneak down the servant's stairs to the kitchen phone. But that was the point, wasn't it? For him not to know, to not have to make a decision about his disgraced daughter. How would she ask him if he knew? How would she tell him?

* * *

The Saturday 4:00 P.M. Eastern shuttle to LaGuardia wasn't crowded. Dressed in evening clothes, they sat as far back in the plane as they could. The precaution of dressing up was rewarded when Panda was greeted at the baggage carrousel in LaGuardia by a heavy woman in a mink.

"Going to the theater. Bringing some things up for a friend," Panda explained the large suitcase.

They drove through the Midtown Tunnel into lower Manhattan. Beck looked out at the curved canvas awnings over rain-sheen sidewalks, gold-buttoned uniformed men in white gloves illuminated in the light through glass doors on Fifth Avenue. Anger swelled in her throat like two hands tearing apart all she'd known and accepted as her place in life. She wasn't even being afforded the dignity of being told where she was going much less if she wanted to be going there. Helplessly being herded, her sin hidden, submitting to someone she wasn't sure she trusted.

The car turned on 11th and stopped in an open spot on the curve.

"Bring the bags," Panda instructed the liveried driver. The man shrugged as if that was not part of his job but bowed to Panda's officious manner.

"What is this?" Beck demanded.

Panda blinked, pressed her lips together, and quickly cleared her throat. "We'll have to see. I'm not certain they will take you," she said as if delivering an untouchable to the home of a Brahmin.

"Who? What?"

"Just make a good impression. Remember, we are doing this for your father."

"Does he know?" She finally asked.

"The fewer the people who know a scandal the better to contain a scandal."

A political aphorism—neither yes nor no—a response that could be redefined later depending on outcome. Another lesson for Beck to learn so she could be...what? Like her grandmother caring more about what people might say than for someone she said she loved.

Panda put the handwritten address back in her patent leather handbag. "This is nothing I wouldn't do, didn't do," she softly added a secret, the details Beck knew she'd never reveal.

This is growing up, Beck thought, *secrets and lies–life as a coward hiding from the truth.*

The driver opened the car door for them and carried the bags after them up the stone steps of a nondescript brownstone without identification or doorman.

Panda extended a leather-gloved finger and pressed the center of a round brass buzzer.

The cacophony of cars and trucks in the city assaulted Beck. She looked past the driver and imagined joining the people hurrying to lives in buildings crowded together. She'd call Randall, find Robbie. She had friends who would come to her. Her breathe caught in her throat, choking in the albumin of her obedience.

A small woman, gray hair pulled tightly around a narrow head, opened the door a crack, and examined them.

Panda beamed with her pleasant, public personality. "I believe you are expecting us."

The woman swung open the door with the grim visage of a crypt guardian. She spoke rapidly with a New York guttural *aw*, "Leave your bags in the hallway. They will be tended to if need be."

Panda turned to the driver. "Wait for me."

He nodded, an anonymous witness to Beck's exile, set the bags down in the vestibule and returned to the car.

The slight woman led them down a dimly lit tiled hallway that smelled of wet rags, through an open door she closed behind them.

"You may hang your coats there." She nodded toward a wooden coat rack in the surrounding darkness of the office.

Panda removed her mink. "I'll hold mine, thank you." Beck knew Panda would not hang her mink on a peg.

"Sit." The woman nodded toward two worn dining chairs facing a gray metal desk.

Beck slouched into a chair, eyes lowered, her new red pea coat draped across her lap. Her shoulders bare in her green chiffon evening gown.

Panda with her mink also in her lap, elegant in a full-length gown, perched forward beside her. "Thank you for seeing us on such short notice. I've heard wonderful things about your school," she gushed.

The woman glowered from the other side of the desk, hands clasped together in the center of a red leather-lined ink blotter, reading glasses hung over a buttoned Cardigan sweater—a warden inducting a new prisoner.

"You know why we are here Mrs...?" Panda asked with a lilt and drawing-out of vowels of her patrician Virginia accent.

"We don't use names here. I explained that to your lawyer. We go to great lengths to protect the identity of our guests," she spoke as if Panda should know this.

Was Beck to be a guest—someone who could leave when she wanted?

Stripped by anonymity of her usual tools to obtain what she wanted, Panda stiffened and looked down her nose at the woman's condescending attitude. "Yes, so I was told. The very reason I am considering enrolling my granddaughter in your school."

"But otherwise, by all means, let us be frank."

Beck shivered, the room cold enough to have kept their coats on.

Panda assumed a more businesslike demeanor. "We were told that your school might shelter my granddaughter during her time...of trouble."

The school matron spoke more slowly, "We are an old institution. Our roots are in the French order of nuns, the Sisters of Saint Joseph."

Catholics—the ones Panda was afraid to offend.

"Our mission is to defend the sanctity of life, to restore and grow the faith of our students in the blessings of forgiveness and redemption. Is that what you seek?" the woman directed the question to Beck.

She was to be a student–of what–falsehood, self-sacrifice?

Panda leaned forward. "I believe God has guided her here."

Beck raised her eyebrows at her grandmother's pandering.

"Tell me what you are seeking at L'Ecole?" the matron again tried to engage Beck. The words for the school were spoken with a full French pronunciation of vowels–la coal a.

Beck exhaled through her nose. Could faith–forgiveness and redemption– be found in submission?

I don't want to be here. I hate everything I sense about you and this terrible place.

"Answer her, dear," Panda said lovingly.

Beck sat more erect and spoke barely above a whisper. "I have faith in forgiveness and...returning to the sort of life I had." She heard her response as a confused jumble of what she thought the matron wanted to hear and what would please her grandmother.

Panda leaned back into the interview, dispensing with pretense other than her mission. "We want to hide her indiscretion."

The matron spoke with the confidence of one guided by God. "If the young lady obeys our rules then you may be certain that no institution is better equipped than L'Ecole to keep her transgression between her and our Lord." The stern focus returned to Beck. "Do you feel that it is the Lord's guidance that has brought you here to us?"

Anger and confusion tinged her answer. "No. I don't believe I do," she said with lowered eyes, not daring to look at Panda's reaction to her renunciation.

"You are not Catholic," the matron said as if that was already two strikes against Beck.

Panda hurried to interject, "We are Episcopal, High Episcopal, very close to Catholic. We are a devout family. She has been training for the youth ministry."

"Do you want to stay with us?" the matron came to the point as if the choice truly was Beck's.

No, no, no. How could she find spiritual strength in a lie–in hiding from Randall? She wanted to run, to not be Richard Lyons' daughter. She hated her grandmother and her false righteousness. If she was going to have a baby, she didn't want to do it alone, here in this dark, cold hole. Beck pulled her lower lip into her mouth and closed her eyes.

"She wants to," Panda lied. "And I am prepared to make a healthy contribution to your order."

The matron's eyes flashed to Panda. With gnarled lips she scorned the naked bribe. "If we take her, I promise she'll come back enlightened, immune to the coarseness of her former life."

Panda huffed at the implication that L'Ecole would rescue Beck from the failing in her upbringing.

The matron appeared to dismiss Panda's reddened complexion and stiffened posture as she turned her attention to Beck. "You are going through a great change, the greatest change you've ever experienced in your life. I believe we can help you, guide you with the teachings of our faith. Do you want our help?"

Weak. She was weak, obedient to authority even when wrong. Beck nodded.

"Very well I think you've come to us in great need and we won't turn you away."

"Thank you," Panda said and relaxed back into her seat.

The woman's lips pressed together into a frown as she looked at Panda.

"Then it is only a matter of the deposit, in cash as I told your lawyer."

Panda reached into her purse to pay for Beck's banishment. What feeling did the matron have about her—that she was weak and easily molded?

Without counting, the shriveled woman placed the stuffed envelope in a side drawer and took out a single piece of typed paper. "Your family and friends should be told that the young lady has gone to the village of Les-ax-Foix in the Pyrenees to live with a French family. All mail will be forwarded from the village. Here's a list of French names and addresses." She passed the page to Panda. "The only telephone in the house is here." The matron looked at a rotary dial telephone illuminated by the desk lamp and turned her eyes back to Beck. "Once a week you will be allowed to make a telephone call to your family. You must not try to telephone anyone but your family."

With a stiff back and upturned nose, Panda said, "I'm *certain* she will obey. She *was* properly raised, I assure you." She folded the page and put it into her purse. "I do have a plane to catch," she said as if she could not stand the loathsome woman a moment longer.

The matron ignored Panda as if she no longer mattered, keeping her focus on Beck. "We are very strict with our rules. You must never tell any of the other guests who you are or where you are from. Once you leave or attempt to leave before your time, or if you tell anyone you are not supposed to tell about where you are, you will be asked to leave our cloister immediately. Do you understand?"

Beck nodded.

"And you will obey our rules?"

How many opportunities did she need to say no, to escape?

"She is very obedient," Panda promised.

The matron leaned farther over the desk as if to more closely examine Beck. "We have many girls seeking your spot. Do you wish to stay?"

What else was there for her to do? She acquiesced to a complete answer over her questions. "Yes, ma'am."

"And you'll obey our rules."

Beck nodded. "I shall."

The matron sat back the matter settled.

Panda stood and put on her mink. "My driver is waiting. Don't want to raise too much suspicion at home."

Beck left her coat on the chair and followed her grandmother to the office door if possible more stunned by her rush to abandon her than her dread to what she'd just committed.

Panda gave her a quick hug. Beck pressed her face down on her grandmother's shoulder. "Don't leave me here," she whispered into the scent of Panda's perfume.

Her grandmother stepped back and contracted her lips in an expression of purposefulness. "We both must be strong. I know you can do it. You're made of good stuff. Do what they say and we'll be together when it's over. We'll write to each other while you're in France." She smiled through the lie, turned away and back with one final admonition. "You are doing this for Randall too. Imagine what this would do to him."

Oh, the masterful politician, identifying and exploiting her opponent's weakness. Randall could go on with his self-directed life instead of being bound to weak Beck and their young child. She would do this for him.

"OK," she barely whispered.

"Stay here." The matron ordered and left Beck while she escorted Panda out.

The smell of the old home, dust and furniture polish, abandoned in the dark—never so alone. The front door clanked. Visceral twisting, panic and sorrow raised Beck's shoulders as if to ward off a blow. How was she to have her baby here?

The matron soon returned and closed the office door behind her. "Sit down," she said and crossed back to her desk where she gazed at Beck with the appraising eye of someone who must clean up a mess. "Do you know why I accepted you?"

The money, Beck thought, but only shook her head.

"Because you were honest. I saw honesty in you. Not like your grandmother."

Beck looked at the matron to judge if she was being ironic, unused to being complimented in comparison to Panda.

The matron's clasped hands rested in the illuminated middle of the blotter. Her face and shoulders remained shrouded. "Do you know how to lie?"

The question was so odd after being complimented for her honesty that Beck didn't know how to answer. Was the matron seeking more evidence of her corruption? Being here was a lie. "Yes, I've lied. "

"There are many kinds of lies, aren't there? White lies, the kind you tell to make someone feel better. What I want you to do is to think about the consequences of lies. Do that and answer the question I asked when your grandmother was here. Do you believe that you can be forgiven and redeemed?"

Beck didn't remember being asked that. Maybe she'd not understood. Uncertain, she replied, "I want to be forgiven. Yes, yes, I do."

"And redeemed."

To go back to her old life, to pretend she loved her grandmother, that her father cared more about her than anything else, that she'd marry Randall? Would Beck Lyons be reborn out of the shell of a girl who no longer existed? Were Catholics more adept at repairing broken souls than her church?

Beck shrugged. "I don't know."

"Do you know those saving stamps they give at stores? If you save enough you can redeem a present. Do you think that is what I am talking about?"

Beck thinly smiled because she thought the matron was trying to amuse her. "No."

"When I speak of redemption, what I mean is the faith that you can make yourself better. Can you make yourself better?"

"If I try."

"Now, tell me again, why are you here?"

Beck responded with half-certainty. "To make myself better. To grow stronger, more self-reliant."

Unforgiving and quick with her correction, the matron snapped, "You are here to seek the Lord's guidance."

Beck huffed, her anger seeping into her response. "I'm here because I'm pregnant."

"Were you raped?" the matron's gaze bored into her.

"No, I quite liked it." She challenged the woman more than she'd dared her grandmother.

"You sinned. You fornicated. Gave into temptation."

Was L'Ecole about more shame?

The matron opened the desk and took out a card on which Beck saw the image of the Holy Mother. "I want you to say this prayer with me. Go ahead bow your head." She waited for Beck to place her hands together. Did the Catholics think Episcopalians didn't know how to pray?

"O Lord, Jesus Christ, Redeemer and Savior, forgive my sins," Mrs. V. read and waited for Beck to repeat each phrase. "Just as You forgave Peter's denial and those who crucified You. Count not my transgressions but rather my tears of repentance. Remember not my iniquities, but more especially my sorrow for the offenses I have committed against You. I long to be true to Your Word and pray that You will love me and come to make Your dwelling place within me. I promise to give You praise and glory in love and in service all the days of my life."

The drone of the prayer was just words without conviction. Beck felt no forgiveness. She was too confused for Jesus to dwell in her.

"Was that hard for you to say? Say it again, yourself."

Beck couldn't remember exactly what she was supposed to say. She missed some words, but when she looked up the matron nodded. "Yes, your own words suffice. It is not the words, it is the asking. God does forgive you. You are forgiven. You don't have to lie to yourself anymore and say that it did not happen or that it is somebody else's fault. You have sinned and Jesus has forgiven you. You never have to lie to Him. He knows all your sins. And when you confess your sins to Him, He forgives you."

Did Jesus know and forgive her grandmother for sending her away before she could speak to her father?

"You will be hiding the truth about who you are when we go inside. Is that a lie?"

Beck looked down and up. "You want me to."

"If the girls inside knew your name and if you knew their names they would have to lie for you, wouldn't they? You would be asking them to lie for you. That would not be right would it?"

Beck shook her head.

"I like to call those lies a better lie–a lie we tell for the betterment of others."

"A better lie." Beck smirked.

"Yes, now you're beginning to understand our Lord's grace. You must never lie to Him. Do you have a Bible?"

"It's not Catholic."

Mrs. V. smiled appearing more friendly. "It's the same Bible. You and I will talk about this some more before you call home on Sunday. You don't want your family to have to lie for you either, do you?"

"Sure, like they aren't all ready."

The matron's gaze was unwavering. "Your attitude will improve when you adjust to our ways. You will call me Mrs. V. You will be called E. Can you remember that? We have five girls. A, B, C, D. You will be E. The next girl who joins us will be an A or sometimes a B or a C depending on who leaves next. When you speak to the other students just the initial. What are you going to call yourself when you go inside?"

"E, I guess."

"Yes, E. Not I guess. Just E. Carry your suitcase. I'll take the other."

"What will happen to my baby?"

Mrs. V. sat back in her chair and looked at Beck with a tilted head, still taking her measure. "That will be up to you or your grandmother it would seem. My understanding from the lawyer is there is to be an adoption."

Sweep the problem away. If that all there was to it? She could have had the abortion and been back at school before anybody noticed instead of this rigmarole about going to France.

As if sensing her apostasy, Mrs. V. said, "Your grandmother showed piety by bringing you here to us so that we may help you regain a righteous path."

Panda was relinquishing control over her to another authority to command what she did with her body, her baby.

"Now, I'll show you to your room so you can get a fresh start in the morning."

With a fatalistic sigh, Beck followed Mrs. V. into the hallway. She put on her coat and leaned to pick up the bigger suitcase. She'd find the strength to leave her childhood behind and become an independent woman free of her family's expectations, able to make her own choices.

At the other end of the dank hallway, Mrs. V. unlocked then re-locked a door behind them.

Darkness gave way to a brightly lit vestibule that opened into a parlor with a marble fireplace, polished mahogany table set with a flower arrangement, an old oil seascape painting, a vase with a fall arrangement of dried wheat, a gilt-framed mirror. The homey, upscale decor comforted Beck.

She hauled the suitcase past a living room across the hall from a carpeted wooden stairway. Three girls watched television. Beck heard the opening refrain to Gunsmoke, a television western about the town of Dodge.

Young, under twenty, dressed in loose casual clothes covering various stages of pregnancy, the girls appeared to Beck to be as unconcerned about their appearance as if they'd been home. Her eyes were drawn to a strong-chinned redhead sitting in the center of the couch who pursed her lips in a low descending whistle at the sight of her. Beck looked away imagining how she much appear in her evening dress as if she was returning from the opera. The Catholics in school and the neighborhood had not seemed that different—bigger families, fish on Friday, worship at a different church on Sunday. Angélique was Catholic, heroic not weak and helpless like her. The Nun's Story with Katherine Hepburn—who people said she looked like—showed the strength of their faith. What did Catholics do? What mysteries were here? Mrs.

V. had spoken as if God had guided Beck. Did He want her pregnant so she'd come to the Catholics instead of living in sin in her own faith?

Beck strained to carry the suitcase up the stairs and followed Mrs. V. down a hallway line with three doors on one side and two on the other.

Mrs. V. opened the center door and stood aside for Beck to enter a room that combined the commonness of a hotel with the personal touches of a relative's guest room. Beck set her suitcase on the edge of a throw rug on the hardwood plank floor and quickly surveyed the furnishings—a bureau, stuffed chair with lace dollies, a radio and lamp set on a table beside a desk with carved claw and ball feet, a framed pastoral print, a crucifix over a single white panel bed.

Mrs. V. carried in the overnight bag containing Beck's Bible and a picture of her mother and brother.

Mrs. V. stood inside the open door and said, "In the courtyard we have a lovely garden. Of course, you will not be permitted to leave the premises. Should you leave, you may never return. Do you understand?"

If I find the courage to leave, I'll never return.

"The Sisters will continue your education with a special emphasis on conversational French. A doctor will come to see you when necessary. We have our own chapel. We rarely have non-Catholics here. Perhaps Father Mahoney can provide you with spiritual guidance, to have conversations as we did tonight, about God's will and free will. Would you like that?"

Is submission to God's will what this is about? Did God really not want her to have an abortion?

"OK," Beck softly said.

In her cawing elocution, Mrs. V. seemed to finally express sympathy. "The time will go quickly, E. I like to think that being here is like having a nice long afternoon nap. When you awake you are refreshed and ready to lead a redeemed life closer to God."

Never in all the dreams of her life had Beck ever imagined herself in a place like this.

"Do you have any questions?"

Why am I here when I so strongly don't want to be? "No, ma'am."

"Breakfast is served at 6:45. Classes begin at 8. If you need anything, I or Mr. J. are always available."

Who was Mr. J.? What kind of dangers lurked in this hideaway? A fear of the unknown raised a tremor in Beck's legs, an urge to run, but to where?

Mrs. V. closed the door, leaving Beck alone or alone as she could feel in New York. Long dark muslin drapes barely muted the raucous bustle of the city. She'd been to New York with her family. She liked the theater, art galleries and museums. Not long ago, before she'd been expelled from that life, she'd thought a daring future would be to come to New York to study art or music. Now the roar of trucks and cars seemed to extend to a distant horizon, unbearable compared to the quiet of Lake Barcroft. How had she fallen so far so fast? Her confidence seemed as flimsy as the Freer Gallery rice paper walls. Her dreams of becoming a woman, of going to college, of marrying Randall and having pretty children seemed like somebody else's. She must rebuild herself.

With her hand, Beck brushed lint and dirt to the edge of the drawers, laid her new underwear, socks, stocking and garter belt, night clothes, shirts, sweaters, and gloves on yellow lining paper. She hung dresses and her new heavy jacket in a closet pungent with a mothball pesticide smell, set the Bible and silver frame of the picture on the nightstand beside the bed. On bathroom shelves layered with white paint, she arranged a brush, bobby pins, and toiletries, washed and dried her hands and face with a green towel smooth from use.

Still dressed in her evening dress, she sat on the ivory chenille bedspread.

A neighbor's radio murmured,

Hello darkness my old friend

I've come to talk to you again.

She looked into the peaceful, confident eyes of her mother's picture. *Help me, Mama.*

Beck laid her hand over her stomach. Was this thing a baby or a seed with no way to live on its own? The Catholics were sure it was a separate life distinct and apart from her. When the time came for her give away her child there would be no doubt.

She should have asked Randall. What would he have told her? Let's run away together to San Francisco and be hippies? Probably nobody would ever love her as Randall had. Would he love her when he found out she'd not trusted him? Maybe Panda was right, she was doing this for him. Nobody had to make choices but her. Was that fair?

Father Dorfman had said to never lose your faith. She had no faith. She was bad. She'd called her mother upstairs so she didn't stop Colin from going out onto the ice where they'd drowned when her mother went to rescue him. She'd been mean to Gail when her father had introduced her.

She thought of Mrs. V.'s prayer. Accept domination for forgiveness. Was faith submission? She prayed for the strength to walk out of L'Ecole and take charge of her life, sighed, feeling no comfort or courage, put on a new nightgown, turned off the lights and lay in a bed that smelled of another—a feral wet cat scent—a girl who'd lain here grown big, been taken to the hospital maybe only hours before.

She went to sleep thinking of Randall and dreamed of him. They were living in a small room in France. A baby cried from a crib in the corner. *"I'm going out,"* he said and left her alone. The baby wouldn't stop crying.

TWELVE

THE JOYFUL MYSTERIES

The explosive hiss of truck brakes shocked her awake. She quickly scanned the small room in the gray crepuscular light bordering thick green drapes. The truth of the strange furnishings and continuous agitation of Manhattan raised a deep sigh. She closed her eyes staring vacantly at a bas-relief of angels around a dirty glass light shade holding bug remains. The radio on the other side of the wall played the Mamas and Papas, "Monday, Monday, can't trust that day."

She'd spend eight months here. Might as well make the best of it, put her best foot forward, make that all important good first impression–show her good stuff.

The shower was old but clean chipped porcelain. Beck shaved her legs, one foot propped on the side of a towel-covered toilet, worn white towels wrapped around her drying hair and body. Condensation cleared in shades of reflection from a full-length mirror attached to the back of the bathroom door.

She removed the towel and examined her body now a host of someone new and distinct inside of her. Was there something about her that would lead to a miscarriage? If so she'd feel liberated, freed from a burden she didn't want to carry.

Her nipples perhaps had swelled a bit, the dark areolas were slightly tender. She could be imagining more visible veins. Her belly was flat. Nobody who'd seen her before she came here would ever have reason to suspect. Not getting an abortion was self-sacrifice, for her father who might never know what she'd done for him.

She teased and sprayed her Jackie Kennedy bouffant, placed a barrette in the center above her forehead, and stepped into the dress and dark pumps she'd worn to the election night party.

The house was quiet. Downstairs, the empty dining room smelled delicious of cooking cinnamon pastry. A tarnished candelabrum with naked spikes sat on a lace center cloth on a mahogany dining table large enough to serve a party of ten. A copy of the *New York Times* lay at the end of the table. Was she supposed to order food, wait here?

She pushed through a swinging door to a kitchen larger than the one in Lake Barcroft but not as large as Heatherford. A hallway with a chalkboard on the wall led to a side room and a rear door.

A stocky man with kinky white hair around a bald crown pulled a tray of cinnamon buns from an open oven with a gray cooking mitt. Cinnamon smell was lifted by the heat.

Beck's tight expression relaxed around her mouth.

Dressed in a white chef's jacket closed at the collar, the colored man set the tray atop the stove, turned and smiled brightly at her, revealing large white teeth. "Hello, pretty lady. You must be E. Are you ready for your breakfast?"

"Why yes, that would be lovely."

He chuckled. "Lovely it is. You're a polite lady, I can see. *Yes siree*, a real lady, yes you are. They call me Mr. J. One thing you can count on here is a fine and varied fare. I was trained by the United States Navy."

The expression of interest came naturally to her in the way her father would listen. "Did you go on ships?"

"I surely did, from Pearl to England, from the Atlantic to the Pacific, I crossed the equator six times. Now, you strikes me as a type of lady that I can really cook for. You tell me what you want, anything at all."

"Do you have croissants?"

Mr. J. frowned and looked perplexed. "No, I'm sorry, I was in the *U.S.* Navy. We didn't do much that type of foreign cooking. Any kind of eggs, bacon, steak, anything like that? How 'bout some these sticky buns?"

"I believe I'll have a bit of tea and some toast, lightly buttered please."

"White toast?"

"That would be lovely."

"Lovely it is. *Yes siree* you're definitely a white toast, lightly buttered lady for this old house. Now you go back and sit at the dining room table and I'll bring your breakfast right out. Miss Kitty should be joining you soon. She's usually the first one awake."

"Thank you, Mr. J."

"You're welcome E."

Who would be called Miss Kitty when everyone was supposed to have letters for names? Nobody was at the table when Beck returned. She sat and opened the *Times,* reading about a meeting at the White House with President

Johnson. If her father went to the meeting, the President would ask about her. *Gone to France.* The lies about her would extend to the President. What if the Leader went to visit her in France? He might if he didn't know this was all a ruse. How would L'Ecole handle that? This scheme to satisfy social standards that barely existed seemed foolish and easy to expose. Who would care? A few of Panda's hidebound friends and the Catholics who she was certain to get a load of during her time at L'Ecole.

""I don't believe it! Somebody is reading my paper."

The exaggerated female voice behind her caused Beck to flinch.

"I'm sorry." Beck rapidly refolded the newspaper.

The redhead she'd seen last night watching Gunsmoke, as tall as Beck, heavier, about her age, wore a tattered blue robe hung open to reveal the beginnings of a pregnant shape beneath a flannel nightgown. She had a handsome face, a firm square chin, a wide forehead.

"Have you been eating my porridge, too?"

Beck smiled.

"How are you?" the redhead asked with exaggerated politeness and stuck out her hand. Beck noticed bitten fingernails, fingers as thick and ill-used as a domestic servant. She remained seated and politely returned the greeting.

"On behalf of the criminally insane, I wish to welcome you to *L'incubator,*" the redhead pronounced the name with an exaggerated French accent, stepped back and swept her eyes up and down on Beck's figure. "Is it the Macy parade you're going to be in today?"

"Why no. I don't believe that's until Thanksgiving."

The redhead excitedly waved her hands in front of her chest and then formed them into fists that she clapped together. "I'm sorry. I didn't recognize you. You're Lynda Bird Johnson!"

If anyone, Beck thought she more resembled Luci Baines, the younger of the President's daughters. "No. That's not me."

The redhead sat next to her and leaned on her hand staring at her. "Then who could you be?"

"I'm not supposed to tell you that."

"No, that's not true. Everybody tells me who they are."

"I'd rather not."

The redhead sighed. "Well, I'm going to have to call you something. How about Lynda Bird? May I call you that?"

"I believe you should call me E."

"You mean like *EEEEEEEEEEEEEEEEEEE*." The redhead again waved her hands. "Like when you see a mouse?"

The girl was just a plain heckler. Beck's mouth drew back in a snarl. "I don't really know how you treat others here but leave *me* alone."

"You want to fight?" The redhead stood up, eyes narrowed, fist raised. "Put up your dukes. Go on give me your best shot."

Beck breathed harder. The tension and anger bottled inside released in a violent explosion of blind rage. With an "arrrr" she launched herself at her shocked antagonist.

Beck was on top, fist raised over the wide-eyed redhead when her senses came back to her.

Mr. J. carried a tray with a tea service and a rasher of toast into the dining room. "Ladies, ladies, ladies. Jesus H. Christ. What the..."

His voice expanded Beck's narrow focus back to what she was doing. She stood, panting and trembling. Sanity returned to her like waking from a nightmare. "I'm sorry," she cried and turned to flee. She hadn't reached the living room when the commanding voice of the girl barked, "Hey where you going? Get back here!"

Beck slowly turned to see the girl had picked herself off the floor.

Mr. J. put the tray down on the table. "What's this all about?"

"Oh nothing," the redhead, her robe disheveled said, "Lynda Bird here is just trying to set the land speed record for getting thrown out of here."

"She was teasing me."

Mr. J. shook his head. "Yes sir, you sure can never tell about this place."

The redhead laughed, "Come back and have your breakfast with me. I like a gal who stands up for herself."

Beck reflexively patted her hair to restore its shape and returned with as much dignity as she could muster.

Mr. J. looked at Beck as if to judge if she was too dangerous to leave alone, then back at the redhead. "Your usual?"

"I like my buns hot, in more ways than one." She said patted her belly and laughed. "I'm eating for two."

"I'm going to leave you two alone. No more fighting, hear?"

"I won't," Beck said, remorse in her voice.

"Miss Kitty?"

The redhead sat in her place, leaned back in the chair and carelessly exposed her nightclothes clearly showing the outlines of her body. "Jacques you're looking good this morning. Might fight her for you."

Mr. J. shook his head and laughed "Hee-hee. Miss Kitty you *are* naughty."

"That's why I'm here." She winked at Beck.

When Mr. J. had returned to the kitchen, Beck tried to apologize. "I don't know what came over me. I've been under a lot of pressure."

"Ain't we all," the redhead said. "Don't worry about it."

"They probably *are* going to throw me out," Beck said and stared at table unable to fathom what she'd done.

"Naw. Jerome is cool. He won't tell. Me either. I like you. Smart and feisty, just like me."

Beck shook her head. "I'm not usually like that."

"And on the Lord's day too. They call me Miss Kitty around these parts," she said like a cowgirl and stuck out her hand.

Beck again lightly shook the girl's hand.

"We're going to have to get you a name. E doesn't work for me."

Beck twisted her lips. "I'm in enough trouble without breaking any more rules."

"Like it here then, hunh?"

Beck relaxed into the humor Miss Kitty was offering and smiled slightly. "Hate it."

"Planning on clearing out?"

"I rather not say."

"Confused, hunh? That's all right I'll straighten you out. Me I'm here because the bastard who did this to me said he'd killed me if I didn't."

Beck slightly nodded unsure if she wanted to share confidences.

Being expelled would force the issue with her family. Strangely, she found the experience with Miss Kitty exhilarating. She'd been complimented for standing up for herself. Maybe it was time to do more of that. She imagined telling her grandmother she'd been expelled for fighting and to leave her alone because she was perfectly capable of making her own decisions.

Mrs. V. had said she'd be able to call her family on Sundays. She planned to tell her father she needed to speak to him about something very important, to buy her a ticket home.

* * *

Midday, the door to her room opened and Mrs. V. entered Beck's bedroom without knocking. Her eyes widen with apprehension. Had the fight been reported?

"Come to lunch," she said in a tone more order than invitation.

"Yes, ma'am." Beck put down the novel and stood.

"Father Mahoney will be available to see you in our chapel after he's heard confession from the other girls," was said as if Beck didn't have a choice.

"Yes, ma'am."

The fight must not have been reported. Beck's shoulders relaxed. Her disappointment at not being forced to leave balanced by relief not to have face her grandmother.

At the bottom of the stairs, Mrs. V. warned again, "Remember no personal information."

"Yes, ma'am, no personal information," Beck repeated.

Mrs. V. turned to her office, leaving Beck to enter the dining room by herself.

Three girls she'd not met were at the table. All eyes turned to her with interest. A rustle behind caused Beck to turn to see Mrs. Kitty. She wore a plaid dress, hair combed and set, eyeliner, mascara and lips colored, nails polished, looking much better than she had this morning, Beck thought.

A girl at the table with long stringy hair hanging loosely around a puffy red face, laughed. "Miss Kitty, why you look like you're fixen to go out? Why all the makeup?"

"The President's daughter is here." Miss Kitty extended her arm toward Beck. "Didn't you dummies recognize her? It's Lynda Bird Johnson."

"Is that what you want us to call you?" the stringy-hair girl asked?

Beck sat at an empty place setting and smiled politely, trying to be friendly. "Aren't we supposed to call each other by our letters?"

"That's too boring," a girl with an accent that reminded Beck of the Kennedys, said. "We make up stories about ourselves. It's betta."

Miss Kitty sat across from Beck and said, "It's a tradition. Do you want to be only a letter, EEEEEEEE?"

Beck looked away from the mocking challenge, unfolded and placed a cloth napkin in her lap.

The girl with the Boston accent raised her hands as if it was simple. "I'm Molly McGuire. I was a gangsta's girlfriend, not a whore exactly, but pretty close."

The girls giggled together in a knowing way that inferred the camaraderie of a shared plight.

"We all make names up for ourselves, or else someone does it for you," Molly McGuire said.

"We don't like to be called just letters," said the stringy-haired girl.

"You don't have to say who you really are," Molly McGuire encouraged. "Make up a life. That's what we do."

"You make up a life," repeated a very pregnant girl so small she hardly looked old enough to be in high school.

The comments rolled around the table, ganging up on Beck.

"The girls who've been here the longest teach the new arrivals."

"That way it's not so boring."

Beck said. "I don't mind being called E."

"We'll call her Lynda Bird," Miss Kitty announced.

The other girls looked at Beck as if to confirm that was all right with her.

Molly McGuire tried again. "Make up a story about yourself. You can do it. Otherwise, we don't have anything to talk about. It's going to be pretty boring for you and all of us if you don't."

"Start with a name," pressed the small girl.

Beck thought it better to be a good sport and play along with their game. "I guess I could give it a try. Now, let me see. My name is Dodge," she slowly said.

Miss Kitty laughed at her. "Because I'm Miss Kitty?"

Beck had forgotten that Miss Kitty was a character on the television show *Gunsmoke* in the western town of Dodge.

"No, not exactly."

"That's going to make us a team. But that's OK. I can use a sidekick."

Beck pressed ahead despite Miss Kitty's amused look. "I'm an orphan. I was left at the door of a rich man when I was born."

"Where?" Molly McGuire asked.

"In Richmond, Virginia. The rich man wanted to adopt me but his wife would not let him. She made him take me to an orphanage. Sometimes, the rich man would come and take me to his home, mostly when his wife was traveling."

"Is he the one who knocked you up?" Miss Kitty asked.

Two of the girls laughed.

Crude and vulgar, Beck thought and ignored her.

"You don't have to tell us that," Molly McGuire said.

"Yes, she does," Miss Kitty said. "That's the best part."

The other girls appeared fearful of Miss Kitty.

Mr. J. passed through the swinging door with a plate of chicken salad sandwiches. "How many of you gals wants pickles?" he asked.

All but Beck wanted some.

After Mr. J. had gone back to the kitchen, Beck said, "He did not do this to me. He has a son, ten years older than I."

"'I'" Miss Kitty interrupted. "You see how well educated Lynda Bird is?"

Beck overrode the heckling, pushing ahead with her story. "His family wanted him to go into their family business, but he wanted to be a professional musician. We were very close as children. I love him."

She lowered her head, wondering if she was too close to the truth.

The small girl said, "That's a good story. Which soap opera do you like the best?"

"What happened?" Molly McGuire asked. "Does he know?"

"Last month I was a virgin. My patron died. I was staying at his house for the funeral. Of course, we were all very sad. His son came home. Our grief made us careless."

Several of the girls nodded their heads.

"Only one time, and he was very sorry, begged my forgiveness. I remained at the orphanage. We purposely stayed away from each other because we did not want it to ever happen again. A week after he returned home, he came to visit me at the orphanage and told me that he was going to marry and go into his family's business in Argentina. A week later I realized that I was late."

Miss Kitty shook her head. "That's not your story. You're Lynda Bird Johnson, the President's daughter, and Richard Nixon knocked you up. Now, that's a story we can live with."

* * *

Back in her room after the meal, Beck spoke to Panda. With unseeing eyes staring at the wall, the intensity of her declaration caused her to lean forward, imagine hands chopping through the air as she told Panda she was going to marry Randall. She was bigger, stronger, looking down at her grandmother with confidence, in charge.

* * *.

Saturday afternoon the faint sound of man's voice came up to Beck's room. She'd become attuned to subtle changes in the quiet order of the house of girls waiting out their time, the lessons taught by the nuns, the meals and television shows they watched together in the living room.

An hour-and-a-half passed and Mrs. V. led her to an arched ceiling room in an alcove beneath the stairs. A priest dressed in a black gown and a white collar sat in a wingback chair beside a coffee table at the far end of a small nave with an alter set before a cross.

"Sit down please," he nodded to a wooden chair like the one in her grandmother's office where the servants sat.

He considered her with watery blue eyes as if to see something not visible with a less educated perception, or maybe for her not being Catholic. The chapel with an oily smell of burnt church candle wicks, seemed close, his knees nearly touching hers, as if he would lean forward to whisper to her. The priests at Christ church would not have sat so close to her.

"Is there something you would like to talk to me about?" he asked.

The cross embroidered on his vestment burned into her with the eyes of God. Uncertain what she was supposed to do, she looked down at her hands, disloyal to her faith.

"Can't think of anything." She bit her lower lip and slumped in the chair.

He considered her, searching deeper. "Try to imagine that I'm a doctor and that you are sick. You have come to me and I'm waiting for you to tell me why you have come."

"Because I'm pregnant," she murmured.

He nodded encouragingly. "How do you feel about that?"

The stupidity and cruelness of his question straightened her back. She squinted at him with consternation. "Terrible."

"Bearing a child is a blessing. You are doing the best for the child by placing it up for adoption."

Her baby was an *it*, not *her* or *he*–not Randall's child to be given away.

The priest leaned over and removed a rosary and pamphlet from a briefcase by the leg of his chair.

"I don't want a child," she said.

Father Mahoney straightened. "Abortion would be a mortal sin. You have chosen a righteous path."

He misunderstood. Where would she get an abortion if she wanted one?

She looked at her twisted hands before raising her eyes to him. "Children go away. They die."

"We'll pray for the Lord to protect your child and deliver him or her to a better life than you can provide. Someday when you are married, God will give you other children that you can love and give them life in a family."

Where was God when her mother and brother were struggling in the upturned shards of triangles and slivers of ice? They had a life in a family.

Her time was up. Father Mahoney had other souls to save. He handed the pamphlet and cross to her. "I want you to read this and we'll spend some more time together next Sunday."

Beck carried the small booklet and rosary to her room, and sat on her bed. *How to Pray the Rosary* was printed in color with a picture of Mary. The Virgin's arms were crossed. Angels placed a crown on her head. Inside were three panels and pictures of the life of Jesus. *The Joyful Mysteries, the Sorrowful Mysteries, the Glorious Mysteries.* Beck read the second Joyful Mystery, The Visitation–*Blessed art Thou among women and blessed is the fruit of Thy womb!*

Beck thought of herself as a tree–her baby was the fruit of her womb. God would give her child to a better mother who wouldn't stand on the shore, her screams going unanswered.

She read the Apostles' Creed...*I believe in the Holy Spirit, the Holy Catholic Church, the communion of Saints, the forgiveness of sins, the resurrection of the body, and life everlasting. Amen.*

"I believe in the forgiveness of sins," she whispered.

A knock on her door startled her.

"Who is it?"

"A man who loves you very much," came a muffled voice.

Miss Kitty walked in, dressed in a pair of jeans that allowed for her expanded front.

"What ya got there?" Miss Kitty picked up the pamphlet. "Aren't you Catholic?"

Was that giving too much information? If she said yes, she might have to prove what she knew. "Not too much."

"What the hell are you doing here then?"

Beck looked away, uncomfortable at blaspheme around holy articles.

Miss Kitty dropped the pamphlet on the bed. "They're trying to show you the righteous path? Don't worry–I have the perfect answer. I *am* Catholic. I know. Beat them at their own game–tell them that you're a virgin, Immaculate Conception Number Two. Tell them that."

The idea was so preposterous Beck laughed.

"What's that I just heard?" Miss Kitty acted concerned. She bent over as if to examine Beck.

Beck laughed harder–first a giggle and then a release that grew to near hysteria.

"She lives. She lives." Miss Kitty imitated Dr. Frankenstein and stomped around the room with her hands in the air.

* * *

That night after dinner Beck was in her room. Outside the thin barrier of wall and window a truck horn blared above the constant movement of traffic. She sat at the desk and read the ten typed pages.

WHAT TO TELL YOUR FAMILY AND FRIENDS ABOUT WHERE YOU ARE IN FRANCE. NOT TO BE REMOVED FROM THE PREMISES.

1. SAY THAT IT IS HARD TO MAKE PHONE CALLS AND IT IS BETTER TO WRITE.

2. USE DETAILS PROVIDED IN THIS MANUAL. REFER TO THE FAMILY'S NAME YOU ARE STAYING WITH.

3. ALL LETTERS ARE SUBJECT TO REVIEW BY L'ECOLE STAFF.

4. NO LETTERS ARE TO BE SHARED AMONG L'ECOLE GUESTS.

5. APPROVED LETTERS WITH NAMES AND ADDRESSES WILL BE SEALED IN AN ENVELOPE WITH YOUR INITIAL ON THE COVER AND THE CITY IN WHICH YOU ARE A GUEST. EXAMPLE: "A-NEW YORK". STAFF WILL FORWARD THE MAIL TO FRANCE TO BE OPENED AND MAILED.

6. MAIL WILL ONLY BE FORWARDED TO AND FROM APPROVED PARTIES ON L'ECOLE LIST (NO BOYFRIENDS!).

She had to write Randall. If she didn't come up with a good excuse, he might try to pester her father. She didn't want Randall coming to the house saying he loved her or some other crazy thing.

She sent a letter to Sonia-Barton with a note in it for Randall–*give Butch*
this but not my address.

Dear Old Friend:

So how's it going? I am sorry that I have not been able to talk with you
but many things have happened to me.

I have traveled to France. I am living with a wonderful family. They have
a daughter just my age. Her name is Kitty.

You don't have to write me. I'll see you next year some time.

Your Friend,

Beck

What would Randall think about a letter like that from her–that she'd lied
when she'd pulled him to her body and said she loved him?

* * *

The week went slowly, like being kept inside while you're sick until you
give into the lethargy and sleep. Television, reading, talking with the girls, being
amused or shocked by Miss Kitty–*L'Ecole is really an illegal baby selling*
operation.

Schooling was conducted by nuns in flat-topped black and white habits,
cloaks of irreproachable purity and protection against evil surrounding pale
faces. Their teaching was at a level of education below what she was used to.
They'd give simple tests and never a grade. L'Ecole did have a good library and
the nuns would bring her books she requested. She asked for more novels
about Angélique which they seemed happy to give her because they were about
a devout French heroine who flirts with but avoids seduction.

* * *

On the following Sunday after she'd arrived, Beck was allowed to call her father for the first time.

Mrs. V. sat in the chair facing the desk, their positions reversed from when Beck had arrived. The student manual was open beside her with details of what to say about where she was.

He answered as if he was waiting for her call.

She imagined him in the living room, newspapers spread around him.

"Well, if it isn't the world traveler. How is it over there?"

She was protecting him from having to lie about her. "It's OK," she said weakly.

"What's that? I can hardly hear you. It must be the connection. How do you like the Pyrenees? A fascinating part of the world—did you know that the Basque have their own blood type and language? Fascinating place. I want you to tell me all about it when you come home."

His voice was political, ebullient. He didn't ask how she'd come to make a sudden transfer to a year abroad. He knew. They would share a lie so she could return to a warped version of herself.

"I'm proud of you for doing this. I think it's the perfect age to go abroad. When you come back you'll be ready for your senior year. Give me your number so I can call you in case I need to."

She gave him the number in the village. According to the guide, the phone would be answered, and a message would be forwarded to her in New York.

"I'm sorry I'm going to miss your birthday with you," she said.

"Me too. Gail and I are going on a trip to Japan, anyway. We'll celebrate when you return. How would you like a string of Mikimoto pearls for Christmas?"

She pressed her lips together. Her anger spreading from her grandmother to him. If he really cared about what she was going through he wouldn't bribe her with pearls. The confirmation of his betrayal opened a wound of loneliness that cut off her breath.

"I'll have them for you when you get home. Love you more than I can say."

But you care about being the Leader more.

"Thanks. That would be lovely. I love you, Daddy. I have to go. It's late over here. I'll call about this time next week."

"Can you call any other days? I might not be here."

Maybe he didn't know. He was masterful at playing a part. She wouldn't be sure until she saw him.

THIRTEEN

THE DREAM OF UNKNOWING

L'Ecole was a dream she could walk through without seeing. Time was marked by changes in her body. Life outside was a fantasy that grew more complicated and disordered the longer she was governed by the strict routines and confinement of the school. She'd see Randall react when she told him why she couldn't keep the baby. Her body would tense, she'd laugh to herself, explain–*it was best for you*. That's what Panda had said. She *did* know best. Then, with a frown and downcast eyes, lips pressed together she'd admit real and false were merging and she was losing track of the difference.

Panda had sent her to L'Ecole to learn the art of the lie. The separation between lying to God and a *better* lie told for the benefit of others–for herself so she could return as if this had never happened. What was real? True? The baby growing inside her was a mistake to be corrected. Beck Lyons was an untruth told for the betterment of her family. She could never be real. Whatever she did, whomever she met, the facade of the lie would separate her from the truth.

During Christmas, the girls opened gifts together and laughed at the clothes few could wear because of their size. Beck received presents and cards sent to her in France and forwarded to New York. Janey wrote in a childish handwriting about–*all the frends who calls and asks for you.*"

Beck bet she meant Randall. Neither he nor Sonia-Barton had written. Her grandmother probably had not put Sonia-Barton and surely not Randall on Beck's mail list.

* * *

By February, her stomach had swollen slightly. She received a letter with the name and return address removed. But she identified Randall's neat handwriting. She rushed to her room to read,

January 7, 1967

Dear Beck,

How are you? Fine I hope. I finally got your address. I saw Sonia-Barton at a party right before I went back to San Francisco. She told me that she would give me your address and then I had to call her a couple of times before I could find her. That's why I haven't written to you before.

Also I guess you would have written me if you wanted to hear from me. (Sob, sob).

Alot has happened to me since you left. Remember the band the Express with the creepy drummer we opened for?

Her eyes widened and she read faster, as if she wouldn't remember the night she'd gotten in so much trouble.

After you went to Europe. I went back to New York and auditioned to be in their band. They hired me! Yay!

Mick, the drummer, is all right. I don't talk about you to him. All I know is they're a band with a recording contract playing originals. I spent the

November in the studio and learned alot. It was too late to use any of my

songs but they promised me that I could put some on the next album.

Let me know if you hear our record in France.

We're going to be playing around New York and doing some shows around

the country. Then if the record takes off who knows we might get to Europe.

I'm jealous of those French boys. Don't be teaching them to much English,

or should I say, I hope that they are not teaching you to much French.

Love ya,

Butch

She read the letter again. Maybe they were not screening for someone named Butch. The nuns had made a mistake letting this letter through. She examined the words *Love ya.*

The letter had taken nearly a month to reach her. She wondered about the letters he'd tried to send. This one was different from the ones she'd received from him at home. Maybe he was suspicious. He was crazy enough to come to France looking for her.

She slept with his letter under her pillow and had a dream where he held her hand. She told him the truth of where she'd been. He turned her gently and kissed her lips. Behind him Father Mahoney smiled, waved and looked at someone behind her. She turned and Randall disappeared.

Six-thirty the next morning, she read his letter again, put on her robe, and went to the small writing desk beside the windows that looked out on 11th street. The words flowed. *Dear Butch...*

She described her friends in the house, only changing them to French girl's names without boyfriends so he'd not be jealous. She used material from the manual, describing the French family, the village. She told him about a rock

band that played in the town who could sing but not speak English. At the
bottom of the fifth page of the lavender stationary, she wrote:

*I'm sorry about the way I had to leave like that. I knew that if I saw you,
I would not want to go to France. I couldn't get away when I was with my
grandmother those last days. I guess I was just sort of confused.*

She knew that she would not send the letter. The nuns would never let it
through because she'd said she would not have gone if she'd seen him.

There are many kinds of lies–helpful and hurtful, big and small, *better lies.*
Some lies were sins. Not telling Randall she was pregnant was a sin. He should
know he was going to be a father and that they were going to give away his
baby. Only God could forgive her for not telling Randall the truth.

His child kicked and pressed against her bladder.

The nuns knew what they were doing in not allowing her to talk to Randall.
If she told him the truth he'd want to keep their baby.

She went to the bathroom to shower. Shampoo washed over her closed
eyes when she remembered she'd left the letters out on the desk. She quickly
rinsed, put on a robe and went into the room to find Miss Kitty bent over her
desk readings.

"What are you doing?" Beck rushed to seize the letters.

"I came to see why you weren't down for breakfast."

Beck turned from her, clutching the pages to her chest.

"Is he the one?" Miss Kitty asked.

"Leave me alone. Get out of here!"

Miss Kitty appeared to perceive the crazy anger building in Beck. "Jeez, like
I really care." She retreated, closing the door behind her.

Beck tore up the letters into small pieces and flushed them down the toilet. If she reported Miss Kitty, she'd reveal that she'd been writing her boyfriend.

Beck hesitated joining Miss Kitty at their usual spots at the dining room table. She sat and avoided looking at Miss Kitty.

"You want to hear about the son of a bitch that did this to me? Miss Kitty asked.

"I most certainly do not!"

Miss Kitty flaunted her disregard for the house rules. "He was my next door neighbor, some mob guy who passes around payola. *I promote da records, get dem played on d'radio. Without me nothin' happens for da record, capiche? I can get you any record you want, no suck me softer, use your tongue over the top, that's it.*"

The horror in Beck's expression appeared to prompt Miss Kitty to give Beck unasked for equal time. "What about you? I just can't see you with a lover, especially a musician. I'd like to meet this guy."

She gave Miss Kitty the intense stare her father used when he was deadly serious. "He doesn't know and must never know. Never. Do you understand?"

Miss Kitty shrugged. "Yeah, I get it. That's what's L'Ecole's about. Right? So forget what I told you about Carmine and I'll forget about Butch."

Beck doubted Miss Kitty would forget about Butch but might never find Randall.

"But I'll probably run into him. When I get out of here, I'm going into the music business. That's one thing I can get out of knowing Carmine."

Beck picked up the newspaper, hoping Miss Kitty would get the message.

"What was the name of his band, the Express? Bet you'd like to have him express against you right about now?"

Beck put down the paper. "I never said anything about a boyfriend–*you* did."

"He says he's in New York. I'll look in the *New Yorker* to see when he's playing. We'll sneak out and go see him."

Beck put down the newspaper, breathing heavily through her nose, on the verge of losing control. "Shut up," she warned and fought to push down the rage.

"Yeah, sure. Forget him, forget you."

She'd be glad to forget Miss Kitty, and if she ever saw her outside of L'Ecole she'd look right through her.

* * *

"Is there anything you'd like to tell me?" Father Mahoney repeated his usual probing.

She cradled the growing arch of her underbelly as she sat facing him in the L'Ecole chapel beneath the stairs.

She was more trusting than she'd been at first. He'd drawn her into a belief of the power of confession and forgiveness.

"I'm thinking I should keep the baby." The speaking of a growing reality of a definite presence–Randall's baby–girl, boy was honest.

He folded his hands together, glanced down and nodded. "Do you have the strength for that?"

She sensed his confusion on what he should say, pushing the dilemma back to her.

She touched her hair. She'd made her choice. Nothing had changed.

He squinted and pressed his long fingers together, "God has forgiven you and is giving you this chance to go on."

"To redeem myself."

"Yes."

"A better lie."

"To go on with your life confident in your decision."

"I'll try."

He examined her as if to see beneath her good-student repetition of what she'd been taught by him and Mrs. V.

She relented, releasing the truth that filled her thoughts in a hurried whisper. "I want to marry the boy, the man who did this to me...have more children with him."

Father nodded with the seriousness of a doctor who'd made the correct diagnosis. "This man led you to sin and would lead you back. It would be better to having nothing more to do with him."

She knew that would be his answer, Panda's answer for how she would threat Randall when she left L'Ecole. The other side of the argument was what she wanted. How much choice did she have?

"Turn to God for strength to guide you. Let us pray as I've taught you."

She bowed her head over her hands as his voice filled the small room with a dipping musical cadence, *"Hanc igitur*–Therefore, this. Turn your eye to God's will and see how He wills all the works of his mercy and justice, in Heaven and on Earth and under the Earth,"

"Therefore this," she repeated the homily, but her voice caught in a lament that God wanted her to forsake Randall.

"Turn your eye to God's will and see how he wills all the works of his mercy and justice, in Heaven and on Earth and under the Earth. Then with profound humility, accept, praise, and then bless this sovereign will, which is entirely holy, just, and beautiful."

She was little, small and weak against the will of God and her family. She must obey and find the strength to turn Randall away.

"I accept and praise my Lord with humility," she finished her part of the prayer

L'Ecole was about her rebirth. She would be reborn, empowered with her faith. Obey and in obedience find the strength to follow a righteous path.

* * *

Sunday night she went to Mrs. V.'s apartment and called her father. For once he was home.

"*Comment ca va ma jolie fille?*"

She laughed and responded in French.

He complimented her on how much better her accent was and said they must go to *célébrez le 14 Juillet à l'Ambassade de France* when she returned.

She was his perfect girl gone to France for the school year. She'd never be the one to tell him the truth.

* * *

Saturday morning the first week of March, Beck found Miss Kitty at her usual early morning spot at the breakfast table before any of the other girls were up, the laminated pages of a magazine open beside her.

"Guess who's playing at the Spotlight on St. Patrick's Day?" Miss Kitty jabbed a finger at the copy of the *New Yorker*. "The Express–your boyfriend's band."

Beck raised her chin and in a dismissive tone said, "I *don't* have a boyfriend and if I *did* he certainly would not be in a band."

Her scorn appeared to stump Miss Kitty for a moment. "It *is* hard to imagine you doing anything fun, but you're not that bad looking in a kind of Gothic way."

Later in her room, Beck looked at herself in the full-length mirror behind the door. She certainly didn't feel attractive–Gothic yes, gloomy and grotesque. Her stomach rounded from within with a shape and life of its own. Her clothes no longer fit. She wore hand-me-downs of former L'Ecole students. Her hair reached below her shoulders and for the first time had a natural curl. Her skin was pink with a scrubbed look. She'd run out of makeup and did not want to ask her grandmother to send more.

What if Miss Kitty *did* find Randall and tell him her secret, the ruination of her grandmother's scheme to protect the family's reputation? What if she was forced to confess to him? Would he marry her? Would he still love her–their baby? She was sure he would. Maybe God's plan *was* for her to marry Randall and not give away their child.

Panda would scorn her as a disgrace to the family to be talked of in lessons to future daughters as warnings, but Beck would have Randall. As soon as the thought of happiness entered her mind a stern inner voice corrected her. She could never be with Randall, never tell him the truth.

FOURTEEN

THE EXPRESS

B eck looked eagerly in the small stacks arranged on a marble table top in the foyer. Beside a big box for Miss Kitty was one lavender envelope with her name written in grandmother's distinctive cursive. Panda was the one whose letters reached her. Sonia-Barton had written once to say she'd decided to attend Tulane instead of LSU. Beck hadn't responded because she was sure Sonia-Barton would sniff out the lie. Then everyone would know Beck was an unwed mother who had given her child away.

She took the letter up to the desk in her room and read,

Try as hard as you can to be the best. Nothing is ever given to you that is not better to earn, including the love and respect of your family.

Beck took a flimsy blue sheet of an international letter with PAR AVION printed on the front and wrote her grandmother as if she was in France.

I went to Catholic Church today and I'm reading more about being a Catholic.

That would send her grandmother into a tizzy and generate a warning about the Catholics who in old Virginia society were just above the Negro.

Her grandmother had a capacity to mime the Virginia colonialist from whom she drew her lineage. *Maryland and the mountains are for the*

Catholics, she'd think as if the continent was yet unsettled and there was room
for the religions and white immigrants to sort themselves and stay apart from
the proper Church of England colonist who'd gotten there first.

Her bedroom door opened, and Miss Kitty came in with a crazed look in
her eyes, her hair, a wild, red mass around her flushed face. "What are you
going to wear tonight?"

"Close the door."

Miss Kitty ignored the command. Beck moved around Miss Kitty's
cantilevered belly and shut the door.

"You want Butch to see you that way?"

"Quit talking that way!"

"Suit yourself. Here's the plan." Miss Kitty, face flushed nearly the shade of
her hair, ranted. "At nine o'clock, we'll go out through the kitchen. I've got it
all mapped out. I can almost taste that beer."

Beck sighed and tilted her head in sympathy, trying to talk Miss Kitty back
from ledge of sanity. "You're almost done. Then we can go on with our lives.
You can drink as much beer as you want."

"Yeah, I'm done and I'm taking you with me." Miss Kitty nodded like she
was doing Beck a favor.

"Now you just calm down. It's going to be all right. Let me finish this letter."
Beck put her arm around the girl's thick shoulder and steered her to the door.

Miss Kitty pulled her around and gave her a full hug, pressing their babies
together. Her voice caught with genuine emotion. "You're the best thing about
being here. Let's stay connected afterwards OK?"

Beck squinted a thin smile. "That'd be nice."

"Want me to see what my mom made me to wear tonight?"

"I will later. I promise.

Beck closed the door behind Miss Kitty. She'd be somebody else's problem very soon. More than ever Beck was grateful for Miss Kitty not knowing her name.

* * *

That night, Beck was with the girls watching Hogan's Heroes on the big color television set. Miss Kitty stepped into the doorway of the living room, wearing a green velvet maternity dress, her lips coated with bright red lipstick, her eyes dark with mascara.

"Lynda Bird, come on." The intensity of Miss Kitty's expression radiated from darting eyes like a pursued escapee.

A new girl asked, "Going out on a hot date?"

Miss Kitty ignored her, turned and strode toward the kitchen.

Beck glanced at the other girls. Why was it up to her to stop this crazy girl? She launched herself from the couch and rushed through the swinging door with a dizzy feeling of events rushing out of control.

Miss Kitty had laid a coat and purse near a butcher block. Jazz played through Mr. J.'s partially open bedroom door. "Go up and get your coat. I'll wait for you."

"Now, Miss Kitty, you calm right on down, do you hear?"

"I'm going."

Beck gently took her arm as she imagined you were supposed to do when someone who'd lost their mind. "Let's go watch television. Twilight Zone's gonna be on soon."

Miss Kitty pulled her arm away. "We're living in the Twilight Zone. Do you have any idea how sick I am of this house, these people?"

Miss Kitty moved with careless steps to the rear kitchen door. "I found out the code to the alarm box," Miss Kitty whispered. "I stayed with Mr. J. when he received an order of food."

Miss Kitty opened a grey metal door on the wall.

"Damn, it takes a key." Miss Kitty looked ready to cry, her swollen face squeezed with frustration.

"Come on now, Miss Kitty. You might have your baby tonight. Then everything will be over. You're gonna be out of here before you know it."

"I sure as hell am."

Miss Kitty yanked open the rear door. A strident bell rang over their heads.

"Close it quick," Beck said.

Miss Kitty stepped into the darkness beyond the door, grabbed Beck by the hand and forcefully dragged her into the cold alley.

"Let me go."

Miss Kitty was too strong and pulled her into the dark. "Mr. J. is coming. You're outside now. You might as well come with me." She dragged Beck waddling like a giant goose down the alley.

"Stop!" Beck pleaded in an exaggerated whisper.

Miss Kitty reached the corner and waved her arms over her head.

Beck pulled free and begged, "Please come back into the house."

"Don't worry. I have enough money for both of us." Miss Kitty's big chin thrust forward.

A cab passed them, stopped, and backed up.

"Get in," Miss Kitty ordered.

Beck looked back and saw Mr. J. and Mrs. V. hurrying down the alley.

"I'll tell your boyfriend I saw you," Miss Kitty said.

Mr. J. and Mrs. V. were almost there.

"C! E!" Mrs. V. called.

"Come on, I'm leaving," Miss Kitty said.

One choice was more horrible than the other—have Miss Kitty reveal where she was to Randall, ruin everything, or risk being kicked out of L'Ecole.

Beck entered the cab and closed the door.

Blocks of the terrifying city sped past, each farther from L'Ecole. If they turned around, an excuse could be found. She had only been going out to stop Miss Kitty. Every minute she didn't return would be harder to explain.

Beck's eyes were wide with panic. Her breaths came in gasps. "We must go back. Immediately. They know. They saw us. Called our names."

"Might as well have some fun then."

It was not fair. What difference if Miss Kitty was expelled? She only had a few more days, maybe hours left anyway. Where was Beck supposed to go for the next four months? How would she explain coming home like this? And look at her. This was a genuine nightmare—on the streets of New York dressed in a red sweater dress borrowed from the house collection, black leggings provided by Mrs. V. Her grandmother didn't send her clothes because she wouldn't want to be seen shopping in the maternity section. No makeup, her hair looking like a rat's nest, going to expose her lie to Randall.

The cab stopped and Miss Kitty pulled herself out.

Beck should go back, make up an excuse, but she had no money.

A neon sign flashed SPOTLIGHT over stairs that descended below street level.

Kitty paid the driver. "Get out," she ordered Beck.

Beck stood on the sidewalk, shivering, pregnant for all to see. Ugly, fat– what would Randall say when he found out she'd lied to him, was going to give his child away?

"I've got thirty dollars," Miss Kitty said. "We can have some kind of fun."

"You call this fun? I am going to get in *so* much trouble."

Miss Kitty laughed a cry of liberation. "YaHAAA. Have you seen your feet lately? You already *are* in trouble."

A line of restless people straggled down a stairwell that smelled of old cigarettes and stale beer. Some wore funny hats and green clothes. A sign announced a St. Patrick's day beer special.

The muscular man seated on a stool examined the identification of a pair of boys in front of them.

Miss Kitty showed him a driver's license.

The man motioned for Miss Kitty to pass and waited to see Beck's identification.

"She's pregnant, for God's sake." Miss Kitty dragged Beck past him.

The man loosely held Beck's arm.

Miss Kitty pulled harder and they were in the nightclub.

He called after them.

Beck looked back to see him looking for someone to go after them.

Men and women drank and talked around a bar. An empty dance floor was lit by stage lights.

A keyboard, microphone stands, a drum with THE EXPRESS painted on its front were arranged on the stage.

Miss Kitty moved to a table near a rear brick wall. "Would you mind?" She showed a couple her radically swollen profile.

"Are you sure you should be here?" A woman asked and made room for them.

No, we most certainly should not be. Beck scanned the crowd but didn't see him. She sat as low as she could. Some of her and Randall's friends from Virginia might be here, maybe his parents.

"Two beers," Miss Kitty ordered from a green-clad waitress. "Make 'em green!"

A candle burned in a glass bulb atop a checkered tablecloth. The room was loud with conversations and laughter. Gray tobacco smoke curled in beams of light.

She couldn't go back to L'Ecole. Mrs. V. would surely expel her. What would her grandmother say? No words could ever explain this. Randall would have to care for her now. She had no choice.

A man walked on the stage and said in a soothing voice, "Ladies and gentlemen, please welcome recording artists, the Express."

With her head down to hide, Beck raised her eyes to look for Randall. The band was mostly the same she'd seen at the Elk's Lodge. Mick was adjusting his drum set. She avoided looking at him. What if he recognized her? Randall had told him her father was a senator.

A man in a lavender shirt that looked like part of a tuxedo with ruffles on the front and big cuffs took his position behind a keyboard. Relief and disappoint mixed in a whirl of confusion. Randall was not in the band.

"Which one is your guy? The keyboard player right? He's the cutest. Way to go Lynda Bird."

Beck stared at the table not giving Miss Kitty any more clues.

The band started to play.

Don't you hear me calling,

Baby?

This was not happening. The singer with a mischievous smile and twinkle in his eyes was doing a little dance step and bobbing for the microphone to sing harmony on the word *baby*.

Make you feel good?

Baby

It's all for you.

Baby

Don't let it go.

It's what we've been waiting for.

This is our time.

Beck slouched low against the wall, disappointment supplanted by despair at having broken the rules for nothing.

Miss Kitty whistled and clapped as if she was at a baseball game. "BUTCH," she screamed loud enough to be heard over the music.

If anybody heard her in the band, they showed no reaction.

"You're horrible." Beck hated Miss Kitty's cruelty while admiring her confidence.

It's what we've been waiting for,

BABY, BABY, BABY.

Suddenly, Miss Kitty lurched to the dance floor. Only two couples were dancing. Miss Kitty frenetically shook her head and waved her hands in the center of a bright light.

Some in the bar clapped for her. Others whooped and whistled. Miss Kitty swung her hair and whipped her neck around. Her preposterous belly, the size of a weather balloon, vibrated before her.

Beck plotted a course to the door.

Then, Miss Kitty spun and fell to the parquet floor.

Beck stood to help her, but others were guiding her back to the table.

Miss Kitty plopped down and spread her legs out before her. "Jeez, that's hard when you're carrying an extra forty-five pounds. Let's order another round. You drinking that beer?" She reached out and plucked the glass of green-colored brew from the table and took a deep pull. "Ahhh!" she slammed the beer down. "You should tell him," she shouted at Beck.

"You *are* crazy."

"Might as well tell each other who we really are now. You're a lot of fun."

Beck ignored her.

"I could ask Butch who you are."

"Why are you so terrible to me?" Beck glanced at her tormentor and then away.

"Go on. Do it." Miss Kitty motioned with her head. "Live for *yourself*. This is *our* lives, *our* time, like the song said. Not the nuns', not our parents', not our babies'—*our* time." Miss Kitty stood. "I'll go with you."

"He's not here."

Miss Kitty considered her as if to judge if she was telling the truth.

"OK leave it up to me then." Miss Kitty moved to the side of the small stage beside the keyboard player. When the song ended she shouted up at him.

"Hey Butch!"

The keyboard player leaned over and had a quick conversation with Miss Kitty before the band launched into a new song.

Beck watched Miss Kitty plod back to the table with a dour expression.

"Bad news about Butch."

Beck's heart clenched as she leaned forward, no way hiding the concern in her furrowed brows.

"He was drafted. On his way to Nam."

Beck's first thought was her grandmother had arranged to have him legally murdered. Randall–the gentlest seeker of beauty at war? Beck sat back in her seat. At least the colonel would be pleased his son was shaping up. If Randall were to die serving his country, he'd be proud of him in a way he never would of a beautiful song written by Randall. The thought of Randall dying caused tears to well in her eyes.

With seemingly genuine concern, Miss Kitty reached for her hand. "I'm sorry. That war is a lousy deal. But he might be all right. You never can tell."

"I have to get out of here." Beck stood.

"Yeah, it might be time. I'm not feeling too good." Miss Kitty paid the bill with a $10-dollar bill, picked up her coat and purse Beck followed her out of the club.

A cab stopped. Beck climbed in to return to L'Ecole and somehow explain where's she been and why she'd disobeyed the rules. The city passed with thumps and shudders. Lights stacked in rows as high as the night—each a life, a plan, nowhere for her. What if she just walked into Manhattan with faith that God would protect and provide for her? Even if there was only a thin hair holding her to the chance she'd be allowed to complete the course at L'Ecole that seemed a stronger rope than the unknown.

"Jesus, my water just broke. Feels like I just peed in my pants. It's getting in my shoes," Miss Kitty said.

The cab driver looked in his rearview mirror at them. "You have baby?" He sounded Greek.

Miss Kitty did not answer him.

"I never have baby in my cab," he said.

"No baby," Miss Kitty said.

"Where you go?" the driver asked.

"I told you, it's somewhere near Fifth Avenue, on 11th. I don't know the exact address. Look for an alley." Miss Kitty said.

"Many alleys. You want go to hospital?"

Miss Kitty did not answer.

Beck felt her own baby move.

The cab drove slowly down the block. "There it is," Miss Kitty said. "Park by the alley."

Miss Kitty clutched her stomach as if to hold the baby in.

Beck waited to see if she needed help.

Miss Kitty motioned with her head and waddled down the alley. Halfway to the kitchen door, she stopped and turned with a contrary expression of twisted lips and narrowed eyes. The dark cold smelled of rotting garbage, a hiding place for muggers.

"Do you think I should do this?" Miss Kitty asked. "I never really believed it until now. Maybe I should keep the little booger."

"I have to." Beck shivered and moved down the alley.

Miss Kitty's hand pulled her around. Beck saw in her narrow eyes and half-smile a mix of emotions—love, relief, gratitude, pain. Miss Kitty's hug was complicated by their stomachs, like embracing across a table. "You are a lot of fun, you know that? When I'm done with this, I'm going to find you."

More of a curse than promise. "Sure," Beck said. "Come on. We have to get you some help."

Miss Kitty tried the kitchen door, turned, smiled and shrugged. "It's locked. Time for plan B."

She banged her open hand on the window loud enough to wake Mr. J. who dressed in black pants, his full round tummy pregnant beneath a white T-shirt, came around the table in the middle of the kitchen. He turned the key in the alarm box and opened the door for them.

"I'm having our baby, Julius," Miss Kitty said.

"Contractions start yet?" He closed the door behind them.

"My water broke."

"We'd best get Mrs. V. You go on upstairs Miss Lynda Bird. Get that beer and smoke smell off you."

Halfway up the stairs to her bedroom, Beck turned.

Miss Kitty, with Mr. J. at her side, looked up at her and smiled. "You're a lot of fun. You know that?"

Beck frowned. "God protect you, Miss Kitty."

With a final uproarious laugh, Miss Kitty said, "You're a riot."

God protect her too from her grandmother's wrath and the loss of love and respect of her family. Randall would never understand if she ever told him that if he'd been there, she'd have gone with him.

FIFTEEN

THE STORY OF A SOUL

S leep came in fits to be broken by wide-eyed fear and concoction of lies. Miss Kitty made her go. Miss Kitty had a knife, held it to her back. Beck went out because Miss Kitty had said she would tell everyone about L'Ecole. The lies rose up only to be pushed down by their improbability.

Beck was at the dining room table at her usual early hour. The New York Times lay unread on the table. She could sense Miss Kitty was no longer in the house and was surprised a wistful longing for the unruliest person she'd ever known. Sonia-Barton had tutored Beck like an older sister genuinely seeming to care and show her how to behave in a lively manner. Miss Kitty, with wit and exuberance that challenged anyone or anything that stood in her way, had treated her like a plaything needing to be shocked into standing up for herself. She should hate her for what she'd done to her, but Miss Kitty had given her a chance to go with Randall. Beck had chosen fear and now must face the consequences.

Mr. J. in white chef's cap carried a small porcelain teapot. "Drink this," he said. "Just the thing for the morning after." He winked, giggled, and returned to the kitchen to prepare her breakfast.

What had he thought she'd done? She poured a cup and a smell arose that reminded her of Christmas eggnog. She took a sip and tasted alcohol, perhaps rum, scrunched her lips and left the concoction to drink orange juice. Mr. J. returned with a big breakfast of ham and fried eggs. "Mrs. V. say you should go down and see her 'fore the nuns arrive," he delivered the bad news with a frown.

Beck left the table barely touching her breakfast because her stomach was so tight. She was going to be expelled but where could she go? Maybe if Randall had been at the Spotlight she could have gone with him, but now her fate was totally in the hands of Mrs. V.

Maybe Panda would abandon Beck, leave her to be cast out on her own. She imagined calling her father or Gail, explaining why she was alone on the streets of New York. Robbie was in New York. She could find him, explain...no never that. A stranger would take her in and when she had the baby she'd....what? Go home like before she'd ruined the plan.

Mrs. V. didn't offer a seat. Beck stood, head lowered, before the perfectly arranged desk–not a paper out of place, letter opener and scissors in a holder.

"Where were you last night?"

Beck shivered at the coldness in Mrs. V.'s voice though the room was warm. Beck's prepared answer came out in a quavering rush. "I went out to get C. She was trying to run away. She was scared. I didn't even have time to get my coat."

"And you stopped to drink beers?"

"I didn't know what else to do." She flinched at the stupidity of her answer, the failure of her rehearsing.

Mrs. V. pressed her hands together atop the desk. "I was clear with you about our rules. You understood that once you leave, you cannot return?"

Beck lowered her gaze. "Yes, ma'am," she whispered.

"I've called your grandmother. She will be arriving in a few hours. Go to your room and pack."

Beck looked at the matron. Her voice trembled on the verge of begging. "May I please stay?"

Mrs. V.'s upper lip curled with disrespect, scorn not so much for her but for the idea that a rule could be flagrantly broken and then ignored. Mrs. V.'s world and the life at L'Ecole was based on obedience. Beck wanted to say how she would obey. She was not rebellious like Miss Kitty.

"That's not possible," Mrs. V. said simply and completely as if Beck had asked if she could become a Catholic priest.

There was no room for argument, but Beck had to try. "I didn't do anything wrong. I didn't try to leave. It just happened."

Mrs. V.'s tone was pedantic. "E. From our very first conversation I have tried to explain to you that you must not be afraid to admit and take responsibility for your own acts. Trust in God and embrace His forgiveness."

God may forgive her but most assuredly her grandmother would not.

Mrs. V. made a noticeable effort to put compassion into her voice. "You are not a bad girl, E. It grieves me to do this, but I have to think of the other girls. You will have no further contact with the girls. You will stay in your room until your grandmother arrives."

* * *

Beck imagined her grandmother's anger slowly boiling, stewing words to be slung at her when they were scalding hot. How long would it take for her to come up from Washington? Would she drive or fly as they'd done when she'd taken Beck to L'Ecole?

As the interminable morning dragged on Beck was not sure which clothes she could take since she'd borrowed most of what she now wore from the house collection. In the middle of the afternoon at her desk reading *Pride and Prejudice* from the house library Mrs. V. entered.

"It's time for you to leave us. Mr. J. will come for your bags."

Despite her apprehension, Beck hurried to follow Mrs. V., wanting the confrontation with Panda to be over. She'd soon have the answer to where she was to go. Dressed in the print dress she'd worn the night before, she carried a tweed burgundy cloth coat from her old life that barely covered her expanded stomach.

"Hi Panda!" Beck tried to put warmth into her greeting.

Her grandmother arose from the same chair she'd sat in five months before. "Harrumph." She looked at Beck's pregnant shape as if to confirm there had not been a mistake, exhaled and turned her eyes away as if repulsed by the sight. She curtly thanked Mrs. V. and strode to the door.

Mr. J. was outside loading her bags. "Goodbye, Lynda Bird," he said.

One person at L'Ecole was not judging her.

Before she could respond her grandmother was at her side. "What did he call you?" She quickly placed her hand on her hat against a strong gust of wind.

Mr. J. hurried inside to escape her.

Beck didn't answer as if she'd not heard either of them.

In the back of the cab, her grandmother repeated the question. Beck didn't know how to begin to explain and engaged her new lying skills. "I don't know. It's nice to see you, Panda. I missed you."

Her grandmother evidenced no interest in being cordial. They rode in silence to Broadway. "Where are we going?" Beck asked.

"I suppose we are going to have to find some kind of place for you to stay for the next couple of months."

"What kind of place?"

"Any place that will take you is what I figure. I understand you went to a bar?" Her voice trembled with reproach.

Beck stared ahead. Though phrased as a question the accusation sounded as if she'd stripped and offered herself to men on the street.

"Where that low creature who took advantage of you was performing?"

Miss Kitty must have told one of the girls. There was no point in lying. Beck closed her eyes in helpless resignation to the cruelty of being completely misunderstood, incapable of defending herself against her grandmother. She wanted to obey, would obey if given the chance.

"How exactly do you expect decent people to fathom behavior like yours?"

"He wasn't there," Beck could barely get the words out the excuse was so inconsequential.

Panda condemned her with her own whisper. "I pity you."

Beck pressed her lips together. If she spoke she was afraid her feelings would escape in a single explosive scream.

The cab moved slowly through the evening traffic. Beck couldn't tell what direction they were traveling in Manhattan. Aside from her misadventure last night, Beck hadn't been past the sheltered patio at L'Ecole. The movement of the pedestrians and vehicles, the buildings, the late winter air seemed hostile— as if she'd been born helpless and alone in a confusing, harsh world. Who was Beck Lyons? She knew herself in a way nobody from her past would recognize.

The cab let them off before a two-story brownstone.

Beck carried her bags up dirty stone steps to a checkered floor in a narrow entrance. Panda used a key to open a door on the first floor of what Beck assumed was a place to confine her. Who would be her new jailer?

Panda turned on the lights to reveal studio apartment. A combination of stale smells of life in an unaired closed space wafted over Beck.

"Don't touch a thing except what you must. Clean up what you dirty. We will replace anything you use."

"Who lives here?"

"Never you mind. You will stay here alone until I make other arrangements."

The idea of being left alone, a true outcast, caused a tremble to run up Beck's legs. She clutched her coat to her chest and turned to her grandmother. "But where are you going?"

"Where do I usually stay when I'm in New York? I'll be at the Plaza."

The disregard in her grandmother's haughty reply caused Beck to pull her head back. There was no point in asking if she could go with her. A year before Panda had taken her to the Plaza for high tea and told her about the train ride up from Washington when she'd met Eleanor Roosevelt. No longer was Beck suitable to stay at the Plaza. Someone might recognize her and report her shame. She watched her grandmother hurry to the black painted door as if being in Beck's presence was too great a burden. Beck's mouth was open but she couldn't think of what to say. The ideas were too big, the injustice too enormous when all she really wanted to say was *don't leave me. I'll be good. I promise.*

Panda hesitated at the door and turned as if to prove she was not heartless and was doing what was best for Beck. "I'm sorry I can't coddle you about this. We can't have you in public. I have to return to Washington and make other arrangements. I was fortunate to find this apartment available. I'll be back in the morning. Don't go out. If you leave here, don't ask me to help you again."

When the door closed leaving her in the strange apartment, Beck slowly turned, seeing but not focusing on the books and what looked like African art. Her eyes rested for a moment on a piece of dark carved wood depicting a pregnant African, then shifted to an open door to a bedroom. Perhaps a man lived here alone. A grandfather clock ticked in the corner as if to count the moments of her confinement. She might as well have been in a single cinder block cell.

She collapsed weakly onto a couch. A deep fatigue overcame her. She was weak and was called on to be strong. She removed her shoes and coat and pulled an afghan over her. Lamps and ceiling lights cast bright patterns on ivory carvings and black onyx statutes. The smell of dust and old books mixed with a stale scent from the bedroom and past cooked meals. What if the owner returned and found her sleeping here? Did he know someone was in his house?

Random creaks, doors closing, footsteps on the floor above shot her from her fantasies to the dangers of reality with fearful starts, rapid heartbeats, eyes wide, to fall back into another fitful dream. *At Beach One "I'll marry you," Not Randall but Robbie is holding her.*

In the morning, she turned off the lights and found a small kitchen but didn't look for food or use a glass to drink water.

Panda returned mid-morning carrying a brown paper bag. Beck stood with her in the kitchen while her grandmother unpacked bread, eggs, milk, orange juice and lunch meat.

"This apartment will be available for some time. You will stay here until I've made other arrangements for you."

In the fluorescent glow of the ceiling light, Beck hugged herself. Her voice trembled, "Do you think I'm bad, Panda?"

Her grandmother stood before the refrigerator and considered her as if trying to decide. "I think something happened to you that we must protect ourselves against. I hope you are learning some lessons. Life does not like to give second chances. If you try to leave here or call anyone, I swear I shall tell your father the whole story and I shall wash my hands of you."

Then he didn't know. At least she could be thankful her father would see her as she'd once been.

When her grandmother left, Beck understood she was truly alone.

* * *

The third morning in the apartment, she borrowed a London Fog overcoat and his tweed driver's cap from a hall closet. The coat was bulky, many sizes too big for her. She caught a glimpse of herself in a hallway mirror and thought she looked like what Panda would call a ragamuffin. But the disguise was effective. Nobody she'd ever known would recognize her.

She had no key and left the door unlocked. The crowded city hid her. She looked through windows of stores at clerks inside, wondering if there was a job she could do. For all she knew, her grandmother had abandoned her completely. What if the baby came early, and nobody had come for her? Where would she go to have the baby? She paused at the Museum of Modern Art but had no money to go in.

When she returned, the door to the apartment was locked. Had the owner returned, her grandmother? She thought of leaving the coat and hat at the door, but where would she go? She lightly knocked and heard someone on the other side looking through the peep hole.

Her grandmother opened the door, her face contorted into a now familiar expression of anger and scorn.

"Where have you been?" Panda demanded. "Have you been in contact with that boy?"

Beck walked past her. "No. I just went for a walk."

"And you stole the coat?"

When she was younger, her grandmother had said, *Don't lie because nobody will ever trust you again.* Had all the love and protection she'd once known been a lie? If her grandmother could turn on her like she had, whom could Beck ever trust?

"I only borrowed it. Mine doesn't fit. This was the first time I went out, I swear."

Her grandmother told her how to clean the toilet and kitchen, make the bed, teaching her like a new servant.

Beck did not ask where she was to go. What difference did it make?

* * *

Panda drove her to West Virginia in a rented car stopping only for gas and to use the restroom. She lectured Beck on how she must behave–a variation of L'Ecole rules–not use her real name, no communication with anyone *especially that creature who did this to you.* Panda had made a deal with L'Ecole to have her mail forwarded from France to West Virginia. Every Sunday Beck would call home to her father as before.

Does he know? The words hung on her tongue but weren't asked. Perhaps she didn't want to know, wanted to believe he didn't know, that he still thought her pure.

At times Panda spoke like before Beck's disgrace–talking of family history, what her father was doing in the Senate, description of a social event she'd attended. During long silent passages Beck looked at the passing countryside and wondered what her life could be without her grandmother's supervision– if she went off on her own? She lacked the courage to find her own way like Randall. He was braver than her, had more confidence because he was a boy or maybe he knew better what he wanted to do, and she didn't.

They arrived that night at the home of Dr. Winston Colby.

"Do not tell him anything about us," Panda repeated. "I'm going to leave as quickly as I can. Aside from the Greenbrier, I have never understood this state. They should have stayed part of Virginia."

Panda never took off her coat or hat. She leaned into Beck at the front door not to kiss her but to say clearly, "Be good. This is absolutely your last chance. Do you understand?"

"Yes, ma'am." She kissed her grandmother quickly on the cheek and watched her say goodbye and thank Dr. Colby for taking in Beck.

When she was gone, Dr. Colby showed Beck where she would sleep, how to move a glass-top table to unfold a sofa bed set against the wall beneath prints of horses, told her she should close the sofa every morning because this was both his library and his children's playroom.

He sat in a leather reclining chair and watched her make the bed like her grandmother had taught her in New York, folding the corners of the sheets up and tucking them under.

Dr. Colby was blond, wore glasses, had red cheeks. He puffed a pipe and blew a cloud of smoke above his head. She liked the cherry aroma of the tobacco more than the cutting smell of cigarettes or cigars. She thought he looked like someone who was happy with his life. He told her many girls had come to him and that he was part of an *underground railroad*.

The underground railroad was how runaway slaves were smuggled to freedom in the North. She supposed she was being smuggled from an abortion.

"What should we call you?"

"Theresa." The name popped into her mind without hesitation.

"*Mm-hmm* good, St. Thérèse. Are you interested in becoming a Carmelite?"

Was she? The idea suddenly seemed plausible. She would be purified, find the separation from the sins of the world that she'd sensed when she first encountered the nuns at L'Ecole.

"I don't know."

"Girls like you sometimes make the best nuns. Here." He stood and pulled a book off the shelf and handed it to Beck. "Have you ever read *Autobiography of a Saint*?"

"No, sir."

"Take your time with it. By the looks of it you'll be with us a good four months."

What were *girls like her?* Girls fallen from grace who knew sin? Alone in the study, the sounds outside the house were of quiet winter in contrast to New York—more like Lake Barcroft. Beck sat in Dr. Colby's chair and began *The Story of a Soul: The Autobiography of St. Thérèse of Lisieux.*

She thought she was reading about herself. Thérèse's mother had died when she was four. Because of the shock of her mother's death, *"my happy disposition completely changed. I became timid and retiring, sensitive to an excessive degree...."* The memory of praying to her own mother in heaven united Beck with the French saint.

Thérèse had to pass through many trials before tasting *the delicious fruits of perfect love and of complete abandonment to God's Will.* She'd wanted to enter the Carmel Convent at fifteen. When the local bishop had said she was too young, Thérèse had broken with protocol and begged the Pope's permission to enter a convent.

Beck devoured the book like a message from God how to live beyond sorrow, return love to those who mistreated her, and grow closer to Him.

* * *

During her four months with the Colbys she was a maid's assistant—cleaning, watching the four children. She tried to *miss no single opportunity of making some small sacrifice, here by a smiling look, there by a kindly word; always doing the smallest right and doing it all for love.* Her devotion to the practices of Thérèse endeared her to the Colbys. A devout Catholic family, they were pleased Beck wanted to attend Mass with them, never asking why she didn't take holy communion.

No mail reached her. The plan her grandmother had thought would pass on her mail to her from France did not work and Beck was cut off from all but Panda who wrote every week to lecture and not waver from the plan to have the baby and return to her life as if nothing had changed.

On Sundays, she tried to call her father. The phone only rang or she spoke to Gail since it was Janey's day off and the Leader was mostly out. She carried on the act of being in France and nobody bothered to question her more than how was she feeling—how were her studies? She could probably write to Randall if she knew how—perhaps through his parents—but that would have been disobedient, and she was committed to following the word of those who knew better than she did what was good for her.

She prayed every night for Randall's safety and told herself that if God would spare him, she'd treat him with spiritual love as she would everyone else, and if he ever found out what she'd done, he'd forgive her. She thought about asking Dr. Colby if a nun could be a liar but could not overcome her fear he'd ask about her past and she'd give away a clue that would expose her. Perhaps the virtue of obedience was its clarity as opposed to the complexity of finding your own way and hiding the lies you told yourself and others.

SIXTEEN

THERESA

S he pushed a vacuum cleaner through the shag of the Colbys' white rug. That morning when she'd closed the sofa bed, a sharp pain different than the pressure she'd been feeling around her waist had shot across her lower back.

She was setting the table for dinner while the Colbys' real maid, Corrina, was over the stove stirring a spaghetti sauce for dinner.

Beck told her she thought her time had come.

"What are you going to name your baby?" Corrina asked.

"Theresa."

"Like her mama, Theresa junior?" Corrina had a high, nearly hysterical laugh. "Guess if a man can do it, a woman can too, can't she?"

Beck flinched from pressure in her lower abdomen and placed her hands on her stomach to hold the baby. "When Dr. Colby comes home would you please ask him to come back into the playroom?"

She was taken to a hospital in a suburb of Charleston but could have remained at the Colbys for another day. Stuck at five centimeters, no matter how many contractions, she could not enlarge enough to give birth.

Alone, behind green curtains, she listened to the sounds of women in labor–groans, cries of exertion, the soothing murmurs of mothers and husbands, the rattle as a cart pushed into the delivery room.

A fear she was doing something wrong made her pray, "St. Thérèse protect me. I love you, St. Thérèse. Protect me and my baby."

Dr. Colby had said he'd call Panda. Where was she? Beck didn't want to be alone now. She needed someone she could cry to, who would tell her everything was all right, that she was doing a good job.

A contraction spread around her back, reaching over an arch of nerves. Beck cried out. You could wail here, bleat like a wounded animal. Nobody expected you to do anything but vent pain.

A nurse lifted the sheet and said, "Finally."

"What's the matter?" Beck gasped.

"You're making up for lost time. You're going to have a firecracker baby."

Beck was rocked by a stronger contraction. Nobody could help her. No relief. She twisted her neck in a contortion and groaned a prayer to St. Thérèse.

A nurse placed her hand atop her forehead. "You're going to be fine. A young strong girl like you should have no problems."

A doctor she did not recognize came to her. "Breathe and push," she coaxed.

Beck felt the baby come into the world like a *firecracker*–an explosion of sparkling aura. The pressure passed out of her. She heard a faint gasp, shallow irregular breathing. Was it dying? The worry had barely formed in her mind when she heard the magical cry.

"It's a girl," the doctor said. "And very healthy."

Beck crooked her head to watch the medical staff wash the naked small body and spread an ointment over her eyes.

A confusion of emotions swept through Beck. The baby hadn't died. Beck was now a mother. No matter what happened she'd be this baby's mother.

Another nurse pushed on Beck's stomach. "Contract to push out the placenta," she instructed.

Beck focused on finishing the delivery.

A nurse held out the blanket-wrapped baby to her.

Beck was surprised by the solid weight as if expecting something like a doll.

The sight of the pinched red face swept away her remorse with a warm flood of love.

"Take her to your breast," a nurse said.

The soft, virgin mouth touched Beck with complete union. She'd never felt a connection like the joining of two souls. Who she was, what she was supposed to do for a moment faded into a bliss of being.

"Take this pill," the doctor instructed.

A nurse tilted Beck's head to swallow the pill with a small sip of water.

Reality returned as Beck was wheeled on her back from the bright lights into the recovery room to be left alone with her daughter behind drawn green curtains.

Beck knew the plan. Someone was coming to take her child. She arose, clutched the bundle to her chest, swayed, steadied herself against the rail of the bed, and pushed through the curtain.

Air was cold on her naked backside exposed by the flimsy hospital gown. Across a room lined with curtained compartments, she saw Panda being escorted through a wide door.

Beck spun but could not control her momentum and was falling, desperately trying to protect her daughter, caught herself enough to slump onto the floor. Hands reached for her baby, and helped Beck back to the bed.

"What are you doing?" Panda asked.

"No." Beck groaned, "The baby..."

"I thought she was to be sedated," Panda said.

"She is. She should be out."

Beck reached for her daughter.

"I want the child taken from her immediately," Panda said.

"No, no." Beck could not speak. Chemical hands closed her throat. An irresistible weight pulled her into a deep sleep.

* * *

When she awoke, her perfect baby was gone. The longing for her was a cave.

Daylight came through two picture windows. Sunlight and shadows fell in patterns on a table, two chairs, a reading chair, yellow walls and brown carpet. Beck arose and felt a muscular ache. Dressed in a fine nightgown she didn't recognize, she went into the hall.

A nurse came to her from a station set in the middle of a square area.

"Where is my baby?" Beck asked, her voice hoarse and dry.

The nurse held Beck by the arm. "She's in the nursery. I was just coming to see how you're doing. Back to bed now."

"What's wrong with her?"

"Just a slight bit of bilirubin, jaundice. We put her under a light. It's very common. Absolutely nothing to worry about." The nurse's strong arms guided her to the room.

"I want to see her," Beck said.

"You stay here."

"Please try to understand I can't do this."

The nurse set Beck on the bed and pushed her until she lay down. "Take this. It's to help you relax." The nurse gave her another pill from a small white cup set on a rolling table positioned by the bed. "I'll bring the baby back when you wake up."

Beck dreamed an alligator had come into the hospital and was looking for her baby.

She awoke when a man brought in a tray of food.

Panda was seated across the room in an upholstered chair reading *Rosemary's Baby*.

"Where is she?" Beck's mouth felt full of cotton.

"Well, look who has joined the living." Panda came to her.

The table was swung over the bed for the food.

"I have to get up." Beck pushed the table away.

"Leave the food over there." Panda placed her hand on Beck's shoulder until the man had left the room, then went to a closet and pulled out a pink quilted robe with blue ribbons stitched across its bodice. "If you want to eat at the table put this on."

There was something forgiving in her grandmother's voice. Beck understood. She could come back now, back to her old life. That was the arrangement. All she had to do was give up her baby and everything would be like before.

Panda followed her to the door of the bathroom. "You didn't thank me for the new clothes and toiletries I bought for you."

"Thank you, Panda."

Her grandmother combed and set her hair as she had when Beck was a little girl.

"I believe we can finish this up tomorrow. I've arranged for you to spend a few weeks at a spa. Then, I have a wonderful surprise for you. We are going to meet your father in Rome in August. We are to have an audience with the Pope. Can you imagine? I am so thrilled. We are to go to the Gondolfo Palace, the Pope's summer home. It's a great honor."

The door opened. A young nurse came in with the baby. "Here she is and so hungry for her mommy."

The feeling of something precious having been found filled the gaping pit with joy. She rose against the edge of the table and reached for her daughter.

Panda grimaced and looked away. "I thought she was to be kept in the nursery?"

"But she needs her mother..." The young nurse looked perplexed by Panda's angry tone.

Panda stormed from the room, leaving her purse on the table. "I intend to speak to your superiors."

"Thank you for bringing her to me." Beck's eyes narrowed with a smile of appreciation. "I just want to have her for one day. That's all, one day."

Panda's voice outside her door demanded, "I want her watched every minute, do you understand?"

Another nurse picked up Panda's purse and took her coat from the closet. "Your grandmother wanted me to tell you that she had to leave. She'll be back to pick you up in the morning."

* * *

Beck stood by the window and looked out at a dark woods bathed by a three-quarter moon. She held the sleeping Theresa Lynda Malloy. Beck lowered her nose to just where the tiny ear lobe lay neatly separated from thin fairy-spun tufts of hair, and inhaled—the pure unaltered scent of her, like a delicious soup, chocolate, pure and sensual—*the splendor of the rose and the whiteness of the lily* as St. Thérèse said.

Some moments must last a lifetime. Only through the love Thérèse had showed her could Beck give her child away. She must trust God that Theresa would be placed in a good and loving family.

Beck recalled a television show about a cowboy who blew on the nose of a newborn calf so the calf would follow him. She gently exhaled over Theresa's face, and prayed God who had delivered Theresa from heaven to a life that He knew would not be with her would plant the sense of her in Theresa so that when they met on earth or in heaven, they would know each other and be together.

Beck was surprised and disappointed she'd fallen asleep. The strong-armed nurse awoke her, and Beck was able to spend a quiet morning with Theresa until her grandmother arrived.

"Not dressed? Not packed?" Panda asked.

"Isn't she beautiful?" Beck lifted Theresa to her.

For an instant, Panda's icy demeanor melted, and her pupils shined with love. The moment slid irreversibly into pained confusion. Her azure eyes turned away from the infant. "I can't, Beck. Please try and understand that I really can't. Don't make this any harder than it has to be."

Beck returned her attention to Theresa. She did not want to waste another moment away from their contact. She willed herself to be peaceful and calm, confident so that Theresa would not sense any problem or grow upset.

Panda called the nurse. "Please take the baby."

The young nurse took Theresa from Beck.

A great sadness too heavy to ever be lifted fell on her. The baby was carried from the room. *Thérèse's love, Thérèse's love,* she repeated to herself.

Panda spurred her to quickly shower and dress. When she came out of the bathroom, Panda had finished her packing.

"Thank you, Panda," Beck said but could not stop an escaping sob.

"Stop moping. The best thing to do is keep moving. Come on, let's get this over with and get on with our lives."

Panda dressed her in a turban similar to the one she wore to hide her hair.

Outside the room, by the nursery, the baby was returned to Beck. The nurse who had brought Theresa to her from the nursery watched them leave with a frown of pity.

Panda pushed the wheelchair in which Beck carried Theresa out of the elevator and turned in the direction of a sign marked "Administrative Offices."

"Put these on." Panda handed her a pair of dark sunglasses that made seeing difficult in the artificial light. Panda also put on a pair.

Inside the office, Beck saw the darkened shapes of two men. One was overweight with puffy skin around his eyes.

There were no introductions. The fat man had a file. "Why don't you take the child?" he said to the other man.

Beck did not want to give Theresa to him. She wanted to run, to hide.

The man reached for Theresa. Beck resisted for a moment and the man used more force to take the baby who started to cry.

"Please no," Beck said and reached for her child.

The fat man looked at Panda. "The relinquishment of the child must be voluntary."

"It is," Panda said. "Don't make a fuss. Do what you must do."

They were holding her daughter like a product to be traded or sold. What if Miss Kitty had been right and this was a baby-selling operation?

Beck looked at her grandmother, pleading, but saw only determination in her pressed lips. This is what she had to do. She had her chances to make her own way, to be strong enough to say this is what I want, not what's good for the family—what's good for me, for my daughter. The answer had always been the same. She was too weak, too obedient.

The fat man handed the open file to Beck. Typed pages were attached by two thin folded metal strips. **Independent Adoption Placement Agreement** was across the top.

The fat man said, "This is all that we need to complete the adoption. Sign where the checks are."

Beck had trouble reading the pages through the sunglasses. A note had been written on the inside cover of the file–*adopting party: Nicholas and Judith Fusco*. Was she supposed to see that? She would now always know who had adopted Theresa. And under guardian of minor parent was her father's signature. So, he did know. He'd been part of the conspiracy to give his granddaughter away. To whom? What kind of people were Nicholas and Judith Fusco? Were they foreigners? Was her baby being taken to Italy? Beck glanced at her grandmother.

Panda spoke sternly, "You've done just fine. Do this and it will be over."

Beck read, *father unknown*. Oh, the lies, monstrous lies, how could God forgive these lies?

"I'll take her into the next room," the man whispered to the fat man.

As if hurtling to impact with a window, Beck saw clearly she would soon pass into an unimaginable afterlife without knowing where her daughter was. "May I hold her one more time?"

"Sign," Panda commanded.

Beck quickly wrote her name by two check marks without reading further what she was signing.

The fat man took the file from her and nodded at Panda who rose and pushed Beck's wheelchair toward the door. "Don't think about it. Let it pass. She is going to be fine. They are a wonderful family. I promise."

Beck started to weep.

"Please, I beg of you, Beck—my heart will break—please don't cry." Panda wrested open the door and shoved the wheelchair out of the office.

Beck barely had time to twist for one last glimpse of her bawling daughter being taken into an adjoining office to a man and woman. He had dark hair, young, Italian she thought. She was blonde. Someday, somehow she'd find them and her beautiful Theresa.

Cold and numb, as weak as death, Beck sat in the wheelchair while Panda had her car brought to the curb. Beck did not hate her, did not even see her as the one who was taking her baby. Panda was hurting. Beck's agony was too great not to inflame her grandmother.

An attendant helped Beck into Panda's car.

Beck pressed down sobs, turned to the passenger window as the car pulled away from her baby, placed her hand on the rain-streaked pane, and silently mouthed, "I'll find you."

SEVENTEEN

DREAMS AND VISIONS

Did her father know? She'd almost asked Panda once as they flew across the Atlantic, but hadn't the nerve, did not want another lecture or more scorn of her guilt. Had he really signed the adoption paper? She'd worked in his office at an auto signing machine used for letters congratulating constituents for graduating high school, college, any special event that a letter with the official seal of the U.S. Senate signed by their senator would be treasured—another lie to make someone feel better and vote for Richard Lyons.

In Rome that morning, she'd been happy to see her father, surprisingly joyful. He'd entered the lobby of the Palazzo Dama hotel his eyes searching for her, and when he'd seen her he'd not noticed she was overweight or the sorrow that spread liver shadows beneath her eyes. She wished he'd asked her what was wrong, someplace private away from Panda so Beck could get a full read of him.

If her father had asked why she looked so old and tired, she'd planned to say something like, "Well, you know I've been through a lot."

She'd wait to see if he seemed to understand or sympathize. If he did, then her future silence, her effort to forget what she'd done would be a direct act of complicity with him. If he wanted her to, she'd be the Vestal Virgin, goddess of the hearth, and maintain the sacred flame of his reputation.

She'd not been alone with him through an afternoon of quick special tours, a reception and dinner at the ambassador's residence. He'd introduced her with apparent pride to diplomats, politicians, and business leaders. He'd told the ambassador and his wife when they met them at the door of the residency that she'd spent the last year in France.

By the time they'd returned to the hotel after ten, he was exhausted and had gone straight to his room with a quick "goodnight – see you in the morning."

"Nite daddy," she said as casually as if they were home and gone to her bedroom in a suite for kings and heads of state.

Alone for the first time since her grandmother had picked her up at the spa, Beck lay in a canopy bed reading the last pages of Daisy Miller, a short story by Henry James about a young American girl in Rome during the last century who dies from a fever caught during a foolish illicit nighttime visit to the Colosseum.

The air of other ages surrounded one; but the air of other ages, coldly analyzed, was no better than a villainous miasma.

The phrase described Rome with her grandmother–a Seeing Eye dog who would bark at her, "Don't mope. Get over it."

Breathing the air of other ages, the museums and churches, the castles and ruins, the way mummies in the catacombs below the Vatican reached with gruesome long fingernails and hair that kept growing after the body had died– everything sad, allegorical and doomed.

She was Daisy Miller, fatally infected. Her solitude only intensified the pain. Too sad to pretend, she refused to forget the sense of Theresa. The memories were always waiting for the smallest mental opening–shocking and terrifying– she'd lost her baby. Someone had taken her child.

In visions and dreams, she'd explain to Randall, saw their reunion, wept as he held her, forgave her, said he understood. Or she'd feel his anger and disappointment in her not trusting him. *I would have married you. We would have found a way, but not now.* Her emotions would rise and fall to despair as she imagined him leaving her forever.

She turned off a light set in porcelain vase beside the bed and was in her state of vision and dreams, barely aware of the European staccato siren bleeping outside the tall drape covered windows amidst the sounds of downtown Rome.

As she fell into sleep a tingling of a warning stirred in her subconscious – a heightened sense of reality–a failure to distinguish if she was moving in the conscious world or in a dream.

* * *

In her nightgown, she walked out of the room without doubt, question or thought of consequences–not taking her purse, passport or money.

An indoor fountain was the predominant sound in the lobby.

Uniformed staff watched her from behind a polished wood and brass counter.

A liveried doorman tipped his hat, "Taxi?"

She did not respond.

She walked down the cobblestone driveway, past the line of Fiats with lights on their roofs, to an alley, a small piazza lit differently than the squares she'd gone to with Panda–no fountains, restaurants or outdoor cafes, no music, no tourists, no diners drinking wine and espresso.

Before three small hotels marked by neon signs were women wearing tight, short skirts and scant tops.

Beck stood beside a fat woman who wore everything in red from shoes to earrings.

"What are you doing here?" the whore asked.

"God is showing me what I must do." Beck said.

The women laughed and shouted to the others, "God wants her to be a whore!"

Their laughter stopped when three French sailors, distinctive in their blue uniforms and round caps, turned the corner around which Beck had just passed.

The sailors stopped. The women surrounded them. Beck wondered if she could awake. She didn't want to be a prostitute.

*Five whores strutted around the sailors like peacocks, saying, "*Vengo con te, se vuoi.*"*

One of the sailors, beautiful, an angel with tight gold curls protruding from his cap, looked directly at Beck. She did not blush or turn her gaze. His eyes were wonderful, deep lights that made Beck tremble.

*He stepped past the whores and said to her. "*Venez donc!*" He took Beck's hand and led her into a door above which a sign shown in neon, Hotel Avila.*

Beck followed not so much being pulled as lifted. She had the sensation of having lost contact with the senses of weight and feet. She concentrated on the feel of his hand around hers, cool and warm, strong and yielding. He was leading her to new understanding and strength.

A small, old woman sat behind a counter made of thin wood. Small compartments held keys.

"Une chambre," *the sailor asked for a room and took a passport from a pocket cleverly cut at an angle by the breast of his tight shirt.*

The woman looked at Beck and said "Il passaporto..."

"Elle est avec moi."

The woman gazed at Beck with eyes that judged.

"Non mettere le mani su di lei," *she said rapidly, her hands also signaling Beck not to go with him.*

The sailor handed the woman money, colorful lire. The old woman looked at Beck, hesitated, shook her head. "Eccola," *she said with disgust and handed the sailor a key.*

Beck heard a baby crying from a room down the hall.

They entered a small apartment that smelled of body lotion. A cheap printing of a snow-capped mountain hung beside a crack on a dirty wall above a couch covered by an old shawl. A door opened inward. A child of no more than ten held a baby. Beautiful black hair parted in the middle, her pale complexion heightened the coloring of red lips. She sat on a large chair, smiled modestly but proudly.

The sailor laughed, put his arm around Beck's waist, and led her to another room away from the baby.

A worn red cover lay across a round bed. A small bathroom with a bidet was visible through a partially open door.

The sailor threw a pile of lire on a nightstand by the bed.

"Est sufficient?" *he asked and started to peel off his uniform.*

Strangely, she did not feel threatened. She was in control. She only had to wait for God's plan for her to be revealed.

The sailor pulled the cover off the round bed and lay naked on his back.

The sight of his body, the way his muscles were detailed in rolls and ridges under pale skin, thin legs topped by the phalanx of his erect penis, a purple snake pushing through the cover of his foreskin, made her feel warm and loving.

She sat beside him.

He reached for her.

With complete confidence she was able to push his arms away from her. She caressed his cheek and explored his body, pleased at the way he shuddered and closed his eyes when she gently held his penis.

"Ah c'est marvelous," *he gasped.*

The sound of the baby crying pulled Beck's attention back to the hall. The lost concentration broke her control over the sailor. The strong arms she'd been able to admire, the fine hands were now removing her nightgown.

The sensation of having a purpose, performing a function released her from the somber trap. She was a whore.

The sailor ravished her, pushing and pulling her about the bed, kissing her in ways that she'd never imagined, falling to the floor still atop of her, giving her such pleasure that she cried and screamed, laughed and groaned, chasing away the devils that whispered sorrow, draped themselves around her until she could see no light, feel no joy.

She saw Panda's face surrounded by shocked, dark, shrouded mummies reaching, trying to draw her back into their death grip. Never. She threw back her head and laughed with such force that the sailor stopped, perched atop of her on his elbows and gazed at her.

"Il y a belle lurette," he said.

She was the most beautiful. She clawed at his back and shuddered with him on the worn rug.

Then, he disappeared–with a breath he was gone. She was naked, had just had sex with a strange man. What if she was pregnant again? God, this can't be your plan for me. Please don't give me another child.

The door to the room slowly opened. Beck pushed herself into a crawling position, on her hands and knees. What if another sailor or man wanted her? She was no whore.

The old woman from the desk entered, very small and heavy, legs fat and pocked, deformed beneath a frayed dress that hung to below her knees. Loose stockings reached above her ankles. A black shawl hung over her head and around her rolled chest. Behind her stood the young girl holding the baby.

Beck stared at them, waiting to see what they'd say to her. She remained in the position of a crawling child or an animal.

The woman cautiously moved toward her as if Beck might leap up and chase her from the room.

The woman moved toward the money the sailor had left by the bed.

Was the old woman going to rob her?

The hag set a book atop the money, looked down at Beck and said, "Chi non è con me è contro di me." The dwarf hurried from the room as if she had just performed a dangerous but necessary task.

The old woman was crazy. Beck had to get away, dressed quickly and hurried from the room.

The old woman was waiting outside. "Lo libro," *the old woman said in a disgusted voice as one would to a child who refused to obey a simple instruction.*

The book.

Beck went back into the room. The door was open. The old woman watched her.

Beck took the book and left the money. The old woman stepped aside, opening a passage for Beck to depart.

The bag followed her out into the street. The whores were gone. In a streetlight Beck looked down at the title. Autobiography of a Saint *was written in English.*

"È bello." *The old woman smiled and disappeared.*

* * *

In the timelessness of a dream, Beck hurried through the lobby. Dressed only in a nightgown, a whore, shame lowered her gaze as staff and guests looked at her.

Back in her room with divine purpose, she found the book Dr. Colby had given her in a travel bag and reread the story of Saint Thérèse of Lisieux– meaning clear and immediate, awakening from a delirium like St. Thérèse. The dream had been a message from God. The sailor had looked like an angel. She prayed for and felt the Lord's forgiveness and power.

God's Will that in this world souls shall dispense to each other, by prayer, the treasures of Heaven, in order that when they reach their Everlasting Home they may.

* * *

Panda woke her with a bustling entrance into her room.

Beck's eyes flew open and fear generated consciousness rolled to her shoulder to stare at her grandmother.

"Why are the lights on? Someone left the door to your room open last night."

Beck inhaled through her nose and searched for clues if she'd really walked through the lobby in her nightgown. She'd not had a DRC episode since she'd been fifteen and crashed her father's prize Triumph convertible into the Hillard's fence barely a half-block from her driveway. She'd returned to her bed with barely a memory.

When questioned by Fairfax Police investigators she'd said she could not guess which neighborhood kid might have committed the crime. But Wayne Conrad had been blamed. For two weeks, Capitol Hill Police sat in an unmarked car guarding the house until the Leader sent them away.

She pushed herself into a sitting position and her hand fell on the hardcover volume *Autobiography of a Saint.* How much of the rest of the dream had been real? What remained was the ecstasy of her calling, her commitment to *love one another with grateful hearts, and with an affection far in excess of that which reigns in the most perfect family on earth.*

Beck blinked and rolled her feet to sit over the edge of the bed. Her face brightened and she looked at Panda with pressed lips and a loving glint.

"What's that idiot grin for? Did you leave the door open? I hope you didn't have one of your attacks. We may have to start locking your bedroom door again."

Beck felt reborn, refreshed in a way that filled her with contentment and a sense of what Janey called giving it to God. "I had a vision. I was called by God."

Panda squinted as if making a diagnosis. "Let's hope it's just Rome and the audience with the Pope. Tell me now if you're not up to it. We don't need you going crazy in front of the Pope."

With unusual bravo, Beck resisted her grandmother's scorn with a deep sigh. "I've never been better."

Her grandmother's gaze fell to the bed. "What are you reading? Where did you get that book?"

Beck gushed with the happiness of her calling, "Oh it's wonderful, the story of Saint Thérèse of Lisieux. It was given to me by Dr Colby."

Panda frowned and pushed back her blond-tinted hair. "Catholics," she muttered, defending her class. "I've ordered your breakfast. Get ready. We need to leave in an hour. Wear your blue dress with the long sleeves and the new hat. The Castel Gandolfo is like their churches, they won't let women in without a hat or with our arms uncovered."

* * *

The rapture of her vision mixed in her DRC state. She moved through dressing and no breakfast in a disjointed strobe-like perception, in step with Saint Thérèse. The book, the vision last night, her delirium all signs Beck must commit to the saintly path.

She was nearly the age St. Thérèse had been when she'd asked for the Pope's intercession. What would her father say? Would he weep like St. Thérèse's father had when Thérèse had told him what she wanted to do? Would her life as a Carmelite nun be as strict as St. Thérèse's had been? You left your family and friends for good, spent your life contemplating God in near solitude.

She would say to her father and grandmother, "The Lord has a greater plan for me." She was confident now, unafraid. The ruined *self* that had so shamed her, the crudely stitched remainders of her past expectations were meager alternatives to the life the Lord had chosen for her. Unlike Thérèse, she was healthy and would fulfill the saint's ambition to work with the poor in Africa.

Others had pure faith. Beck had needed God to show her the darkness before she would trust Him to lead her into the glorious light that now shined before her. The lack of choice was a blessing. She no longer had to struggle, only to follow, to purify herself behind the walls of a convent, make every act and every thought a devotion before going into the world with the love in Christ.

* * *

A frocked priest drove the car from the city toward the mountains. Beside lake Alban was the Castel Gandolfo, the Pope's summer palace. Stiff Swiss Guards stood at attention, dressed in uniforms with bunched short pants and metal helmets, carrying sharp pointed pikes. Everywhere was iconic sculpture, painting, mosaics, metalwork, embroidery. Beck was certain she was drawing closer to her destiny.

Like Panda, she wore a lace chapel veil they'd purchased on the Ponte Vecchio in Florence. But unlike her family she was here to change her life.

They were escorted down a hallway of frescoes of biblical scenes framed by embossed white arches and pillars, gilded tables and sofas.

In a receiving room resplendent with religious art, fine wood and leather-bound books. Everything was meaningful, pulling Beck into the divine union.

Her gaze fell to a small marble statue on a wooden table. Saint Thérèse, her beautiful face draped in a thin habit, her fine tapered hands clutching a cross in a bed of roses.

Pope Paul VI entered with an entourage of priests. The pontiff wore a red mozzetta, stole and moved comfortably down their small receiving line in red slippers.

Panda didn't bow but stuck out her hand, eyes twinkling with her charm. "So nice of you to see us," she said as if greeting an elected official.

The Pontiff spoke to Panda in surprisingly good English with a heavy Italian accent. "I've heard about you. You are a good woman and have raised a good son and are helping to raise this lovely granddaughter. Bless you."

Panda swelled with the idea that the Pope knew about her.

The Pope stepped to Beck on his way to the Leader.

Now. Show your devotion. Obey God's will. Beck overcame the inhibitions that threatened to paralyze her and fell to her knees, Panda's gasp beside her like a thunderclap.

The Pope's thick white robe moved before Beck's face.

St. Thérèse as a young girl had knelt as she, perhaps in this exact spot. When the Pope had told St. Thérèse to obey her father, the saint had clutched the Pope's knees, begging.

Beck opened her heart to the Lord's will. Perception of time, space self disappeared. In tears, she bowed and pressed her hands together in prayer. "Holy Father I have been called. St. Thérèse spoke to me. I am to be a Carmelite." Too hurried—her words lacked certainty.

Panda's hand touched Beck's back.

The Leader cleared his throat implying something being suppressed.

Beck raised her eyes in supplication. A priest spoke to the Pope in Italian.

In a tone more humorous than reverent, "*Un rosario*," the Pope issued a quick instruction.

"Please stand," the Pope said to Beck.

Beck rose with a locked stare into Pope's dark eyes shining with the confidence of faith. "God loves you," he said and with a brief touch placed a rosary of black beads and a silver cross with a raised crucifixion in her hand.

"Thank you," Beck said, mundane for the complete melding she felt to him.

The pontiff extended his hand to the Leader in an invitation to move away from the nuisance of an overwrought daughter.

Panda seized Beck's elbow. "You...you behave, do you hear?" she hissed and guided Beck to stand beside the table with the statute of St. Thérèse.

Beck looked at the white figure arms extended into a dark bloom of copper roses at her feet as if the image might perform the miracle of speaking for her. No, she must express the truth of her inspiration, return scorn with love, smile with the glow of her enrapture.

Her grandmother stood close, lips pressed together in a battle of mortification and *isn't this amusing?*

Like two mismatched props they stood side-by-side as the Pope spoke to the Leader before a painting of Mary holding the baby Jesus.

The brief audience over, the Pope and Leader moved back to them.

Beck knees trembled. Must she do more to convince the Pope of her sincerity.

Panda seized her hand in a surprisingly painful grip.

The Pope spoke to Beck last.

Like an amateur watching a practiced professional, the love in the Pontiff's eyes and smile of beatification entranced Beck.

"Follow your convictions," he said to her and left the audience.

She'd been anointed by the Pope. She was to be a nun.

* * *

The Leader sat in the front passenger seat of the Mercedes. A priest drove them back through Rome, using the opportunity to reaffirm the Church's doctrine on the sanctity of life and opposition to abortion.

A barrier of nervous anger separated Beck from her grandmother in the backseat. Beck's devotion to her calling did not blot what she'd done to her father. She pushed back her apprehension with the glow of her anointment and pulled the presence of the Pope around her like a magic cloak of summer sunset light. Her smile was thin but rapturous as her grandmother scowled, condemnation bottled with curled lips.

The Leader and Panda had heard the Pope's words, witnessed Beck's commitment. Their disapproval would not compare to the illness and pain suffered by St. Thérèse.

* * *

The doorman at the Palazzo Dama opened the rear door of the car for Beck.

Dressed in an olive colored uniform and leather pillbox hat, he bowed slightly and smiled. "Pretty pretty girl take walk last night."

Hope gasped and flinched with a quick smile.

Panda was close enough to have heard and breathed hard through her nose. Her disapproval had reached an unexperienced high. She led their passage through the lobby with a scornful glare.

Beck was happy to rush after her, head down to avoid the stares of the hotel staff she was certain were being directed at her.

In the living room of their suite, Panda put down her alligator purse on a table and turned, eyes wide with anger, head thrust forward. "What was that foolishness? Are you mad? Remind me to never take you anywhere I don't want to be mortified."

Beck looked down, hurt despite the expected criticism.

"That is enough." The Leader curled his lips.

Beck had rarely heard her father use that tone of command on anyone but her.

Panda straightened her back and tossed her head, unused to being taken up by her son. "You let me handle this, Dickie," she said, promising punishment.

Beck turned to her father her head lowered, eyes raised to plead. "I believe I am in need of assistance."

Her father laughed at their private code.

"You certainly are. Come with me," Panda said with stalking wolf's eyes.

"No." Beck straightened her neck and stood up to her grandmother. "I want to stay with my father."

Panda swelled. "Then, you'll force me to say what I have to say in front of him."

Beck shivered. Good tell him. Get it out, end this doubt and distrust.

In his command voice, the last word, her father cut Panda off. "Enough Mom. I think Beck and I will go out and spend an afternoon together if you don't mind."

Panda twisted her lips as if trying to capture words, panted through her nose. "Oh no, I don't mind. I'm exhausted. I have to pack." She started to turn away then back. "I hope you'll explain to your child that the Catholics would love to get their hands on the daughter of a prominent Episcopalian. Oh, wouldn't they love that?" Panda turned to her room muttering, "Here's gratitude for you."

Her father blinked in relief when Panda closed the door to her bedroom. He turned to Beck with a half-grinned. "Let's have some fun. I've missed my little girl."

She'd be his dutiful daughter, but he wouldn't change her mind no matter what he said.

* * *

Beck tried to relax as they walked from the hotel to the race track-shaped Plaza del Popolo, past the obelisk, down the same streets Beck had seen in her dream. Instead of whores standing before a cheap hotel were windows of fashion and art. Nobody recognized him or treated them as anyone but American tourists, a father and his daughter.

Truth so near, she didn't trust herself to speak, too absorbed in her passion to show delight in the fanciful marble sculptures of the Villa Medici.

She thought of the postcard she'd sent Robbie of Bacchus riding a turtle and inwardly cringed at her naïveté. Only a year ago that girl might have been someone else who wanted a boyfriend.

As they passed the Basilica di Santa Maria, the Leader said as if on impulse, "Let's go in."

"Oh, I'd like that." Beck smiled, hoping the magnificence of the church would inspire him to accept the choice she'd made.

She placed the Florentine lace chapel veil still in her purse over her head and they entered the nave. They stood before a long carpet across the marble floor looking into the rounded sanctuary.

Beck's breathing slowed. Her concerns of the world were blanketed by a deep peace. This is where she belonged. She smiled at her father with Saint Thérèse's love of a perfect family.

He looked down at her from his 6'1" and back at the sculptures and paintings of saints.

"I can see why you want to be part of this. It speaks so clearly of the inspiration of the divine."

Oh, the miracle had showed him what she must do. She would be patient and allow God's love to fill his heart with understanding.

* * *

They sat in an outdoor cafe. He had an aperol. She drank a citrus spritzer and took a small bite of a pear tart from the pastry cart.

He looked across the white tablecloth at her and appeared sad as St. Thérèse's father had. "I was very moved by what you did this morning."

Her father had great empathy. He looked at her without judgement, open, ready to understand, sympathize. She'd heard him on the phone at home talking to someone who was angry or demanding he take some action. *Look, I understand. I get it. But...*

She glanced away then back to look him squarely in the eyes. He wouldn't understand but she had to try. Her complexion reddened as she dug in. "St. Thérèse came to me in a dream. She did, really she did. I'm to be a nun."

The Leader pressed his lips together in a half-smile, half-frown. "Seeing the Pope...it must happen to lots of people. But honey, you can't be a nun. You have to be born into the faith, really understand and believe it."

"I am to be a nun," Beck spoke with the power of St. Thérèse. "That is my conviction," she sought to align herself with the Pope's words.

"You're not Catholic." The Leader pleaded, calling his daughter back from madness. "And I want grandchildren." He went to the heart of his argument, "an heir."

Her eyes widened as she examined him. Either he was the Michelangelo of lairs or he didn't know he had a beautiful granddaughter taken by Nicholas and Judith Fusco. She looked across a metal railing, a filigree or roses. Maybe his heir was in the baby carriage that passed on the sidewalk. Across the street in the recess of a doorway, two infants boys nursed on the teats of a wolf. Truth and lies, dream and waking fluttered around her. She looked back at him, confession pushing like a boil from her brain. "Do you know what happened to me?" Her voice quivered. She raised her chin to his opaque eyes.

"What?" he asked with diplomatic insouciance as if he really didn't know.

She could read and understand his expression as clearly as if he had shouted at her. He refused to witness her corruption, and she retreated. "I meant what I said to the Pope. I had a vision. I did." Beck prayerfully pushed her hands together.

The hardness of the confrontation again turned to compassion, countered by a suspicious tilt of his head that she was describing a DRC event. "One of my best friends is the Archbishop of Washington. He was the one who arranged the audience. He'll be thrilled that you were so moved."

Her father showed her how to dismiss her betrayal with a light heart. Beck breathed quickly. She was either a whore or a novitiate. How could she tell her father of a dream where she understood Italian and a French angel made love to her to be saved by a troll. Or had been it real?

EIGHTEEN

THE CLOUD OF UNKNOWING

The house at Lake Barcroft was quiet in the morning. Beck looked at her bedroom furnished with the trappings of her former life. A matching dresser, two nightstands, a makeup table and desk were scrolled Colonial revival painted white with gold leaf trim. Roses on the ivory material of the canopy over her double bed matched the shades on her lamps. Dolls piled in a corner atop an old toy box. A framed print of A Mother Bathing A Child by Mary Cassatt hung by a tacked Here Comes the Beatles poster–a concert at D.C. Stadium Panda had taken her to. A guitar case, stereo and record collection set beside the private entrance from the side of the house; makeup bottles and perfumes arranged on a lace strip beneath a vanity mirror attached to the dresser beside the bathroom door. An ink blotter, a leather container of pens and pencil beneath a bulletin board on which were tacked clippings of actors and actresses, high fashion models. She longed for the cloud of unknowing, the ascetic security Saint Thérèse the Little Flower of Jesus had described in her autobiography.

Her thoughts were pulled to the material world with a desperate worry. Where was her daughter? She should be looking for Nicholas and Judith Fusco, becoming their friends, seeing Theresa. Maybe she could babysit for them and have time alone with her child.

No, to see Theresa would be to abandon the lie. If she was to do this, she must walk a narrow line, careful not to lean toward the truth.

With a sigh, her throat parched, she climbed the stairs to the kitchen to pour herself a glass of orange juice.

Janey stopped putting away dishes from dinner and breakfast from the dishwasher in the middle of the counter leading from the refrigerator to the stove. She studied Beck. "Ya look a different. Water bad over there?"

Nobody knew her better than Janey.

Beck took a sip and placed the glass on the Formica countertop. "I met the Pope. I asked him to help me become a nun." She clasped her hands and raised her eyes heavenward, giving Janey a reflection of the devotion she'd seen depicted in the paintings and stained glass saints.

Janey pressed her lips together and her round upper cheeks rose like two plums but she didn't release the giggle Beck knew was there. "That good," Janey said and went back to her chore.

Before Beck's father had remarried he would leave Beck alone with Janey for days at a time. Once when Beck was seven, on a cool, fall, Sunday evening, Janey had put on her church dress and hat—a Mae Reeves work of art of brim and lace that nearly circled her shoulders and hung over her left eye. A Yellow Cab driven by a friend of hers had taken them across Columbia Pike, the road that ran by the entrance to the lake. On the other side of the two-lane highway was Lincolnia, a community founded by freed slaves.

Beck had been the only white person. As big an adventure as she'd ever known: the singing–*You love God in every way, every day, that's how to do it*–clapping, hosannas, organ and electric bass guitar shaking the walls of the small wooden church. Janey was an angel. Beck understood Janey had been sent to watch over her to show her the way to love God.

"I love you, Janey." She'd never told her that.

Both of them teared. "Chil, ya my blessed chil." Janey appeared confused. "My good chil." She resumed her work as if afraid to lose her understanding of what she was doing there.

* * *

That afternoon, eager to hear news of Randall, Beck joined Sonia-Barton on their private beach. They sat beside each other in folding aluminum chairs barely off the sand. Lake activities were at their peak–people floating on rafts, children screaming and diving from docks, sailing small boats, partying on electric pontoon boats and private beaches. The intimate neighborhood was the perfect accomplice to shelter Beck–both her enemy and center of her world, like someone you love who had killed your mother and brother. The placid summer surface was soft and yielding, not cold and hard as it had been that winter–the first cold spell. Colin had been impatient to try the ice skates they'd gotten for Christmas. She hated swimming in the lake. Her grandmother had paid for lessons from one of the muscular lifeguards who laughed at her terror of the hands reaching for her from beneath the surface. She never went ice-skating.

She'd lost a year of her life, yet here she could feel as if nothing had changed.

"Another boring day at Lake Barcroft," Sonia-Barton sighed and flicked her cigarette butt into the water.

Beck shifted in her chair and pulled the hem of her muumuu down to cover her ankles.

"So how was *France?*" the mocking tone alerted Beck that she faced a test.

"OK." Beck said, then remained silent, looking out at the lake.

"Like your hair like that," Sonia-Barton tried to open her up.

Beck tugged on the floppy beach hat she wore over her pageboy—short and straight, curled under at the ends. "Thanks. You look as cute as always."

"Haven't really had a chance to talk since you got back."

"No. Still a little wiped out by the trip, I guess," Beck said.

"I heard you went crazy in Rome. Sounds hilarious. Did you really goof on the Pope?"

Beck resisted the urge to turn to look at Sonia-Barton, hiding the shock that froze her stomach.

Sonia-Barton smirked. "The Leader told mama about it. Said your grandmother 'bout fainted." Sonia-Barton giggled, giving Beck time to gather herself.

"I've become religious. Catholic. I want to be a nun." Her tone was serious to the point of being dull as if announcing a doctor's appointment.

Sonia-Barton laughed with whooping glee. "Sure. Good idea." She laughed harder and held her side.

Beck stared at her with consternation.

"Well, I'm sorry," Sonia-Barton said. "I mean you're not even Catholic."

"Why does everybody keep saying that? I can learn."

"Plenty of Catholics back home. They're all right, party like crazy. Mardi Gras is all about the Catholics."

Beck looked back at the lake as if she couldn't be bothered with Sonia-Barton's or anyone else's doubts.

"You told Randall?"

Beck hugged her knees and told the biggest lie. "I'm done with Randall."

Sonia-Barton glanced at her and in a mocking tone like calling a bluff, said. "He knows, everybody does."

When Beck had one of her sleepwalks, the doctor had told her family she should not be awakened but led back to bed so as not to shock her nervous system.

Nobody had told Sonia-Barton whose meanness percolated through the squint in her eyes, and thin sadistic smile as she slapped Beck awake from her dream. Beck's nerves curled like they'd been singed, pain to numbness, paralysis to flight. She fought the urge to flee, tilted her head and with her inherited skill in obfuscation asked, "That I'm going to be a nun?"

Sonia-Barton smirked. "Nooo."

Beck shrugged with nonchalance. "Whatever are you talking about?"

"Mama says we're not to talk about it."

Beck shook her head as a tremor passed up her spine.

"About what?"

"Oh you know, babies."

Beck crinkled her forehead to look bewildered. She was collapsing, disappearing into the pit of her stomach. The scheme of suddenly departing for France in the middle of her junior year seemed as transparent as if she'd said she could jump across the lake. L'Ecole, the adoption had been only to satisfy her grandmother's prehistoric notion of social judgement. Her father was a liar, wanted her to lie for the sake of politics. He had told Gail. Who else?

"Randall thinks that?" The question, barely a whisper, floated on the breeze.

"I don't know. Haven't talked to him about it."

Beck's frustration exploded in a scream. "Then what the hell are you talking about?"

She rocketed to her feet and stood over Sonia-Barton, fist clenched, red fury haloing her eyes.

Sonia-Barton fell back in her collapsible chair, eyes wide with surprise, a fear-raised shoulder.

"Don't ever say that again!" Beck's voice hissed in a guttural growl. Panting through her nose, she spun and climbed the stone stairs up the hill to the house and went through the outside door to her room.

On the edge of her bed, humiliation heated her. She'd failed St. Thérèse's prime lesson—what is the demand of love? Do little things with great love. She'd allowed her ego and concern about what people were saying about her to govern her behavior. Never mind whether her family would permit her to convert, was she fit to follow in the path of St. Thérèse?

But if she was to remain in the temporal world was she strong enough to defend her reputation? The last stand between truth and her lie was her confession. She'd said she was done with Randall. When she saw him and he asked her what had happened to their child, would she confess? She'd as much as admitted to Sonia-Barton by the way she'd reacted to her taunting. She stared at the phone and thought about calling Panda but a kindness to Gail who would be blamed stopped her.

In two weeks, she'd be starting her senior year. Randall was fighting in Vietnam, maybe to die or be wounded there. She must go on with her life, count on the lies of L'Ecole to deflect the gossip. When she was eighteen, she'd enter the order, and leave the soiled world of disgrace behind. Then no one would doubt her commitment. Until then she must find the strength to behave as if nothing had happened, to be a regular seventeen-year-old girl who had spent a year abroad in France and learned how to meet every challenge with love.

* * *

Sonia-Barton dressed for man-hunting in a tight black leather miniskirt that barely reached to mid-thigh. This was a chance to prove to her that they could still be friends, teenagers going to a party.

Sonia-Barton drove the red Mustang her daddy had bought her to the party in Upperville, 50 miles west of Lake Barcroft. Beck sat beside her in a black leather bucket seat. Her dress reached to her ankles. Despite Sonia-Barton's criticism, she wore no makeup.

Up the long poplar-lined drive she parked on the lawn of a colonial mansion fronted by tall columns and topped by a rounded cupola reminiscent of Monticello.

Sonia-Barton turned to Beck for one last lecture. "Try not act like a nun, tonight. Don't go crazy. If you start feeling something coming on, come get me. OK?"

Beck nodded as would someone who had nothing to hide but her meekness. Maybe Sonia-Barton really was her friend and cared that Beck was in distress.

The party appeared civilized enough. Most were rich preppy children from the Hunt Country–many who jumped horses following a pack of hounds chasing a fox over fieldstone walls built by Eighteenth Century slaves.

A midshipman Sonia-Barton wanted her to meet had chosen another girl. Beck sat in the living room with Frank, a premed student at UVA. Frank liked to talk about himself. Beck nodded and acted as if she was listening while Frank explained the details and challenges of his existence. She could stay with him until it was time to leave. Sonia-Barton had promised she'd have Beck home by eleven but Beck knew she wouldn't.

"How about some fresh air?" Frank asked. Did he mean to take her outside to kiss her?

Beck looked through the series of rooms that composed the first floor. Drinking and smoking couples leaned close to each other and sat in groups of drunken conversation. They talked in shouts and laughs that Beck could not join. She didn't want to be left alone so went with Frank to a patio overlooking dark fields dimly lit by a quarter moon.

"Do you have a boyfriend?" he asked, casually probing her availability.

Not another lie–she didn't have to lie to Frank.

"I'm to be a nun." She clasped her hands and looked out on the night.

"Oh, really. Gee that's, well I never knew..." His voice trailed, not expecting that excuse.

Beck felt as if she was drowning in emotion, her words frothing out of her. "I can't live like this. I have to leave now. I shouldn't be here."

Frank followed her down the central hallway. Sonia-Barton was with a group standing by a philodendron.

"I really have to leave," she shouted, tears flowing.

"Oh jeez." Sonia-Barton frowned.

The group around Sonia-Barton were watching her with concern.

Sonia-Barton put her arm around her, "That's all right, honey. It's gonna be all right."

She picked up her bag at the front door. "She's having a bad time," she said to the host in a semi-whisper when he saw Beck's distress. "Got to get her home."

* * *

They rode through the dark Virginia countryside in silence until they reached Route 50. Something about the main highway and the increased speed of returning home calmed Beck.

"Thank you for leaving," she said. "You are a good sister."

"You all right?" Sonia-Barton looked over at her hunched in the seat.

"Sorry I broke down like that.

"Been hard on you. France, I mean."

"Yes, France." Her voice trailed implying much more in the word.

Beck glanced her. Car lights reflected raindrops on the windows against her face. Maybe Sonia-Barton had joined the lie. Maybe, those who really loved her would join the lie if she was good enough a liar.

"I met a man, a real man. Oh god, Sonia-Barton, I never felt anything like that before. I can't live without him. That's why I want to be a nun."

Sonia-Barton looked at her, then back at the road.

Beck told of a lover who lived in the village in France where she'd been.

"How old was he?"

"Old but not too old. Thirty-two."

"Are you going to see him again?"

"Please, Sonia-Barton." She choked a sob. "Don't ask me about France. I'll tell you more when I'm ready."

Sonia-Barton pressed her lips together. "Well, all right, I guess, but damn Beck you don't have to become a nun of all things. I've never seen a girl take it so hard."

* * *

Back in the safety of her bedroom, candlelight flickered against the brown plastic cover on the turntable. She lay on her bed and held the rosary the Pope had given her. Shadows and half-lights altered the shape and sense of her bedroom. Her lie to Sonia-Barton had belittled her conviction. She tried to imagine she was in a chapel, that her mind was clear and ordered by her devotion–*the cloud of unknowing. Thou art the farther from God that aught is in thy mind but only God.* Every act should be a prayer, any hardship bearable, every thought an expression of your love of Christ.

Energy from her devotion filled her–an electrical substance that coagulated in her legs, making her want to jump, run, flee but without permission. She felt medieval and superstitious.

She prayed for St. Thérèse's to intercede, to quickly make her a novitiate before something else happened. Then she felt guilty and prayed for Randall who was in real danger. Will you forgive me if I tell you the truth? Will you understand?

* * *

The ringing telephone awoke her from a deep sleep. The sun was bright in her windows. The house was air-conditioned to a comfortable sleeping temperature despite the damp humidity outside. The phone rang again. Beck sat up on the edge of the bed pushed her hair from her eyes.

"Hello." She couldn't make her voice sound awake.

"Still asleep?" her grandmother asked.

"Hi Panda. Sorry, I'm still having trouble with the time change."

"Are you having trouble with anything else?"

The truthful answer would be to say, *everything*, to alert Panda that everybody knew their lies and they were being ridiculed. "No," Beck lied.

She was given one of the midrange family pride and obligation lectures. Her grandmother's Piedmont accent, the prolonging of the vowels, grew stronger. "I want you to remember who you are, who we are. We are different. Your troubles are not the troubles of an ordinary girl. The world is just waiting to whisper and laugh about you. Do you want that?"

Her grandmother thought she was protecting her. Beck was the one was protecting her grandmother from knowing who was laughing at them. "Of course not."

The defeat in Beck's voice incited Panda who repeated for the hundredth time, "You don't tell anyone, especially not Sonia-Barton. She is just a scandal waiting to happen."

"I won't."

Panda played her ace. "Well, at least we won't have to worry about Randall Malloy for awhile. He might not be coming back at all."

Oh god, dear god, was she to get Randall killed? Her grandmother had the connections to get Randall drafted and placed in the most dangerous fighting. Instead of bringing love to her acts, she was she to bring nothing but tragedy?

She couldn't keep her voice from nearly gasping. "No, please I'll never tell him, never tell anyone. I swear." Panic stripped the guise that she didn't care about Randall.

"And you'll give up this foolishness of converting?"

Never mind becoming a nun, her grandmother was demanding complete abandonment. "Please don't do anything against Randall. It wasn't his fault. I swear I'll never see him. I'll never tell him. I promise."

"I'm sure I don't know what you're talking about. I have nothing to say about what happens to that boy unless my curses count for something. I'm going to see you through this terrible phase of your childhood for all our sakes."

She hurried to be Panda's good girl again. "I love you, Panda. I don't know what I'd do without you. What would have become of me? Thank you, thank you."

No matter how forced or bald was Beck's motivation, her grandmother's voice softened as she accepted her prostration. "I'm doing this for you."

"I know."

Aggression and submission flowed between them. Beck would lead a secret, chaste, spiritual life in her own way. There are many paths to God.

She'd barely returned the receiver to the cradle when the phone rang again. "Hi," she said as lovingly as she could, thinking her grandmother had forgotten a warning.

"Oh god, am I glad to hear your voice. I've been so worried about you."

Beck rocked back on the edge of her bed and tightened her grip on the receiver.

Miss Kitty. How had she found her?

The frail lies of L'Ecole were collapsing. Her first instinct was to pretend she didn't know who was on the line. She tried to disguise her voice putting on a more patrician New England–bordering on a bad British accent. "I'm sorry, who is this?"

"Nice try, Lynda Bird. I'll tell you who I am if you tell me who you are? Oh yeah, I already know who you are."

"I'm afraid that you must have the wrong number."

Despite the worry of being exposed, it *was* humorous to hear Miss Kitty's uproarious laugh.

"Like I don't recognize your voice. Want me to tell you some more about yourself, some other things you might have forgotten?"

"I'm sorry, you must have the wrong number. And I really must go now."

"Oh, ta-ta, tootle-loo. Wait. What should I tell Butch?"

Beck bet she hadn't talked to Randall and didn't know how to find him. "Butch?" she deepened her mixed-up accent.

For an instant doubt crept into Miss Kitty's voice. "You do know Randall Malloy, otherwise known as Butch, don't you?"

"And if I do?" Beck regretted even implying that she might know him.

"Can't wait to tell him how we sneaked out to see him play in New York."

First her grandmother and now Miss Kitty's blackmail—why were people so cruel to her?

"What is it you want?"

"Your first born child. Oh, forgot that's already been taken."

Humor broke through Beck's reserve like an unseen hole that brings down a dam. She wanted to laugh, needed to laugh.

"A senator's daughter and what a senator. I should have known. I was pretty goddamn close, wasn't I?"

"This is wrong." Beck used her normal voice, on the verge of pleading.

"Have you told him?" Miss Kitty asked.

No doubt who *him* was.

"Told him what?"

"About, you know, everything."

Beck stiffened her posture and willed assurance into her voice. "I'm sure I don't know what you're speaking of."

"All right, I guess you'll just leave it up to me."

Oh, the blatant and naked threat—Beck cringed at the torture of those who proffered to care for her. "If you choose to betray me, that is your choice."

"I won't betray you, honey. I'm gonna save you. Just want to see you have some fun. Hey, that wouldn't be a bad line for a song. Maybe it *is* a line from a song."

"Your threats don't scare me. I'm to become a Carmelite."

"A piece of candy?"

"A nun. I asked the Pope."

"Oh, that's perfect. You a...a..."

Miss Kitty's hee-hee laugh widened the crack in Beck's facade. She squeezed her lips together to keep from laughing.

"Mock my faith if you wish."

"Oh Jesus." Miss Kitty guffaws grew to whoops and gasps. "You're not even a Catholic."

"Why does everyone say that? It's the faith, not the religion."

"You have no idea."

"I have to go now. Thank you for calling."

"Wait, wait. We have to talk. I want to see you again."

"God bless you, goodbye."

"God bless you too. You're a riot."

Beck hung up.

The most likely way Miss Kitty could have found her was through Randall. What had she told him? More than ever Beck wanted to leave the lies and half-truths of her life. She craved the clear order and certainty that St. Thérèse had described. Beck lay back on her bed, practicing clearing her thoughts of everything but her love of Jesus, a centering prayer—*mercy, mercy, mercy* she repeated to rest in the presence of God.

The telephone rang again. Who was calling to afflict her now? Beck reluctantly picked up the pink princess receiver from its cradle.

"Hi, it's me. I'm sorry I laughed at you becoming a nun." Miss Kitty sounded sincere.

"I really am going to do it."

"No sex?"

"You learn not to need it."

"They'd have to cut me off at the neck and sew my mouth shut. Want to know how I found you?" She'd given herself a good name. A big cat playing with little mouse Beck. Ignoring Miss Kitty was easier than standing up to her.

Beck did want to know *that* at least. "If you wish to tell me."

"Oh, I wish, I wish. I called the club, got the number for the band's management. All they said was Butch played in a band in Brooklyn–bit of a dead-end. They gave me the name of the band. I got in touch with some guy named Robbie who told me all about you and Butch?"

A rush of concern tightened her stomach. "What did he say?"

"That you're stuck up." Miss Kitty delivered the hurt in a calm, reporting a fact.

Beck blinked rapidly, hurt spreading down her throat. "He did?"

"In so many words. And that's how I found you."

Beck's gaze dropped to the floor. She'd thought they were her friends. She didn't mean to be stuck up. Just because she didn't let him go too far on the beach. Panda was right. Boys were just waiting to lie about you.

Miss Kitty's voice dropped to a worrisome tone. "Robbie says, it's pretty heavy what Butch is going through."

Did she want to know? Wasn't her promise not to have anything more to do with Randall Malloy? But her concern for him overrode her caution.

"I pray for him."

"Yeah, that should do it. You write to him?"

"I think it better if I didn't."

"Does he know?"

Miss Kitty was the most intrusive person she'd ever known.

"No! He must never know."

"I won't tell him."

Beck sighed heavily into the receiver. "Maybe he already knows." As much as she resented Miss Kitty's prying, to be able to talk to someone who knew the secret bridged the spinning wheel of her internal conversations to a live dimension.

Miss Kitty agreed that L'Ecole was a flimsy cover. "People believe what they want to believe. If they want to think you got knocked up, they'll think it. My mom, some people, you could tell them I went to the moon and she'd believe you."

"What did you tell Robbie about me?" Beck mustered the nerve to ask.

"I told him I'd met you in Europe and that you'd told me about Butch. Clever, *huh*?"

"Very."

"He wanted to know all about what you were doing in France."

Beck leaned forward and raised her shoulders. "What did you tell him?"

"That you'd run away and was now a hooker in Marseilles," Miss Kitty said in the same deadpan reporting-the-facts voice.

The girl was so outrageous Beck couldn't help but giggle.

"What was that I heard? Gaiety? Mirth? I'm afraid I'm going to have to report you to the Sacred Order of Misery for this infraction. I'm sorry to inform you that you no longer qualify for service as a nun or for a piece of candy."

She had Beck going. Miss Kitty had a devilish way of making her laugh. "You may be closer than you think. I had a dream in Rome where I was a prostitute."

"Really?"

It was good to have a friend to talk to, someone you could tell anything. She might as well trust Miss Kitty. It wasn't as if the wild girl didn't already have enough to ruin Beck if that was her intent.

"What you need is a vacation. Come on up to Connecticut."

"I'm going to the beach with my family."

"I've got a family, a big family. You'll love them and they'll love you. You can be here in a few hours. You want me to come down there and get you."

"No!"

"Well, if you insist."

"Please, that's a terrible idea.

"Are you ashamed of me?"

"I just don't think it's a good idea."

"Why? I'll be able to tell the same lies. Two are better than one."

"It's against the rules."

"Whose rules? What's L'Ecole going to do, kick us out?"

"They kicked me out?"

"What happened?"

Lost in a maze of lies, Miss Kitty was a compass of truth. Despite the blackmail and risk, she was a prized friend.

* * *

Four days later, Beck was awakened by her father's knock. By the time she'd dressed, he was seated at the table with his back to the bar and cabinets that separated the dining room from the living room. Sunrise glowed through large windows positioned to view the lake. Her habit of early rising had come from childhood when the best time to spend with him was breakfast before he left for work.

She sat where Janey had set Raisin Bran cereal at her place with an empty bowl and pitcher of milk.

"I've received a letter concerning you."

He handed the pink sheets to her.

August 2, 1967

Dear Senator Lyons:

I am writing to invite your daughter Beck to visit our home in Greenwich.

I am a great admirer of you and of your family. It will be a delight to have your daughter as the guest of our daughter, Jacqueline.

Sincerely,

Emma McKenna

"How do you know Jacqueline McKenna? They are a very prominent family."

Miss Kitty's family was prominent in the Leader's eyes? Who would have ever thought? If he knew the fraud of the France story, she'd be compounding the lie by saying where she'd met Miss Kitty.

Beck looked down and shrugged. "From school." She didn't say which school.

"We'll be at the beach. Your grandparents will be joining us. If you'd rather go to Greenwich that's fine with me."

NINETEEN

MERCURY RECORDS

B eck flew to LaGuardia on the Eastern shuttle and caught a limo to Greenwich where Miss Kitty picked her up in an open-top Jeep. Seeing her, the energy and warmth, the hugs and exclamations made Beck happy she'd come. Her pleasure at the reunion lasted until the suicidal pace Miss Kitty drove on the narrow roads past estates so large you could barely see the mansions. Beck held onto the door handle, eyes wide with terror, sure they were going to die.

Miss Kitty swerved into a long driveway bordered with fieldstone walls. An old dock reached into a pond that did not look as was well-used as the docks at Lake Barcroft. A central colonial structure with wings and floors added over generations was surrounded by rocky lawns and woods.

Beck was expecting a horrible environment to have produced someone as disturbed as Miss Kitty. Instead, she found a lively, full family life she'd imagined during her lonely days as an only child. Miss Kitty was right that Beck loved her family and they her. Miss Kitty was the oldest of seven children. Emma, her mother, had dark hair, a full figure and broad face highlighted by sparkling eyes. She spoke in a soft voice and seemed happy holding several children on her lap. Miss Kitty's father had met Emma at a high school dance. Beck had the impression that Emma had brought her own family fortune. Each of the two brothers and four sisters ranging from infants to teenagers had distinct personalities and vied for Beck's attention. Emma was pleased to have Beck provide interest to her children during their summer vacation. Miss Kitty's father, a redhead like her, would honk his car horn when he arrived home from work in a new burgundy Jaguar. The younger children would race and clamor to be the one to sit in his lap and steer the short distance to the garage.

"I used to run out," Miss Kitty said. "I got tired of winning."

Miss Kitty lived in two rooms off the kitchen above the carport. Beck slept in a paneled room with a brown shag rug where Miss Kitty had her stereo, record collection and posters of movie stars.

"Come on, I'll show you the scene of the crime."

Miss Kitty led her across a lawn littered with children's toys, swings and climbing structures, past a swimming pool and gazebo into the woods. "Don't worry. He's not there anymore," Miss Kitty said ominously.

They came to an old child's fort built of discarded lumber, furnished with cast-off patio furniture. "Here it is, our little love nest. I learned a lot here."

"Why did you do it?" Beck immediately regretted asking the question.

Miss Kitty's skin reddened. "Why did you do it?"

"Love," Beck said weakly.

Miss Kitty looked through the woods where a neighbor's Tudor style house could be seen. Sunlight through the leaves partially highlighted freckles on her pale skin. "I started babysitting. You know me and my mouth. Carmine called my bluff. Listen, I shouldn't be telling you this. He said he'd kill me if I ever told anyone. I'm sure he's Mafia."

"I didn't ask you to tell me," Beck stated the obvious, but then felt bad seeing Miss Kitty frown. "I know we can tell each other things, we couldn't tell anyone else."

Miss Kitty brightened and looked at Beck with a sparkle in her eyes. "Yeah, we need that. I do love you, you know."

Beck sighed. "Love you," she said but knew she wouldn't be here if not for Miss Kitty's aggressive bullying.

* * *

The third day of her visit, a Rolling Stones record was playing. Miss Kitty looked at her breasts in a mirror. "At least I didn't have to nurse. They look all right don't they?"

Miss Kitty had a large body. Everything about her seemed exaggerated to Beck. Embarrassed by Miss Kitty's nudity, Beck looked away.

Miss Kitty attached a red balconette bra and put on her blouse. "Sure you don't want to come? You might have some fun."

"No thanks."

A car horn honked. Miss Kitty looked outside. "Come on," she said to Beck.

"No, I'll stay here, I'm tired."

"Tomorrow, I'm going into the city. You're going to come, aren't you?"

"To do what?"

"Get a profession. We'll take the train."

Beck relaxed when Miss Kitty was gone. She turned off the record player and listened to the sounds of the insects and birds. She wondered how someone could come from this serenity and be as unsatisfied and disruptive as Miss Kitty.

* * *

Beck had been asleep for hours when Miss Kitty returned. In the morning, she was awake before Beck. Amazing how much energy Miss Kitty had—how little sleep she needed. They ate honeydew melon on a glass table near the pool. A covered silver rasher of bacon was set on the table by a maid. Beck was excited to be going back to the city. She wanted to go to the Museum of Modern Art.

Miss Kitty didn't dress as if she was going to a job interview. She wore tight jeans rolled up above her ankle over snakeskin clogs, and a black silk boat neck shirt beneath a studded silk bomber jacket. Beck dressed as if she was going to an event with her father in a conservative summer pinafore and flats.

They rode a train carrying the last wave of morning commuters and arrived at Grand Central Terminal at 10:30 in the morning. As they walked north on 41st, Beck compared how she'd felt the last time she'd walked the streets of Manhattan when her grandmother had left her alone. Maybe she *had* changed. Her life *was* improving. Her good humor lasted until Miss Kitty said. "Let's go to L'Ecole."

Beck stopped amid the crowd, ready to abandon Miss Kitty and find a way back to Virginia.

Miss Kitty laughed. "Just kidding. Jeez, you take everything I say so literally."

"You like to distress me, don't you?"

Miss Kitty clenched her fist as she'd done the first time Beck had encountered her. "You want to fight? Go on, put 'em up."

Beck smiled. "At least Mr. J. would be happy to see us."

Miss Kitty put her arm on Beck's shoulder. "That's it, relax. We're here to do some business. I have no interest in ever going back to jail. Let's just forget the whole deal, OK?"

"I want to trust you."

"You *have* to trust me. I'm the only one who really knows you," Miss Kitty said and turned up 42nd toward Broadway.

As Beck walked beside her, she had to admit the distressing truth that people who professed to love her wanted to control her. Where in her future would she be free to lead her own life, find her own future? At least Miss Kitty offered a more exciting and unpredictable alternative than Panda and her father. Beck smiled and quickened her step to keep up, curious to discover what adventure or misadventure Miss Kitty had in store. "What kind of job are you trying to get?" she asked.

"We're going to get jobs in the record business. If an idiot like Patuchi can do it, we'll do great."

"I have to finish school, you know."

"Not me. I'm done with school."

"Don't you want to go to college?"

"Boring. It's the music business for me."

What was it about music that made young people so sure that is what they wanted to or could do? Both Randall and Miss Kitty were certain of their choices, willing to abandon traditional life paths. Maybe someday she might try to do something in music. Panda expected her to be a proper wife to a great man. Music would certainly be different than anything her family had ever projected for her.

Miss Kitty led her through the squalor of Times Square to the church-like golden art deco entrance to the Brill Building. The intense redhead examined the list of over a hundred offices of music publishers, agents, and record companies. Beck suspected she had no idea how to get a job in the music business and no interviews lined up. Beck was there to act as a foil and keep Miss Kitty going forward.

Blackfriars Records treated them like teen fans. A receptionist gave them a magazine and an autographed picture of an act Beck had never heard of, which they left on a bench beside the elevator.

"It's going to happen. We have to aim higher, go to a real record company." Miss Kitty led her back to Broadway to the offices of Mercury Records.

A heavily made-up Spanish-looking woman with a beehive hairdo looked at them suspiciously. Her desk was surfaced with shiny metal strips. An exposed black stairway curved to a second floor. On the walls around a seating area were pictures of old crooners, Negro and Latin, jazz, rock.

"We're here to see Mr. Gibson," Miss Kitty said.

"Is he expecting you?"

Miss Kitty said, "Our father, Senator Lyons, suggested we stop by to see him."

"Who?" the receptionist asked.

"Majority Leader Richard Lyons," Miss Kitty slowly repeated the lie, and then quickly winked at Beck with an amused expression.

Miss Kitty wasn't going to get a job because of her father. What if he found out? Beck leaned toward the door, again on the verge of abandoning Miss Kitty. She lingered only to make sure Miss Kitty didn't make ill use of her father's name.

The receptionist spoke into her telephone.

"Don't you use my father's name," Beck whispered harshly at Miss Kitty.

"Connections. Got to use connections," Miss Kitty said loud enough for the receptionist to hear.

A woman came down the stairs that rose from the lobby. "Hello, I'm Mr. Gibson's personal assistant."

Miss Kitty pumped her extended hand. Beck quickly dropped the assistant's offered hand and looked down, mortified to be identified with this crazy caper.

"Mr. Gibson is busy now, may I tell him what you want?"

"He's a friend of our father, Senator Lyons. We need to speak to Paul," Miss Kitty said.

"About?"

"This is a personal matter," Miss Kitty said.

"I'll see what I can do, if you would like to take a seat and wait," the assistant said and returned up the stairs.

Beck sat far enough away from Miss Kitty on fat stuffed furniture that someone might not think they were together.

"I hope he really does know your father," Miss Kitty said across the table separating them.

"Everyone knows my father."

Miss Kitty pawed through magazines and picked up a copy of Billboard, reading intently until the woman returned. "Mr. Gibson is very busy. He said to give your father his best."

Miss Kitty stood up and confronted the woman. "He's not my father, he's hers. Would you tell Mr. Gibson one more thing please?"

Beck was already up and moving toward the door.

"I'm sorry, you're really going to have to leave. This is an office and..."

"Tell him that Carmine Patuchi would like him to see us."

"Carmine?" The woman looked perplexed.

"Patuchi."

"You can call back and make an appointment. Have Mr. Patuchi or whoever..."

"We'll wait," Miss Kitty said and sat back down, defiant in the face of the woman's authority.

The assistant returned up the stairs, no doubt to call the police.

Bad enough using her father's name now Miss Kitty was using the name of a Mafioso who had threatened to kill her.

"Don't go," Miss Kitty said.

"I'll wait for you out front." Beck returned to the lobby to wait for Miss Kitty, saw no police going into the building, and worried about what else Miss Kitty might be saying or doing. After fifteen minutes, Beck rode the elevator to the Mercury Records' floor. Through glass doors she saw Miss Kitty reading in the reception area as if she'd wait all day.

A man walked down the circular staircase in the office and approached Miss Kitty. He had a narrow face, a tired expression heightened by darkness under his eyes, dressed in a suit that needed pressing. An untightened tie hung from his collar.

Beck backed away to the elevators again.

Miss Kitty came out of the lobby. "Come on, we're in." She pulled Beck toward the entrance.

Paul Gibson escorted them up the circular stairs, down a hallway lined with pictures and framed gold records into a large office with a view of a dark gorge formed by sheer mortar walls.

"How do you know Patuchi?" Gibson spoke with a New York accent.

"We are very intimate," Miss Kitty said.

"Seen him lately?" Gibson asked.

"Lately enough," Miss Kitty said.

The way Miss Kitty talked to adults amazed Beck. The crazy girl wasn't intimidated by anyone.

"Have a seat."

Beck sat beside Miss Kitty in a matching leather chair.

Gibson leaned against the edge of his desk. Piles of new records were stacked on a table beside the tallest record player Beck had never seen. Large speakers hung from the ceiling facing the desk.

"And whose father is Richard Lyons?" Paul Gibson asked.

"Hers." Miss Kitty looked at Beck.

Beck swallowed words that her father didn't know they were here and leaned forward ready to leave.

"I met your father once at a dinner for John Kennedy," Gibson said to her.

"That's nice," she lamely said.

"What can I do for you?" Gibson asked.

"We want to work for you," Miss Kitty said.

"Doing...?

"You know, making records."

"What do you know about the record business?"

"I know what sucks and what doesn't."

Beck's eyes darted to Miss Kitty, again shocked by her public use of foul language in front of an adult.

Paul Gibson did not appear to care. He smiled, "So you want to do A&R?"

Miss Kitty looked at him suspiciously, as if Paul Gibson had asked if she wanted to do what Carmine Patuchi had asked her to do.

Gibson patiently explained, "That's where you go out to clubs and listen to acts. It would mean staying up late. Think your parents would permit that?"

Beck shook her head but Miss Kitty said, "I'm a liberated woman. I go where I want when I want."

Gibson smiled. "Well, you certainly have the attitude for the job."

His phone rang and he went back behind his desk, answered the phone and appeared to be ignoring them as he talked about a contract with David Bowie.

Miss Kitty remained seated in the office as if she'd stay until dragged out unless Gibson gave her a job.

Gibson looked at them as if remembering they were in his office. "Give them the offer," he said, hung up, and remained behind his desk.

"What about you?" he asked Beck.

"I'm still in high school. I don't really think that I can..."

"She's just here to give me immoral support."

Gibson laughed. "You got ID? You over 18?"

Beck shook her head no.

"Got it right here," Miss Kitty held up her pocketbook and stood up ready to show him.

Beck rose ready to be thrown out.

"OK, go down the hall to the last door on the right. Ask for Danny in the A&R department. See if he'll give you a shot."

Miss Kitty beamed, excitement radiating from her eyes. "I'll tell him you sent me."

Gibson nodded. "OK, tell him I sent you."

"You won't regret this," Miss Kitty extended her hand across the desk and shook on her first music deal.

TWENTY

A GOOD GIRL

D eep apprehension disrupted her focus on the problems of chemical bonding. Saturday morning was too distant from the Monday test. She'd keep her place at the top of her class with a late Sunday night study binge.

What if Randall was already dead? Would she hear from his mother that he'd been killed in combat?

Beck's English teacher—a blasphemous Scot—had lectured last week that irony was the laugh God made when you told Him your plans. What were her plans? She'd not found Theresa. Was her calling to be a nun only one of God's laughs revealed in the truth that she longed for Randall?

She intertwined the rosary the Pope had given her and searched for strength in the sight of her Bible and the Encyclopedia of Catholic Saints lying on her desk, to the Madonna on the wall.

She said a prayer for Randall, her daughter, herself. "Strength was God. Certainty was His," she whispered.

The prayers did not restore confidence. She was a misplaced word wrenched from a forgotten sentence–a captive in a land of shadows. Faith, she must keep her focus on God, and obey His will, she lectured herself.

Janey ate a sandwich in the breakfast nook. A small black and white television that had once been in the recreation room was tuned to a soap opera. Beck poured herself a glass of orange juice and returned the waxed container back to the refrigerator. On the television, she watched a pretty young woman sobbing on the shoulder of an elderly lady. "But Nana, I love him." Beck sat by Janey and listened to the advice. "You have your whole life before you. You'll find someone else." *No I won't,* Beck said to herself.

She put on a jacket and walked up the flagstone path to the road toward Beach One. The feel of the air, the look of the neighborhood at the end of fall when the houses stood unshielded by naked trees, promised the harshness of winter. A blue and white mail truck moved incrementally forward without a letter for her from Randall. He'd given up writing when she'd never responded.

Beck shouldn't have been on the road when the mail was delivered. Randall's mother came down their steep driveway as eager as she would have been to receive a letter from Randall. Beck resisted the urge to turn away.

A fraud, she returned Mrs. Malloy's wave, hiding her granddaughter.

They met beside a dark green juniper. Beck said she was fine and school was good.

"Let's see if Randall wrote," Mrs. Malloy said.

Beck watched her remove the stack of envelopes and their eyes settled on a thin blue envelope–evidence that Randall had been alive.

"Do you write him?" Mrs. Malloy asked.

"No. Goodbye." She turned her back to the woman, the coldness pure Panda when dismissing someone beneath her.

Beck was an adult now, defending what was personal. Better to be rude than revealing.

* * *

In June, she received her own letter from Randall wishing her a happy birthday. He wrote as if there was no gap in their relationship, ignoring her cut.

Saigon is a city with a serious attitude. This rich lady who owns a bar where I sat in with a band took me to this kind of seance. Not only do they talk to the dead, but they hand around pots of money like that's how to make the dead feel better or something. Very strange, but rewarding, since I have good "ja" or something like that and when they gave me money the spirits really seemed to like it. The money had to be new money."

Beck read the letter repeatedly savoring his words, *"I guess you know how I feel about you. You are so much more interesting to me than anyone else I've met. Your memory helps me keep things in perspective.*

His words were a mystery she wouldn't clarify with a response. Was he fighting in the jungle, his life in danger or playing in bars in Saigon? Was there really only one love, and if there was, would Randall know he was her only love if she never spoke to him again?

* * *

Her other grandparents, her mother's parents, gave her a trip to New York and two Broadway tickets for her birthday. Beck wasn't sure who to invite but settled on Sonia-Barton.

The bellboy set their bags on the wooden luggage stands at the end of the two double beds. Beck tipped him a dollar for each bag. The bellboy was young but acted as if Beck and Sonia-Barton were older, calling them "ma'am." The room was hardly the suite she stayed in with her father or Panda, but it was the Pierre. Beck was showing Sonia-Barton she could have a good time. That night they were going to meet Miss Kitty. Beck had the apprehension of daring. The idea of Sonia-Barton and Miss Kitty meeting was to contemplate the mixing of two dangerous chemicals that could blow up in her face.

She went to the window and looked over the park. Last year when she'd arrived in the city, she might as well have been six years old as lonely as she'd felt. Now, she was to return in the fall to attend Bernard College. The chance to be anonymous, to disappear into the mass of so many people appealed to her.

Eleven that night they went to meet Miss Kitty at the Cafe au Go Go on Bleeker Street.

Beck showed her Virginia driving license to the doorman and for the first time was legally admitted to a bar. The room was cramped and narrow. Beck felt out of place and easily identified by her conservative blazer jacket over the all-round pleated print silk dress, her neat hair, her makeup a foundation with lipsticks and eyeliner.

She scanned the crowd and saw Miss Kitty up against the bar, dressed in a toga style dress and a pair of sandals laced up around her ankles. A very handsome man stood close to her as if they were together.

"Back for more fun and games, I see," Miss Kitty hugged Beck and barely glanced at Sonia-Barton, treating her like an unsophisticate. "I'm glad you're here." Miss Kitty waved at someone. "I have to run over to the Bottom Line and catch an act. It shouldn't take long, but I promised I'd show. You might as well wait here. I'll be back in a half-hour."

After she was gone, a small, worried-looking man came up to them.

"How ya' doing?" His shirt was open at the collar as if proud of the small tufts of chest hair. A limp handshake matched the lackadaisical manner with which he spoke. "I'm the band's manager. Name's Joey. You know Kitty?"

It was odd to hear someone use her nickname as if something had escaped the confines of L'Ecole, an inside joke carried out into the world.

Beck spoke loudly over the sound of the tightly packed room. "She'll be right back."

Joey nodded. "Come on over. I got a table by the door. We can wait for her together."

The band was playing blues influenced with distorted guitars and an aggressive beat. The singer was tall and skinny, stomach muscles ridged under an open vest. Beck preferred prettier songs, but the band was exciting and the audience looking over each other's shoulders was appreciative. She began to tap her foot and sway to the rhythm.

"What do think of the band?" Joey asked Sonia-Barton and then Beck as if he was not sure that Beck had heard.

"I like them," Beck said.

"A lot?" Joey asked with a tense expression.

"Sure, very nice."

"Tell your friend Miss Kitty that she oughta sign them."

Beck wasn't sure what he meant.

He leaned over the table. A diamond pendant hung below his shirt. "They're going to be big. I wouldn't be fucking with them if I did not truly believe that they were going to be truly fucking big."

Sonia-Barton laughed, eyes wide with wonder and excitement.

"Want to meet the band? They're called the Autotunes, you know, like cartoons but spelled like tune. I'll be happy to introduce them to you at their next break."

Beck was used to people paying special attention to them because of her father. The exposure to the music world was different. Beck smiled to see how eagerly Sonia-Barton agreed to meeting the band.

* * *

Miss Kitty returned and Joey stood to give her the seat beside Beck.

"Sasha," Miss Kitty said to the man with her, "would you be very gallant and see about a black Russian for me and for you?" she asked Beck.

"Coffee, please," Beck said.

"I'll have a black Russian too." Sonia-Barton forced herself into the request.

"*Bien, cherie*," he spoke French with a Slavic accent.

"Ain't that poetic." Miss Kitty leaned over to follow his movement through the crowd. "Russian dancer, defected last year. Ain't nothing defective about that man."

Joey hovered as if waiting for a moment to speak.

Miss Kitty glanced over her shoulder at him. "How ya hangin', Joey? You got anything truly fucking big yet?"

"So you finally came to see the Autotunes," he said.

"The out of tunes is more like it," Miss Kitty sneered and ignored him while he went to the band and whispered to the lead singer. The band launched into the best song they'd played yet. The singer arched his back and squeezed his eyes as he sang. The drummer twirled drumsticks in the air between beats.

"They're pretty good," Sonia-Barton said, which caused Joey, who'd returned to stand behind Miss Kitty, to say, "Yeah, real good, fucking great."

Miss Kitty didn't comment. Sonia-Barton leaned forward and smiled happily. Beck saw how impressed Sonia-Barton was by Miss Kitty.

After working the crowd into appreciation for their music and effort, the band stopped for a break and the singer came to their table.

"Miss Kitty, A&R Mercury." Joey proved his worth to the singer.

"Glad, really glad." The singer seemed as eager to meet Miss Kitty as the girls in the club whose eyes followed him were eager to meet him.

"Sit down," Joey said.

The singer squeezed in beside Sonia-Barton who didn't seem to mind, while Joey stood over his shoulder.

"Sorry about the sweat," the singer said over the sound of the recorded music.

"Sweetheart, we like men who sweat," Miss Kitty said.

Sonia-Barton giggled and rubbed her shoulders against the singer.

Miss Kitty asked where he was from, how long the band had been together. "Ever been in the studio?"

"Not much."

"That's all right, we've signed acts we've heard singing on street corners." Miss Kitty winked at Beck.

Poor Joey, the singer and Sonia-Barton were taking her seriously. Sad that Miss Kitty teased others the way she played with her. Miss Kitty seemed to think that just because she didn't take anything seriously, nobody else did either.

Nearly three in the morning, Beck and Sonia-Barton sat squashed next to Sasha and Miss Kitty in the back of a taxi.

"Did you know that Beck could have a job doing this?" Miss Kitty asked Sonia-Barton.

"I'll do it," Sonia-Barton said.

"No, the record company really likes Beck. I'm serious," Miss Kitty said.

"How do they know Beck?" Sonia-Barton asked.

This was the interaction Beck had dreaded when putting Miss Kitty and her stepsister together. Why did she trust Miss Kitty when she was waiting for the moment she'd betray her?

"Didn't she tell you? When she visited me last summer we went to an interview together. Beck really wowed them."

Sonia-Barton leaned over to look at Beck, "She did?"

"I didn't do anything. I just watched."

"Yeah, but they liked you," Miss Kitty repeated.

"I don't know why," Beck said.

The uniformed attendant opened the cab door at the hotel.

"I'll call you," Miss Kitty said, and drove off with her Russian dancer.

"Gawd! This is a total blast!" Sonia-Barton looked at Beck with new admiration. "I'd quit Tulane in a minute and burn rubber to get up here for a job like this."

"Don't believe everything Miss Kitty says. She makes things up."

"You met her in France?"

Beck nodded in a vague way unsure if *France* was code for where she went to have her baby.

They rode up in the polished wood and mirrored elevator to the fifth floor.

"If you don't want to do it, tell them about me," Sonia-Barton continued to press as if Beck could really get her a job hanging out in clubs with Russian dancers looking for bands to sign to contracts.

"Maybe next summer."

Tables turned, Beck the more experienced worldly one–a fake–distant, fearful in a world of illusion. She wouldn't explore the unknown, leave the guidelines that defined who she was and what she should be. She admired, even envied the courage to be different, the feeling of stepping off a ledge into a depth she could not judge. Not her–she clearly was and wanted to be–a good girl.

But she knew her greatest temptation was coming home.

TWENTY-ONE

LIVING THE LIE

H er personal habits deteriorated. She slept during the day, watched the Tonight Show before walking to Beach One to sit on the sloping lawn–waiting for Randall.

Self-awareness was scorn. She came to this spot without a plan or knowing when he'd return to Lake Barcroft. Alone in the shadows of a netherworld of ghosts and repeated conversations, she'd imagine cutting him off. Then with a wave of emotion, she'd be loving him, sharing everything.

With an absent swat at a mosquito whining by her ear, she stirred the humid August air. Low, night clucking of geese floating on the lake came from the dark. A taxi drove down the entrance through the night. Randall was home.

Her lashes fluttered and a tremor reached down her arms. Emotions swept through her body tightening her stomach to the point of pain, trapping air in her constricted lungs to be cast out with a deep sigh. The reality of what she'd been waiting for now seemed an intrusion on a dream. She breathed deeper and followed the domed car climbing toward his house. Was she capable of not speaking to him, when all she did was talk to him in the loop of obsession that fed her mania?

Unable to resist, she stalked the edge of Lakeview Drive in the shadows of shrubs and trees, hating her weakness, her craven need to see him. She pressed against the Miller's three-rail fence and looked into the tall windows atop the hill—a lit stage of the return of Randall, their only child home from war—joy, pride, and relief of which she could be no part. Mrs. Malloy hands pressed together leaned into Randall as if unable to keep her arms from him. The Colonel stood proud and erect looking eye-to-eye, man-to-man, soldier-to-soldier with his son.

She turned away, head down, her lip twisted with self-loathing.

Before dawn she rose from her bed, didn't stop to dress. Her sleeping shirt hung over her breasts mid-level to her hips. She purposely walked barefoot to his house. Doors were not locked at Lake Barcroft. She went into the private domain of the sleeping and opened his bedroom door.

He was on the bed in a lotus position—muscular beyond her imagination, naked, eyes closed, fingers in the position of the lotus, forefinger to thumb, feet crossed beneath angled knees. She reached out to touch his cheek. She froze when his eyes shot open. For an instant they stared at each other.

"I...I dream," she said and remembered nothing until she woke in her bed.

The dream had the presence of reality, but then so did the memory of so many dreams. She checked her feet and they were soiled by the road. Had she walked out that night? Had she gone to his bedroom? The memory was faint with age, a glimmer of recall. Weakness caused her shoulders to slump. He would think her ill, stuck up and crazy. She took a deep breath and told herself she was better than that no matter what Randall thought.

* * *

Though she waited all day, flinched when the telephone rang, then shrank into a ball of depression and hatefulness of her weakness when he didn't come over. She stared at the phone and thought of excuses, what she would say if she called to welcome him home.

With a growing fear of what she might confess, she packed a quick bag of toiletries and fled to the beach house. He would come to her room tonight, or he wouldn't. He'd understand she didn't want to see him, their separation complete and lifelong. Let him have the memory of a good friend, a first lover, not the stolid truth of L'Ecole and Theresa.

As she drove down I-95, she told herself she'd grow. Distance and strength is what she must have.

* * *

With barely time to pack for her first semester at Bernard she returned from Virginia Beach.

"Randall been round to see you," Janey said in the kitchen with the wary approach she used since Beck had become strange.

"That's nice," Beck said and poured herself a glass of orange juice.

"Hear from their maid at church, he's going to out in California until he's out of the army."

"Marines," Beck corrected her with a hint of pride in her voice. She couldn't hide from Janey but carried on the charade of indifference because she must, or she'd falter and give into selfish desire. "Got to go pack some more."

"Sho, sho," The maid's shiny forehead contracted as she watched Beck leave the kitchen.

* * *

That night in a waking dream, she walked to Beach One with the feeling she was leading him. Why would he come to her? She'd not answered his letters, made no acknowledgement of his homecoming.

She sat on the slope of the lawn and trembled in anticipation. She felt the dew on the grass against her thigh. This was not a dream. She was here and he was coming.

The shadow of a figure walked like a stalking cat by the stand of canoes at the dark edge of the beach.

She looked down and closed her eyes. If this was a dream, then he wouldn't be there when she looked up. She didn't want him to see her like this, but when would she ever not be like *this*? She glanced to the hidden center of the lake and back at the clear shape of him, now close. She closed her eyes and suppressed bolts of energy coursing through her.

"Hey, Beck," he said as casually as if they'd only been apart for hours, not a lifetime of change.

"Randall." She breathed his name with a tremor, tentacles of emotion twisting in her.

"How you been? Missed you."

She was a pure-bred politician. She could handle this.

"So nice to see, Randall." She pulled her shoulders together into a near shrug. "What are you doing out here at this hour?"

"Followed you." He grinned. "Learned some things in the Marines."

She smiled in their old way of joking. "You could have killed me."

He frowned. She'd touched a spot not for joking.

"Yeah, they taught us that for sure."

"I'm sorry I shouldn't been light about that."

He raised hands in helplessness. She had seen him in his room last night, muscular, full, a killer. She wanted to touch him.

She stood and faced him before he could sit next to her and force her to stay, to talk. They were nearly the same height and she met his stare. "Glad you're back."

"I made it. Now, I want to forget it."

"I'm glad you're home, safe."

"I got another nine months, teaching at Pendleton. Turns out I'm a pretty good leatherneck. But hey, what are we talking about that shit for?" He reached for her and she jumped back as if was trying to kill her.

"Please don't ever touch me." Her voice was cold, Panda-like.

In the moonlight, she saw the hunter in his narrowed eyes.

"What happened, Beck? What happened to you?" His voice was low with a rasp.

"That is none of your business."

"Bullshit." He loomed dangerously over her.

She crouched. "Leave me alone."

"No." He seized her upper arm and pulled her to him. "Tell me."

She wrenched away. "Touch me again and I'll have you arrested. You understand that?"

He furrowed his eyes in an expression between humor and anger, before settling into a frown. "Yeah, should have gotten the message. People change."

"Good night and don't bother me again."

She turned and ran before he could hear her sob.

Wake up, wake up. Dream yourself back. She ran through a mirror reflecting another mirror, the images stacking back into infinity, all the times they'd been together.

He was the French sailor. If she'd been a whore in a past life, she wanted to make it up to him, explain why she'd give up honesty and truth.

She sorted through what was real and what she'd dreamed. Had she been a whore? Had Randall returned? Confusion kept her awake. Some day she would ask him—did I come to your room? Did I see you on the beach when you came home? He and Robbie would say how stuck up she was, acting too good for them. He would pity her, find someone honest to love.

Tell him you love him this time, she told herself as she waited for sleep to be with Randall again. She forced her thoughts to the lessons of L'Ecole. God forgives her. She must accept responsibility for her actions. Some lies are for good. *St. Thérèse guide me to merciful love.*

TWENTY-TWO

THE HOMESTEAD

S onia-Barton's voice rang with pride as if she'd accomplished a daring feat, "I invited Kitty to the Homestead,"

Every New Year, Panda's side of the family gathered for a reunion at the Virginia mountain resort–no place for Miss Kitty.

Seated on the edge of her bed, barely home an hour on her first Christmas break from Sarah Lawrence, Beck gripped the phone more tightly. Imminent disaster was near, twisting her nerves, eyes lowered in consternation. What chickens were coming home to roost now? "Is she coming?"

"She is!" Sonia-Barton drew out the *ssss* in her exaggerated Southern sorority glee. "Can you imagine? That's going to liven up that scene. Hew-wee."

This disaster in the making was her fault for putting Miss Kitty and Sonia-Barton together–for letting Randall get her pregnant. Beck's voice was disparaging. "You don't know me at all do you?"

"Well what do you mean? She's the one person I know who *can* liven you up."

"Who said livening me up is anybody's business? Sonia-Barton, are you trying to torture me? I'll be a nervous wreck. You don't know these people. They are quiet, dignified."

"They a bunch bores."

"You have no idea the trouble Miss Kitty can cause."

"Oh yeah I do. That's the whole idea."

Beck looked to the book of Saints. *Lord, deliver me. Constant love.*

"The Leader already said it was all right. Yeah, I told him she was your friend from France, the one you visited in Greenwich."

Beck was convinced that mention of *France* was code by Sonia-Barton that everyone knew she'd not really been in France. Did that include her father? Was this proof he believed she'd been in France for the year? Why would he not ask Beck if she wanted to invite a friend? Suspicion and doubt swirled in her mind. What would Panda say when the Leader told her she had met Miss Kitty in France?

Beck was the good child amongst a pack of miscreants. Should she go along or try to stop the mischief?

"Besides, I want her to get me a job in New York this summer."

"She can't do that. I've told you, don't believe everything Miss Kitty tells you. She a trickster, mischievous."

"Well, I think she's a blast."

Miss Kitty at the Homestead would be exciting—dreadfully exciting. Beck would have to stop her. "I'll call her tell her she can't come."

"I'll pay for Miss Kitty if that's what you're worried about."

The hotel bill would inevitably go through Panda.

"It's not appropriate. You can come up to Sarah Lawrence. Stay with me in the dorm. You can see her then."

"Jeez. The only reason I'm going is because Mama insisted and I haven't seen her yet this holiday. This is going to be a big bore."

* * *

Perched in her usual telephoning spot at the top edge of her bed, Beck tried to be nice about uninviting Miss Kitty. "This might not be the best place for us to see each other. I'll be back in New York in January."

Miss Kitty was not going to make her task easier. "You know my family. I want to meet the Senator. It puts us in context."

"That's not the only context that puts us in. Where are we going to say we met?"

"In New York."

Beck's shoulders hunched. "No. Sonia-Barton and my father think we met in France."

"OK, we met in France."

"I get tired of these lies."

"So what's your grandmother going to say if she knows we met at L'Ecole? She says anything, she blows her own story. I'm looking forward to watching her squirm."

Cruel–not a way to spread God's love. "Don't. Don't say a word about L'Ecole to anyone."

"I won't. Promise."

Beck hesitated, her position weakening.

"Don't you want to see me?" Miss Kitty cajoled.

"I see you in New York all the time. You're doing this to torment me."

"Toughen you up."

"I don't need toughening up. Why do people think that?"

"Cause you're a punk."

"I don't want you to come."

"I'm coming. What are you going to do about it?"

The blood red veil of uncontrollable rage came over her. "I hate you!" She screamed and threw the phone, creating a dent in the shiny lacquer of her bureau.

When the trembling subsided, the weakness, the need to apologize came. Ten minutes later, Beck called Miss Kitty and relented. Beck *was* a punk, always afraid. She only dreamed courage. Was only strong when in a rage.

"We're going to tell the same story, right?"

"*Toujour ma chérie*. We're a sisterhood of bullshit."

Beck needed to mark the parameters of the lie. "How did you find out Randall's name?"

"Robbie. I asked him if you'd ever had a boyfriend. He told me the whole story."

"The whole story?"

"No," Miss Kitty said derisively.

"Robbie doesn't know?"

"Don't think so."

"How about Sonia-Barton?" Beck asked.

"You tell me."

Beck raised her eyes to the ceiling and shrugged. "She implies everyone knows."

"Did you ask her?"

"No, it's like everyone is being too polite to ask."

"Yeah, same here. My father is the only one I know who knows. Listen, if they're not going to talk about it, why should we? Maybe nobody is talking about it because they don't give a crap. If they don't care why should we?"

"I don't ever want Randall to know."

"I see how that could be complicated. Look, let's make a deal, we never talk about it again. Let's bust out of L'Ecole once and for all."

If Beck only could, that was a pact she would join with joy and gratitude. But ruse to cover her pregnancy trapped her in a maze. She couldn't find her way out, could only imagine a life where her paths were open and of her own choosing.

"Don't worry. I'm the heiress from Greenwich—the kind of person you're supposed to be associating with."

"Oh dear Jesus, you and Sonia-Barton together. I don't think the Homestead can handle it."

"We're going to find out."

"You're terrible."

"Terrible as I can be. Love you. See you soon."

* * *

The historic hotel and resort was built over natural hot springs in the Allegheny Mountains of Virginia. Thick snow covered the golf course and the surrounding mountains—old and worn down compared to the young ragged peaks in the West. A porch set with green painted wicker rocking chairs in spite of the freeze and snow ran in two directions from a central clock tower. Porters unloaded the car among other arriving and departing guests, skis, and baggage.

"Welcome back, Miss Beck," a doorman in a jacket with a mandarin collar greeted her and opened the door into the warmth—a scent of lavender, spice, and burning wood from the fireplaces lining the lobby, large as a downtown hotel yet with the ambiance of a comfortable country inn. The illusion was created with tastefully decorated subsets of small seating areas before individual fireplaces, coffee tables, sofas, and chairs upholstered with striped colonial patterns.

She'd barely unpacked when there was the sound of a key in the doorway. Beck turned in alarm, sure she'd locked the door. Of course her grandmother would have a key.

Panda bustled in. "I just wanted to see if you had arrived."

Beck recognized a parry before the thrust.

Panda looked at the two twin beds. "Is your guest here?"

"No, she'll be arriving tomorrow."

Panda shook her shoulders slightly. "I understand you told your father you met her in France." Her cadence built like a prosecutor.

"Yes," Beck said in barely a whisper.

"Does that mean what I think it does?"

"I have no idea of what you think?" Beck rose her chin. She tried to make the denial sound polite but there was sass in her voice.

"Is she from the school?"

Beck blinked. "I met her in New York."

Panda stepped closer causing Beck to lean back. "I do not like being taken for a fool."

"No one is taking you for a fool."

Panda squinted. "So, your friend knows and we are subject to blackmail. I am going to be keeping a very close eye on...what's her name? Miss Kitty? What kind of name is that?"

Panda must be getting her information secondhand from Gail and Sonia-Barton.

"Her name is Jacqueline McKenna. She's from one of the finest families in Greenwich."

"Catholic?" Panda was suspicious of all associations between Beck and Catholics since the Vatican.

"I don't know. Panda. I hope it will be all right. I really want it to be."

"How does Sonia-Barton know Jacqueline?"

"I introduced them at my birthday trip to New York."

Panda turned away and shook her head. "Sometimes, I think you are just stupid."

Beck's lower lip trembled, and she pulled herself more erect, forced strength into her voice, but sounded weak. "Please, don't talk to me that way."

Panda closed in, forcing Beck back until she was seated on the edge of the bed. "Have you told him?" She leaned over Beck, eyes boring into her, daring her to lie.

No doubt who *him* was. Beck pressed her hands together and lowered her gaze before looking up to plead, "I cut off Randall completely. I've told no one. I promise."

"Except for this Cat or whatever her name is. What about Sonia-Barton?"

"No, Miss...Jacqueline, won't tell her."

As if resigned to being at the mercy of others, Panda squinted and bored into Beck's eyes. "I'll be watching. Now get ready for dinner and meet me downstairs in fifteen minutes."

* * *

Whatever hope Beck had that Miss Kitty might play the part of a Greenwich socialite was dashed when she saw the New York hippie in the lobby the next morning. Hair parted in the middle like a red wave breaking over her big head and flowing down to her thick shoulders, dressed in a white full-length cashmere coat over a calico dress and buffalo hunter mid-calf leather boots, heavy Navajo squash necklace and matching silver and turquoise bracelets resting on her wrists, "Lynda Bird!" she cried and pulled Beck to her chest.

"That's Beck to you, please," she begged.

Miss Kitty looked around. "Where's the enemy?"

"Please, please," Beck leaned forward. "This is my family. Don't cause any trouble."

"*Moi?*" Miss Kitty looked perplexed. "I'm on a mission from God to spread light and joy in the darkness of the Lyons den."

Beck shook her head. "You're nuts."

"Fun, fun, fun. Let's go to the spa."

* * *

Miss Kitty calmed her somewhat when she dressed for dinner in a white Organdy fluted skirt with beaded jacket, a pearl choker. Combing her hair only made her curls spring out around her head so that she looked like a red lion prowling the social lambs.

Beck dressed in a pink blouse and blue blazer walked beside Miss Kitty into the large dining room. Columns and false balconies painted white with light green recesses lined the upper reaches of a three-story high ceiling that absorbed the din allowing for intimate conversations among the hundred diners. People she'd known all her life were looking, judging.

A portly black in a tuxedo calmly assigned tables with an authority born of many decisions. "Miss Beck, it's so nice to have you back. The family has already gathered." He extended his arm.

They crossed to a dignified but accessible distance from the dance floor where the Battles had their tables.

Panda sat beside her brother, Judge Harry Battle, who'd retired to live in a community adjacent to the Homestead. Their faces were flush with self-satisfaction in their health and status. "Here's our girl," Uncle Harry chuckled when he saw Beck.

As if not to be outdone, Panda radiated joy at seeing Beck. "Hello, my darling," she said.

Beck introduced Miss Kitty as Jacqueline McKenna from Greenwich, Connecticut, hoping the location would convey her social status.

The older and younger antagonists locked stares like two boxers probing for weakness. With an exaggerated accent bordering on British, Miss Kitty said, "How lovely of you to invite me."

Panda's eyes narrowed and her thin smile barely tipped the edges of mouth. "Pleasure," she said curtly.

They were seated at an adjoining table set for eight with Uncle Harry's daughter, Victoria Adams, her husband and their three children.

"Sit next to me," Sonia-Barton said to Miss Kitty.

Beck sat beside Ashley, Beck's nearest cousin by age at sixteen, a fan of Sonia-Barton.

A sommelier with a key hanging around his neck approached with a wine menu.

Miss Kitty ordered a double martini and a bottle of Foreau Clos Naudin.

The drinkers at the table Jack Adams, Sonia-Barton, and Miss Kitty enjoyed each other, laughing loudly and telling stories that seemed funnier to them than to the rest. When Ashley said she was studying at the Washington School of Ballet, Miss Kitty regaled her with stories of Sasha and the Moscow Ballet.

Beck caught more than one stern glance from Panda, but if anything Miss Kitty was acting reserved. And what exactly did Panda expect Beck to do about the loudness and obliviousness to her standards of polite behavior at the Homestead?

After dinner, like a worried parent ready to intervene, Beck trailed the good-timers to an area of the lobby that switched functions from afternoon teas to a bar. With a snifter of brandy on the piano, Miss Kitty loudly played and sang Danny Boy.

Beck hovered behind her and tried not to appear embarrassed as she saw Panda arch her back as she surveyed the spectacle from where she exited the dining room with her brother. Beck wasn't sure where the Catholics or Irish were on her social scale or there was a hierarchy in such depths of scorn. There was true appreciation for the song among the Adams. A few guests within hearing distance clapped when the song was done.

"I think that's enough," Beck tapped on Miss Kitty's shoulder.

"Want me to stop?"

Beck nodded. "I think you'd better."

"No, more," Ashley encouraged.

Miss Kitty smiled. "Maybe later." She popped up the bench. "Let's get our coats. I've rented a sleigh."

* * *

Beck relaxed into the seat of the sleigh. Red curled iron supported an open carriage facing the back of a great coat and hatted driver on a bench raised to see over the head and haunch of a Clydesdale. Moonlit snow on the golf course reflected in ivory highlights of sparkle and shadow. A cold wind rustled bare branches.

"Why are you so afraid of your grandmother. She is just a bully, you know."

Beck sighed and pulled a checkered tartan blanket over the ledge of their knees.

"You don't know her. She's complicated."

Miss Kitty turned her head to look at Beck. "What can they do to you?"

Beck shrugged. "Make me feel bad."

"Only you can make yourself feel bad."

"Please, no therapy. Let's just enjoy the ride."

Her plea had no more effect on deterring Miss Kitty than ever.

"If you let them make you sad, it's going to urge them on, particularly a sadist like you grandmother. She enjoys tormenting you."

Beck pulled her lips inward. "She means well."

"Don't they always. She's a dreadful old snob."

Panda's sense of order and proper behavior was a good foil for the longhair, let it rip culture Miss Kitty embraced.

"She's very proud of my father. She wants to protect him, that's all."

"And you're expendable."

Beck shrugged. "I suppose. She used to be nicer."

"Until her doll got herself knocked up."

"Don't be like her."

Miss Kitty looked at Beck with widened eyes. "What do you mean by that."

"You don't have to point to my faults."

"Sorry," Miss Kitty settled back into the leather seat and was quiet for a moment. "Do you know what evil is? Not that Christian claptrap about a fallen angel. It's right here, right now. It's people saying their doing what's best for you, sure about what's right. The difference is I want you to be yourself, not some prop in someone else's story."

"Who asked you to save me? I'll find my own way."

Miss Kitty blew out a stream of condensation from her pursed lips. "Don't be so afraid."

"That's what she says."

"Ha! If you ever got your courage up and confronted her she'd back down fast enough. All bullies do."

"Did you come here to pick on me? I see you all the time in New York. And why did you go through Sonia-Barton?"

"You're not making me feel very welcome."

The temperature seemed to drop. Beck pulled a scarf tighter around her neck and wondered if the driver in the red heavy livery coat and top hat could hear them. Would he report what he'd heard the senator's daughter say?

"You don't understand," Beck lowered her voice to a near whisper. Please let's don't talk about it here."

Miss Kitty shrugged. "Why not here of all places?"

Beck nodded at the back of the driver perched on a bench above them.

"Who the horse? Hey! You know what we're talking about?"

His coal colored face shined in the moonlight when he turned to them. "No ma'am."

"What's your name?"

"Jacob, ma'am." He turned forward to show he wasn't there to socialize.

"Hi Jacob. You know who this lovely lady sitting beside me is?" Miss Kitty said to his back.

He looked over his shoulder and smiled. "Yes'm I do. Known her since she was a little girl."

"Nice to see you, Jacob." Beck smiled but did not recognize him—just one of the many who worked at the Homestead.

"Nice to see you, Miss Beck."

Miss Kitty laughed a roar that belted across the fairway. "Miss Kitty and Miss Beck. Tales of the Old South."

She was right in her Yankee condescending way. Beck was part of the South—a culture of standards and discretion. The sleigh ride had turned into a trap. Beck smiled but her eyes were focused on dark shapes of trees. Did Sonia-Barton know about the pregnancy? Did Randall? How many people pretended to believe her charade, the stories, France. Her grandmother's fear of being exposed might be for naught. What if everybody knew and she was a liar that nobody believed? Her life moved in two worlds—reality, Randall, and the dream world of the lie.

* * *

Surprisingly, Miss Kitty appeared to have been waiting for the right moment to broach a delicate topic. Back in the security of their hotel room after the sleigh ride, Miss Kitty tossed her coat across a chair. Her expression softened. "Got something to tell you about Randall-boy. He's good. Really good, like Dylan good."

"Randall?"

"I think could pop him big. That cutie Robbie that I got your number from sent me a tape Butch made in Saigon. The label will flip over a guy like him—soldier and all—did his duty. They got enough of scruffy draft dodgers. I think I can sign him."

Beck breathed through her nose. Nothing would make Randall happier and even if she'd been horrible to him, she could do this for him in her own way. "That'd be nice."

"Just want to make sure it's OK with you. I mean I'm not trying to totally infiltrate your life."

Beck twisted her lips in a faint smile. "You're doing a good job of it. I'm not in touch with him. You know, the secret."

Miss Kitty looked at her with a sorrowful lilt of her eyes. "You gave him up for your family?"

Beck closed her eyes at the simplicity of the statement. "I guess. He'd hate me anyway when he found out I'd given away his daughter."

Miss Kitty heaved a sigh. "Oh, my darling. It's so much harder for you than me. I can't imagine."

Beck slapped her hands together in a manner her father did when making his final decision. "It's over and done. No looking back. Don't tell him, that's all I ask."

"I'm your friend, not his. This will be strictly business." Miss Kitty studied her for a moment, then hung her head to confess. "I don't want to be a bully."

"Then don't."

Beck was flummoxed by Miss Kitty's contrition. She saw genuine remorse in her downcast eyes and apologetic tone, but doubted she'd ever really change.

Miss Kitty enveloped her in one of her hugs that made Beck feel childish in comparison to the girl's strength and size. "I love you so much."

"Love you too," Beck said and lied. "Glad you're here."

Miss Kitty stepped back from the embrace. "You're not a punk really. You have your own kind of strength. Maybe it's first impressions, the way you took me down. I just think of you as someone powerful."

Beck blinked.

"You're such a good girl."

"I try to be."

The rebellious, non-conformer personality snapped back. "Well, I don't. Come on Sonia-Barton is waiting for us in the disco."

"Sounds like pure trouble. I'm meeting my uncle early for a breakfast. I have to go to bed."

"Jeez! Why do you like to sleep so much?"

"Are you going to leave me alone?"

"Why start now?"

"Please behave yourself," Beck begged as Miss Kitty headed to the door.

The prospect of sleep was always mixed with distrust of what kind of dream she'd have. Would she be strong, carefree or wander the hotel as a whore? Would she ever have the courage to be with Randall when awake?

TWENTY-THREE

SLEEPING

The Dream Reality Confusion diagnosis had been left untreated because people would think Richard Lyons' daughter was crazy. She'd been left to learn the difference between mind and body, sleep and waking on her own with no one to ask if she was right.

Wake now, it's only a dream–when the sweats and trembles grew too intense in a nightmare.

Stay, linger–when a tingling warmth bubbled down her spine upon a loving visit from Randall or hard to a remember message of comfort or warning from her mother.

The scratch of a key in the lock of Beck's hotel room barely awoke her. She sleepily thought Miss Kitty was returning.

"Thank god, you're here," Panda said.

The oddity of the visit and relief in her grandmother's voice indicated a dream. Beck's eyelids fluttered open. The lights were on. Panda strode to her bedside with a rustle of wool skirt.

Anger roil up Panda's neck, across her powdered complexion in patterns of red. The compression of her voice, six inches from Beck's head, was more powerful than a raging scream.

"Well! Well! That...that thing you brought with you was caught giving drugs to Ashley. In plain sight, out in the open, a brazen criminal."

The impossible news had the terrifying quality of a nightmare. Beck pushed herself up, ready to run, rescue, escape, stare wide-eyed at her grandmother.

Panda stepped back as if expecting Beck her to get up and do something.

Beck swung her legs over the side of the bed.

"What? I mean...I don't understand," she fumbled for a response.

As if to clarify to a simpleton, Panda laid out the facts, "She's been arrested. We are doing all that we can to keep Ashley out of jail. Of course, Sonia-Barton was a party to the crime. I suppose we must think of something to say about you. At least you were not with them."

Beck had the sensation of her lungs wobbling. Miss Kitty arrested. Sonia-Barton, Ashley?

"She's....careless," Beck said almost to herself.

"What?" Her grandmother hissed.

Beck continued to stammer. "She doesn't do drugs. She drinks."

Panda's complexion darkened as she squeezed her mouth and eyes into a furious squint. "Have you lost your mind?"

Beck's shoulders lumped with the same helpless feeling as when they'd been escaped from L'Ecole. It wasn't her fault. Why did Miss Kitty always get her in trouble? Miss Kitty was in worse trouble than sneaking out. Beck stood but her grandmother kept her pinned to the side of the bed.

"Is she in jail? We must help her."

"We? You mean your father? You expect him to interfere with a criminal investigation?"

Beck gently tried to maneuver around her grandmother.

"Where are you going?" Panda seized her by the upper arm and held her with deadly urgency.

Beck was surprised by her grandmother's strength as if she was struggling to pull a tenacious weed from her garden. For an instant she wondered if Panda would hurt her.

Panda pushed her back onto a seated position on the side of the bed. Rage and indignation poured through her furious expression as she leaned over her. "Why did you bring her? She'll tell the world now. That girl, a common drug fiend, knows. Oh, we're ruined, ruined! Why? Why have you done this to us?"

Beck could swear she heard the faint pop beside Panda's eye. Her grandmother looked as if something had unexpectedly caught her attention. She straightened, pivoted and lay on her back across the bed her feet dangling loosely toward the floor.

Beck sat beside her for an instant not comprehending what was happening. Her grandmother's eyes were open, looking at the ceiling as if to find the source of her trauma.

"Panda, what's the matter?

A tremor moved her grandmother's eyelids.

"Panda, oh Panda," she whispered.

Wake, wake, she willed, then picked up the telephone beside the bed and forcefully pressed the 0.

"Please send an ambulance. My grandmother is very sick. She can't move." Her voice sounded amazingly calm to her.

She willed herself to be strong, think clearly, then slipped into weakness. *This isn't happening.*

A timeless still trapped her in an eddy of emotion. She couldn't save her grandmother any more than she had her mother and brother. She patted Panda's face and cried, "I'm sorry. Really, I'm sorry."

She tried not to be bad, wanted to be good but could not overcome the curse of her being, bringing death and disgrace. Her father was scheduled to arrive tomorrow. He must hurry. She picked up the phone and rapidly dialed home. The phone rang and rang. Finally, Janey answered.

"Lyons residence."

"Do you know where my father is?" There was no hiding the panic in her voice from Janey.

"No, not rightly. What's wrong?"

"My grandmother is very sick. He needs to come fast." Beck began to sob. "It's my fault. She was angry at me and..."

"Oh, sweet child, this is not your fault, you understand? You stay right there, I'll find him," Janey said. "You keep praying, baby, I know you are."

A knocking on the door caused Beck to put down the phone. She took a step, turned and picked up her skirt and blouse from the floor.

"Come in, please come," she shouted and with her clothes pressed to her chest to hide her nightgown, opened the door.

A balding man with a hotel badge looked at her, into the room, then back at her. "I'm the night manager. You called about an emergency."

"It's my grandmother, Mrs. Lyons." Beck stepped aside so he could see the evidence. "I think she's very sick."

""An ambulance has been called. They are close. They'll be here soon," he said in a failed effort to comfort her.

"I need to change."

"Go ahead. I'll stay with her."

Beck abandoned her grandmother into the bathroom to dress but with only a short reprieve to come out.

The manager had placed a pillow under Panda's head and covered her with a blanket. He hadn't moved her legs, leaving Panda fallen, knees bent, mid-heal black shoes resting above the carpet.

They stood beside the bed as if ready to help Panda if she should suddenly stand or fall off the bed.

"I think she may be having a stroke. My aunt had one. She was never the same," the manager ponderously delivered the terrible news.

Beck put her hands together and as Janey had suggested, prayed, "Oh please Jesus. Saint Thérèse, forgive me. Heal my grandmother. I'll be good. I promise I'll be good.

* * *

Beck hurried after the gurney, forgetting her coat, surprised by the freezing temperature as she stood behind the red and white vehicle. The blue uniformed emergency responder invited her to ride in the back. She sat on a bench and watched a monitor showing regular dips and rises of Panda's heartbeat.

At the hospital she was left in a stark room with plastic furniture and a television broadcasting the Tonight Show.

Another mistake, she'd not thought to call her grandfather. Someone at the hotel must have told him. He rushed in eyes searching about before focusing on her. The first white stubble of a beard was on his face. "What happened?" he demanded.

"She was mad at me." Beck lowered her eyes as she made the confession.

His attention moved from her unsatisfactory explanation to a receptionist seated behind a glass window beside the entrance to the treatment area. "I'm here to see my wife Penelope Lyons."

He was escorted back into the treatment area, leaving Beck to sit across from a woman with a small child.

"My man's been in there a long time," the woman said with a thick native Appalachian accent.

Beck nodded but offered no encouragement.

"Was a-changin a tar," the woman said.

"Sorry," Beck said and moved her focus to the television attached to the corner of the ceiling.

She was immobilized by lines of fright that pulled tightly in opposite directions between worry about her grandmother and thoughts of herself. Panda was not the only one in the family who would blame her for Miss Kitty giving drugs to Ashley Adams. Beck hugged herself for warmth and lectured herself not to be thinking of herself at a time like this. Had Janey found her father? What would he say? He rarely got mad at her. She'd have to tell him why his mother had the attack. How many people knew? How could this be contained? Panda had once said to Beck—scandals are to be ignored, looked at with surprise if they force an appearance, explained in a way that confuses the disbeliever, consoles and reaffirms the believer.

She might have killed her, caused Miss Kitty to go to jail, disgraced herself beyond time. She'd brought Miss Kitty to Virginia where people were put in jail for drugs. She was demonstrating how weak and ineffectual she was in a crisis— what her grandmother called her poor decision making qualities.

"God help you," the tire changer's wife said in parting as she was taken to another part of the hospital to her husband's room. Beck shivered alone. Staring at a print of a mountain scene on the wall, she prayed silently for her grandmother, for Miss Kitty, the tire changer, for a miracle. Panda would walk out. They'd make an excuse. Panda would say that Miss Kitty had not been arrested, or that she would take care of it, if only Beck would never see her again. Beck would do that. Anything to rebuild this collapse of reality back to happiness. She'd go into where Panda was sick and tell her that she was right— I am a willful girl.

Her grandfather returned and sat beside her for a moment in stunned silence, his lips pressed together. "Well, it doesn't look good. She might not ever be the same." He covered his eyes with his hand.

As if his presence released her to completely fall apart Beck hunched over and sobbed.

He put his arm over her quaking shoulder.

"It was my fault. She was mad at me. I'm sorry, sorry." Her lamentation heaved from her in gasps.

"We must be hopeful." He tried to calm her. "Let's go see her."

She went with him into the intensive care unit, a small annex to the emergency room, because he led her, forcing her to stop moaning. Refusing to go would have been improper behavior even though she did not want to see what she'd done to her grandmother.

Her grandfather held open a green cloth screen and Beck saw Panda hooked up to an array of instruments. Tubes were taped over her mouth. At least her eyes were closed.

Beck moved cautiously to the bedside. She prayed for a miracle, for Panda to respond, even to criticize her. "Please get better, Panda. I'll never be able to live with myself if you don't." She wanted to hug and kiss her but was afraid to touch her. "I'm sorry, Panda." She started to moan again. "Please get better." She took a gold cross from around her neck and placed it over Panda's heart. Her grandmother's skin was cold. Death was an open door.

* * *

She sat with her grandfather in the waiting room for another hour. He noticed her shivering and asked for a blanket in which she wrapped herself. "Has anyone told Dicky?" he asked.

"I called home. Janey is trying to find him. I think he's in Israel."

He smiled at her. "You've been very brave, did just the right thing. If you hadn't gotten her to the hospital so fast she might have died."

"Thank you, Pawpaw." She pulled the blanket tighter around her shoulders. The hospital smell of disinfectant opened her nostrils. She was tempted to play his good girl, but she had to know. "Did you hear about my friend?"

He tilted his head and looked askance at her as if wondering why she'd ask about a friend at a time like this. "No. I don't believe I did."

"Oh," she said, looked away and then back at him. "She got in trouble with the law. That was why Panda was mad at me."

"Oh," he mimicked or maybe she was imitating him. "Were you to blame?"

"No!" She said with certainty, then guiltily lowered her voice. "Not for that." She pressed her clenched fists into her lap. "Panda was angry with me about it when she got sick. That's why she was in my room." She knew she was repeating herself, but the gravity of her guilt called for confession upon confession. Her voice trembled and she pleaded with widened eyes.

"I don't see why it couldn't wait until morning," he said, seeming to take her side and blame Panda for getting so upset.

The truth came out like a heavy burden she was laying down. "Panda said my friend was caught giving drugs to Ashley."

He sat more erect. "Ashley Adams? Why that's terrible. You say this is a friend of yours? You shouldn't have friends like that. Where did you meet her?"

Beck looked into his crinkled blue eyes trying to read the secrets they hid. Did he know? To honor Panda, she had to keep the lie going. "In France. She got in trouble there, too."

"Why did you invite her to the Homestead?"

Was she now to blame Sonia-Barton by saying it was her idea or her father for giving his permission?

"She's from a good family in Connecticut. I stayed with her last summer. I had no idea she'd do anything like this."

She could see the lawyer in him mulling the facts, containing the damage. "Perhaps there's been a misunderstanding."

The misunderstanding was her family's faith in her goodness. She was a curse on them and didn't know how to be good. She must find a way to fix the wrongs she brought.

* * *

Her grandfather sent her back to the hotel in a cab, telling her to get some rest. As if she could sleep. She watched the dark forest past through the snow-stained window, wished she could run away. How was she going to sleep in the bed where Panda had fallen? In the morning, she'd have to face the rest of the family.

She needed her protective family. She couldn't protect herself, was too weak to defend herself much less help Miss Kitty.

Through the rest of the night, she tossed in bed, occasionally sleeping, plotting what she could do.

* * *

At six in the morning dressed in a skirt, a tan cashmere sweater, and blue blazer she looked like the proper young lady she wanted to be. Her uncle, Judge Battle, was an early riser. She'd rehearsed an explanation, a plea for him to use his influence to either cover up or help.

The large dimensions of the dining room and the number of white-coated crews ready to attend the many tables were more evident at the early hour with so few at breakfast. A rack of toast was set beside a small vase with orchids. A waiter poured hot chocolate from a silver pot. She glanced at the printed breakfast menu—but didn't order anything.

Her uncle, dressed in a brown twill jacket, looked as tired as she felt. The red tinge on his high cheek bones rose to his eyes as he saw her and sat beside her at the family table.

"What do you hear about my sister?"

Beck spoke quietly as he leaned to hear her, "We won't know un..." She stopped mid-word. Her mouth opened as she deeply inhaled and rocked away from her uncle, focused on Miss Kitty rapidly approaching the table.

"That cousin of yours got me in some big trouble," Miss Kitty said loud enough for others in the dining room to hear.

Her uncle sat more erect with a tilted head as he inspected the crazy girl–wild red hair, the jewelry including a cross formée lately favored by the Prussian military hanging from her neck–invading their conversation.

"They're trying to blame me for her..."

Beck nearly rose up from her chair to interrupt the dramatic explosion erupting from Miss Kitty. "This is my cousin's grandfather." Beck accented her urgency with a quick nod at her uncle.

Whatever she was, Miss Kitty was not stupid, and saw an opportunity.

"Excuse me," Miss Kitty turned her attention to the judge. "Are you Ashley Adam's grandfather, Judge Harry Battle?"

"I am," he drawled.

"Sarah Handley." Miss Kitty stuck out her hand. "Sir, you have heard the news about the senator's mother?"

Uncle Harry glanced at Beck then perfunctorily shook Miss Kitty's hand, "We are most concerned, yes ma'am."

Miss Kitty leaned closer to him. "She suffered a serious stroke last night upon hearing the news that foreign agents had used her granddaughter to get to the senator."

"Now, wh..what's this?" Uncle Harry demanded.

"I want you to know that Ashley is completely innocent."

"Of course she is!" The judge's voice carried in the cavernous dining room.

Miss Kitty kept her voice to a conspiratorial low. "They were trying to plant the dope in Beck's room and made a mistake—foreign agents, drug smugglers have set up Beck as a means of embarrassing the senator. We think they're Viet Cong."

Beck flinched and shrank from the absurdity.

Miss Kitty practically put her head against the judge's and said in a near-whisper, "The CIA is already on the case. I've been authorized to request that you do all you can to suppress news of this event until the whole gang can be rolled up to the big boss. This must be accomplished in a manner that will not alert those who are watching. All records must disappear. Do you understand? These people are ruthless. No one in...a...Homestead will be safe."

Miss Kitty took him by the shoulders and pulled him so close it appeared she intended to kiss him. "I am very concerned about the senator. His mother is lying near death. We must protect him. I must go now."

Miss Kitty winked at Beck and rushed from the dining room.

Her uncle shook his head in disbelief. "What in the blue blazes was that? I've never heard such cock and bull in 25 years on the bench."

Beck shrugged and confessed. "That was my friend."

"The one the security guard caught with Ashley last night?"

"Yes."

"I truly believe she's on drugs. You can tell her that the matter has been taken care of. Fortunately, your friend and Ashley were at the Homestead and we do have a bit of influence here. I do suggest your friend leave as quickly as she can and not bring her *hippa* ways around here or you or any other member of our family. I could have her locked up for quite awhile for insanity."

Miss Kitty hadn't been arrested. Her grandmother had taken the story and blown it into a stroke. Why? Why did everything even a mistake always turn out so deadly for Beck?

Her uncle patted her hand on the table. "And please, darling, do be more careful and discreet about who you associate with," he echoed her grandfather's advice.

"I will, Uncle Harry, I promise." She meant to keep her word.

The majordomo approached the table. "Miss Beck, your father, the senator, is on the telephone."

Beck sighed and rose to meet the condemnation she dreaded the most. On the house phone by the entrance, she heard the sorrow and fear in his voice. "I'm on my way. I'll be there in two hours. You should go see your grandmother." His voice caught in a weak register she'd not heard since the days after the drowning. "It doesn't look good. We're having her airlifted to Bethesda. They can do more for her there."

"I'll pray," Beck said.

* * *

After the ambulance had left for the airport, Beck drove home alone. Sonia-Barton and Miss Kitty had returned to New Orleans and New York as fast as if the law was after them. Neither had apologized or taken any responsibility for Panda's attack. Why should they? Beck was to blame.

Down the steep hill of the entrance to the lake, she resisted the urge to look at the Malloys' house for evidence that Randall had come home for Christmas. The possibility of his nearness fed the imagined conversation.

She would talk to him when she was stronger. But she needed him when weak. If she tried to go forward when there was nothing there, she'd fall into space. That was a good concept–falling, falling into space, your love no longer there to hold me, keep me from floating away. Randall could turn the idea into a song.

Only Janey was home. Beck was restless in the house. She felt like walking to Beach One but didn't trust herself to walk by Randall's.

In a winter coat and a mink hat her father had brought her from Canada, she walked down the serpentine stone steps to the private beach below the house. Snow had covered the ice with white as if by a death shroud. Early afternoon sun illuminated orange patterns between gray billows of clouds.

Across the lake, two boys walked on the porous crust. She remembered watching Randall play hockey, hitting a round black piece of rubber between two piles of stones set on the ice. A ping of an air bubbled moving beneath the ice caused her to cringe.

Panda would say confront your fears. Upstairs, in an unopened box was a pair of ice skates Panda had bought her for her fourteenth birthday. Magically thinking that if she did what Panda wanted, she'd get better, be proud of her.

No fear, Beck whispered to herself as she gingerly stepped onto the crunching surface. Her heart rate accelerated, and tears blurred her eyes.

Another ping reverberated like a monster calling her to its icy grasp. She spun back to the railway tie dock and frozen sand.

A movement at the top of the stairs caused her to look up to glimpse a white haired woman in a dark coat turn and walk out of sight on the recreation room porch.

Beck hurried up the gravel path beside the house.

Janey was waiting for her by the phone in the hall.

The compassion that glistened in her eyes forewarned the news.

"Your Panda passed."

Janey arms and soft chest were there for her.

Beck nodded with a fatalistic expression. Her guilt was sealed. She was weak, had disappointed Panda one last time.

TWENTY-FOUR

SOMEDAY

M iss Kitty invited her to the Manhattan recording studio—not Randall. Beck was drawn into herself during the 45-minute bus ride down Broadway from her apartment. She parsed conversations with Randall's spectral presence, told herself she mustn't confuse dreams with reality. Randall hadn't come to see her when he'd returned to Lake Barcroft or New York. He knew she'd not trusted him to tell him she was pregnant. He purposely cut her off.

Did he want to see her or was this just another Miss Kitty manipulation and torture? Two years at college, among girls equal in their displacement had calmed Beck. The anonymity of Manhattan allowed her to walk in her waking dream, endless streams of fantasy conversations with Randall—some angry, others loving, forgiving. If she acted with the intensity and history of her fantasies, he'd think her insane. She was insane. He knew that. Why try to hide the truth.

Why would he want to see her anyway? When they were young, she had a conceit she was special. He was lucky to have her for a friend. She'd thought marrying him would be beneath her. Now, he was famous. Miss Kitty had gotten him a recording contract and was his manager. They'd found their place with direct determination.

Beck was 20, floundering in a someday world–someday she'd join the Carmelites, find Theresa, happiness with Randall.

Miss Kitty had sworn she'd never told him about the pregnancy. Beck had to trust that she hadn't, but she didn't.

The recording studio with its pitched roof and round stained-glass window still looked like the church it had been. A nervous tremor built in her stomach as she waited in a foyer set up like a living room with art on the walls, plants, and a Persian rug on varnished wooden floors. She asked a young man moving into the interior in a purposeful walk if Randall Malloy was here.

"Butch?"

He looked at her as if she might be a stalking fan.

"Please tell him Beck is here." She might have said Dodge. One of his popular songs played on the radio had the line, *Dodge is there when I need her*. An article about him in the Social section of the *Washington Post* reported he'd written the song about the daughter of the Majority Leader. Robbie probably was the one who'd said that. She doubted Randall would. She'd treated the revelation as more quasi-notoriety for being near someone famous, barely anything to do with her.

Miss Kitty, frizzed red hair exploding around her shoulders held by a rope band, calf-length buckskin boots, looking as ready as ever to kick something over, rushed from a hallway and hugged her. "Don't you look fetching." She stepped back to admire Beck's carefully chosen Mexican embroidered blouse, no bra, her hair parted in the middle held back with a golden flower halo.

"Very hip." Beck mocked herself.

"Come on we're doing a mix of a new song. Ever been in a recording studio?"

"No."

"Well you're gonna be. I want you with me doing this."

Did Randall? Beck remembered Sonia-Barton's envy at the lifestyle. For Beck, the music business meant only one thing–Randall.

The buildup to the reunion, the energy that churned up her legs was mistimed. He barely looked up from where he sat behind a board of knobs and levers. His stern glance over his shoulder and perfunctory nod evidenced her visit was Miss Kitty's plot, not approved or asked for by him, likely at the wrong time when he was at work.

Miss Kitty closed a thick door to create a deadened atmosphere to better hear the details of music coming from large speakers hung from the ceiling and a bank of small speakers on either side of a console.

A man with a black pompadour rising above his head like a sculpted wave, sat beside Randall. A window looked out into a larger room with a drum set, a forest of microphone stands and vines of electric cords.

She was a superfluous audience to the clearest music she'd ever heard, powerful, professional, as much a marker of how he'd changed as his long hair, old jeans and plaid wool shirt. Hadn't she changed too? Their relationship could also grow. She was happy to see him, wanted to be part of what he was doing.

"That's the mixing board." Miss Kitty leaned closer to explain in a voice low enough not to disturb Randall. She pointed to a rack of equipment, "Those are volume controls, mid-range equalizers."

There was science, mystery here like a NASA launch control room. The magic of music she loved came from rooms likes this. Did Miss Kitty think she'd be more impressed with Randall than she already was?

The man seated beside Randall pressed a button and the music stopped. He swiveled in his chair and gave Beck an up and down run of his eyes over her body.

"Hey, Beck," Randall casually greeted her.

Was she supposed to apologize? What had Miss Kitty been thinking about inviting her?

"Hi," she said as if they'd just met on Lakeview Drive, and gave him the unwavering attention of her father greeting a constituent.

"Beck's got killer ears," Miss Kitty said as if answering the unspoken question of why she was there. "I wanted her to hear this."

What did killer ears mean? How would Miss Kitty know what she was able to hear?

Randall looked at Miss Kitty with a cocked head and shrugged "Play it from the top," he said to the man beside him.

Two-inch tape began to turn atop a complex machine with its own bank of controls. The voice she'd known from childhood now powered and deepened by reverb broadcast through multiple speakers.

Irony runs through shades of feelings.

She loved the line and felt its emotional pull but thought the music was too busy. He was trying to cram too much in the phrasing. The lyrics were chasing the melody.

When the song had played through its radio-ready three minutes, Miss Kitty looked at her. "What d'ya think?"

Randall squinted in consternation.

She knew he didn't want her criticism. "I think you might bring the music down a bit so I–we–can hear the voice more. I think it might be more powerful that way."

He stared at her for a moment then said with a thin smile, "Usually good for an honest answer."

Usually–he clearly mocked her dishonesty.

Heat of humiliation raised the color in her cheeks. She pursed her lips and looked away from him. "I was just in the neighborhood and...sorry, I shouldn't have come."

She turned to the door.

Miss Kitty frowned. "Wait."

"I need to go," Beck opened the heavy door.

Miss Kitty followed her to the lounge and closed the door behind her.

"That went smashingly," she grinned.

"He had no interest in me being here."

"But you wanted to see him."

Beck frowned and shook her head. "Leave it up to him next time, OK?"

"Sure, but you were right about the song. He listens to you."

Randall came out. She glanced to the front door then back at him.

Miss Kitty stepped back to give him space in front of Beck or to be a better witness to the encounter.

Randall's eyes narrowed, indicating a shared feeling of annoyance at Miss Kitty's willfulness "Tell Cosmo, I'll be back in a minute."

Miss Kitty hesitated as if not trusting them or reluctant to miss the encounter she'd instigated. "Oh yeah, sure." She submitted to Randall's authority.

Left by themselves in the hallway, Randall ran his hand through the long strands of hair hanging over his broad forehead. "Didn't mean to chase you away." There was kindness in his expression, maybe pity.

"I know, just wasn't a good time," she said.

"Want to meet some other time, when I'm not working? This is expensive."

She crossed her arms in front of her chest. "We'll see. You better get back to work."

"You have a boyfriend or something?" He peered down in an expression of concern she found familiar. The remnant of his jealously made her smile. "A few. Bet you have lots of girlfriends."

His eyes twinkled. "A few. Thought you were going to be a nun."

Her eyes narrowed. "Who told you that?"

He shifted his weight. "Sonia-Barton."

What else had Sonia-Barton told him? He knew about the France charade, disdained her for her dishonesty, for not trusting him, hiding his daughter. "It's a not a joke." She hid shame with anger.

He lowered his gaze and shrugged. "Sorry, didn't mean to make light of it."

"Next year, I'm still thinking of taking my vows."

He considered her like he used to when he wanted her do something and she wouldn't. *Get thee to a nunnery.* She was Ophelia scorned by Hamlet.

He offered a way back. "Let's get together sometime."

"Why?"

He smirked. "Still mad at me, *huh*?"

"I didn't say that."

"Be nice if you'd talk to me some day," he laid the blame on her, probably rightly.

To repulse his intrusion, she took direct aim at a weakness "Want to talk about Vietnam?"

He examined her as if to determine her intention then attacked back. "No. Look I know what happened. I'm sorry. We...I should have been more careful."

His assumption on why she'd cut him off, the escalation of the use of their intimacy, snapped up her barriers. "I have no idea what you're talking about. But hey, it was nice seeing you. See you around." She turned to leave but felt his hand on her upper arm.

He stepped in front of her. "I want to see you. Really see you."

"Why?"

"Give me your number."

Probably Miss Kitty had told him everything or Sonia-Barton. "Get it from Miss Kitty."

"I don't want to chase you."

Instinctively, she knew he did.

"OK, we see each other. What then?"

"And we'll marry."

He was not going to let her go. He'd use every secret, all her frailty to overpower her. She heard in his laughing tone willingness to make the memory of their childhood promise a joke. He must have known how much she'd missed him, sensed her years of obsessive thoughts of him. He knew her weaknesses as well as she knew his. Her eyes misted and her voice trembled. "Don't. Some things are too sweet."

Corrected again, he nodded. "Yeah, sweet." He sighed. "We can have our secrets. We can have our places where the other won't go."

"Is that one of your songs?"

He saw her resistance dissipate and smiled. "You're right. That's a good lyric. And you were right about Shades of Feeling." He nodded back at the control room. "It needs more space in the lyrics."

"Dancing in the shades of feeling. It's a great lyric."

"That wasn't in the song, but it is now." With a perplexed tilt of his head, he examined her as if trying fathom a mystery. "Don't make me bad."

"Don't make me good." She swallowed a rush of emotion swelling in her. "We have our own spaces."

He pulled his lower lip in and nodded. "So long as there's space for us."

She smiled. "The lines keep coming. Better get to work."

"Yeah, it's flowing. I need to catch it."

She took his extended hand for a shake and he pulled her gently toward him.

"Don't." She pulled away. "Give me time."

He grinned and shook his head in bemusement. "That's the name of the song, *Give Me Time*. Got a tour coming up. Robbie will be glad to see you too. We'll get together when I get back. Right?"

She nodded. "Someday."

In the way a look can express more than a hundred words, she thought they were back in touch and would be forever.

He leaned forward as if he might kiss her and if he had, she would not have pushed him away.

"See you soon," he said and turned back to his work.

* * *

On the bus back uptown, her fantasies of future happiness, fulfillment waned. He'd said he couldn't spend time with her because the studio was costing money. What was she worth to him? Why had she come to him? He could see through her, knew she longed for him.

She'd been played, taken advantage of. He only wanted to gain the upper hand, revenge for the white trash treatment, the snobbery.

Foolish girl–she heard her grandmother's voice–felt her disappointment. She was not thinking clearly.

* * *

Beck's grandparents came up to New York in the spring and took her to dinner at Lutèce. They sat before a marble fireplace and spoke in low tones as not to disturb the intimacy of other diners in a room that held the ambiance of a Fifth Avenue mansion.

Her grandmother, Jean Carroll, was a horsewoman with a tanned, lined face. Beck's grandfather, Peter, looked at Beck over a highball with a perplexed expression as if he had forgotten what he wanted to say to her.

If they felt like second-class grandparents to the Lyons, they were always happy to see her and she felt relaxed with them, as they were not always trying to teach her something like Panda. She loved the time she'd spent in New Kent, a replacement for their daughter in her childhood room still containing her furnishings, toys, old books, records, art, atop a curving flight of stairs in a house that had been in the family over 200 years, the trips to Stuckey's, riding a Buckskin named Savvy that was *her* horse, swimming in the pool.

Jean Carroll had a distinct tidewater accent—a southern drawl that drew out the vowels and *r's*. She exhaled cigarette smoke dragon-like from her nostrils and said in a tobacco-cured voice, "She would have wanted to know you were happy."

Her grandparents had a way of acting as mediums, asking her questions in her mother's name. Telling her stories as if their duty was to see that Beck had a strong sense of her mother. Beck didn't know how to tell them her mother was a loving spirit without the power to do the things she'd missed and needed in a mother—to tell her things would get better in time, to forgive her. You may be able to find happiness or love, but never another mother.

"I get down sometimes."

"Oh, that's normal enough, I suppose." Her grandmother waved her Pall Mall by her head.

"You're just growing up." Her grandfather looked sad, as if empathizing with Beck's melancholy response.

"What do you think you want to do after college?" Grandmother Jean asked.

"I'm interested in religion."

"Really?" Her grandmother tapped off the ash of her cigarette. "What kind of religion?"

Beck channeled the peace she felt into a modest nod. "Taking a vow."

Her grandmother eyes widened. "Really? You mean a minister?"

They wouldn't have been able to fathom she meant to become a Catholic nun. There were Anglican nuns. "Something like that."

Without trying to outright dissuade her, Jean said, "You are in the in-between years. Now your mother at that age wanted to play music in concerts in the worst way. Do you still play? She would want you to keep your piano up."

"I should practice more."

Grandfather Peter said, "You play a lovely Debussy. Every time I hear you play I think of her."

Beck was sorry she'd spoken of sadness to them.

"How is your personal life?" Grandmother Jean asked.

Meeting a proper husband was behind the question. "I have lots of friends," she lied.

"A beau?" Jean asked.

Beck looked away, hesitated to reveal a secret or half-truth. Randall was her fiancé more by hope or forsaking, a giving up. He had his secrets too, horrors he wanted to forget. He would never ask about their child and she would protect her family secret. There was a weird gap in their love, their need to be close, like they'd gone too far off a trail and were trying to find their way back using old landmarks. But to where? Go forward or back to memories?

"No."

"Oh, well," Jean Carroll waved her cigarette. "You're still young. I didn't think that your mother would ever marry. Then one day she comes home and announces that she's marrying a congressman and moving north. Imagine."

Her grandmother said north as if their daughter had moved to Massachusetts instead of a hundred miles to Fairfax. Maybe they thought there was more ice in Northern Virginia and their daughter would be alive if she'd stayed in the South.

Her grandfather took another long pull on his cocktail and looked drunk. They had other children and grandchildren who Beck thought would make them happy and were less a cause for concern than she was.

* * *

Beck entered the narrow walkway into the cloister as nervous and excited as if joining her lover. She *was* joining her lover–a complete love of Christ. She'd told Gail she was going to stay with a friend. To go to the Carmelites with a lie seemed sinful and a bad way to start, but it occurred to Beck that God had taken extra care to teach her the shades and nuances of lying. Next month, she'd turn twenty-one and be free to do whatever she wanted.

A sister, tall and stooped, her face narrow and unlined by smiles, led her to a room with four metal bunk beds. "This is where the aspirants stay. Leave your bag by the dressers. You can choose a bed tonight."

The thin lumpy mattresses did not bother Beck. Earthly comforts were a distraction. She'd read of the life, knew that every minute of every day must be a devotion.

Saturday and Sunday she worked at St. Luke's in Southeast Washington, played with children, helped fix and serve meals, felt blessed and protected.

Sunday evening before she left, the Reverend Mother spoke to her in the courtyard formed by the four sides of the compound.

Beck lowered her eyes humbly before the nun's gaze.

"I understand that you want to join us? May I ask why?"

Beck knew her answer must be as sincere as a response to a proposal of marriage. She'd studied the stages of admittance to a life of contemplation. "I wish to pursue my own spiritual formation without interruption."

"Do you understand what it means to join our order?"

"I am here to learn."

Her mind clear and ordered by devotion; the cloud of unknowing–*Thou are the further from God that aught is in thy mind but only God.*

* * *

Sunday of her third and final visit to the Carmel, Beck prayed in a chapel lined with sculptures of the Holy Mother and saints. Sisters in their brown habits knelt with their backs to her. The gilded altar glimmered faintly in candlelight. She wanted to belong here, never to leave, but felt nervous–an impostor. Doubt lingered what she would do if she fully submitted to her love for Randall. But that was a fantasy. They spoke regularly and when he was not on tour, he would take her to dinner, dancing in Manhattan. Going out with him was a variation of being with her father–the status, stares, eager contact by fans, little to do with her.

Randall treated her with old-fashioned propriety, an understanding that they would not be lovers until they were married. Miss Kitty too had grown strangely quiet and non-manipulative. Were they waiting for her to come to them in their world? Here was the opposite of that–a cloistered life of prayer. She was drawn between two opposing paths unable to commit to either.

When the nuns passed, Beck walked behind them, down a stone corridor across the quadrangle to the cloister, paintings of Christ and wooden stations of the cross in the dim light.

"Beck, I'll see you in my vestibule," the Reverend Mother whispered from an alcove as Beck passed.

The unexpected voice from the shadows and the faint coloring of the nun's face surrounded by her brown veil caused Beck to shiver.

She climbed the staircase to a stark room furnished with two chairs, a bookshelf containing a small library, and a low table on which an open book of prayer was perched on a stand.

"Please sit," Mary Vivian spoke softly as if to respect the silence of those trying to keep their thoughts on God. Beck focused as before a test as she faced the nun. The Mother Superior pondered her for a moment. "You wish to remain with us?" she asked.

"Yes." Beck also spoke softly. Words in the sanctity of the carmel had deeper meaning, carried a greater weight. She would never have to lie here.

"Is there a reason why you may not join the cloister?"

Beck stiffened. Randall? Her family? Her doubts?

She'd been to a priest at St. Anthony's who was guiding her on the formal steps to conversion. She'd already explained to the Mother Superior she was not yet a Catholic. But she'd not told them who her father was. Beck did not give the Mother Superior the political stare, but looked down modestly at her hands, "I have some conflicts, yes."

The face, framed by a white wimple, was not attractive. The pressed lips topped by a faint but distinctive moustache were tense in a way of suffering, not peace. Beck had a disturbing sense of foreboding as when she was admitted to L'Ecole.

"You are very beautiful. Have you known men?"

Beck was flustered by the question. She blinked. "One, a man who says he wants to marry me. Others in college." Ben Cowper, the class president at Columbia, had been a two-year boyfriend when she was *over* Randall. The scion of a wealthy North Carolina family, a real comer of whom Panda would have approved. Three who'd she slept with because she liked sex and they appealed to her.

"You've had carnal knowledge?"

A hint of eagerness in Mary Vivian's voice caused Beck to look at her. "Yes."

The Mother Superior nodded. "That is good, so you know what you're giving up. Did you enjoy sex?"

Beck felt as if Mary Vivian wanted sordid details, like girls talking about a date.

"Yes, most of the time. I became pregnant at a young age and stayed with Catholics to give up the child for adoption. I spoke often to a priest, was taught by nuns, learned of Saint Thérèse from a doctor." She ran through her prepared arguments of how she'd been called to be a Carmelite not filling in the details of being expelled from L'Ecole.

The nun–a tilt of the head, a steady gaze as if trying to see what lay within her thoughts–appeared to doubt Beck was suitable for a life of prayer.

"Some come to us to escape a bad memory, or a bad situation." She raised stubby fingers as if submission. "We don't judge why you seek a life of contemplation and prayer. We have watched you and wonder are you're fit to bear the burdens of our sheltered life. And I use the word burden with purpose. The burden on those who you have left to come behind our walls. Does your family know you mean to consecrate yourself to a religious life–will your family accept your decision?"

Beck sat more erect. "I'm going to be 21 in June. I can do what I want."

The Mother Superior leveled a stern look as if criticizing Beck's willfulness. "The bishop spoke to me of you. He's heard from the highest authority...from Rome." The nun looked at her as if Beck was a freakish liar.

Beck's hope dimmed. This was not to be.

"There are other ways to serve the church, something more in keeping with the gifts God has given you. We have great need for those who can speak for us in the halls of secular power."

Halls of power sounded odd coming from the nun as if she'd been told the term and imagined Beck's father as an autocrat who could benefit or harm the Church with a wave of his hand.

"We must always be open to God's will and the majesty of the path He has chosen for us. Please be sure of what you will be leaving behind if you choose to join us."

Beck refused to back down and mustered her earnestness into an intense statement of faith. "I believe God has called me to a Carmelite vocation. I wish to spend the summer here as an aspirant."

The Mother Superior shrugged at Beck's use of language from *Becoming a Carmelite.*

"You know the words. You may stay with us so you may better understand our way of life, and the community can discern if you are called to Carmel and will begin Postulancy."

Beck bowed her head.

* * *

Beck rose early to tell her father she intended to be baptized into the Catholic faith and spend the summer living with the nuns. Mornings were the time when she could be with him alone, have his attention. The split level wall of windows looked out at the lake cast in pink hues by the rising sun. The New York Times and Washington Post lay unread by the pile of mail at his place at the head of the yellow wood table.

The sound of gravel being disturbed in the driveway indicated his driver had arrived. She would not have long with him.

Dressed in a blue suit and red tie suitable for television, he hurried down the hall past the front door and did not sit. "I've a breakfast meeting," he explained to her as he poured a cup of coffee from a porcelain server.

He stood beside her, so she had to turn and look up at him to speak. Rushed, she said. "I've spoke before to you of my wish to join the Carmelite order to become a Catholic."

He pressed his lips together into a half-frown. "You want to talk about this now or when I have more time?"

"You never have time."

He slowly took a sip of coffee. "Is this because of me?"

He was blaming himself as if her aspiration was a failing.

"No, it's what I want. I've been to a cloister. The Carmelites have accepted me for a trial."

He set the cup on a saucer and switched into political negotiation mode–mid-focus, sympathetic. "What about Randall?"

The counter so threw here back she didn't respond with other than widened eyes and stared at him.

The Leader praised Randall as he would a prized political ally. "I saw him last week. He came to see me with a veterans group. He's a remarkable young man. My staff, particularly the girls were lined up to see him. I know he cares for you, has for a long time."

The Leader looked at the thin gold watch on his wrist. "Sorry, I'm running late. May we discuss this more when I have free time?"

When would that be, at the beach in August? "Daddy, I really might want to do this."

The use of *might* betrayed doubt. To have her way would require certainty.

"I believe Randall wants to marry you. That would make me very happy."

What was this manipulation? How were these men ordering her life, deciding her future, interfering with her celestial calling as if from another time when women were chattel?

The Leader put his mail into a tan soft briefcase embossed with the Senate emblem. "Can't wait to see my grandchildren if you accept his proposal."

His cynicism crushed Beck. The wall he'd built around the truth that he had a grandchild, now five years old, was impenetrable. She looked up at him, tears misting her eyes. "Don't you know?"

He smiled at her. "I know I love you and will be proud to be your father whatever you do. I'm sorry I have to run."

After he was out the door, Beck remained at the table staring over a box of Raisin Brand at the calm of Lake Barcroft. Where was God's will? Where was the magnificent path He had chosen for her?

Janey came in through the swinging door from the kitchen and stood over the Leader's barely used breakfast place setting. "What dis I hear 'bout ya a marryin' Randaaa? Dat true?"

Beck wistfully shook her head and sighed. "I don't know what's true."

BOOK THREE

TWENTY-FIVE

TRASH

T he 75 miles drive from the Roanoke airport to the Homestead seemed to grow longer the closer Beck and Randall came to the resort and her family. She was twenty-eight, married to Randall, and in therapy for her sleep walking. Her therapist had worked a lot on guilt. Beck wasn't to blame for her mother's and brother's death. She hadn't killed Panda.

Beck had never told the psychiatrist that she'd given her child away.

As the limousine drove through the low mountains, Beck's apprehension showed in an unconscious curling of her lower lip over her lower teeth. Why had Randall decided *now* he wanted to accompany her to the annual reunion? Wasn't their marriage enough proof her family had accepted him? She'd said he didn't have to come, knew he wouldn't have a good time, said she was looking forward to spending time alone with her family. He either wasn't listening or didn't want to take the hints that she didn't feel comfortable with him there. As usual, she didn't know how to tell him what he didn't want to hear.

She turned to him and lectured, "I would very much appreciate your not getting high while we're here, and please shave."

He continued to look out the side window at the stands of thin Appalachian pines. "Randall, are you listening to me?" She waited for a reply with her hands bunched in her lap. "Randall, you never listen to me."

With a tilted head as if surprised, he softly apologized, "Oh, sorry. I was just kinda lost in my world."

"Of god!" she exclaimed and put her hands together in a mock prayer. "We're both a couple of dream walkers."

He grinned. "You always give me good lines for songs."

She didn't take that as a compliment. Everything for him was an idea for a song. She wanted to talk about how he treated her and now, more importantly, how he behaved around her family. She didn't want another Miss Kitty episode.

"I was thinking about some lyrics, about when your mother and Colin died."

Her jaw dropped and she bobbed her head forward. "Why that of all things?"

He looked at the padded gray headliner as if he could see some mystical apparition. "That's when I met death."

The memory of those black days came back with terrifying force charging her body with anger. She launched herself and had her hands around his neck squeezing before he could respond with marine hand-to-hand combat training, splitting her grip on him with an upward thrust of his hands.

"I don't want to hear about that from you or in a song," she raged.

He squinted, too highly trained a soldier to take his eyes off an attacker. "Calm down. It's just an idea, nothing real."

With an exhale of anger, she seethed, "What's more real than me watching my mother and brother drown?"

"I'm sorry."

She rubbed her wrist. Bruises were forming. "You hurt me," she said in a childish *how could you* tone.

"It was instinct."

"You live by instinct. You're a lizard."

He smiled. "I love the way you think."

She breathed deeply, pouted. "You're supposed to be sensitive.

"I am. Give me a chance. Once you get to know me, you'll see."

His humor was infectious. Beck pressed her lips together and lowered her chin to her chest, relaxing into her seat.

"Haven't seen that hellcat for a while."

She raised her head. "What do I have to do to get your attention?"

"Show me some love."

"Or use a bullwhip."

He chuckled. "What do you want to talk about?"

"Not now." She nodded at the back of the head of the driver who'd witnessed her explosion. She wouldn't be surprised if the fight was reported, *BECK ATTACKS BUTCH IN BACK OF LIMO.*

The senator's daughter married to a rock star was irresistible fodder for the gossip rags.

Sometimes she wished she'd stayed in the Carmel. Memories of the nuns returned with a cringe that was as fresh as the day Miss Kitty had come to "rescue" her with loud profanities, referring to the sisters as *honey lickers.*

Both the community and Beck knew she wasn't going to be a nun. Mother Superior had counseled Beck that there were other ways to serve in the spirit of Jesus and had sent her to Catholic Charities.

The organization, whose mission was to lessen poverty, had been happy to hire someone who could easily and effectively meet with elected officials, explaining their mission, helping to insure legislation was written to fund organizations and programs the Church supported. While she'd found the work rewarding, she hadn't thrown herself at the feet of the Pope to be a lobbyist.

Four years earlier, the voice she wanted to listen to for the rest of her life had come through the phone from a hotel room on the road. "I'm not asking you to spend your time with me, just our time. Besides it's the only way I'm ever going to get you back in bed."

"Old as Eve," she'd said.

They'd been married by a Catholic priest in the same garden where she'd confessed to her grandmother that she was pregnant, surely sending Panda spinning in her grave.

Perhaps, approaching the Homestead triggered Beck seeing Randall through Panda's eyes, and the feeling that being him was a moral failing.

* * *

The limo let them off in front of the central bell tower of the hotel where she was greeted by name by the porter. On the front balcony as they entered the lobby, two men carrying skies stopped short and did a familiar double-take at sight of Randall. She knew Randall didn't like being noticed, yet he was dressed in a Hawaiian shirt and a black-banded Panama hat more suitable for the tropics.

As soon as they'd checked in, Randall escaped to their room and passed on going down to the family table. While her father thrived on contact, Randall hid, treating the adulation as an unfortunate byproduct of his profession.

* * *

She returned from dinner and the excuses.

I thought Butch was coming, Ashley Adams had asked with an all too eager gleam in her blue eyes.

Randall was lying on the bed watching television. A tray from room service rested on a table. He'd eaten some fruit and soup, drank a half bottle of wine. A languorous scent of marijuana came from the bathroom.

"I asked you not to get high while we're here." She breathed through her nose, fist clenched, anger dangerously rising.

He didn't respond but kept focused on the television.

"Randall...Randall!"

"What?" The word slurred.

Her face reddened and her heart thumped. "I asked you not to use drugs here. You know what happened with Miss Kitty."

"Killed the wicked witch of the East?" He smirked in a way that fueled her rage. She grit her teeth in a snarl and fought not to lose control. "Why did you come? To torment me?"

"To make love to you."

"What?" she nearly shouted.

"That's what we always do after we fight. Let's just cut to the chase."

His boorish seduction succeeded in transferring anger to sexual energy. But first she wanted to make her point. "We need to talk before we kiss. We spend all our time in *your* world. This is *my* world. I want you to respect it."

With an attitude of *if you want to fight, we'll fight*, he looked up at her and said mockingly. "You hate this world. It's always tried to make you something you're not. What about *our* world?"

"I'm talking about you, not me."

"I'm talking about *us.*"

"God, you make them sound like they're my enemies. They're my family, for goodness' sake."

"You think I'm dying to be holed up in another hotel room?"

"Then why are you here."

Exasperated, he squinted. "To be with you. OK? You want me to leave?"

Her resistance melted. "No. I want you in that bed."

He was right, but so was she. Sometimes the dimensions of their lives became too confusing. She stripped her jewelry and evening dress, her arousal growing as his eyes never left her.

* * *

Afterwards, he was energized ready to escape the confinement of the room. "I hear there's a honkytonk in town. Let's go have some fun."

Sure and be up until closing time. He still hadn't accepted that she was here for her family. "No. I'm meeting Daddy for breakfast, early."

"We're out of tune." He glanced at her as if to gauge if she'd understood what he was trying to say.

She walked naked to the bathroom. "Don't use that line in a song. It's a cliché."

"Yeah. Breaking up is always a cliché."

"That's better."

When she came out in a hotel robe, he was wearing his Panama hat.

"See ya," he said and reached for the door.

"Don't get in trouble."

He didn't respond and left her to ponder how they could stay together. He'd never broached breaking up before. She was surprised he'd dared. He'd never leave her, at least overtly. He'd sulk and withdraw making her feel she was mistreating him, like when she wouldn't go out with him in high school and he wanted her to know that other girls liked him. Plenty of girls liked him now.

Maybe he'd take Ashley Adams with him tonight. The cause of one calamity at the Homestead would be happy to go.

Hopefully, Beck had satisfied him so she wouldn't have to worry about him making love to another woman tonight.

If she loved him, she should be more willing to share living in hotel rooms, the months of travel on buses and planes. But she wouldn't. Tears misted her eyes as she thought of him leaving her.

* * *

Dressed in a full-length sable mink coat and fox fur headband, there was something about being outside with her father, sun rising through the bare branches of the trees, smoke scent of birch resin, breath condensing around them on a brisk but leisurely pace that said she was a go-getter—an *early bird who got the worm* as Panda would say. The worms came to Randall. He worked hard but on his own biorhythm, energized and active after the world had done its work—a minstrel, entertainer of the masses, more comfortable in bars and clubs than dinner with her family.

By the time she'd returned her coat and hat to the room where Randall still slept it was 8:30 and she was ready for one of the Homestead's big breakfasts.

Sitting at a table for two in the cavernous dining room, she put down her china teacup. "Catholic Charities is sending me on a speaking tour next month, to some college campuses."

"I'm so proud of you."

Nothing pleased her more than his praise. She blinked as if to suppress a tear. "Thank you, daddy. I'm proud of you too."

"You'll be at the Women's Club for the unveiling on the 12th?"

Panda had been one of the original members founded to rival the Washington men's clubs. An oil painting of her was to be hung. "Of course."

"Will Randall come?"

She shrugged and frowned. "I don't know, depends on his mood."

His father ate a bite of trout. "He's caught between two realities, isn't he?"

As much as she appreciated his praise, she liked more evidence her father was paying attention—saw her and tried to understand what she was experiencing to the point of echoing her thoughts. She nodded and sat more upright in her chair. "Remember when he ran away?"

"When he was a boy? Sure do. His father called me and we put out an alert to find him."

She frowned at the memory. Did he remember her part? "I think he's running away in some ways again."

"From you?" Her father cocked his head to question her.

Beck lifted her shoulders. "Yes, I suppose I'm a part of it. I represent what he's running from—the straight life, Washington."

Her father looked down at his hands on the table as if focusing on his gold embossed University of Virginia class ring before raising his eyes to her. She knew he was going to say something he wanted her to understand. "I don't know. He uses his fame well, works on issues he cares about. He's a real leader in his way."

Typically, her father weighed the good against the bad, starting with the positive. She waited for the other side.

"Randall can engage in criminal activity, but I don't believe you should be an accomplice."

Beck slumped in her chair. That was a hard clear shot. He wanted her to leave Randall if he didn't clean up.

"I'm not that much of a fuddy-duddy. I know the drug laws are not enforced equitably and he may well feel immune. But people tell me what he does, people who threaten me." Her father spread his hands to open his palms. "They can you use him and *you* against me. I'd hate to see you dragged into something like that."

"And particularly after what happened with Panda," she said. With the comment Beck demonstrated her agreement. "I'll speak to him, try to make him understand that I can't, I *won't* be a part of that lifestyle."

"Good for you, Beck. Believe I'll read the papers in the library. Join me?"

She was happy for this time with her father, reminiscent of when they'd rise early at Lake Barcroft to read the paper and discuss the events of the day.

A man and woman with two children approached them.

With a start that took her breath away, Beck saw her daughter.

Finding Nicholas Fusco had been easy. A widower congressman from California, Beck had lobbied and met him at parties and conferences. Until now, though sorely tempted at times, she'd managed to avoid seeing her daughter.

Beck fixated on the face she'd last seen in a hospital in West Virginia.

"Nick, I'm so glad you came." Her father's greeted the man with usual effusiveness.

"Glad to be here," Nick said with a wide smile showing whitened teeth, friendly in the charismatic way of a politician.

"This my daughter, Beck," the Leader introduced her.

Somehow, though she felt like she was going under a rushing river with the blood pounding through her ears, Beck managed to turn her eyes away from the eleven-year-old girl and compose herself enough to shake hands and say, "Congressman, we've met before in my work."

"Of course, Beck. Catholic Charities, a great group. Your father has mentioned you often. This is my sister Lil," he introduced a thin woman with straight unevenly cut hair.

By rote, Beck shook Lil's hand.

"This is Betty and Frankie."

Beck's eyes again rested on her daughter.

"This is Senator Richard Lyons, the Majority Leader of the Senate and his daughter Beck. She's married to a rock star," Nick said.

"Who?" Betty asked.

Nick looked helpless for a moment, obviously not remembering.

Eyes turned to her, but Beck was struck dumb.

"Butch Malloy," the Leader covered for her.

"Oh," Betty said and considered Beck with a natural eerie mimic of Panda.

The Great Arranger moved Beck along a notch. Was God reminding her of the promise to find her daughter?

"Nice to meet you," Betty reached out her delicate hand.

At her touch, Beck swayed back in a near faint. "Theresa," she sighed.

"My name is Betty."

Beck pulled back with an idiotic grin as she fought to recover her composure. "Nice to meet you, Betty."

The Leader's gaze also lingered on his granddaughter. If this was theater, performers like this rarely came along. He knew. He'd always known, she decided. How else would he know Nick so well?

"We're going skating," the little boy, Frankie, said with guileless wide dark eyes.

"Very good," the Leader chuckled, displaying no evidence that he'd lost his son to skating.

"Nice seeing you Leader, Beck," Nick said. "We have a full day of family fun ahead of us."

Family fun indeed. Did Nick know she was the birth mother? Had Panda picked the parents in the private adoption? Had she known Theresa would be raised by a congressman? The questions only grew more complicated, the answers harder to fathom.

"You know him?" her father asked as Beck walked in a daze to the hotel library.

"A bit from work."

"I sent him to Ethiopia where his wife was murdered."

Her father's downward gaze and slumped shoulders reminded her of the days after the drowning.

"I'm sure you couldn't have known, had your reasons," she mumbled meager reassurance.

"His wife Judith was kidnapped in Ethiopia. He tried to rescue her. It was terrible. I suggested he bring his family down here."

"Had you met the children?" She tried to hide the answers she sought behind the question.

"At the memorial for Judith."

"There's something familiar about Betty," she probed deeper.

"Yes. I had the same feeling."

* * *

Beck sat beside the Leader in the paneled room, an unread New York Times hiding her face.

Some things lie below your consciousness and when they come into focus you ask yourself how you could not have known? Congressman Nick Fusco had been all over the news two years ago. A real hero, he had the square jaw line and dark Italian good looks she'd briefly glimpsed through the door when they'd taken Theresa from her.

God had returned her daughter to her.

But what if you lack the courage to accept a miracle? Who was Beck afraid of displeasing? What censure silenced her now? Panda the enforcer was dead. Why couldn't she be as clear as her father had been about Randall?

Daddy, there's something I've been wanting to ask you for a long time.

When better than now? But what if he *really* didn't know why she'd gone away, who'd adopted his granddaughter?

She should tell Randall. Mostly, she and Randall were good at keeping their worlds apart. And she had multiple states of mind to track—waking and dream, truth and lie. She was uncertain if she'd gone to his bedroom at Lake Barcroft when he'd returned from Vietnam. Had she met him on the beach that summer?

She *had* gone to the recording studio to see him while in college.

"We should have been more careful," he'd said. And she'd lied that she didn't know what he was talking about.

He'd never pressed for the truth. Wasn't that proof that he loved her?

She owed him the truth, should trust him with her confession. But the lie was too inviolable. Maybe she didn't love him enough. No, she couldn't love, had never loved anyone more. Maybe he didn't want to know. Maybe she didn't want to know if he was faithful.

"I'm going to go speak to Randall." She rose from the leather club chair.

Her father set down the Wall Street Journal and took off reading glasses to look up at her.

"Don't be afraid to admit you made a mistake."

She frowned at the similarity to his mother. Panda may be dead but her son continued to view Randall as a threat. Was hiding Randall's daughter from him another mistake?

* * *

Randall was still asleep when she returned to the room. Drawn by an irresistible urge to see Theresa again, she retrieved her coat and hat. Could she declare she was the birth mother, demand her rights? What were her rights? What did she really have to go on–a feeling, a coincidence? What if she was wrong? She'd look foolish.

* * *

The outdoor resort activities were given to winter sport. Sunlight shined bright on the white square of the skating rink set at the foot of ski slopes, more hills than mountains. Bing Crosby dreaming of a white Christmas broadcast from speakers on poles strung with holiday lights. Betty with an intense expression moved skinny legs covered in dark tights, wearing only a pink hello Kitty sweatshirt and no hat–half-step, half glides not yet skating, beautiful, prettier than Beck had ever thought herself to be.

Nick, handsome in a blue blazer, his charcoal white-streaked hair slicked back on the sides of his head, slid to a stop with his feet together sending up a spray of ice by the railing where she stood.

"Beck, wonderful to see you here."

She smiled, "We're happy you came and brought your family."

He gave her a smile she found attractive, white camera-ready teeth.

"You're a good skater, she said."

He raised his dimpled chin. "Grew up in Ohio. We used to skate all winter on ponds. You grew up at Lake Barcroft didn't you?"

Her focus narrowed, startled he knew about her, evidence perhaps he knew more. "Yes, how did you know that?"

"Your father's been telling me about you since I met him—a proud father."

"I don't skate."

Nick's smile dimmed. "I understand."

His response conveyed he knew, more sensitive than Randall not to bring up the drowning.

"Daddy, watch!" Betty had taught herself a skating motion that sent her toward them so fast Nick had to catch her to keep her from crashing into the railing. "Good, honey."

"Hi," Betty looked up at her and was off again to teach herself more skating skills.

Her daughter was Betty not Theresa, Beck told herself. They looked alike but probably not enough to be identified as mother and child. She could see herself in the chestnut hair, long neck, wide shoulders, the spread of high cheekbones, Randall in her mouth, Panda's eyes.

"She learns fast." Beck tried to maintain a light timbre.

"Oh yes. She's amazing. After her mother died she had to grow up fast—me too, in my own way."

"I'm sorry." She was veering into personal space, sharing tragedies, but he was the one who had brought up his wife's death.

He cleared his throat indicating the wound hadn't fully healed. "If it wasn't for the kids, I don't know if I wouldn't have completely fallen apart. They have to put up with a lot with a father in Congress, but you know about that."

"We're special," she said with a thin smile.

"I couldn't have done it without my sister, Lil," he nodded at a woman with gray hair and glasses sitting in one of the white plastic chairs before boxes to put skates on.

"Daddy, help me."

"OK, Frankie, hold on." He smiled at her. "Duty calls." He skated to the little boy who was holding onto the railing trying to pull himself along without falling.

There had been no good-bye. He needed help raising his children, her child. He didn't know she was Betty's mother. He wasn't that good an actor. Panda wouldn't have let the adopting parents, especially a congressman know Betty's grandfather was Richard Lyons. There could be a mistake. Maybe Betty wasn't Theresa.

Beck sat beside Nick's sister and with practiced listening skills soon had Lil telling about the polio she and Nick had when they were children. He'd recovered. She still had a weak leg so skating wasn't for her. Their father had been a Romance language professor at Tiffin College. She'd worked as a librarian at Oberlin before coming to help Nick with the children. Their mother had been from Santa Barbara which Nick now represented in Congress.

"Lovely children," Beck said.

"Delights," Lil said.

Nick smiled at them as he skated backwards pulling Frankie by the hands.

"Terrible about his wife. Judith, right?"

"Yes. You can't prepare for something like that."

"Tragic. Such a vital woman. I think we spoke once about adoption. I work with a group that does a lot of adoption work. I think she said that she and Nick had adopted."

Beck tried to delve in an offhand manner but was worried she'd been too obvious.

Lil raised her eyebrows and turned to her. "Really? Judith spoke of that? I'm not sure Betty knows she's adopted. I don't know if Nick has told her yet."

Beck abandoned the questioning before she made a more revealing mistake. "I won't say anything, of course. I better be pushing on. Nice talking to you, Lil. Bye." She waved at Nick and walked through the snow-capped cabins certain Betty was her daughter.

She imagined telling Randall she had a surprise for him. Eleven o'clock he should be up.

A group of teens were gathered like dogs sniffing at a gopher hole in a little used area of seats at the end of the hall, waiting for a chance to see Butch Malloy.

In the room, Randall was buttoning a denim shirt. A guitar lay against the side of the bed. The unmistakable, illegal sweet incense scent of marijuana smoke was in the air.

The bathroom opened and Ashley walked out. Beck looked quickly at Randall, who issued his stupid boyish grin.

"Oh hello," her cousin said. "Just dropped by to use the loo."

Appearing to sense the danger, Randall stepped between Beck and Ashley, wrapping both arms around Beck in a strong grip.

"I was just playing her a new song."

Beck's fury emerged in a shout, "And smoking pot?"

She wretched herself free so Randall only held her by the wrist. "You did this on purpose. What are you trying to prove? You're so famous you can disgrace my family. And you," she glared at Ashley. "Trash."

Hearing herself echo Panda turned fight into flight. She pulled free and left the room.

Randall caught her in front of the young fans who moved to be near him as if he might talk to them. Who knew what rumors of scandal they'd spread?

"She was just using the bathroom, that's all."

"We'll talk about it later," Beck whispered.

Ashley joined them, her pale skin rosy on high cheekbones.

"I'm going to be late," Beck said as if that was all that was wrong.

"What are you so uptight about? Butch was just playing me a song," Ashley said.

Only his fans called him Butch instead of Randall. Beck didn't believe he would make love to her cousin, but to let her in the room, couldn't he see she was dangerous?

TWENTY-SIX

LIGHTHOUSE

B eck understood Randall's offer to go with her to the family dinner that night was his way of attempting to make up but now she wished he'd stay in their room. He tied his hair back into a ponytail and wore a Navy double breasted blazer.

Anxiety tightened her stomach. Heads turned and looked at them as they passed, a whispered chant *Butch Malloy*.

Uncle Harry at the head of the oblong table looked at Randall with pursed lips. "Nice of you to join us, sir."

Randall appeared to enjoy not being treated like a celebrity. "Glad to be here, judge. Nice to see you again."

Randall knew how to behave when he wanted. He sat beside Gail across from Beck and the Leader.

Ashley arrived with her family and started to sit beside Randall.

"Let your mother sit there." Beck said in a crisp voice.

The oddness of the direction brought attention to tension between the cousins.

With a scrunched up face, the young blonde looked at Randall as if to ask *do you believe her?*

Randall's impassive stare conveyed she had no ally there.

Uncle Harry nodded with the gravity of a high priest presiding over the annual rite of ancestor worship.

With a haughty shrug Ashley moved to sit beside her father with five other relatives at the other end of the table.

Beck watched Randall engage the Leader in a discussion on farm policy, evidence of the "good work" Randall did in her father's eyes. Her uncle also appeared to take Randall more seriously, asking a question about where the funding went from the Farm Aid concerts.

Beck thought Randall could be a regular, working man, but then, that wouldn't have been him. Why wasn't she satisfied with a husband who was lauded around the world as a great artist?

Beck drank wine and was beginning to relax when she saw the Fuscos take a seat across the dining room in an area away from the regulars. She couldn't take her eyes off Betty, dressed like a budding teen in a black pinafore and stripped shirt. She'd curled her hair and wore makeup, beautiful, sophisticated. In five years she'd be the age Beck had been when she'd conceived her. Would Aunt Lil warn her about the dangers of her budding sexuality?

Beck became aware of her father following her gaze. With a sudden change of focus of being caught, Beck made a display of returning her attention to the table.

The Leader asked Randall, "Hunger is one of your issues isn't it?"

Beck's back straightened. Randall put down his double straight bourbon. "It's one of Beck's priorities at Catholic Charities. I did a benefit last year." He continued to try to show himself in their best light–working together for good causes.

The Leader looked at Randall like a doctor evaluating a patient.

"You know Congressman Fusco?"

Beck inhaled quickly, raising her eyebrows.

"Not sure."

"He's chair of the Hunger Caucus in the House."

"Oh yeah, good man," Randall tilted his head and narrowed his eyes trying to suss out where the Leader was going.

"He and his family are here. We saw them this morning."

"Oh, that's nice," Randall said and looked at Beck for help.

"Lovely family," she said.

Appearing to be satisfied Randall had not been told about Betty, the Leader turned to his uncle and asked about conservative Democrats in his part of Virginia switching to the Republican Party.

She saw Randall's eyes glaze as the gravity of his thoughts pulled him into his fantasies.

"Need to go," he said leaving an uneaten chop in front of his place.

She quickly shook her head to convey her displeasure. He ignored her, barely said good-bye to her father and Gail, mumbled "Judge," and walked away from the table.

"He's working on a song," she feebly implied a new Butch Malloy song was worth the insult of abandoning her.

"An artist." The Leader's smile indicated he understood.

Randall appeared to become disoriented snaking through the maze of tables. She watched as if a higher consciousness led him to within inches of his daughter.

Nick smiled and nodded at him. Randall didn't respond, maintaining a straight-ahead stare, ignoring the expressions of recognition from strangers that regularly greeted him.

Nick said something to Betty and Frankie. Betty turned her head to watch her father walk away from her.

Did Betty's adopted family communicate in innuendoes and lies like her birth family? Was Nick telling her about a rock star they'd just seen?

Nick looked to the Lyons family table and met Beck's gaze. For an instant they stared at each other. She looked down at her plate of Dover sole and tried to act as if this was a normal family meal.

* * *

When she returned to the room, Randall was picking his Martin, scratching lyrics on a pad in front of him.

"Going for a walk," she said and took her coat and hat.

"OK," he vaguely replied.

She left the hotel by the rear entrance near the outdoor pool. She'd not gone ten yards, still in the light beneath the overhanging porch when she heard her name.

Nick stepped toward her.

"Oh well, I just saw you," he said as if needing an excuse to talk to her.

"You'll get cold out here."

"Oh, I don't mind. I'm actually hot."

She started to walk into the darkness away from the hotel with a feeling of sleepwalking–a disorientation of order and visions regardless of time and space. She could have just stayed in the light of the hotel to have a conversation with him. How far would he walk with her?

"I was hoping to meet you at the World Hunger Concert last year in Chicago."

"We were just talking about that," she marked the coincidence, wanting him to know they thought alike.

"You were there?"

"No, I had other business."

"With Catholic Charities? Great organization."

He seemed to know more about her than published stories about the daughter of the Majority Leader and Butch Malloy? "What's your interest in hunger?" she asked.

"Well," his voice assumed a practiced air on one who had told a story many times. "During the war, I was blown off my ship by a kamikaze. We nearly starved before we were rescued. I know what hunger means."

He was from the World War II generation like so many of the parents, teachers, politicians she'd known. They'd built the world she was raised in, rarely revealing the horrors they'd witnessed–maybe because there were so many of them and they were mostly silent about the nightmares they shared.

"I was very young when I went to war."

She looked down feeling awkward that he seemed to want her to know he wasn't that old. They walked farther into the darkness of a cleared path bordered by snow leading to the golf course.

"I met Butch in Chicago. He's a great guy," Nick said.

"Sometimes." There was enough scorn in her voice to convey her disapproval. "He's hiding out in our room," she tried to explain.

"Why's he hiding?"

She wanted him to know why he'd ignored him in the dining room. "He wanted to be famous and now he can't stand it."

"It must be exciting being married to him."

"I suppose." She sounded disappointed, too revealing that much of her life with Randall had become a boring retreat. "He likes to go to clubs and bars, kind of a night owl.

"And you're not?"

"No, mostly not, we're on different schedules."

"You sound unhappy."

She didn't have anything to be unhappy about except Nick was raising her daughter.

"What about you? Are you happy?" she parried.

"For the most part." He hesitated and with a drop of his voice into sorrow said, "I miss my wife."

She felt like an idiot asking a man in mourning if he was happy. "I'm sorry." She tried to make her condolences sound sincere by speaking in a more compassionate voice.

"You knew her?" he asked.

Lil must have told him. Beck hadn't been careful enough. Her lie was exposed. She'd never met Judith. "I think so."

"And she spoke of us adopting Betty?"

Was this lie a *better* lie to protect someone—his dead wife, Judith? When stretching truth give away as little as possible. "In the context of Catholic Adoption Services." Her evasiveness was rewarded by him wanting to explain, not question or doubt her.

"We tried to tell her she was adopted when she was young." He told a poignant story that shifted Beck's apprehension to gratitude that he'd shared the tender moment when they'd told Betty she was adopted.

He and Judith had been sitting beside her on her bed after reading Doctor Seuss *Horton Hatches the Egg*.

"Am I the egg?" Four-year-old Betty had asked.

"And I'm Horton," Judith had said.

"And my mother didn't want me?"

"She wanted you," Judith had pulled Betty against her side. "We just wanted you more and God gave you to us."

Beck's words slipped in a whisper, "I wanted her."

"What?" Nick pulled out of storytelling.

Beck rapidly shook her head and blinked. "Where did you do the adoption?"

He turned his head to her and said as if wondering why she'd asked, "West Virginia."

"I do a lot of work with adoption with Catholic Services," she covered her tracks.

Confirmation thrilled and confused her in a spiral of emotions.

She was tempted to ask if he remembered the name of the hospital, but that would have risked too much exposure.

Nick sighed and returned to his explanation. "I'm not sure she remembers. We didn't think we could have children and then Frankie came along. I couldn't love her any more if she was my own child. Do you think I should tell her again?"

The irony of the question was like a falling elevator through the levels of meaning. She needed time to find a safe landing. Nick was waiting. To delay would be to confess.

She stopped and looked up at him. "I don't know. What if her real mother wants to meet her?"

Once asked, the question seemed barely relevant, revealing of another motive.

Nick's voice was disembodied in the dark. "I've thought of that. I always thought it should be up to Betty when she's ready. There are ways she can find her birth mother when she wants."

Beck was a prospector who'd hit a rich vein of precious ore. "You don't know who the birth mother is?"

"No. A friend handled the adoption. It was a private placement. The adoption papers were sealed."

"And this was before you were elected to Congress?"

"Yes, I was just a lawyer, living in Santa Barbara then."

With typical expression of one talking about his own history, Nick didn't appear to sense her question had confirmed a revelation. Her family could not have known that Theresa would be brought to Washington, back to her real mother. God had returned Theresa to her.

At the moment she should declare the miracle, truth knotted in stomach and she protected her father's reputation. The *better* lie–to sacrifice her interest–one truth for another. Why disturb or try to replace Betty's memory of Judith? How to explain to an eleven-year-old girl why she'd been given to another mother? Or that a man with long hair who'd ignored her tonight and sang for his living was her real father?

"Better to leave it up to her," Beck softly said.

Nick appeared to approve of her answer. "She's been through enough. She and Judith were extremely close. I hope to find someone someday that can help me raise her, someone that she will feel close to."

In an autonomic response Beck's hand slipped forward and touched his.

He moved to hold her hand–a gesture which could still be interpreted as friends walking hand-in-hand. Enclosed in darkness beneath the night shadow of an elm, he turned toward her still holding her hand. When she didn't pull away, he kissed her lightly on the cheek, still well within the realm of friendship.

Was she supposed to stop him from going farther? The intimacy grew to a fever, as he pulled her to him.

For a moment she stiffened, before placing her hand on the back of his strong neck and moving farther into the embrace.

She liked the size of him, the way she fit against him, the slight scent of cologne. Randall would never wear a fragrance.

Nick released her as if to confirm intention. She slumped with knee-weakened passion. Wind blew a wisp of her hair. In the darkness she saw the shape of a figure with a Panama hat watching them from a shadow. Was her dream now a nightmare?

"I'm sorry, I shouldn't have done that," Nick said.

She sighed. "I felt it too."

His eyes glittered with lustful appreciation as he considered her as if trying to determine how far he could go.

Beck looked past him and the figure in the hat was not there.

Nick appeared to land on the side of morality. He hunched his shoulders. "I'm not like that, you know."

She raised her eyes to his.

"I don't mess around with married women. Don't mess around at all really."

She looked away from the intensity of his stare. She'd tempted him. He'd mistaken her interest in Betty for a come-on.

She put her hand out, almost reflexively childlike and he pulled her to him. Her passion was fed by elation that here was the majestic path God had chosen for us, a miraculous second chance.

She floated in his embrace and if he'd pulled her down she's have made love to him on the snow.

As if sensing her weakness, he detached from her and she awoke to awareness of the danger of his attraction. The modern sexual morality for congressmen she guessed was not too different than the music business. She knew that Randall was regularly offered sex by strangers, maybe even her cousin. Would a player talk about his dead wife?

As they walked back to the hotel, he spoke of his love for his children, saying he needed a partner. He was an easy mark, a clear offer if she wanted to be Betty's mother in life as well as fact.

They entered the lobby without speaking. "Well, good night then," he said and rapidly climbed the stairs as if embarrassed for being too obvious.

Beck returned to the hotel room, wondering if Randall would be there. Would he say he'd seen her kissing another man?

Randall sat on the end of the bed, working on his song.

She put away her coat and hat and sat on the reading sofa feeling disoriented like she'd come to the wrong room. She'd just been kissed by a man, a real man, not with the hazy artistic sensitivity of Randall. Both scary and complimentary to think that Nick Fusco wanted her, that she wanted him. If he knew her better would he still want her? At least Randall knew her, or most of her anyway.

"Do you miss not having a child?" she asked.

He looked up at her with interest. "Are you ready to?"

She'd not been clear on her verb tense. A child could be taken from her again. Now, more than ever she wasn't sure of her marriage. She'd strayed into a dangerous opening.

"No."

He considered her for a minute as if contemplating if he wanted to go down that road. "You know I want to have more...I mean children with you."

He corrected himself, respecting the sanctity of her secret. He knew. She should tell him his daughter was here. But like a curse that silenced confession, she blinked and said, "You know I love you."

"Love you too," he gave an automatic response. "Here, listen to this. Think it's called *Lighthouse*."

He played his new song for her, a private premier, the perk of being married to a star—beautiful, sure to be a hit, a crowd-pleaser—an allegory to a lighthouse beaconing an old lover home.

Somebody's calling you,

Turn around to see

A boat is waiting

To take you to me.

Like a lighthouse in the rain,

I will feel your pain.

Like a lighthouse in the rain,

We will start again.

Innocence and strength of love were the hallmarks of his songs. If she left him, would he write about lies and deceit?

* * *

The Women's Club was in a converted mansion above Dupont Circle in a neighborhood of embassies. Most of the guests were women. At a glance Beck was able to identify who she knew and would be useful to speak to, who were lawyers dressed in matching skirts and jackets, who were socialites and dilettantes in more feminine colorful attire, drinking martinis and glasses of wine in the middle of the day. The men in similar suits and ties were more difficult to sort, their age and the manner indicating who had power.

She saw Nick in the hallway leading to the dining area, certain he'd come to see her. Out of the corner of her eye she was aware of him staring at her for an instant too long. She walked to a part of the club with smaller rooms and sensed him following her down the hall.

"Beck."

She stepped into an empty office, pulling him in her wake. He closed the door behind them.

Beck loved his large sleepy Italian eyes. "You had better be careful, my father's here," she said as he pulled her to him. He kissed her as urgently as the first time and she pressed firmly against him. Insanity, deliciously insane, to risk so much for a kiss. Beck heard muffled voices, enough to scare her.

"I'll leave first," she said.

He looked overwhelmed and pursed his lips. "I must see you."

* * *

At nine that night, she drove into the parking lot of the Jefferson Memorial. He was dressed in a full-length black cashmere coat, scarf, and newsboy cap, waiting for her beside a tour bus. She lowered the window of her Jaguar. "Hey sailor, looking for a good time?"

Inside the car, she found his nervousness charming.

"Thank you for coming. I can't tell you how much it means to me. I've thought of nothing but you since the Homestead. May I ask you," he hesitated as if making one last internal argument, then looked at her with an embarrassing passion and sincerity. "Is there a place in your heart for me?"

His deep limpid eyes were portals into an honest soul.

God, you are giving me back my daughter. Her awe at the thought caused her to catch her breath. "Yes," she whispered.

His kiss, the gentle pressure of his hands, the day's growth of his beard and shape of an older man seemed blessed, an anointment. She leaned to be closer to him. But the lie was a curse. Would he want her if he knew her deeper motive to be reunited with her daughter? If she told him now, perhaps she could explain, make him understand. But if she told him, she must tell Randall, Betty, everyone. Panda's secret, all they'd done to protect her father would be sacrificed for what? People would know she was with him to be with Betty. The stone of her silence refused to move from the crypt of her complicity. She sat back in the seat. "No. I'm wrong for you."

The veer emphasized with a matter-of-fact tone exposed her flaw. He stared at her with his sad, beautiful eyes, and said—as if she needed to know—"I'm sorry, I felt so strongly there was something between us."

"More than you know. But it's wrong. I can't, won't."

Gone was the ardent lover, replaced by an embarrassed gentleman who'd tried to seduce a married woman, mistaken why she'd refused.

384   JEFFREY MARCUS OSHINS

TWENTY-SEVEN

THE HAND OF GOD

Perhaps because she'd turned 33 and felt older, Beck's relationship with Randall had increasingly seemed like something of the past, of childhood. They no longer tried to live together or span the two realms they lived in. He didn't like Washington and when he wasn't touring preferred tropical climes. They'd talk nearly daily by phone, and the sex was good when he did come home—maybe better to compensate for the time apart. Though she was a legendary figure in the music press and among the fans who knew or thought they knew the story of Butch and Dodge, she kept her distance, leaving Miss Kitty to tend to his life as a performer.

She was in an imaginary relationship with Betty. Her daughter was now sixteen, the age she'd gotten in trouble. She worried about her obsessively, the way she used to think of Randall. She told herself the same stories. Like a bully repeatedly tormenting a fool, she'd repeatedly fall for the same mental tricks. Her throat would tighten, eyes glaze, rehearse confessions, devise plots of reconciliation and explanation.

Her role as a lobbyist for the Catholic Church occasionally brought her in contact with Nick. She'd meet with him in his office, see him at conferences and social events. With a tinge of embarrassment over a past indiscretion, they'd talk policy, act happy but not too happy to see each other. She'd casually ask about the children, hungering for news of a child she fought all temptation to spy on, befriend.

Nick was a legislative star, the object of great sympathy and admiration until he wasn't.

On a winter evening, in 1982, the second year of the Reagan administration, feet tucked beneath her on a Victorian sofa in the study of her Capitol Hill brownstone, Beck watched the news anchor report that nine members of Congress and a senator had been filmed taking bribes from FBI agents posing as Japanese businessmen. Among the official photos of smiling, confident looking men was Nick.

The video cut to him in handcuffs being led by FBI agents from Pamela Harriman's P Street mansion.

She picked up a phone atop a carved elephant end table beside the sofa and dialed her father. They regularly talked on Sunday, a remnant of her days at L'Ecole.

"NBC just showed Nick Fusco being arrested," she said.

"I know." His voice was gruff, "Damndest thing I've ever seen, beyond anything I can remember."

"Was the press there for any of the other arrests?"

"Not that I know of. Obviously there was a leak. Someone must really be after his seat. I'm sick about the whole business. This is an attack on the legislative branch. They got Bobby Rogers too," the Leader said of one of his closest friends in the Senate.

"Nick never remarried, did he?" she asked. The question was too personal, too irrelevant and revealing. She knew Nick hadn't.

"Don't know that much about the man's personal life." The Leader negotiated with greater minds than hers. He wasn't going to show he knew Nick had adopted his granddaughter by a mere feint like that from her.

"Wonder what will happen to the children if he goes to jail?" She gave away her hand, but her father refused the bid of Betty's adoption.

"Anybody who knows these men believe they're innocent. It's rotten. The whole business stinks. The FBI set them up. This is a gross attack on the Congress. I'm going to ask Rogers and Fusco to sit at my table for the National Press Club dinner next week. You want to come?"

She stared at an abstract round face Paul Klee on the wall. She hated when Washington devoured its stars and was suspicious of the invitation. If Nick was put in jail, Beck should be there for Betty, at least as a friend.

* * *

Dressed in Panda's full-length silver mink coat, Beck stepped from the far side of the Leader's official limousine at the ballroom entrance of the Shoreham and followed her father through the crowd of arriving guests as he moved in a practiced manner through the many who wanted to speak or be seen with him.

Nick Fusco in overcoat and tux was waiting for them inside.

"Leader, how are you?" he greeted her father with a bravado that seemed forced given his destroyed reputation.

Her father made a point of heartily shaking his hand as the Director of the FBI passed. Only in Washington would the hunter and hunted come together like this to be made fun of by their peers.

The Leader said loudly to Nick, "Raferty's the President's tool."

Whether the FBI director heard him or not was not evident as Raferty moved farther into the hall.

"It goes deeper than you might think," Nick said.

The Leader nodded but this was not the place or time to share a conspiracy theory.

Bobby Rogers, the senator caught in the sting, stepped out from the milling crowd of tuxedos and ball gowns.

"Bobby, good to see. You know Congressman Fusco." The Leader passed him off to Nick and moved expertly to another quick conversation.

Nick and the senator nodded at each other, appearing to share a reluctance to be seen together as if they were in a police lineup to be identified as part of the same gang.

Beck pondered the shaky pinnacle politicians stood on—what Panda had defended for her son.

A thin handsome man, Rogers' eyes shone with kindness as he took Beck's hand. "I've known you've since you were a little girl. I've been to your house at the lake. We're going to be sitting together this evening."

They walked as a group through a ballroom as large as an airplane hangar to a table near a raised dais where the hosts and speakers were seated. Few had taken their seats, busy with political and press mingling.

Nick, a sheen in his large eyes, visibly admired Beck as they stood by their table.

She knew how to dress to blow away the style police of Washington in a Versace sleeveless silk sequin gown with a tight bodice accenting her breasts, her hair styled with a chignon of Dolly Madison curls down the back of her long neck, diamond teardrop earrings below her ears.

"You look gorgeous. I can't tell you how many times I've wanted to call, to see you." Nick looked enraptured.

She smiled and nodded, caught between not wanting to encourage his attention or talk to anyone else. "Lovely seeing you."

An elderly lady stepped to their table. "Well look who's here. Have you decided to come home?"

Beck beamed at the upturned rouged cheek of Andrea Vorpel–Panda's college friend from Mary Washington–a bridge between Virginia and Washington society.

"I'm here. We have our place on Capitol Hill," Beck said.

An angry old aunt, Andrea lectured. "I'm too old to waste words. Your grandmother would want you at Heatherford." She referred to Panda's estate as if to Beck's birthright. "Time to come home to Virginia."

Beck smiled whimsically, not bothering to say that after her grandfather had been placed in a rest home, Heatherford had been leased to the embassy of Saudi Arabia and was now a fortified compound. "Do you know Congressman Fusco?" Beck attempted to shift Andrea's attention.

Andrea gave Nick a disdainful glance and quick nod. Nick ignored the slight and zeroed in on the man with her, George Bennicini, Washington bureau chief of the New York Times. After a token greeting, Nick said to Bennicini, "I have reason to think there's a relationship between the FBI trying to remove me from Congress and the firing of Clark Kerr."

"The former chancellor of the University of California?" Bennicini twisted fat lips and squinted at Nick.

Nick spoke quickly, as if anxious to have his say before they were interrupted. "Go back into your files on the relationship between Reagan and J. Edgar Hoover. Look for the role of James Ashmore."

"*Humph*. Yeah, OK."

"Ashmore is running for my seat. I beat him 12 years ago and he's never forgotten it."

Beck heard Nick talking too fast, sounding paranoid, seeing ghosts in closets. The family man she'd been attracted to at the Homestead had been driven to distraction. She was wrong to criticize his behavior. Who knew how she'd be if she was 57 facing criminal charges and jail?

Bennicini shrugged and looked for his next conversation. Nick had lost him.

As if waiting for her chance, Myrna Toll from the *Washington Post* dropped into Bennicini's spot in front of Nick and Beck.

Beck was looking to sit down but remained standing beside Nick as Toll introduced herself.

"I was wondering if you'd mind mixing a bit of business with pleasure? I could not pass up this opportunity to find you both together," Toll said to Beck more than Nick.

"Hello, Myrna," Nick said.

"The congressman and I spoke at your husband's concert Saturday," Toll said.

Beck tensed and set her Gucci opera purse down on the table. What was Nick doing at Randall's concert? Had Betty gone? Randall hadn't said anything about seeing them.

"When I saw you at the concert," Toll said to Nick, "I was only working on a piece about Butch Malloy, Washington's contribution to rock. My assignment has grown. I want to do a piece on you, a personal piece about your family."

"My family's off limits," Nick said.

Toll leaned closer to him. "I want you to know that I am not a scandal writer. Just a reporter who does her homework. I want the opportunity to ask you about some things I've uncovered, give you the opportunity to deny or elaborate."

"And what is that?" Nick pressed his lips together.

"Everyone has secrets. You two appear to have your share." Toll stared at Beck.

Being married to Randall, Beck was used to prying reporters from fan and celebrity magazines, but not the *Washington Post*. What, if anything, did this newshawk have on her?

Stephen "Brownie" Brown, star of a weekly television talk show, pushed between Nick and Beck.

"THANK YOU, THANK YOU, MYRNA TOLL!" His theatrical voice carried across the hall.

Beck stepped back in apprehension of being caught in a spectacle as heads turned and conversations stopped to watch Brownie perform.

"You have just given me a topic that will no doubt make even the most ardent defenders of the First Amendment understand that we have become as callous and obsessive as hooded priests. You self-righteous Torquemada! By what scale of sanctity will you judge these good people?"

"Come on, Brownie." Toll tried to stop him before he built up too much steam—too late.

"No, you come on! This man, this man," Brownie boomed and pointed at Nick, "could very well be innocent. But we shall have lost his fine services by then. He will be trivialized, laughed at, and financially ruined, and why? What will we say then? That he is no longer newsworthy? Will you not even leave him the dignity of his family? Where was your interest in this good man and his family when he was working to relieve the despair of millions? Is there a greater humanitarian in the Congress? Shame, shame," Brownie's voice quivered, and disappeared into the depths of his condemnation.

Beck was ready to leave. She hated the small-town gossip and overacting bit players of Washington. What *secrets* had Myrna Toll uncovered? More than ever Beck was grateful for her grandmother sparing her the whispers that would have followed her if she'd not hidden her pregnancy.

Lights momentarily dimmed. Brownie stalked off and Toll shrank back as attendees sorted themselves by numbered sticks in floral centerpieces on tables crowded with silver, glasses, and plates. Ten people to a table, they sat to a roll and salad, a long-running production—the upper end of the rubber chicken circuit.

Each February the National Press Club Salute to Congress parodied a topical issue. A program at each place read—*How to Succeed in Politics Without Really Trying*. A Monopoly-type drawing of a happy man with his feet on a desk blowing a smoke ring from a cigar through three other smoke rings. After dining on *Gerrymander Garden Salad, Born Rich Crab Soup*, and *Unopposed Veal Medallion*, waiters served the dessert, *Glace Deceased Opponent*. The master of ceremony rose from his seat next to the podium and the entertainment began—a cross between a roast and a bad late night television opening monologue.

The female president of the club introduced a senator whose family name was on grocery shelves around the world. "Tell us, Senator, what was the most difficult thing about your election?"

The senator walked to the podium from the dais. A good legislator who worked hard, he and the other guests of honor were to be set up as comedic straight men for the evening.

"Let me see, the hardest thing I had to do to get elected was to speak to my daddy 'bout 'creasing my allowance so I could pay for the TV ads."

Polite if not enthusiastic laughter filled the hall.

"But things didn't get any easier once I got to Washington. People kept trying to give me things. I thought to myself, well, this seems normal enough." He paused for more laughter. "But I was told that now that I was a United States senator, I just couldn't take anything that was offered to me. If somebody was to try and give me money, I was to call the FBI immediately."

Nick stared ahead, not joining the laughter, the object of a roomful of bullying and ridicule.

"So," the senator continued, "one day some foreign fellow gives me this briefcase full of money, just like my birthday back home," more laughter, "and I said, 'I can't take this; I'm afraid that I'm going to have to call the FBI and tell them about this.' Imagine my surprise when the man said, 'Senator, you don't have to worry about that. I am the FBI.' I was right relieved to hear that, and I said, 'Well does that mean I can keep the money?"

Appearing to be aware of people looking at him, Nick forced a shallow chuckle.

"No,' the FBI foreign fellow said, 'we have to keep this money to see if there are any crooked politicians out there.' I said, 'Well sir, you don't have to act like a foreigner to find out about that, just go down to the *Washington Post*. Ask them–they'll tell you."

After the laughter subsided the senator continued, "I read the *Post* now. Didn't used to, but I have to now that I spend so much time up here. I read it to find out who's getting divorced, married, indicted. It's a great newspaper. You understand, though, back home we're more polite about that sort of thing. See, we find out about those things from our friends. We don't read about them; it's kind of like up here you don't have any friends, just the *Washington Post*."

He waited for laughter to roll back and forth across the large room. "What I don't quite understand though is who's gonna watch out for you? Now down home, say you stray a bit from the true and narrow, a friend is likely to come up to you and say, 'Billy-Boy, as your friend, I have come to tell you that you had better straighten up and fly right."

The senator had the good timing of a professional entertainer.

"Can you imagine the *Post* printing a warning–'Senator seen cavorting with a woman not his wife last week, watch out–we're on to you."

Beck glanced over to see Nick frowning and looking down.

The next speaker said he understood one of the congressmen indicted in the sting planned to plead that he thought the Veterans of Foreign Wars were paying him to speak–"Because they sure did look foreign."

Was laughing at Nick's and Bobby Rogers' misfortune therapeutic? The saying goes, comedy is someone else's tragedy. Would they make fun of other misfortunes? What if Nick had been blinded–*They say that justice is blind, but I know a congressman who...*" Those laughing thought that he and the other politicians caught in the sting had brought their trouble on themselves and were fair game. Few believed they were innocent. Nick and Rogers loved their jobs too much to take a bribe. By having the indicted members of Congress sit as his table, the Leader was sending a message to the Justice Department–don't use these sorts of tactics to take down members of the legislative branch. She should be willing to do her small part. Her father probably only wanted Nick at the table to cover his support of Rogers. But why did he need her there for that?

Beck leaned over and said to Nick, "Would you take me home, please?

He blinked in surprise. "Now?"

"Please."

"Of course." He stood and held the back of her chair while she picked up her purse.

She nodded to the Leader and walked beside Nick across a room of 70 tables. Their departure together seemed to attract more eyes than the four female reporters dressed like bees on the stage, singing,

I'm gonna sting ya, Congressman,

Yes, I am, Yes, I am.

I'm gonna sting ya, Congressman..."

She wished she'd stayed and stuck it out. Washington gossip would be full of the Majority Leader's daughter, Butch Malloy's wife, leaving with Nick Fusco. She wanted to be alone with him to hear about Betty meeting Randall.

Outside in the quiet of the foyer, Nick retrieved their coats.

"Are you, OK?" he asked as he held her mink for her.

"Oh, I'm all right." She slipped her arm into the silk-lined sleeve. "I don't have much tolerance for the silliness of it all. The way they take themselves so seriously." She looked up at him and smiled. "Washington just seems stupid and cruel sometimes."

"Thank you for getting me out of there," Nick said. "It was hard to endure."

He'd thought to ask of her first, but she was willing to accept his gratitude for what she'd done for him.

In his car, she examined his profile. He glanced at her and smiled. She reflexively turned her gaze, worried he'd misinterpret her look for the attraction that had come so seductively at the Homestead. *What did you think of the concert?* She rejected the question knowing he would think she was asking about Randall.

With his eyes on Rock Creek Parkway, he said. "You know I didn't do what they say I did."

"I know. My father does too." She hoped he wouldn't try to give his defense when she wanted to talk about Betty.

He launched into an elevator pitch of a defense he'd have to make repeatedly in public and court. An old military buddy who was his campaign treasurer had taken money from the FBI agents and deposited it in Nick's campaign account. If they'd found the bribe in his campaign account, he was going to have a hard time avoiding blame or jail.

"How are the kids, Betty?" she changed the subject to her liking.

Nick hunched over the wheel, face gray and old in the lights of oncoming cars. "They might put me in jail. I can handle it but I worry about Frankie and Betty."

"Me too," Beck said softly, nearly to herself.

"You remember my sister, Lil? She's become a member of our household. She can watch them if I have to go away."

Beck sighed. "I hope it won't come to that. Did Betty enjoy the concert?"

Nick seemed to brighten, "Oh definitely. She's been a huge Butch Malloy fan ever since she saw him at the Homestead."

Beck raised her hand to cover her face, hapless, unable to avoid catastrophe. She'd wafted Randall in front of Betty like a poison potion.

"He was her first rock and roll crush. She has a friend at school whose aunt works for his manager and got them backstage passes last week for the show at the Capitol Center."

Beck's shoulders slumped. She turned to look at Nick's profile. "And you let her go?"

Nick appeared to not understand her alarm. "Why? I took her."

Beck quickly shook her head to compose herself. "It's quite a scene backstage. I don't go to his shows very often. Probably should though."

"Betty's a songwriter. She and a chum at school have formed a band. I think Betty's going to be a star."

Genetics, her carelessness, a friend—irresistible forces were pushing Betty toward her father. Was there no retribution for her lie too horrible?

Beck put urgency into her words as she trained her eyes on Nick. "You don't want that for her. It's a terrible life." She rallied to sound more positive. "I'd be happy to help, perhaps, you know, mentor, be there for her. A young woman can face a lot of challenges today."

He glanced at her with a thin smile, liquidity in his beautiful sleepy eyes. "I would appreciate that more than I can say. Funny, I see some of you in her."

Beck turned from his adoration with a slight nod and kept her gaze locked ahead. He didn't know, couldn't know she was Betty's mother or Randall, whose creative talents she'd apparently inherited, was her father. "I'll call and leave my contact information at your office," she said as his car approached her rowhouse.

He parked and looked at her with the tentativeness of teenager on a first date. Afraid he was going to try to kiss her again, she dispassionately said, "Thank you for being such a gentleman. No need to walk me in."

Opening the iron gate to the brownstone, she could not be locked inside quick enough. Her relationship with God had loosened until she no longer felt her life was in His hands until this. Was He sending her a message? Adopted by a man who would become a congressman, brought from California to Washington. Of all the rock stars why would Betty's friend's aunt work for Miss Kitty? She knew the woman—a cousin of Randall's mother. Had Betty been reunited with her father by a celestial hand or a demon?

* * *

Dressed for meetings on Capitol Hill in a Talbot tweed, Beck was ready to leave when the phone beside her bed rang with an accusatory tone of someone trying to catch her. She almost didn't answer but thought her father's people might be calling about using the brownstone for a fundraiser.

Nick spoke in a hesitant manner. "I hope I'm not disturbing you."

After the cold shoulder she'd given him last night, she doubted he was calling to make love to her.

"It's about Betty."

She pressed the phone tighter to her head.

"She ran away. No, not exactly ran but didn't ask my permission, just left word with her aunt that she was going to Boston. It's a school night. This is very much unlike her to miss school. She's a very good student." He tried to bolster her, act the proud parent but Beck shared his concern at her behavior.

Randall was playing at the Garden in Boston tonight. She didn't want Betty around the drugs, sex, criminals who preyed on the innocent and naive at a Butch Malloy show.

Nick confirmed why Betty was in Boston. "Apparently, she met a woman backstage at the Capitol Center who says she's part of the band family, whatever that is."

Beck frowned. Butch Malloy and the Bloomers attracted *Bloomheads* who followed the band from show to show, mostly a harmless traveling party. All ages from early teens to aging hippies would congregate in the parking lot outside the venue, sell handmade knickknacks and drugs, help each other with food, places to camp or couches to *crash* on, beg for tickets to always sold-out shows. Beck had thought Betty was too sophisticated for that.

"They're family, friends, staff." She was making excuses. The *family* also included band girlfriends—like sailors with a girl in every port—some random, others regular. Had she been an Electra delivering her daughter to her father? What if Randall took Betty as his road lover? No he wasn't like that. Or was he? The way women touched him—hugs, blushes, young seductresses primed by nature to sacrifice their innocence. No, Randall, never—but if not him the band or worse, the depraved roadies who thought that moving equipment was show business and girls part of the food chain.

Nick's voice sounded constrained. "We don't know anything about this woman who invited her. Betty is very mature for her age and I do trust her. I'd just feel better if someone was there to watch for her. I was wondering if you could give me Butch's number?"

She honestly didn't know. When he was traveling with the band he was the one who called her. He'd called from Cleveland two nights before. "I'm sorry. When he's on the road he's nearly impossible to reach. They are very secretive about where they stay, you know, rabid fans and all." She was putting him off and rushed to add, "Let me give you his manager's number. She calls herself Miss Kitty. I'll try too."

"Sorry to involve you in my dysfunctional family."

Beck twisted the headset cord. You have no idea, she thought. "I'm glad you did. I want to protect her too. I may go to Boston myself. I've meetings in the Senate this morning. I'll fly up this afternoon, make sure she's OK. I'll talk to her, try and act a good influence." Her shameless misrepresentation could not have offered a more attractive seduction than a promise to help his—their—precious daughter.

"I can't tell you how much I appreciate the interest you show in my family."
He reverted to being her suitor. "Is it wrong to tell you how I feel about you?"

"Not now." She cut him off with a businesslike retort. "I'm happy to do
what I can."

Betty was the age she'd been when her life went off the rails. Beck had tried
to be righteous, married Betty's father. Everything was out of order. When she
and Randall could have had another child they didn't–she too busy with her
career–a lie told to cover her fear having another child.

Many times, he'd implied he knew why she'd gone to France. She should
have told Randall long ago where their daughter was. She could honestly say
she'd tried, but not that hard. She doubted he would understand what she still
protected, why she'd waited so long to tell him.

* * *

Her lobbying dragged through most of the day with a hearing, visits with
congressmen and an opposing *America first* senator who wanted support for
a crop bill in exchange for not blocking federal funding for the Food Stamp
program. She'd not been able to get through the many times she'd called Miss
Kitty and when she caught a crowded five o'clock shuttle from National Airport,
neither Randall nor Miss Kitty knew she was coming.

TWENTY-EIGHT

BALANCE OF FIDELITY

N early showtime at the Boston Garden, she went to the backstage door beside the loading dock. A gaggle of Bloomheads were trying to talk their way backstage past security and tour staff. Beck approached a burly guard with a walkie-talkie and said, "I'm Butch's wife."

The man looked at her Louis Vuitton overnight bag and red Russian Princess coat before speaking into his walkie-talkie.

While she waited, a woman shivering in a thin coat, black mini-skirt, breath condensing in the cold, spoke to her.

"He's really near, man, I mean, I know I'm going to get in. Butch and I have like this thing, you know. I've been listening to his records since, you know, like when I was a little girl. He was the first record I ever bought and anyway the other night, I just got this message from him—I don't know like how, somewhere—to come here and be with him, I mean really be with him."

Five minutes passed with no response from inside. Standing with the psychotic fan and a teen who said that Charlie from the lighting crew had said she should come backstage for a pass, Beck might as well have been holding a sign or finger up to the scalpers out front. She'd never had to beg to get in anywhere, much less one of Randall's shows.

An expensively dressed couple with an air of entitlement arrived. The guard spoke into the walkie-talkie. Barely a minute passed before the door opened a crack and Pluto, who'd hitched a ride from school dances around the world tending to the band family, stuck out his head.

The door opened to admit the couple and Beck stepped forward.

The guard put out a muscular arm to stop her. "Please step back, ma'am."

"Pluto!" she called.

He looked out again and his eyes expanded with surprise. "She's in," he said to the guard.

The psychotic with a thing for Randall grabbed Beck's arm as the door opened. The security guard pulled her away. "Tell Butch I *have* to talk to him," the woman pleaded as Beck walked into the back of the arena.

Beck waited while Pluto gave the couple two patches *Untouchable Tour* written in circus style across a silhouette of palm trees and a camel, *BOSTON* stamped across the bottom of the shiny white rayon. "Don't have one for you." He scrunched up his face. "I'll walk you back."

"Is Miss Kitty here?"

"Not yet. Butch expecting you?"

His officious attitude surprised her given his past respect if not reverence. Years since she'd been to one of Randall's concerts, she felt out of place, not that she'd ever felt comfortable in the weird distortions of performance and idolization of his shows.

Roadies stacked now empty equipment cases. A buzz of anticipation and a thousand conversations, claps and whistles arose from the hidden audience, indicating the show was about to begin.

Pluto walked her through a backstage party area with a pop-up kitchen and bar, now nearly empty, no Betty.

"The guest area is over there." Pluto pointed to a curtain guarded by two men.

"Where's Randall?" she asked like a woman catching her husband cheating.

"You know, getting ready for the show, about to go on."

"Take me to him."

"Well, I mean, you know..."

She gave the smaller man a sideways glance.

"OK." He sighed like he was going to get in trouble for obeying her and escorted her into a locker room lined with stalls.

"Better wait here," he said and knocked on a door marked Visiting Coach.

A woman stuck out her head. Pluto nodded in Beck's direction. He tried to whisper but Beck heard him say, "Tell him Dodge is here."

The door closed and they waited with no immediate response from inside the office. The sound of the crowd grew more restive as they clapped for the show to begin.

The door opened and a redhead sauntered out dressed in a sheer silk peasant crop top exposing a flat belly and tapering of her waist. Elegant, confident in looks and charm, she passed Beck with a frank stare that combined curiosity with a mocking expression. To dress like that in this cold was to be putting your sexuality forward. Where was her coat? Why did she have to leave before Beck could go in? Only the band's wives and families would be allowed in the inner sanctum before a show. The redhead was someone's lover in the band. No groupie would be allowed in. Who else other than Randall's lover would be sent out before Beck could come in? A twisted knot of sorrow and anger tightened in her stomach. No wonder nobody wanted her here. The scene was so common—wife comes home unexpectedly, catches husband cheating.

"OK," Pluto said.

The office had a utilitarian look of multiple users, a desk, office chairs, and a large television screen built into the wall. A woman's coat and bag lay beside an antique leather saddle bag Randall used to carry clothes and notebooks.

Randall, dressed in his everyman denim work clothes and boots, took her hand. Was his slight tremor normal pre-show nerves or more proof she'd caught him with a mistress? "Hey, Beck, nice surprise," he said.

Robbie, her first lover, put his arm around her shoulder in a sideways hug. "Dodge, you're looking better than ever."

"Oh, I just was in town unexpectedly, thought I'd catch a show."

"You should have called someone," Randall said with a hint of exasperation.

"I tried," she said.

He followed her as she set her coat and bag beside his lover's.

The sound of the crowd grew with stomping feet almost to match her anger. "Better go on," she said in a cold voice.

"Yeah." Randall turned his attention to the band. "OK, let's do this."

The band huddled like a sports team ready to take the floor. Randall, coach, star, guru closed his eyes and said almost in the tone of prayer, "Let thoughts go, just play."

"Play," the band repeated, clapped.

She followed as they moved as a unit through the locker room and up metal stairs to the raised stage.

Houselights went dark and a pre-recorded soundtrack from Elgar's *Salut d'Amour* elicited a raucous response. Positioned by the onstage mixing board, Beck watched stagehands with small low-power flashlights guide the musicians to their instruments. In the dark, Robbie spoke to Randall who nodded. Robbie turned to the drummer set up on a riser and a message was passed through the band.

With a nod from Robbie, stage and spotlights flashed on and the band roared into *Dodge*.

The crowd responded to the opening chords off his first album, rarely played, and cheered for a song avid Butch Malloy fans knew he'd written about his high school sweetheart, the senator's daughter he'd married, and if she was right about the redhead in the coach's office, would soon be divorced.

Dodge's there when I need her,

Nobody can touch her,

Cause she's my friend,

What comes after that,

Don't matter much,

Don't matter much,

Don't matter much in the end.

Randall looked offstage and smiled at her before turning back to the microphone pointed at his mouth.

She didn't doubt he still loved her, would always love her like nobody else could. She owed him the benefit of the doubt and an explanation of who was the redhead with her coat and bag beside his. She was Dodge, a star in the

Butch Malloy firmament. Let the redhead try and usurp that. Beck would claim her rightful place in the Bloomer pantheon and do what she'd come to accomplish–find and protect her daughter.

In the illumination from the stage, she could see into the front row area reserved for the backstage crowd–not Bloomheads, but leathered record executives, local dignitaries, family and friends–more interested in the scene than the music.

Among the partying crowd, Betty looked somehow regal watching the spectacle with a bemused smile. Straps hung a floral print blouse on thin shoulders. Her round face and high cheekbones, Panda's emerald eyes and Randall's mother's strong jaw, melted Beck with a memory of the newborn she'd held for so short a time.

Standing beside Betty, sharing an elegant high-class look was the woman who'd invited her to run away. The redhead caught Beck staring. Their eyes met for a contest of wills that Beck lost, stepping into the darker recesses of the stage, shifting her gaze back to the performance. The strumpet had infiltrated her life, possibly seduced her husband and constituted a promiscuous threat to her daughter. Beck hated her.

* * *

Ninety minutes into the show, Randall was singing one of his pretty sad songs.

I lost you,
In the night.
I lost you,
In the light,

Of a passing day.

Miss Kitty arrived.

"Lynda Bird, what are you doing?" she asked, lips pressed together in an expression Beck recognized as trouble.

Beck raised her voice over the music, "I tried to call you."

"And I tried to call you back a bunch of times. So?"

"Aren't you glad to see me?"

"Mostly," Miss Kitty examined her with narrowed eyes. "And what's so important that you called me five times?"

"A friend of mine asked me to look out for his daughter. That one over there." Beck pointed to Betty.

Miss Kitty glanced at the swaying, smiling girl. "Let's get a drink," she said and led Beck down the single flight of metal stairs at the edge of the stage.

A full bar was set up in the lounge. Spicy scent of curry wafted from an open kitchen behind checkered-clothed-covered tables. "What you drinking?"

"Stoli with a twist," Beck ordered.

"A Chablis," Miss Kitty said and turned to Beck. "Who's your friend so important to get you to a road show?"

"Nick Fusco. I gave him your number. Did you talk to him?"

"He left me a message."

"You call him back?"

"No," Miss Kitty said with scorn. "Why should I?"

"He's worried about his daughter."

Miss Kitty exhaled a quick laugh. "You know how many calls we get from parents wanting us to fix things because little Jill or Johnny has run off to be a Bloomhead?"

"You know who Nick Fusco is?"

Miss Kitty took a sip of Chablis. "One of those crook congressmen, isn't he?"

"He says he's innocent."

"Don't they all. What's it to you?"

"The redhead who came out of Randall's dressing room when I arrived, brought Betty Fusco."

Miss Kitty pressed her lips together. "She's my cousin Monique Fleischner, took the young lady under her wing at the Capitol Center show, asked if she could bring her up for the Boston show. Monique's no Bloomhead if that's what you're worrying about. She's got more money than you do."

"Monique's very attractive."

"Yeah, it runs in the family." Miss Kitty took a deep pull of wine.

"And she's Randall's lover," Beck said between question and statement.

Miss Kitty contemplated her for a moment. "You run up here to protect yourself or the young lady?"

"I came for Betty, but that's not what I found."

"And what do you think you found?"

Beck glanced to see if anyone was near enough to overhear them. "Let's go for a walk."

They picked up their glasses moved deeper into the cavern of the Garden loading dock.

"Please don't play me for a fool. Tell me. Is Randall faithful to me?"

Miss Kitty squinted. "You want me to be your spy?"

Beck looked at her intently. "I want you to be my friend."

Miss Kitty shrugged. "Not that I know of, but I'm not the morality police. L'Ecole put me off telling people how to behave."

Beck spoke calmly, hiding the anguish she felt at being close to confirming her suspicions. "There have been others, haven't there?"

Miss Kitty shook her head. "You really that clueless?" She set the wineglass on an equipment case marked with the band's name. "I'll try to explain your man to you 'cause I *am* your friend; otherwise I'd say *c'est la vie,* baby." Miss Kitty looked toward the stage. "The man has got a foot on the floor and his head in the bed–your house-of-mirrors senator's daughter's life and this..." She passed her extended arm in a semi-circle, "...dream time. Butch dreams for people–ugly people, beautiful people, Monique people, Betty people. He shares visions with them, puts into words things they know but can't say. That's what he does. That's why 19,000 people are out there floating around this building for a few hours. He doesn't fuck them. You understand?"

No, she didn't. Did Miss Kitty mean he was faithful to her? Beck looked into her vodka glass and then up at Miss Kitty. "He dreams with me too. It's like I'm not there most of the time."

Miss Kitty shook her head in disgust. "You're thick as a bag of nails. Are your nerves so dead? Don't you listen? He's written a hundred songs about you. He feels you in ways you don't feel yourself. You're the root of his images and pretty words. No Monique can be that for him. Isn't that enough?"

Beck exhaled deeply. Miss Kitty was clever. She hadn't denied that Randall took lovers, that Monique was one of them. "That doesn't mean I'm happy."

Miss Kitty shoulders slumped. "I guess I always figured his love would get you through all the other lies in your life. But then I never understood what he saw in you."

What was one more lie? To not abandon Betty again, she had to be rid of Monique. Beck leaned closer to Miss Kitty. "I do love him. More than I show. I know that but...oh, I don't know, maybe if it had been different, if we had a more normal life. Help me hold onto him. Help me understand him."

Miss Kitty scrunched her cheeks into an expression of sour distaste. "How long I know you? You think I'm buying that? Talk about playing someone for a fool. God, you're corrupt. Is it something in a politician's blood? I don't know why I keep thinking of you as some kind of victim. Usually I can see people so clearly. Not you. You always confuse me."

Beck blinked and looked beyond Miss Kitty with a distant focus she assumed when Miss Kitty insulted or bullied her.

Miss Kitty continued her attack. "You're pure Washington. I don't know any other way to describe it. Not evil for evil's sake, not like Nazis. It's a kinder, gentler evil, a lie, a crime always done because it's better that way—better for who? That's what you evil bastards can't ever see—it's always just better for you more than anybody else."

A roar arose with a steady wave of clapping as the band left the stage for the ritual of being called back for an encore. Miss Kitty looked intently at Beck. "Just don't go crazy about it, OK? I've got to go collect some money for you."

Miss Kitty turned to leave, then turned back. "If you want to find Miss Fusco, Monique said she was going to bring her to the aftershow party. You can see Monique in action there." Miss Kitty gave her one of her troublemaker smiles and left her alone on the cement floor.

Beck had to keep her focus on befriending Betty and guiding her away from the dangers of this fantasy world where women were seduced by the allure of men playing songs. To leave now would be to abandon Betty to drugs, careless sex, and illusion. Clapping and cheering rolled through the backstage. At least Miss Kitty had given her a clue where to find Betty.

Beck retrieved her coat and bag and was waiting when after a two-song encore Randall hurried to a limousine parked at the back of the stage to whisk him to the hotel. Otherwise, he'd have to wait backstage for the crowd to clear.

"You're coming with me?" he asked as if surprised.

Beck got in the backseat of the stretch limo beside him.

"I don't know where we're staying," she said.

The Town Car exited through VIP parking on a six-minute trip through downtown Boston to the Millennium.

She didn't say anything as he wiped off with a towel, a laborer finished with a hard job, pulled on a hoodie and leaned back into the seat.

"Good show?" she asked as they drove down Beverly.

"All right."

They rode in silence a few blocks while he decompressed.

"Sounded good," she said.

"The usual train wrecks. Drink?" He nodded toward a stocked bar behind the front seat.

"No, I'll wait," she said.

"To what do I owe this honor?" He was ready to talk, sounding as perturbed as when she'd arrived unannounced at the show. "Come to break up with me?"

She looked out the side window and then at him. "Is that what you want?"

"Not this minute," he said as the limo pulled into the garage of the hotel.

One of Miss Kitty's assistants carrying a soft leather file case was waiting by the service elevator. He reminded Randall that he was Bart, assistant tour manager. "Great show," he said.

Randall was barely responsive in his detached manner. The beaming and eager young man escorted them to the concierge floor avoiding the lobby where enterprising Bloomheads were sure to be gathering for a chance to tell Randall how much they loved him.

In the hallway outside the door to their suite Beck asked Bart, "Do you know where the after show party is?"

Randall turned his head in surprise.

"1104, it's a suite," Bart said with hint of pride that he was in on the secret location.

Inside their room, Randall put his saddlebag on a desk. "Since when do you want to go to a band party?"

"Nick Fusco's sixteen-year-old daughter is supposed to be going. That's why I'm here." Beck set her bag down beside the door.

Randall squinted and cocked his head but seemed to accept her explanation. "You going down there now?" He picked up the kit.

"I'd like it if you went with me."

"All right let me clean up and change. They'll have food down there. We can eat."

While he showered, she sat before a gas-fired fireplace, a needless extravagance in the heated hotel. Large windows on two sides of the room gave an expansive view of the dark harbor.

The *better lie*-morality and truth–lying to protect reputation competed in her mind. For every reason to tell the truth there was an argument to remain silent. Others seemed to be able to live outside the truth–Panda to protect her son. Miss Kitty surely wondered where *her* son was, but she wasn't trying to find him. Fate hadn't forced her hand the way Betty had come to Randall.

Pressure rested in Beck like the bag of nails Miss Kitty had accused her of being, growing heavier the longer she waited. Her silence had been to protect her father. She lacked courage not morality. Familiar arguments looped through her mind. What if Panda had never told her father why Beck had gone away? How could he not know? Her grandmother couldn't just make her disappear in the middle of a school year without her father knowing the reason. Why was she still protecting him and from what? What harm would come to him now? Only his view of her, but if he already knew, what difference would it make?

What if Betty didn't know if she was adopted? If Beck's main purpose was to protect her, disrupting and casting suspicion into her relationship with Nick might cause more harm than good. Betty would be unlikely to trust her then.

Perhaps there was a middle ground, an external revelation. Betty might try to find her birth parents and would come to them.

Myrna Toll from the *Washington Post* had implied she'd uncovered secrets about Beck. The music press and fan magazines would eat up a story about Butch and Dodge's lost child. Randall would hate that. Would he understand why she hadn't told him she knew where his daughter was? Betty might like the idea of having Butch Malloy for a father, but how would she feel about her?

If she confessed, would that get her off this mental Tilt-A-Whirl? She'd wait to see how he behaved at the after show party and maybe tell him then. Maybe they were already broken up and he'd moved to another or multiple relationships. If they broke up, then she'd tell him. What difference would it make?

Lost in her turmoil, she meditated on her centering prayer–*mercy, mercy, mercy.*

Her eyes were closed when Randall came out the bathroom. She kept meditating through the noise of him dressing.

"You OK, Beck?"

She felt him touch her knee and opened her eyes to find him kneeling before her. Dressed in a fresh pair of jeans, a Pendleton shirt, and mod-style dress boots, looking strong, handsome, desirable. Sometimes he surprised her that he wasn't the skinny teen who'd seduced her and they'd somehow instantly leaped forward seventeen years. She tried to put her love of God into her expression. "Yes, I'm OK."

Randall rose from his kneeling position. "Why are you here?"

The question, though asked with concern not accusation, caused her to frown and pulled her from the calm of her meditation.

"I told you Nick Fusco. He was worried about Betty."

"I remember her when she was a little girl at the Homestead." Randall turned his gaze from her and looked out a window-framed view of the Custom House Tower.

Her eyes widened. "You remember that?"

Like a lawyer before a jury, he turned to offer a key piece of evidence. "I saw you walk outside with him. I followed you."

Her breath caught. How long had he doubted her fidelity?

She stood to defend herself. "I've always been faithful to you."

He took her hand and pulled her to him. "I believe you."

She pressed into the familiarity and comfort of his embrace, smelling the mixture of pot and hotel shampoo like an open box of wet herbs. "Have you been to me?"

He let her go and looked at her with his large, brown Randall eyes–full of sympathy and sincerity–eyes so many women loved. With a tremble of his full lower lip, he asked, "You want me to lie?"

The simple question was fraught with consequence–to know and leave, delude and stay. Here was the justification for the *better lie.*

She looked out at the twinkling lights of the city merging into the darkness of the harbor and back at him. "Tell me," she asked, as if for a death sentence.

He sighed and released his own burden. "We haven't talked for a long time, maybe since we were kids. When you got pregnant and went away."

She stiffened and reflexively denied. "Whatever are you talking about?"

The question had been answered. The moment to open herself, truly share her life with him had been forfeited for the sake of the lie, too embarrassed to confess, too far to backtrack.

With a tone of pleading, he said, "I'm used to feeling like I can never be good enough for you. I need honesty. My life is weird enough. I can't come home to that anymore."

She turned toward the fake fireplace, pride overcoming her sorrow. She would leave him before he left her. "We're so different. And we just keep getting more different."

"I don't really feel like I've *ever* known you. You're a mystery to me. Anyway, if we're going to break up, do you still want to go to the party? I'm fine with ordering in."

He was being flippant, trying to paper over a confession.

"Have you been faithful?"

"In my own way."

Anger, sorrow swirled in hearing what he'd trapped her with evidence of her guilt into asking. "What do you mean by *that*?" her voice clipped.

"I can't live with only part of you." He looked into the faint reflection of them in windows, then back at her to deliver his ultimatum. "I'm too far beyond that now to keep going."

She saw the sympathy he'd showed since they were children waiting for her to acknowledge that she understood he was going to leave her.

A freezing cold gripped her and she trembled like the floor was crumbling beneath her. She missed him like she'd missed her mother and brother, blamed herself for the end, and tried to scramble to sure footing. "I didn't come here to break up with you."

"There's never been anyone but you in my heart."

All he had to comfort her was a cheap line from a love song.

He reached for her and held her near but not close, offering a chance to go on. The *better lie* would have been kinder, protecting. She blinked back tears. What did she expect? Why was she surprised with them becoming lovers so young, being apart for months, him the object of idolization, the fountain of dreams, a magnet of delusion? Cut your losses, move on. To stay would be to confess.

"I do love you." She raised her face to him. "I don't know where you begin and I end."

He gave her an offer of reconciliation, a balance of fidelity.

"You forgive me for being bad sometimes?"

"No. I'll never trust you again."

The stupid grin was back. "You never did."

"You're horrible. Why do you have to be Butch Malloy?"

He frowned and shrugged. "I ask myself that more than you can know." He reached for her but she refused to go back to him. "Was Miss Kitty's cousin one of the ones you strayed with?"

"No, she's Robbie's."

Her eyes expanded and voice rose. "Robbie! What about Suzanne? He's married with children."

"You know Robbie. I got to tell *you* that? He's always been that way."

She looked around the room. "What am I doing here? What am I doing with you...you degenerates?" Anger conquered forgiveness, propelling her.

"You sound like your grandmother."

Beck raised her chin. "I *am* like my grandmother. And proud of it. How dare you talk of her that way? She was better than you could ever be!"

She burned the bridge, destroyed the route back. Still, she knew he'd be willing to reconcile if she would. "Don't you touch me." She pushed his hand away.

"Come on Beck. Would you rather I lie to you?"

"No and I don't want you sleeping with our daughter."

He lowered his neck, face scrunched. "What?"

"Robbie's whore is with our daughter."

His mouth gaped and he shook his head.

"Betty Fusco is our daughter." Truth sliced like a ray into a dank grave to reveal a rotting corpse.

Randall stared at her as if to see if she was psychotic. His eyes narrowed and hardened.

She'd done what she came to do. He wouldn't sleep with his daughter, would protect Betty from Robbie and the other low life in his troupe. "I tried to tell you once. I saw the adoption papers, knew who had adopted her."

"Have you told her? Anyone?"

A caught criminal, she pleaded extenuation. "I don't know if she knows if she's adopted. I was protecting her too."

"Is that why you were with Nick Fusco?"

The accusation restimulated her anger at his faithlessness. "Don't turn this back on me now!" She nearly shouted.

Anger met anger. His voice rose and she saw the warrior. "Did I mean so little to you that you would choose your lies, your corrupt family over me?"

"Stop it," she screamed. "If anybody should understand me, it should be you."

He hung his head as if to confess. "Yeah, God forgive me I do. Why did I ever marry you? I knew. I knew."

"Goodbye, Randall. I'm sorry." She picked up her bag and coat and left him on her own broken terms.

Truth out, she felt no relief. Up to Randall now, the burden of the lie had been passed to him.

She had no place to stay and still must find her daughter.

TWENTY-NINE

TRUTH

The elevator opened into the lobby. Milling groups of Bloomheads were distinguished from hotel guests by their casual attire, sloppy grooming, and partying attitude.

Beck waited in a line at the front desk while the guitar player from the band stood with an excited, tall young girl by his side. He picked up his key, saw Beck, and shrugged as if to ask *what can I do?*

"I'd like a room, please," Beck said when it was her turn.

"Are you with a group?"

She hesitated, on the verge of saying *with the Butch Malloy tour* but that could easily lead to questions of why she was not with Randall. "No, single."

"I'm sorry ma'am, we're completely booked. Would you like me to see if we can find you another accommodation somewhere else?"

Beck frowned, trapped. She couldn't go back to Randall and wouldn't leave without finding Betty. "Do you have a Betty Fusco registered here?"

"If you would like to use the house phone over there, the hotel operator will check and put you through or leave a message."

Beck stepped back into the lobby and saw Robbie arrive through revolving front doors with Monique and Betty. Beck stepped into an alcove reading room and watched her daughter set a daypack by her feet and take off her coat and gloves.

Robbie, carrying a small bag, was dressed in keeping with Randall's casual *I'm not a rock star* jean jacket and plaid shirt. Heads turned and fans moved to stare at him as if a continuation of the show. Beck was sure Robbie loved his wife and children and would not want them to know he was in the company of Monique Fleischner or a sixteen-year-old runaway. Was Robbie going to sleep with both Betty and Monique or cast out one of them to find her own place to sleep tonight?

Beck moved toward the elevator to intercept them.

"Hey Dodge, what you doing down here?" Robbie asked.

With fans gawking, Beck felt the familiar public spotlight. Bart, the assistant tour manager, gave Robbie a room key. He looked at Beck carrying her coat and bag.

"Oh, just checking on something," she said.

Bart told Robbie where the party was and took his bag and coat.

Monique tried to hand him her bag and coat.

"You got a room?" Robbie asked.

Monique looked confused. "No."

"Got a room for these ladies?" Robbie asked Bart. "We always book a few extra in case we have to move," he explained.

Though tempted, Beck couldn't ask for her own room without announcing her terminal marriage.

The psychotic who'd talked to Beck outside the Garden stepped from the milling fans and confronted Beck. "Did you see Butch? Did you tell him I was here?"

Beck reacted with the polite reserve of a lifetime dealing with strangers who acted as if they knew her.

Robbie moved between her and the stalker. "Hey, Maude. Off your meds? You don't want to get in trouble. Back off now."

A security heavy came to them. Maude retreated a step with a desperate look of being close to her goal yet thwarted. "Hey," she said to Monique. "I met you at the Capitol Center. Tell Butch I'm down here. He wants to see me. Not her." She gave Beck a hateful stare.

Betty raised her eyebrows at the exposure to the underside of rock and roll fame.

Beck hoped Betty was seeing that little separated Maude from Monique. Had Randall slept with someone he knew and cared for or taken advantage of delusion? How easy to dazzle young girls who'd just seen thousands cheering your performance—cheap and unsatisfactory? A bit of truth made you hunger for more no matter how much pain you appropriated.

In the wood-paneled elevator, Beck couldn't think of a way to pry Betty from Monique. "How's Suzanne and kids?" she asked.

Robbie smiled at her blatant call for fidelity. "Oh they're good. How's things with you and Butch?"

"Good as long as he's faithful to me."

"*Mmm*," Robbie appeared to be enjoying the game. "He is on a bad day." He lasciviously winked at Monique in a manner Beck found repulsive. How could a woman, much less Betty, find anything attractive about men who were no better than whores?

The elevator door opened. "See you at the party," Monique said seductively to Robbie and left with Betty.

Robbie ignored her and glanced at Beck when the elevator closed. "Crazy life," he said.

What if Betty was as attracted to Robbie as she'd been at her age? "That girl is the daughter of a friend of mine. She's only sixteen."

"Never stopped me."

Beck squinted at him, fury in her eyes.

Robbie smiled. "Kidding, Dodge, just kidding. You know me."

"Yeah, I know you."

The elevator opened. He put his arm around her shoulder. "Now a married woman."

She shrugged him off. "Not funny."

He laughed. "Don't want Butch attacking me again for trying to kiss you."

"I'm serious. Keep your hands off Betty Fusco?"

"Which one is she?"

"The young one."

"They're all young."

"Don't you take anything seriously?"

He stopped in front of the door where the sounds of music and conversation were too loud for a hotel hallway and looked down at her. She remembered loving that look, longing for those lips. "It's a party, OK? You come home from the party and you're serious. Not about this," he said and opened the door.

When they entered the living room of a two-bedroom suite, Randall was seated on a sofa against the far wall with a plate of ribs, coleslaw, potato salad and a beer before him. Miss Kitty stood by the couch guarding who could approach him.

Friend and husband faced Beck as if from inside a bubble of distorted reality.

Beck set her coat and bag by the door and moved with Robbie into the circulation of talking, drinking, and smoking. Let Randall think she'd gone to Robbie. Maybe he'd still be jealous.

The band's entourage, while more conservative than some bands, was still rock and roll. The burning rope scent of marijuana wafted through the thirty people in the room. Beck didn't want to be where a knock on the door could be the police, didn't want to feel as if she had to defend against the seductions that had taken her husband and now threatened her daughter.

A man on the catering staff waited on her like the queen, clearing a place at the dining room table and bringing her a plate of smoked barbecue brisket, salad and a glass of wine. While she ate, a small morality play transpired in front of her as a college-age girl held the Bloomers' drummer's hand and looked beseechingly at him as he shook his head refusing her invitation to go into one of the adjoining bedrooms.

Beck shifted her gaze to a very talented guitar and mandolin duo standing in a corner, performing intricate bluegrass numbers. The duo played with intense nervous expressions as if this was their big chance. They were no less talented or dedicated than the Bloomers. The differences were so slight and so great in what Miss Kitty and the record industry could create for musicians. If that was Randall, competing with the laughter and conversations, the line to see him would stretch for blocks. Maybe these musicians had more sensible lives than Randall with real jobs as teachers and children at home to raise. But that didn't stop Robbie's immorality. What if Randall quit the music business, would he be faithful then?

Beck's eyes turned to the door when Monique and Betty entered. Betty surveyed the party with interest and poise as opposed to Monique who smiled too eagerly, waiting for someone to entertain her.

Beck's gaze went to the couch where Miss Kitty leaned over and whispered to Randall. He put down a rib, wiped his hands on a napkin. Like a team Miss Kitty and Randall, the king and knight walking through his court, came to Monique and Betty.

Panic burned in Beck. Was he going to tell her? Here? Now?

Beck rushed to join the group unsure of what she would say.

Monique appeared excited that Randall had apparently come to greet her. "That was a great show. Marvelous," she said and reached out to touch his upper shoulder.

"Thanks," Randall reflexively responded and glanced at Beck and as if to prove Monica wasn't her lover said, "This is my wife, Beck."

Monique extended her hand in a ritual greeting. Beck stared at the finely done nails as if something loathsome and weakly returned the shake.

"Betty," Monique had the temerity to introduce her daughter to her.

They shook hands. Betty nodded and pulled her hand away with a frown.

Beck met the challenge of Betty's diffidence by putting her hand on her hip. "I understand you didn't have your father's permission to come here. Do you think he'd approve of this woman who brought you?"

Her hatred of Monique bled into the tone of reprimand. She could be Mrs. V. confronting a wayward girl.

Betty blinked rapidly, startled by the attack. With an image of Panda's scorn for those beneath her, looked down her nose at Beck. "That's between my father and me."

"Why didn't you tell him you were coming up here?" Beck pressed.

Betty frowned and stood more rigid. "That's none of your business."

Randall shifted uncomfortably and glanced nervously at Miss Kitty who Beck could tell was enjoying the drama.

Beck's plan to be Betty's friend and guide had been possessed by Panda's hectoring manner.

Monique smiled thinly. "Come to cause another tragedy?" she challenged with a narrow gaze.

Anger in body and mind—Beck recognized the symptoms of her IED but could not control the explosive fury that this whore had been told or knew about her. With a "RRRROWL!" shriek like a Virginia fox, she leapt at Monique who retreated so suddenly she tripped over her heels and fell on her back with Beck following reaching for her neck.

As a team, Miss Kitty and Randall reached down and by major force lifted Beck off the shocked woman.

"You come with me." Randall hustled her away with a strong grip on her upper arm.

As the red fog cleared Beck saw Betty staring at her with her mouth open in amazement. The party was silent all eyes on Beck.

"Rock and roll, Dodge!" Robbie whooped as Randall steered Beck out the door.

After the explosion came the weakness and regret as Beck meekly acquiesced and left the party with her masterful husband, joining Randall's final performance of the evening.

If her purpose had been to befriend and guide Betty away the likes of Monique, she'd failed, showed herself to be crazy. Stories would spread about the attack. She might be arrested.

As they waited for the elevator, Beck tried to apologize. "I'm sorry. I thought I was over that." Her head hung lower as she glanced at Randall looking at the up arrow.

"*Sheesh.*" He twisted his lips in resentment.

The elevator arrived and she followed him to their suite. He opened the door and stood aside for her to go in. She went first and turned when the door closed behind her without him.

Alone, like a child sent to her room, she wondered if he would return, but knew he wouldn't. He didn't like to fight with her and there was too much they needed to say or would never say. She thought about going after him but as always didn't.

Sorrow clamped her chest and her lips turned down as weakness warned of a lengthy depression. She needed to talk to Randall. She could tolerate the loss of physical intimacy, but not the sharing that drew them together.

She sat in the chair looking out at the harbor and prayed for him to return, talking to herself in imaginary conversations, acting out scenarios like before when she'd tried to leave him after Betty was born. The fifteen-year interlude when they'd been together had been like an island of mental health in a sea of psychosis on which she was now lost. If he was really gone, to what levels of mad solitude would she fall?

Her mood shot from sorrow to happiness when the door to the suite opened but fell immediately when Miss Kitty entered carrying her bags.

Beck stood. "Thanks," she said with a thin smile to not give Miss Kitty an opening to torment her.

Miss Kitty set the bags down. "Yeah, thanks for blowing up my tour."

"Sorry."

"Yeah, well at least we'll get some good songs out of it-living the lie comes to mind."

Beck turned from her, but Miss Kitty wouldn't back off and followed her into the room. "You going to tell me what's really going on or do I have to demonstrate once again my amazing ability to see right through you?"

"What do you think it is?"

"I don't know. It's almost as if you're jealous of that teenager. But even you must know Butch would never do that. It'll come to me."

Miss Kitty had been so close to figuring out the truth ever since she had trapped Beck into going to hear Randall play. From the time that she and Miss Kitty had been at L'Ecole the truth had always seemed a slip away. Now after all these years of guarding the secret, the confession seemed easy as if stating something obvious that had nevertheless been overlooked.

In a soft voice that seemed to echo, Beck asked, "Do you ever think that no matter what, a mother will find her child?"

Miss Kitty stared at Beck with wide eyes. "Jesus, you're still not trapped back at L'Ecole are you?"

"Don't you see? Betty is Randall's and my child."

Miss Kitty closed her eyes and her chest heaved with a deep breath.

Beck hurried on to convince Miss Kitty she wasn't crazy, had broken no rules, had tried but had been unable to resist the forces of fate that had outed the facts. "She came to me. It was a miracle. I didn't try to find her. The Fuscos were in California. I saw their name at the adoption. Nobody could know he would become a congressman, come to Washington."

Miss Kitty shook her head and stared at Beck in amazement. "Once and for all, you have finally outdone yourself. Have you told Butch, completely blown his mind?"

Beck nodded and looked down for an instant. "I just did."

"Big of you to not let him be seduced by his own daughter. That was truly a righteous decision."

Beck's eyes widened. "He wouldn't, you said so."

"It sure wouldn't be because the kid wasn't willing."

Beck straightened her back. "I don't know if we should tell Betty."

"Yeah, hey you know that lady that just tackled your friend is your mother."

Beck's eyes misted. "It's about fear, paralysis, not insanity." She twisted her hands together, "Maybe a little insanity."

Miss Kitty's snorted, "A little. Can't blame it all on yourself."

"I think Randall has left me," Beck said as if to say *isn't that enough punishment.*

"You're damn right he's left you. He's finally seen you for what you are...a complete nut."

Beck's mouth turned down, and tears welled. Then, she looked at Miss Kitty's tilted head of crazy red curls and gleam in her eyes and the ice shard piercing her chest was shattered by a tickle. "Oh god, I can't do anything right. I'm a wreck."

"Ha!" Miss Kitty started the laugh and said through her growing mad giggle, "But man, I'll tell you this, if I didn't love you already, seeing you knock my cousin on her fat ass was worth the price of admission."

* * *

Living the lie was a good title for her life. A stalemate of action, a waiting for a sign to proceed, marinated in a tart sauce of self-loathing, weakness presented with false pride, a victim of her fears.

Randall had not returned to the room. The illusion of their intimacy was shattered. Why wonder which of the women at the party he'd slept with that night. They were through as a couple if they ever had been since she'd kept the truth from him. Either he or Miss Kitty would tell Betty.

Beck would have to explain why she hadn't told her. Not that it would make a difference in how her daughter would feel about her. Of all that had happened last night, the image of Betty's shocked look as Beck attacked her friend remained. Betty would think, perhaps rightfully that she was crazy. She'd been a good mother for the time she had Betty, would have been a good mother if she'd had the chance. Or maybe she wouldn't. What did she know about being a mother?

After a fitful night of sleep alone in the king-sized bed, 4:30 in the morning she left the hotel suite, put one foot in front of the other, a frail pilgrim to a life without Randall.

She stood by the front door of the hotel for the first airport shuttle to arrive when she saw Betty walk the lobby with her small bag. The appearance of her daughter was a shaft of light in Beck's dark mood.

Betty returned her smile of parental pride and cheery greeting with a diffident, "Morning."

They stood in the cold outside as the other passengers bent and contorted to board the van. Beck had the feeling Betty was hoping she'd get on and she'd not have to sit by her.

The last passengers to board, they sat beside each other on the rear bench row. The van was cold and stuffy, smelling of winter coats and perfume. Beck didn't speak until they were on the freeway. She wanted to know where Betty had slept last night and with whom? Had Miss Kitty or Randall told her? Possible but unlikely, how would she behave if they had? "You have school today?" Beck asked.

Betty turned her head slightly with lips compressed, replying as if to an idiot. "It's Thursday. I go to school on Thursdays."

Beck refused to be put off by her scorn. "Where do you go?"

"Potomac," Betty disparaged as if the word was difficult to release from her tight lips.

"We used to play them in sports. I went to Madeira."

As if Beck was a bothersome stranger telling her about her ancient childhood, Betty didn't respond, hugging her arms to her coat though the van had started to warm with dry, blowing heat.

"You going to try and make classes today? We should be back in time. I can drop you off if you want." Beck pandered to her.

"I have a car at the airport."

"Oh, you drive?" Beck instantly regretted the assumption of her immaturity.

"Yeah, I drive."

Beck endured a minute of cold silence before turning her head to Betty. "Sorry if I was a little crazy last night."

Betty pulled her cheeks into a smirk. "Did my father ask you to come look for me?"

Beck cautiously replied, "Not exactly."

"He told me about going out with you. I think he's in love with you." Betty delivered the line with the skill of a boxer.

The impact knocked Beck back. "He told you that?"

"He tells me a lot."

Beck was confused by Betty's maturity, sensing the ruthlessness of an infighter she'd dare not expose a weakness. "He was worried about you."

"Why? He's gone half the time. Doesn't worry about me then."

"I'm sure he does."

Betty glanced over at her as if to ask how she would know or why she cared.

"Does he leave you and your brother alone?"

"You mean like when he goes to jail?"

Beck was surprised by the brutality of the response and shook her head.

"My Aunt Lil, my father's sister, lives with us."

"I remember meeting her at the Homestead. Lovely lady, very gracious. You're lucky to have her."

The mention of the resort seemed to warm Betty a bit. She opened her arms from her side. "I remember meeting you then. I thought you were totally cool."

The compliment was an unexpected opening. "Guess I'm not so cool now."

Betty joined Beck with a half-smile. "You think I'm a groupie?"

Beck glanced about at the three other passengers sitting in front of them who could hear them and leaned closer to Betty.

"No, I mean." She shrugged sensing an honest answer was critical to earn Betty's trust. "Yeah, it happens."

"And that's why you came after me?"

The girl was maddeningly insightful. "I was worried about you because well you know, what's going on with your father and all. When he called I wanted to help."

Betty hung her head and looked down. "I should have told him."

Impulsively, Beck reached over and squeezed Betty's gloved hand. "I'm not worried about you. You can handle yourself. Maybe I was just seeing myself in you. I got in trouble when I was your age."

Betty looked at her with a narrowed focus in her Panda eyes. Beck felt caught in a crosscurrent of time and personality as if speaking to her grandmother.

"I had to go away from home for a while."

Betty waited for Beck to go on, but that was all Beck could say in public.

Betty leaned closer to her and pursed her lower lip. "Politician's kids, you can't be a regular kid. If you go out and do something crazy, it gets broadcast because your father's a politician. You don't have to worry about me. I was looking for a chance to connect with some music business folks."

Beck recalled Randall at her age saying he was going to be a musician, running away to New York. "Your father told me you're a very talented musician. I may be able to help."

She heard the irony of speaking of two men as *father.*

"Thanks, anything you can do. Butch and Miss Kitty also said they'd help."

The van was pulling off the freeway on the airport exit.

Beck's breath held in her chest. "They did? When?"

"Last night, when Randall came back after the fight, he and Miss Kitty spent some time with me. I'm going to do a show case for them, see where it goes."

"That'd be nice," Beck said in a lethargic tone, unable to hide her concern. "It's not all fun and games, lots of travel, people taking advantage of you."

"That's why it would so great to have Butch and Miss Kitty's help. Yours too," she said as if to not hurt her feelings on the chance that Beck might know someone else who could help.

She couldn't compete against Randall and Miss Kitty. Were they to have a closer relationship with her daughter than her?

* * *

The 06:00 A.M. air shuttle from Boston to DC was nearly full but they were able to get seats together—Betty window, Beck aisle. She leaned closer to Betty, speaking loud enough to be heard over the engines.

"I lost my mother when I was young. I know what it's like to, well you know, sometimes you want...I just want you to know that I'd be happy to be there for you if you need me," she added the new qualifier.

Betty eyes pulled together with empathy, sharing what only motherless children can know. "I'm sorry. I get defensive."

Beck rode the wave of sympathy. "It's hard. I understand."

"I want to be a musician. It's something I have to do."

Beck nodded. "Randall was like that when he was your age."

Betty leaned closer eager to hear tales of her father. Beck mixed in the lore of Dodge and Lake Barcroft that was part of the Butch Malloy story with nuggets of him practicing piano before school, the early bands, Robbie. She could not have a better subject to entice Betty into viewing her as a friend and confidant. But then with uncontrollable compulsion reverted back to her mania.

"I know I can't replace your mother, but I hope you'll think of me as someone who you can turn to if you need to talk to someone."

Betty shrugged with apparent lack of concern for hurting Beck's feelings. "I'm not looking for another mother. I had the best mother in the world."

Pain pierced Beck's chest, jealousy of what Judith had, and she never could. "Do you know you're adopted?" The question was propelled by anger more than concern.

Betty squinted at her and raised her cheeks. "What?"

All the years Beck had rehearsed when and how she'd explain had been squandered with an off-hand approach. "I mean, I worked with your mother on a program to bring orphans into the United States from poor countries." The lie first told to Lil grew ghastlier as she floundered.

A shield dropped across Betty's expression conveying her intuition of Beck's duplicity. "My mother would never have told you that."

"I may have misunderstood." Beck stared at the back of the headrest in front of her. Should the truth emerge, when her lies were revealed, Betty would never trust her.

* * *

Sunday after she returned from Boston, Beck went to 9:30 Mass at Our Lady Queen of Peace in Arlington. The church seemed unadorned and less formal than the basilica of the church she attended in Washington.

She arrived late and sat in the back, scanning the predominantly Latino congregation until she found Nick and his family sitting together in a wooden pew illuminated in sunlight shining through a wall of tall oblong windows. Nick, Frankie and Lil were dressed in suits, Betty in a white blazer and a dark turtleneck sweater that framed her long neck. They looked wholesome, devout, hard to imagine their trouble.

After the service, Beck waited until the Fuscos passed up the aisle.

Betty saw her first and her eyes expanded with a breath of apprehension, eyebrows raised in surprise and pressed lips in suspicion.

When Nick saw Beck, his smile was between joy and embarrassment.

Beck walked with them onto the lawn. After being reintroduced to Lil and Frankie, Nick invited her to join them for breakfast at the Pioneer.

"I can't this morning," she said and stepped to the side of the sidewalk to allow the congregation to pass. Nick and Betty stayed with her while Lil and Frankie moved to conversations with their own friends.

Nick glanced at Betty and back at Beck, "Thanks for bringing Betty home," he said with a tinge of humor in his voice.

"Glad to have been of service," she tried keep the mood light.

"What brings you here?" Betty challenged.

"I wanted to see you again." The answer was too heavy not to be true.

Betty raised a single eyebrow in another eerie rendition of Panda. "Why?"

If Randall or Miss Kitty had told Betty she would have known why.

"I missed you." Beck joked. "And you too." She looked up at Nick.

Betty looked at Beck with a bemused twist of her lips. "Nice seeing you," she said without conviction and moved to join a gaggle of girls her age.

With a hopeful droop of his pretty eyes, Nick said, "Great to see you. Thanks again for going to the rescue."

"Did Betty tell you what happened?"

Nick shifted uncomfortably. "Yes, I was surprised. She says you're tough."

Beck looked down and back up at him. "Not crazy?"

"No, well maybe a little. Maybe in a good way."

"Would I be crazy to say I want to see you?"

Nick rapidly blinked and smiled. "Not too crazy for me."

THIRTY

UNDERSTANDING

Washington was late to the news that she'd left Randall and was dating an older indicted congressman. Leave it to the music press to be first with a story that Randall had left her for a younger woman after a violent breakup in Boston.

In June, Beck reluctantly met Andrea Vorpel for lunch at the Women's Democratic Club. The dining room, down the hall from where she'd kissed Nick during her first flirtation with him, was empty enough for them to sit in privacy. A white-coated waiter set a straight vodka with a twist of lemon before Andrea and a tomato juice for Beck.

Andrea took a long pull on the drink with the relief of an alcoholic, set the first drink of the day on the white tablecloth and looked across the table with mirth in her eyes. "I must admit, Beck, I'm at a lost to how to proceed." Her accent was high-brow Virginian with a touch of Tidewater that slid into and out of long vowels.

Beck didn't meet her surrogate aunt's probing gaze, looking without seeing in the direction of the library where the portrait of her grandmother hung in unwavering judgement.

"You know what I'm going to say." Andrea's smile wryly lightened the mood. "Look at me," she ordered not unkindly.

Beck focused on the age lines around her eyes–an expression of seniority and superior judgement.

"Why are you here if you know I'm going to give you hell?"

Andrea's sensitivity to what Beck might be feeling, relaxed her a bit. "I guess I thought it better to hear it from you than whispers and stares."

Andrea took another sip, nearly finishing the vodka and put her drink down on an doily engraved with the club's logo. "You do know that because of your first marriage to that musician you have managed to garner a bit of glamour to go along with your social birthright. Washington is a provincial village. We like to think of ourselves as the center of the universe. But where power and greatness is not that uncommon, glamour here is rare. Jackie had it. You have it. People will talk because you are different."

To be compared to Jacqueline Kennedy, a first lady born into a *good family*, was high praise from Andrea. Beck took a sip of her tomato juice. "And what will they say?"

"How interesting you are. And you *are* interesting Rebecca Lyons."

Beck noted Andrea's use of her maiden name and the reference to Randall as *that musician*–like Panda in her snobbish view of the social status of an entertainer.

The waiter came and Beck ordered fillet of soul, Andrea soft shell crabs.

"Please do an old family friend a kindness by telling me why?"

"Why?"

"Well, if you're going to be coy, I'll just have to be satisfied with my sordid imagination."

"You mean, why am I going to marry Nick Fusco?"

Andrea smiled as if to a clever child. "That would be a wonderful place to start."

Beck replied in a flat tone of stating a fact. "Because he needs me and I love him."

Andrea raised a mascara drawn eyebrow. "Extraordinary. I mean I suppose I shouldn't be so callous as to not believe that love conquers all, but I do."

"Sorry," Beck said softly.

"And so the mystery remains, leaving pity no admiration."

"I didn't ask anyone for their admiration...or pity."

Andrea sighed. "Then, I'm going to say my piece and invoke your grandmother who would be pulling her hair out to understand your behavior. Is this one of your acts of penitence like when you threw yourself at the feet of the Pope?"

Clenched in anticipation of a coming blow, Beck was shocked into lowering her guard by the memory of the Vatican. "My grandmother told you?"

Andrea laughed with her sophisticated trill, a run up a scale of short exhalations. "She swore me to secrecy. Said it was the most mortifying thing that had ever happened to her. I tried to make her see the beauty of what you were doing, as apparently your father did, but Penelope as you know was a proud if not devout High Episcopalian. We old Virginians take that seriously, and to declare yourself a Catholic, you might as well have declared yourself a Negro in her mind."

Now, Beck understood why she'd come. She leaned forward, looked Andrea in the eye then down as she asked. "Did she tell you why I went away?"

Andrea responded with such sympathy in her watery eyes that Beck felt as if Andrea really did love her. "Oh dear," she lowered her 84-year-old voice to a conspiratorial whisper. "Do you think you are the first one to leave school in the middle of the year for France? There was a time when one didn't mention these things."

What else had Panda told her closest friend? If just another person knew then perhaps Beck could be done with the lie. "Did you know there was an adoption?"

Her words were such a stark clue, Beck was certain Andrea would surmise the answer to her question as to why she was with Nick.

But Andrea only shrugged and testified to Panda's discretion. "I assumed there was. That is generally how these things are done. I knew the Catholics were involved."

Panda must have divorced herself from the idea that the child was a Lyons to give her to a Catholic family. To send Beck to L'Ecole, a Catholic institution, then to have Beck come out saying she wanted to become a Carmelite must have driven her to paroxysms of regret.

Andrea leaned toward her in a gesture of emphasizing her words. "Your grandmother did this so that you would have a better chance at life. She picked you up and carried you by her will to higher ground. I know you resented her at the time, but you should recognize and honor the sacrifice she made for your benefit by not throwing it away by tying yourself to a crooked congressman old enough to be your father. There, I've said it."

Like her grandmother, Andrea was working herself into a righteous lather, ignoring any pretense other than her scorn of Beck's behavior and Nick.

"You're like one of those Hindu who throws themselves to be burnt on their husbands pyre. It's like a prison romance, marrying a convicted murderer on death row." Metaphors mixed and tumbled from the agitated old lady.

"He hasn't been convicted of anything."

"He is *moyen, moyen, moyen*. He had nothing when he came here, except his wife's money. Don't you know people are who they associate with? Nick Fusco is certainly not the first crooked politician in this town and won't be the last. He's a *stupid* crook who got caught. He associated with unsavory characters who brought him down. I don't want to see the same thing happen to you."

Andrea leaned over her plate to instill and defend the last redoubts of social propriety, the mythical standards of whom someone of Beck's *station* should associate—as if an exclusive and rare civilization would be lost if she didn't.

"You are the bearer of centuries of tradition. Nobody can gain what you have been given, but only you can lose it. That would be a great shame."

"Washington makes me feel like a child who can never please—the endless grouping of who was in and out. Smart if you didn't get caught, stupid if you did. Did my grandmother tell you I wanted to be nun? I'm sorry I'm not the one to carry the tribe's fire for another generation."

Andrea tilted her head and pouted in disappointment. "I'm sorry, dear. I can just imagine what your grandmother would be thinking of this silly stunt of yours. Noblesse oblige, but to subject yourself to this...this circus." Andrea pleaded, "I don't think I or anyone of your friends will be able to stand the sight of you beside that man during the trial. Please, please do not play the dutiful wife. It will be too awful and of no avail to him or you."

"What if he is found innocent?" Beck asked.

Andrea raised an eyebrow. "Come on, who do you think you are trying to kid?"

"You are depressing me, Andrea."

"Sorry dear, but don't ask me to hold your hand. He doesn't have a chance of being re-elected."

"That's not the reason I'm with him. I love him...and the children."

Andrea sighed. "You have really found your way into a mess. You will have all the sympathy and understanding in the world if you would just walk away, say you were overcome with something–god knows what. Think about your own needs. Think about the people who matter, who are going to be hurt and ashamed if you stay by this old crook through this ridiculous trial. Don't let him pull you any deeper into the slime. There is no reason on earth you have to go with him like those shell-shocked ninnies hanging onto their husband's arm as they walk out of the courthouse to begin their sentence."

"Please."

"What horrible theater," Andrea said and bit down on a crab, shook her head and scowled. "I find the idea that you should sacrifice so much for a man who has made his own bed and must lie in it ridiculous." She waved a crooked arthritic finger at Beck. "Don't be afraid to admit that you've made a mistake, that's all. The longer you delay, the worse it becomes."

Beck reached out and laid her hand on the table. The beautiful Cartier brilliant-cut diamond and platinum three-stone ring Nick had given her glinted in the light. "I know you think my life is a mess, and maybe it is, but please believe me I have my reasons."

"And they are?"

"Nick and the children."

"I know the easy way to understand your behavior is it's part of your condition, but I'm old fashion. I think weakness of character can be corrected by exercising good judgment."

Beck smile wanly in the direction of her grandmother's portrait. Panda had never admitted that Beck was mentally ill. Her telling Andrea was another revelation of a family secret. She was speaking to Beck through her best friend. Beck could hear her telling her to *face your fears.* Beck was afraid to tell Betty, the world that she'd found her daughter because they would think she was crazy. But didn't they already?

Randall hadn't told anyone Miss Kitty, perhaps theatrically, not wanting to ruin a good show, had told no one, either out of cruelty or friendship. Beck slumped slightly in her chair, still cowering before the lies that had started with her pregnancy.

* * *

Beck would keep the Washington townhouse and Randall the New York condo. Randall was on tour and she was in Manhattan to supervise the packing and removal of her things.

Beck told the movers to take a Basquiat street art piece.

"Excuse me," Valerie, the sister of Randall's new girlfriend said, "They didn't say anything about the art."

"It's mine." Beck's disdainful look dared the young woman to challenge her.

The small, nervous woman went into the bedroom and Beck heard her on the phone reporting to her sister.

Valerie returned to the hallway and said, "Butch is on the telephone. He would like to speak to you."

Beck glared at the interloper. Valerie stepped back into the living room as if to give Beck privacy.

Strange bottles of perfume and a jewelry case were on a dresser top, clothes in the closet. Beck stood beside a bed covered with a bedspread she'd bought where Randall slept with another woman and picked up the phone receiver.

She could hear crying and screaming in the background. "If I leave now, I'm not coming back."

Randall said, "OK, stay. Why are you so insecure?"

Something about the distress in his voice made Beck pity him. "Hello?"

"Beck, *um*, hi...I just wanted to tell you that you can take whatever you want, anything you want."

"Just my belongings, thank you."

"The divorce is just about stuff."

She could hear his girlfriend crying near him.

"I'm sorry I didn't call you or anything."

That caused another scream and was quickly followed by the sound of a door slamming.

Beck wondered if he had his soldier face on or hurt boy. She pitied anybody who tried to get close to him now. With her gone he'd be able to shut the door completely and live in his own solitary world.

"I didn't mind," she cruelly responded.

He was giving her, himself, one more chance. "I was thinking maybe we should try some counseling, not just give up like this."

She stood straighter and thrust out her chin. "I can't see that."

He sighed and accepted their fate. "So much for romance. Guess I never could be good enough for you."

"You know I never thought that," she lied.

"How's Betty?"

He knew why she was with Nick. If he wanted vengeance, he could use their daughter to get back at her in many ways.

"She's fine, starting her senior year next year."

"I told her I'd get her in a studio if she finished high school."

They were negotiating over the affections of a teenager who didn't know they were her parents.

Beck pulled in her shoulders and hunched over the phone. "You want that for her? That life?"

"You mean my life? It's not too bad if it's what you have to do."

"Like you?"

"Yeah, like me. Better I'm there to watch out for the sharks."

"You should know about that."

He giggled. "I've been bit a few times."

"And you can be with her and not tell her?"

"Tell her what?"

Randall didn't usually tease her. He was being obtuse because he didn't want to fight.

"You know what I told you in Boston."

"Oh that."

"You know."

"I *don't* know."

"Good, don't lay that on her. She has enough going on without any of that."

"Yeah."

So easy to fall back with Randall, the safety of a space where she knew every curve and sharp edge. Doubt spread through her and her knees sagged.

"You think I'm wrong not to tell her?"

"Well, it is a bit of false pretense. What about Nick?"

Anger swelled in Beck like a repercussion and she straightened. "That's between us."

"Well then..."

"I need to do this, Randall." She regained her certainty.

He hesitated, as if searching for one more argument, then gave her the separation she wanted. "Well, goodbye. Nick's a good man. I'll always love you," he said and hung up.

* * *

The temptation was to cut everyone from her life who didn't understand her, thought they understood, questioned her motives or sanity but that would leave her removed from her family and friends. Better, she thought as she left the condo to meet Miss Kitty and Sonia-Barton for lunch to keep tabs on what was being said. She needed the warning if Betty was told to know what to do when she was exposed.

The restaurant was around the corner from the condo on W. 72nd street. She'd gone so many times with Randall, the owner greeted her by name and asked about him.

"He's on tour," she said, not caring or needing to tell him they were getting divorced. If she returned to New York, she'd live in a different neighborhood.

Miss Kitty and Sonia-Barton were waiting at a rear table with white tablecloth, rose in a vase, bottles of olive oil imported from the owner's village near Venice.

Miss Kitty, topped in a fedora laced with braid and feathers a style that said, *I can do whatever I want,* greeted her with a trepidatious nod as if knowing Beck was on edge.

Sonia-Barton wore a Scout button-down blouse open enough at the top to show her cleavage but appropriate enough for the brokerage clearing house where she worked with junk bonds. She made enough money to live well in Manhattan but still appeared to long for Miss Kitty's rock and roll lifestyle of late nights with adorable young men.

Sonia-Barton mimicked Miss Kitty's subdued greeting.

Beck sat facing the two and put her purse on the empty seat next her.

"Darlin' you look beat," Sonia-Barton began the inquisition.

Miss Kitty did a poor Neil Sedaka imitation, "Breaking up is hard to do."

"Comma, comma, down dooby doo down down," Beck sang, trying to go along with the joke.

"You done with the move out?" Sonia-Barton asked.

"About."

"What are you going to do with it all?" Sonia-Barton asked.

"Put it in storage, I guess."

"Jeez how much stuff do you have in storage?"

Beck frowned. "With my grandparents' estate enough to fill a museum."

"I can probably take some of it," Sonia-Barton said.

"Whatever you need. Hang some of the art. It's a shame to keep that in storage."

A uniformed waiter poured Beck a glass of the chilled chardonnay.

Sonia-Barton took a sip of her wine and placed the glass beside the empty space awaiting her lunch plate. "And tell me again, why you're doing this?"

At least her stepsister was direct. Beck glanced at Miss Kitty whose mirthful gleam showed her usual enjoyment at watching Beck squirm.

"Time to move on," Beck said.

"To a political scandal?" Sonia-Barton asked with a wrinkled forehead.

Beck was the weak sister to be tormented. "I spoke to Randall about Betty today." Beck cut Sonia-Barton off before she could move into Nick and directed the comment to Miss Kitty. "Says he's working with Betty, going to take her into the studio."

Miss Kitty shrugged. "She has the look...kinda like you." She huffed a short laugh.

Sonia-Barton was still intrigued enough by the music business to stop her questioning and appear to try and get the inside conversation.

"I don't want that lifestyle for her."

"How you going to stop her?" Miss Kitty challenged.

"Be there for her, talk to her...when she's ready."

"That should work," Miss Kitty mocked with a sneer.

"Really. I want your help. She's not cut out for that life."

"She's got natural talent. Any of her relatives musician?" Miss Kitty's eyes narrowed.

Beck's face reddened. The molten heat rose in her chest. "I'm serious."

Miss Kitty had witnessed and been the object of enough of Beck's rage to recognize the signs and backed off with a shrug. "The road isn't for well-bred young ladies like her."

Beck's rage could not be deflected or controlled. The trembling in her hands wouldn't subside and the explosion could not be contained. In a loud, near scream that cut through and rose above the quiet conversations in the small restaurant, Beck shouted, "Don't tease! Torment!"

"Shh, shh, shh," Sonia-Barton held up her hands in a position of surrender. "Calm down."

Beck panted trying to do the breathing exercise her therapy group had practiced.

The room came back into focus. She was standing. The owner of the restaurant was moving to their table with a stricken expression.

"Rrrraugh," Beck exhaled a loud cry, picked up her bag and fled in shame.

People didn't love her, couldn't understand her. They didn't tell Betty because they thought Beck was insane.

THIRTY-ONE

FACING FEAR

B eck sat on a couch in the living room of Nick's Santa Barbara ranch. Large trapezoidal windows reflected the interior lights against the darkness outside. She felt unmoored as if she was in a sphere of light floating in space.

Nick was seated at a desk set against a river-stone wall, talking on the telephone with his campaign manager. She'd flown out with Betty and Frankie yesterday for the campaign finale. Against her advice and better judgement, he'd taken the children out of school so they would be with him on election night–another example of his total focus on winning–showing himself a family man might be worth a vote or two. In Washington, Betty and Frankie had been spared direct exposure to the harsh campaign and continuous disrespect to which Nick was being subjected. They'd just returned from a rally that had been disrupted by youthful workers from his opponent's camp who'd showed up in prisoner's uniforms.

Nick survived the June primary. He had too many friends, had done too much good work for the local Democratic party to turn him out. Now it was November. The general election was in two days.

She read a column by Brownie, the Washington Post columnist who had defended him at the Press Club dinner. Nick's staff had it reproduced on slick copy to be handed out as campaign material. Beck was uncertain if a defense by a Washington pundit was too self-serving and of little value in the district.

A DOER IS SET UP

Seated over our morning coffee we read of more politicians allegedly caught in criminal activity.

Imagine you are a congressman who is approached by a foreign businessman who wants to invest in your district, activity that will provide jobs and increase local tax revenues. You are asked to support legislation favorable to the foreigner's interest. Does this seem criminal? Is this all Congressman Nick Fusco has done?

Fusco is a hard working "doer" in the House. As a founding member and chair of the Select Committee on Hunger, he is directly responsible for the saving of thousands if not millions of lives and relieving immense human suffering. Though he does not call attention to it, Fusco is not satisfied to sit in capitals, talking about the problem. Once as a new member of congress, he made an arduous trek to a remote part of Ethiopia, an area ravaged by civil war and mass starvation. There, with his own hands, Fusco helped build a feeding station and a hospital.

Congressman Fusco is a decorated war hero; not one of the glamour boys, but the one you will see working late to hammer out a portion of a bill too difficult for most of his colleagues to tackle.

Fusco refused to accept the FBI bribe attempt, this is on tape.

Was Fusco set up by a man who wanted his seat?

His opponent, James Ashmore was Lieutenant Governor of California when President Reagan was governor. Back then, J. Edgar Hoover was convinced the United States was infiltrated with communists...

Brownie dutifully went on to describe Nick's theory of how Ashmore had worked with the FBI to remove the Chancellor of the University of California and implied, though there was no proof, that Ashmore had been paid back by the FBI setting Nick up.

Beck found the conspiracy theory to be paranoid yet believed Nick had been setup. But how then to explain the other elected officials caught in the FBI sting? Were they only collateral damage in a plot to ensnare Nick? Beck doubted it.

They climbed the wood and metal stairway to the white hallway on which a Ray Strong oak landscape and a Hank Pitcher surfer hung. The only illumination in the bedroom was atop an old wooden horse from a carousel still on its pole in the center of a table. A collection of weathered wind vanes hung from the high-peaked ceiling. Lamps, wooden washstands holding house plants and mirrors, large dark cabinets, frail wooden chairs with embroidered seats, polished tables covered with lace holding vases and framed pictures, two couches, a love seat, and heavy drapes around the windows. This had been his wife's room. Nick hadn't removed or added furnishings since her death. Sleeping here was like being in another woman's bedroom in a nightmare or mistake.

She was a bad lover. Nick tried. He would caress her for hours if she allowed him. "It's the stress," she said as an excuse.

"Does it bother you that I'm probably going to lose?"

"Only that it would be wrong. You're a great congressman."

"Do you have any idea how much it has meant to me to have you with me these days? I don't think I would be able to stand this if it was not for you."

She lay awake long after he'd gone to sleep and felt nothing good could come of her charade. She watched moonlight shadows on the ceiling and thought of Betty and how being here was the best chance she'd have to watch and shape her daughter's emerging views of herself and the world. But what if she was only a version of Panda acting as if Betty's judgement was flawed and she knew best when she didn't?

* * *

They arose early to attend a prayer breakfast hosted by the Council of Churches. Beck was seated next to the mayor of Santa Maria. When it was time to pray, they stood, and the mayor reached for her with a moist hand. She could feel the hair over the top and felt swallowed by an animal. This was what she was supposed to have become—a valuable asset to a politician.

The room's dimensions were an illusion created by a sliding plastic partition on rails embedded in the ceiling. The table was crowded with assorted condiments, thick silverware, plates in descending concentricity, with the upper desert plate holding a fruit dish chilled in ice, water glasses, baskets of rolls and pastry covered with napkins. Out the windows was a view of strawberry fields.

While extemporizing the prayer, the Baptist minister at the head table appeared to have a Southern accent, though when he'd met them at the door, he'd spoken like a Californian. He addressed the Lord in a slow, folksy manner with a beat and accentuation of words to coincide with his exhalations, giving the heavier rhythms an explosive burst through the air. He inhaled on "Dear" and exhaled on Ga'odd. "We ask you most humbly to gi'ave our elected offi'cials the wisdom to fulfill with honor and inte'grety the trust bestowed up'on 'em by the cit' tizens...And dear Ga'odd, please give special guidance to Con' gra'us man Ni'ick Fusco, and his companion Beck, in the na' ame of Jeee' usus, the Sav'yoar, aaamen," the mayor gave Beck's hand a squeeze.

"Amen," the rest of the men intoned. Beck mouthed the word but felt no elation or peace.

Is that what she was in the eye of the Lord–a companion? Perhaps because of her work on the business-side of the Church working as a lobbyist–*seeing the sausage being made*–her relationship to God had become transactional–*if I do this will You do this?* More than guidance or blessing she prayed for forbearance.

She supposed her appearance at Nick's side so late in the campaign in a community that had raised and knew his wife was confusing and hard to digest. No matter how much gratitude Nick expressed for her being there, she doubted her presence would do him any political good.

* * *

"You look so beautiful tonight," Nick complimented before they entered the victory party.

She didn't feel beautiful, more of a distraction in a Sacs red Moa-collared jacket with large brass buttons down the front.

Like victory nights with her father, a group of supporters and close friends shared the wait for the election results with them, drinking and watching a television in the living room of a hotel suite.

Beck dropped more ice cubes into her soda water and lime. There was a noticeable lull in conversations as a couple entered and heads turned to look, then away as if embarrassed. Beck guessed who they were by the size of the man. The woman's hair was frozen in place like a blond motorcycle helmet. Beck thought her designer gown and full regalia of jewelry overdone for the occasion.

Nick crossed the room to greet them. "Hi guys!" He beamed. "Beck," he called her to introduce Paul and Marcia Annunzio. Beck wished he hadn't included her in his too obvious public welcoming of the man who'd ruined him.

"I'm so happy to finally meet you." Marcia enthusiastically beamed at Beck.

"Hello, dear," Paul looked down on her as if she was his favorite person in the world.

Beck's expression remained blank. She, as Panda would say, *looked right through him.*

"Any returns yet?" Paul asked appearing intent on demonstrating he was still a player in local politics and Nick's trusted confidant. He and Nick moved toward the television broadcasting the news that Ronald Reagan was crushing Walter Mondale, leaving Marcia with Beck.

"You must be so tired," she said to Beck.

Was it that obvious? Beck had not slept for more than four hours at a stretch in weeks.

"Has Nick told you about us?" Marcia asked guiltily.

"No," Beck said to imply the Annunzios were insignificant.

Marcia spoke like a plaintiff pleading for leniency, telling how long they'd known and loved Nick.

Beck remained with the woman in the center of the party aware of people watching them—some with sympathy others condemnation. Beck stayed with her, listening to offer counseling if needed or wanted. They were both—at least on the surface—standing by their men.

"Paul was the one who found Betty for them to adopt."

Beck's interest focused. Her eyes narrowed and she leaned closer to Marcia.

But Marcia was on to the way Paul had worked on Nick's campaigns through the years.

Here was another natural opportunity to explore did Betty know if she was adopted. Was Betty interested in learning who her true parents were? But Beck remained silent. She was committed to keeping the secret now, least of all revealing clues to this woman.

"Do you know what they're doing to poor Paul?" Marcia whispered. "They are trying to make him testify against Nick. Well, you can imagine how badly Paul feels for doing anything to hurt Nick. He's just devastated, and it's nothing less than cruel for those federal prosecutors to treat Paul this way. I don't think Nick knew; I really don't. Paul thought he was just raising money for Nick's campaign. He thought the only problem was to get around the campaign laws."

She hoped Marcia was not saying to others—*we broke the law just not that law.*

"I don't think, we should be talking about this. Good-bye and good luck," Beck ostracized Marcia to stand with Paul.

"OK, here we go," one of those watching the television said.

Tom Brokaw, the NBC anchor, announced, "We are projecting that twelve term congressmen Congressman Nicholas Fusco, one of the most powerful men in the House of Representatives, who is to stand trial for allegedly accepting bribes from FBI agents posing as Japanese businessmen has been defeated by James Ashmore, a former Lieutenant Governor of California. James Ashmore, a Republican, will be the new congressman from the 19th district of California."

Beck went to Nick's side. He was on the phone hunting for a miracle. She assumed he was speaking to his campaign manager at the county elections office. "*Ah*, what about Lompoc?"

She and other guests watched him like the central character in a tragedy. She could see the fight drain from him as the ends of his shoulders dropped as the certainty of what he should have known was coming settled on him. He hung up, looked at her and shook his head. "We're losing everywhere. James got me."

She squeezed his hand as she leaned into him in an awkward almost embarrassed embrace.

"Well, we better get downstairs. I'll call James and concede."

"I'll tell the children." She went to the bedroom. Betty was lying on the bed, Frankie on the floor with a group of children watching television.

"Did Daddy lose?" Betty looked up from the book she was reading.

"Yes," Beck nodded. "We need to go downstairs. Do you want to come?"

Betty scrunched up her mouth as if weighing the pros and cons of the loss. Frankie stood and looked at Beck as if for guidance,his large eyes filled with sorrow.

"What do you think?" Betty asked, "Should we?"

"I don't know," Beck said. "I'm going with him."

Betty stood up. "Come on, let's do it," she said.

Beck followed Betty into the main party. Nick was on the phone. Beck noticed him stiffen and his lips press together as he listened to Ashmore. "Good-bye," he said curtly and set the phone down.

Betty went to Nick and laid her head against his suit when he hugged her. "It's OK, Daddy," she whispered.

He pulled Frankie into an embrace, stepped back and said. "Come on let's go down there. No long faces. Let's show them what the Fuscos are made of!"

* * *

Beck and the children stood behind Nick around a lectern and microphone on a stage set up in a hotel ballroom. Lights illuminated them not only for local television but network news covering his concession speech. Beck thought they should not have had the victory party in the ballroom, which now looked nearly empty, more morbidity than celebration. Balloons and streamers were tied to empty chairs. The few remaining supporters were mostly young people and older women faithful to Nick. A Hispanic woman wiped away a tear.

The Annunzios stood in the back of the ballroom watching the consequences of what Paul had done. Beck tried not to look like one of the *shell shocked ninnies,* Andrea had abhorred.

Nick stepped to the microphone. In an almost apologetic voice he said, "Thank you, thank you my dear friends. You can never know how much your support has meant to me and my family during the fourteen years that I have had the honor to represent you in Congress. I just got off the phone with the new representative of the 19th Congressional District, James Ashmore. I congratulated James and assured him that I and my staff would do our best to insure a smooth transition so that people of this district, which I've been so proud to serve, will continue to have the best representation in Congress."

Beck assumed he was going to give a quick speech and they could leave. "James said something to me I think people should know."

Beck saw his face redden as the fight and anger returned to him. He'd been passive but in control. He'd known this was coming. Would his paranoia further disgrace him? *Please go out with dignity*, she prayed.

He looked down as if struggling not to speak his mind before shrugging in defeat. "Well, you know, *ah*, *hmm...*" He cleared his throat. "James and I've known each other a long time. He fought hard and he won. I wish him the best of luck. God bless you all. God bless our great nation. And thank you one more time for giving me the opportunity of a lifetime to serve you."

He waved his hand over his head as the meager crowd clapped, without saying what Ashmore had said to him, probably a taunt of some kind, turned away from the cameras to his family. The picture in the paper the next day was him hugging Betty as Beck looked on expressionless as if bored.

* * *

When the children had gone to their rooms, she sat with Nick in the living room of his ranch with the triangular windows looking out on the night.

"What did Ashmore say to you?" she asked.

Nick looked to the vaulted wood beams and didn't answer right away as if not wanting to give the words the dignity of repetition. Anger returned to his expression as he pressed his lips together, ready but nowhere to fight. "He said that he learned a long time ago not to take me for granted. It was the way he said it. He set me up, got me out of the way, the only way he could beat me."

"Oh." She looked away from him, sorry she'd prompted his futile remorse. She was happy he'd not tried to run his theory of the FBI and the Chancellor of the University of California during his concession speech. She looked back at him and softened the tone of her voice. "I was proud of you tonight, the way you handled it."

He genuinely took her compliment as a ray of light in the dark night, smiled, and slapped his hands on the top of his thighs. "Well, it's over now. On to bigger and better things."

* * *

Nick went to work every day the remainder of his term, not shirking his duty as many of the lame duck members did. He appeared to want to treasure every minute he had left, even the packing of his office. The last day of 97th Congress, he was in his study in Arlington unpacking mementoes from his long congressional career.

Lil was traveling, ostensively happy to have someone cover for her, but clearly making space for Beck.

From upstairs in Betty's room, Beck heard Randall singing,

Shadows dance, wind sings,

Open your heart to what my love brings.

Beck climbed the stairs and stood in Betty's open bedroom door.

Dressed in a red Stanford sweatshirt, Betty was propped with pillows on her bed, schoolwork piled around her. The room was a combination of childhood dolls and accoutrements of a musician including a Martin D-18

JEFFREY MARCUS OSHINS

acoustic guitar and a Fender Rhodes electric piano. Stereo speakers on a bookshelf loudly projected Randall's new album.

"Come in." Betty said.

"Would you mind turning down the music a bit?"

Betty's pretty pout opened into sympathy. She hurried from the bed to lift the needle from the black vinyl disk. "Sorry."

Beck stood at the foot of the bed. "Have you spoken to Randall about going into the business?" She heard herself sounding accusatory, distrustful.

Betty's eyes narrowed. "He's invited me to go ice skating at Lake Barcroft."

"When?"

Betty shrugged and squinted as if at the stupidity of the question. "I don't know. I guess when the lake freezes. You want to go?"

Beck rapidly shook her head in a near tremble. "I don't ice skate."

Betty stared blankly at her.

"I just hope you keep it in perspective," Beck tried to explain.

"Keep what in perspective–ice skating?"

Beck refused to respond to Betty's sardonic humor. "This whole idea of being a performer."

"He and Miss Kitty like my songs. I sent them a tape. We're going to talk about Butch producing a professional demo. Might get some of the Bloomers to play on it." Betty's eyes were glowing with enchantment at the idea of the Bloomers playing her music like she was describing the best thing in the world.

"You don't want that lifestyle." Beck repeated her criticism of Betty following her dream.

Betty easily saw Beck's real intention and threw up her hands. "What are you talking about? Why are you so weird about me and Butch?"

Beck realized she'd been too obvious with her suspicions. "I just don't want to see you hurt."

"How am I going to get hurt? Because you are? I don't get you. In fact I don't get this whole deal. You mope around here like you lost your best friend." She was growing more indignant as if something she'd wanted to say could finally be spoken. Her hands raised as if to push Beck back from an unwarranted intrusion. Her words bit. "Nobody understands why you're here, even my dad."

"I came for *you*." Beck voice trembled.

"What are you talking about? Jesus." Betty looked at Beck with eyes narrowed with distrust.

"Because you're my..." Beck froze, the words trapped inside an ice cage.

Betty looked at her with a downturned mouth and contracted eyebrows as if she thought Beck might really be crazy.

"I've always cared about you," Beck weakly said to fill the empty void.

"Why?" Betty's voice rose in pitch.

Beck looked down in weakness. "You'll understand some day."

Betty shook her head, sighed, and put her hand on Beck's shoulder in a manner the Leader often used when trying to bond with someone. Maybe Nick did it too. The affectation was a common stunt by politicians.

Betty spoke soothingly as if she was the adult comforting the child. "You're not weird. I'm happy you care about me. I care about you too."

Looking into Panda's eyes, the same height, hands and wrists identical to hers, Beck felt disoriented, in dream time.

Beck pulled her into an embrace and atoned for all the hugs she'd missed.

The hug went on too long to be casual and Betty stepped back. "I'm really glad you're here for my dad. I know it means a lot to him."

"I'm here for you too," Beck repeated as if that was all she had to say.

"I know, thanks. I won't play Randall's music around you anymore."

Beck noticed she'd used his name not Butch. "I want you to think of me as your mother." She heard Gail saying the same and saw the same reaction she'd had.

Betty frowned, looked away and back at Beck as if wanting to make something clear. "I had a mother and she died."

Beck sighed at the cruel delineation. A tightness filled her chest so she thought she might cry. She was too cautious to declare herself Betty's mother. All her efforts to grow closer to Betty had been misperceived. Her hidden motivation, acting as if she had a right to oversee Betty's behavior, had only made her *weird*. She'd crowded Betty, made a terrible mistake by not letting Betty come to her on her own accord.

As if recognizing Beck's pain Betty returned to sympathy. "Look, I'm sorry. I just don't understand. It's probably me. I just am kinda of my own person. I just don't need another parent."

Kinda is not a word, Panda's correction popped reflexively into Beck's mind–the model of behavior she was tied.

Randall and Butch, Betty seemed to have delineated the two characters. Who was she attracted to? Would Randall have more success in treating her as his child than Beck. Everything she'd tried to do to protect Betty had resulted in the opposite effect. Betty would now hide her *relationship* with Randall as Beck had once. Another of her grandmother's haunting adages—*one good turn deserves another*—came to her. Betty's behavior was the fruit of Beck's deception. Panda controlled Beck and through her was attempting to control her great-granddaughter. To free Betty from that cold, dead grasp the best was to let her be ignorant of those who sought to design her deportment and values.

* * *

Nick stirred beside Beck as if fleeing something in his dream. She listened to the sound of traffic, a distant siren and felt the disorientation of cause and effect grow until she thought she'd never be able to right herself and find a course to redemption.

The wife of a politician was not what she wanted, what she'd avoided.

She didn't belong with Nick. She'd made a mistake and longed for Randall who knew her imperfections like no one else and still loved her.

THIRTY-TWO

READY AND WILLING

The news from Miss Kitty was shocking. Myrna Toll, the reporter from the Washington Post had contacted her about Betty.

In her bedroom on Capitol Hill, Beck squeezed the phone tighter, stood with a frozen back.

"You told her yet?" Miss Kitty pressed

"I haven't told anyone."

"Somebody is talking."

"You know who?"

"Yeah, I know," Miss Kitty said as if weary of the subject.

"Was it you?" Beck challenged.

"No, it doesn't mean a pile of jalapenos to me."

"Was it Randall?"

"Not sure he believes it. I have to admit the girl does look like mama Malloy–more than you. I just mess in your life, nobody else's."

"This is my life."

"And it's about to get a lot weirder. Your father is going to testify on Nick's behalf. Does he know?"

"My father?"

"Yeah, your father, not mine, not the colonel. At least that's what Myrna Toll told me."

Beck sighed as it to release another secret. "That's one of the big questions in my life. I don't know if my father knows about any of it. He's always tried to cover for his mother and act like he didn't know about L'Ecole. He's a good liar."

"World class. But he won't be able to lie on the stand. What if they ask him?"

"Why would they do that?"

"You know impeach the witness, say he has ulterior motives for speaking on Nick's behalf?"

"Where are you getting this?"

"I've got my sources."

"Who?"

Miss Kitty harrumphed. "All right I'll tell you. Your stepmom told Sonia-Barton...thought you might like to know," Miss Kitty teased with her usual joy in tormenting Beck. She knew all the players and was loving the drama.

Beck heaved a sigh. Anger percolated below her words. "Stop playing with me."

"What are you so afraid of? That nobody will like you or say my god, she got pregnant like that's never happened."

"You talk about it?"

"No. I keep the sisterhood, always will. How many times I told you that?"

"Why do you accuse me then?"

"I don't. I understand."

"Thanks for all your understanding...and the heads up."

"Your father testifying? I may come down for that."

"It's not a show."

"Oh yes it is."

"Will Randall be there?" Beck asked.

"You think we're tied to a string? Want me to invite him?"

"No!"

Miss Kitty laughed. "I find you endlessly entertaining."

"So glad to entertain you."

When she hung up, Beck thought maybe she should see her life in the same humorous mode. But she was bred and raised to be serious about protecting the reputation of herself and family. She'd thought that by letting Randall and Miss Kitty know the truth, her confession would be easier. She was not going to be the one to bring scandal and notoriety to her family. Beck thought of Panda's preternatural premonition that Beck would get in trouble. *Scandals will happen. There are ways to deal with them if they can be contained early enough. Do you understand?"*

Beck had done all she could to contain the scandal, but truth still lurked only a whisper away.

* * *

What is the use of foresight and not be able to avoid the foretold?

The day her father was to testify to Nick's good character, Carl Cox, his lawyer thought Nick should bring his family. Nick asked her to join them.

"Of course," Beck had said though she would have preferred not.

They were led by Cox down the marble-lined hallway to the courtroom. Beck walked beside Nick. Betty and Frankie followed.

Myrna Toll was waiting with a group of reporters outside the tall set of dark wooden doors to the courtroom door.

"Is Butch Malloy putting on a benefit for you?" Myrna Toll called.

The question almost stopped Beck to say *no*. Nick glanced at Beck. She scowled her response.

Nick's lawyer, Carl Cox held the courtroom door open for her. "It's important you're here," he reassured her as she passed. She looked at him to confirm he was serious. If Miss Kitty was correct, Beck being there would only add weight to the argument that the Leader was biased in his opinion of Nick. Nobody had asked for her ideas about Nick's defense strategy.

They entered the packed courtroom like a band going on stage. A hundred eyes followed her as a young associate from Cox's law office rose to give her a front row center seat. Nick was paying for this highly educated space holder. The cost of the legal team was taking all Nick's savings. Since leaving Congress he'd worked full time on his defense with no income. Judith had left him some money, but most of her fortune including her half of the Arlington house and the Santa Barbara ranch had been left in a trust for Betty and Frankie. Nick refused Beck's offer to loan him money saying it was enough she was standing by him. She would get Miss Kitty to set up a defense fund and if necessary make a secret contribution. But wasn't hiding money what this trial was all about— one contribution illicit the other anonymously admirable?

"All rise," the bailiff called.

Judge Deirdre Wagner, an unsmiling excessively serious woman with narrow eyes, her hair pulled tightly back around her unattractive face took her seat on the raised dais and the show began. The courtroom was a windowless stage designed to inspire awe. Each side had a team of three lawyers at tables before the judge separated by a wooden rail from the watchers—Justice Department officials, the press, and public. Lines formed early in the morning to get a seat to witness the disgrace of power and fame—a cathartic cleansing of the body politic.

The lead prosecutor, U.S. Attorney Jay Aldin, with a thick wave of hair, his presence bespeaking the authority of government, called Kevin Kiyosaki, the undercover FBI agent who had entrapped Nick. The jury, judge, and other trial participants donned headphones and opened notebooks to read the transcripts of what was being said on the film of Nick and Paul's first meeting with the undercover FBI agents.

On the film, Kiyosaki, a Japanese man in a sports jacket identifies himself as an agent of the Federal Bureau of Investigation. After giving the date and location, he states, "In a short time I am expecting to meet Congressman Nicholas Fusco. In front of me is fifty thousand dollars in five packets. I am placing the money in this briefcase to be given to Congressman Nicholas Fusco in order to secure his support of amending a telecommunications bill to allow foreign ownership of U.S. media and telecommunications companies."

The foundation of the government's case against Nick, was broadcast on multiple television sets around the courtroom. Black and white, indeterminate focus, almost like an art project or porn, shot through a small hole in the wall, you could hardly tell who the figures were as they moved in and out of the static frame in a dimly lit room.

Awkward from the start. Randy Gaithers, a lobbyist later revealed to be working for the FBI, moves Nick from the seat he chose to one directly facing the secret camera. In the crude footage Nick looks tired, impatient and unsure of the purpose of the meeting. He explains why the Congress would never vote to allow foreign ownership of U.S. telecommunication companies.

"My clients are willing to invest in your district, utilizing local labor, of course, and financial institutions. Perhaps some language could be written into the report about levels of foreign investment..." Gaither shoves the briefcase with the cash toward Nick. "Go ahead, take a look," he encourages.

Nick appears distracted. He glances at the briefcase, and says he has to make a telephone call and leaves the room.

With Nick off frame, the focus is on Paul.

Gaithers asks him to look in the briefcase.

When Paul sees what is inside, he snaps the briefcase shut, and stands. His eyes narrow. His wide thick shoulders expand beneath his suit jacket. "There is no way Congressman Fusco should be around this." He acts angry, insulted that they would try to bride him.

The party leaves the living room and the range of the camera. Paul can be heard off camera saying something unintelligible.

On the stand, Kiyosaki was asked what happened in the hallway away from the camera.

"Hearsay, your honor," Cox objected.

"Your honor," Jay Aldin, the U.S. Attorney, said, "the witnesses are all available to be examined on the veracity of their statements."

"You may testify what you observed," the judge ruled.

"Mr. Annunzio told Congressman Fusco that they should leave."

"And they left without the bribe in the briefcase?" Aldin, the prosecutor asked as if he was defending Nick–testimony so favorable to Nick that it caused Nick's lawyers to lean their heads toward each other at the defense table for a quick conference.

Beck began to feel more confident that Nick would be found innocent. Why would the government even bring the charges? Paul had acted honorably. Perhaps he should have reported the bribery attempt to the FBI as a senator had done, but Paul had not taken the money.

Then, the prosecution showed the second film of a meeting the next day with Paul on a yacht moored in the Maine Street Marina.

In the second film Paul comes without Nick. He's more expansive and relaxed–a salesman promising he can deliver Nick's cooperation.

"And this is for Congressman Fusco's benefit?" Agent Kiyosaki asks. "You are authorized to speak for Congressman Fusco?"

With the bored voice of one used to wielding great power, Paul answers yes to the questions and says Nick will do whatever he asks him.

The briefcase is passed. Paul quickly opens it to confirm the packets of 100 dollar bill are inside and says, "I'll see this is put to good use."

"For Congressman Fusco?"

"Of course. Now about investing in the district. I think I can be of great help there." Paul spends the rest of the grainy film setting himself up to be the real estate agent of the supposed Japanese investors, in particular a golf course development beside Lake Cachuma.

"And Congressman Fusco will help us if we need him?"

Paul smiles and spreads his boxer hands across his belly. "I think we can all do good business together."

The devastating recording of Paul accepting the bribe was proof a million good words could not dispel, a shadow so dark as to cover anyone associated with him. Nick had just been in the wrong place at the wrong time, with, as Andrea had said, a disreputable character who'd bragged Nick would do whatever the undercover FBI wanted, taken their money and deposited it into Nick's campaign account. That is why he was probably going to jail.

There was no question Paul was guilty. The defense had to separate Nick from him, show Paul to be acting on his own.

* * *

The Leader didn't testify until the afternoon. His arrival caused heads to turn as he was escorted by a marshal to a chair near the bailiff on the other side of the courtroom from her. She was unable to catch his eye until he was called to the witness stand. She barely shook her head and pressed her lips together, trying to convey her apology for wasting his time, for utilizing his good name in the flimsy hope his testimony might help prove Nick's innocence.

Cox stood before the witness box where the Leader sat at the side of the judge facing the courtroom. He seemed proud to call the Leader as a witness. "Senator Lyons I appreciate very much your taking the time to come and vouch for Nick Fusco's good character."

"Glad to."

"You are the Majority Leader of the U.S. Senate, is that correct."

"Yes."

"You're very busy, aren't you?"

The Leader grinned quickly in his handsome manner, "Often, yes."

"The court appreciates your taking time from your busy schedule to share with us your opinion of Nick Fusco. Have you ever observed any act or indication that Nick Fusco might be prone to accept a bribe?"

"None," the Leader said forcefully. "I have no idea why the FBI might have tried to entrap him."

"Objection!" Aldin called out. "Motion to strike the last remark."

Now Beck understood that bringing the Leader to testify was more than just speaking of Nick's character but to forcefully introduce the idea that the government had illegally induced Nick to appear to commit a crime.

"Your honor," Cox said, "Expert observation. The Majority Leader is a highly trained lawyer and senator with oversight of the FBI. He knows what entrapment is."

"Jury will ignore the witness and counsel's reference to entrapment. You will be instructed later on the defense of entrapment."

The lead prosecutor Aldin tried to impeach the veracity of the Leader's opinion because of relationship to Beck.

"I've known Mr. Fusco a long time," the Leader said.

"Is it true, Mr. Fusco is engaged to your daughter."

"That is my understanding, yes."

"And you knew Mr. Fusco before that?"

"Yes."

Beck tensed ready for him to be asked if he knew Nick had adopted his grandchild?

"Then you approve of your daughter's intention to marry Mr. Fusco?" Aldin asked.

Beck stared at her father, wishing Cox would object. The Leader glanced at her and a look of bewilderment flashed across his practiced neutral expression. He didn't understand why she'd left Randall for Nick, why she'd put him in this position.

"Yes, I just wish that it could have been under better circumstances," he answered.

She conducted her own silent examination. *Do you know your daughter gave birth to a child? Do you know she has found her daughter, your granddaughter?*

As if to answer her questions, the Leader looked at Betty with a wistful expression of remorse.

"Thank you Majority Leader Lyons," Aldin dismissed him, apparently satisfied he'd demonstrated the Leader's bias if not the truth.

* * *

Beck didn't go to court with Nick for the verdict didn't play the role of the *shell-shocked ninny hanging onto her husband's arm as they walk out of the courthouse to begin their sentence.* He didn't call her to tell her he'd been convicted.

She heard the news on WMAU while driving by Sibley Hospital. Her heart beat faster as if there was an emergency and she must respond, go to Betty.

Lethargy, leavened by fear crushed her. She took a breath to see if she still could, held down by Washington and the shifting illusions by which people judged themselves and others, not truth but ego, governed by rules without sympathy or remorse.

She dropped down into the band of nature along the Potomac set aside as if a reminder of what had been lost, driving by instinct rather than consciousness. She should cross Chain Bridge and go to Betty, but her conniving plot seemed as blighted and misguided as not telling Betty she was her mother, waiting for someone else to tell her so she could confess. She drove out past the beltway, not going anywhere just to be in the country.

Winter was still and life sheltered from the cold. Darkness came early over the fields and she drove far into the Blue Ridge before turning back to Washington. If she was going to break off with Nick now was the time. Too timid to call him, fearful to be exposed as the fraud she was, he'd think her cold and hard for cutting him off when she was merely craven. Everything seemed wrong, day was night, she guilty, Nick innocent, injustice and misunderstanding reigned.

Only Randall understood her, accepted her with her flaws, knew her when she was innocence, ready and willing to love. The greatest wrong was that their love was self-corrupted, ruined by silence and misunderstanding. They should be able to talk, not part like strangers. But how could he know her, when she didn't know the words–simple words that as by a damaged brain wouldn't come to her?

* * *

By the time she drove down the entrance to Lake Barcroft, the houses were dark in their regular order of sleep. The temperature was below freezing, too unseasonable for teens to be sneaking out to meet at Beach One.

She drove by Randall's house and slowed. Mrs. Malloy would understand if she knocked and said she needed to talk or maybe she'd find Randall, naked and strong meditating in his room.

She recognized the dreamscape, the feeling of floating between realities, magical appearances and emotions too close to the flame, open, feeling more than if awake. She'd learn how to ice skate, not be afraid, be ready to join Betty and Randall when they went skating.

Her father's house was still, everyone asleep or gone. Janey was married to the taxi driver who would take her to church, with a daughter of her own.

In the darkness, the sound of the furnace coming on slightly shook the house in a way that was deeply familiar and comforting.

Downstairs, her old bedroom had been changed into a guest room. A rear door in the room lead into an unfinished hollow in the hillside where the family memorabilia was stored. Rebecca found the closed box of the ice skates Panda had given her for her. She turned off the light and stepped out onto the porch into the cold.

Her eyes adjusted to the radiance of the quarter moon as she descended the stone stairs to the private beach behind her house. Frozen sand crunched beneath her feet.

She sat on the edge of the retaining wall, took off her boots, removed the white figure skates from the box. The skates were too small for her but she forced her feet into them and laced them around her ankle with fingers tingling from the cold as they became numb.

The voices she'd been hearing were coming from the darkness in the center of the lake, female voices, sounding strong, assured, laughing as in intimate and delightful conversation.

Tears raised and were torn from her eyes by a northern wind. She forced herself to stand on the ice. The skates slipped from beneath her and she fell hard onto the olive surface.

Her breath caught. She waited for the break, to fall into the cold, but the ice held. She clumsily pushed herself to her feet, remembered the movements her brother had taught her, putting down serrated edge of the toe to push off, the slight pushing to the side.

She was away! A miracle, gliding over the shiny reflection of the moon as if flying. Yes, she was dreaming. Fear was for wakening. Into the darkness, the voices now numerous as if a party in the dark middle of the lake.

She reached the spot thirty yards in front of her house, the place where everything had changed and heard the ping, a terrible victorious god claiming her, moving from the other side of the lake straight toward her.

The sound made her wake, forget how to skate. She slipped and fell. The impact caused the ice to break with a crinkling like a wine glass fallen off the table.

The water was first a shock, then a strong heavy hand filling her clothes with weight, pulling her down. She reflexively cried out for help, saw Randall speeding toward her, his feet barely touching the ice.

"Don't!" she cried out. The cold was over her head, filling her nostrils and mouth. She fought the choking, then a pleasant relaxation loosened her. The darkness, the depth of Lake Barcroft became a comfort, a soft blanket tucked around her.

She drifted down into the dark. Her last breath asked, "Mama?"

Jeffrey Marcus Oshins is a multi-instrumentalist who records and performs under the name Apokaful. He is the author of numerous novels and a travelogue. He lives in Santa Barbara, California.

Praise for the 12 series of novels by Jeffrey Marcus Oshins

12: A Novel About the End of the Mayan Calendar

Never a dull moment, this was a hard-to-put-down, exciting tale written by a talented author.

5 star Amazon review
–Shell Forest Melody

The novel 12 is filled with magic, fantastic visions, invented words, chase scenes through mountain lakes in the Sierras and school campuses...and even music: A CD by Oshins' band Apokaful, which is also the name of a band playing at a nightclub in the novel...(Apokaful is an adjective describing someone who is preoccupied with thoughts of the end of the world.)

–Santa Barbara Independent

If you're looking for the standard doom-and-gloom world-ending catastrophic calendar-end story--look somewhere else, this is not it.

–4 star Amazon review
Mallory Anne-Marie Haws

12 is a beautifully written, remarkably original book.

–David B. Stockwell
Author of Tanks in the Wire

Read other books by Jeffrey Marcus Oshins

12: A Novel About the End of the Mayan Calendar (Book One – 12 Series)
And We Shall Perish (Book Two- 12 Series)
Hippies in the Andes/Freedom Pure Freedom
Women in Politics

Listen to Apokaful on YouTube.